HOT CARGO

Nicki Bennett
&
Ariel Tachna

Dreamspinner Press

Published by
Dreamspinner Press
4760 Preston Road
Suite 244-149
Frisco, TX 75034
http://www.dreamspinnerpress.com/

Hot Cargo

Cover Art by Dan Skinner/Cerberus Inc. cerberusinc@hotmail.com
Cover Design by Mara McKennen

ISBN: 978-1-935192-49-7

Printed in the United States of America
First Edition
February, 2009

eBook edition available
eBook ISBN: 978-1-935192-50-3

To Jess, without whom we never would have embarked on this sci-fi journey and whose suggestions and encouragement got us to our destination.

✦ PROLOGUE

"Do you see that?"

"See what?" Richard Jeffers turned from his console to his partner, Nguyen Li, who was scrutinizing a patch of starfield—the same patch he'd been studying for the past three days, for all Richard could tell. Leaning forward, his head bent alongside Li's darker one to peer at the display panel. "I don't see anything. Maybe it's time to take a break, Win."

"It was there, just for a second. Something moving. Fast." Sitting back, the spectographer rubbed his eyes and stared at the screen again. "I swear it was there, Richie."

Richard shrugged his shoulders and ruffled Li's short-cropped hair. Stellar spectography duty on Confederation Science Outpost CX-2114 ("a place so boring they couldn't even come up with a name for it," Li had complained) wasn't the galaxy's most exciting posting, situated as it was on the outskirts of inhabited space. Of course, that's what allowed them to escape the light and electromagnetic pollution that interfered with astronomical observations in more densely populated sectors. They'd made good progress on the galactic mapping project and captured some especially clear images, and they only had another five weeks to go before their tour was up and they could hand the station off to their relief crew. Richard couldn't wait.

"Okay, I give up," Li sighed finally. "Let's call it a night and we can search the images tomorrow with fresh eyes, for whatever I saw and for whatever else is there. How does that sound?"

"As long as you promise to actually sleep and not come back in here to stare at the screen all night, that sounds great," Richard agreed. "Come on; neither of us is going to do any more good here tonight. We're both so exhausted our eyes are crossing."

Li had to admit that was certainly true for him. Resolutely setting the recorder to auto and the computer to pick up and note any changes so he wouldn't have to look through the entire night's footage in the morning, he pushed away from the console and smiled at his partner. "Your turn."

"My turn for what?" Richard countered with a grin, just starting to rise from his station when a klaxon sounded, the harsh scream so unexpected that he dropped back into his seat in shock. "What the—"

"There!" Li shouted, pointing to the spark of light moving across his monitor. "Proximity alarms. I *told* you there was something there!"

"The supply ship isn't due for over a month. I can't imagine who else would have business out here in the back end of the galactic arm," Richard countered. Moving to the comm console, his fingers flew over the keys and knobs, trying to lock onto a signal. "Unidentified ship, this is ConSci post 2114. Please identify yourself."

Silence greeted his words. He switched to a wider frequency in the hopes that the silence was an inability to hear them rather than an unwillingness to respond. "Unidentified ship, this is ConSci post 2114. Please identify yourself. Repeat, please identify."

A blast from the unfamiliar ship's weapons was the only reply. The station rocked precariously, knocking Li to the floor and almost sending Richard there as well. "Unidentified ship, this is a science station, not a military vessel. We have no hostile intentions. Desist immediately."

Again, there was no response. Fingers flying, Richard ran a diagnostics check, transferring as much power as he could from the sensor arrays to the station's energy shields. He hoped whoever was firing on them was just trying to get their attention. Their shields were designed to deflect space dust and the random asteroid, not a deliberate attack. And they had no weapons, because who'd want to attack a two-man research station?

Apparently whoever was out there, Richard realized, as another barrage shook them only seconds later. Turning back to the comm, he reconfigured the frequency to a Confederation channel, even though he knew they didn't have the signal strength to reach anyone in real time.

"Richie, we've got to get out of here," Li insisted, pulling himself up off the floor, his lips bloody where the impact had caused his teeth to break skin. "The shields on this piece of junk might keep out the space drek, but they aren't going to do anything against weapons fire."

Richard looked back once more at the ship and snapped a final image, shooting it off via the space waves toward home. If they didn't make it out alive, hopefully the image would get through and give somebody somewhere an idea of who to go looking for. "Let's go."

The narrow corridors that usually felt so cramped seemed endless now as they raced toward the docking bay. Another impact slammed them from one wall to the other, the lights flickering and then going dark, replaced slow seconds later by the dim glow of emergency lighting. "Faster!" Li shouted, reaching for Richard's hand to pull him along behind him.

"Hit my knee," Richard gasped, moving as quickly as he could despite the pain in his leg. Rounding the last bend in the corridor, he skidded to a stop, unconsciously gripping Li's hand more tightly. "Shit," he whispered, the word echoed by the slow hiss of a pinhole leak, their precious air escaping into space. The door to the docking bay was buckled, the paint melting away and dripping in gobbets to the floor. "Shit, Win...."

"Richie...." The two scientists stared at each other, acceptance darkening their eyes. Richard reached out his other hand toward Li, but before their fingers could meet, a final blast from the unknown ship hit the main power core, the resultant explosion tearing the fragile metal apart.

It took three days for their last message to reach Confederation headquarters. The Admiralty commanders studied the image, but could find no familiar markings on the unusual ship. In the face of an inexplicable, untraceable new threat, they did what they always did.

They blamed the space pirates.

CHAPTER 1

CAUGHT WITH HIS PANTS DOWN

ADMIRAL PETER KELLER rubbed his hands together in grim satisfaction. He had just received word that his men had succeeded in capturing the *Golden Stallion*. In a matter of hours, the despicable pirate would be his. He cracked his knuckles. That space trash was about to pay the price for messing with the Admiralty. He didn't know yet if the *Stallion* had anything to do with the destruction of the CX station, but even if it hadn't, he agreed completely with the Confederation crackdown on piracy. It would be a pleasure to wipe that scum out of his sector.

On the other side of the solar system, Blaise Risner was not nearly as sanguine. For years, he had successfully eluded the Confederation, his precious ship sleeker and faster than anything they could throw at him, but that hadn't mattered today. They'd caught him with his pants down, and now they had him with enough contraband to convict him for sure.

"I didn't know what was in the containers," he told the soldier holding him prisoner. "I simply loaded them and took off. It's just my job to haul cargo, not to check every package that comes on board for the accuracy of its manifest. Whoever cleared these for shipping off-world should have done that."

"Save it for the Admiral," the soldier growled. "I'm just following orders."

"Are you sure we couldn't work out a deal?" Blaise asked persuasively. "After all, I've got all this good Betelgeusian wine. I'd be glad to turn it over to you personally, Lieutenant…."

"Freeman," the soldier replied.

"Lieutenant Freeman, if you'd look the other way just long enough for me to get back to my ship...."

"Bribing an officer, pirate?" Freeman asked.

"Privateer," Blaise corrected.

"Smuggling and now bribery," Freeman continued, ignoring the other man's words. "The list of charges is growing. Let's go. The Admiral is expecting you."

Blaise cursed silently. Why did he have to be boarded by the one honorable officer in the entire fleet? *In for a penny, in for a pound.* "Surely there's something I can offer you?"

"You already have," Freeman replied. "Your capture just guaranteed me a promotion. I'll have my own ship in no time."

Resigning himself to his fate, Blaise fought nonetheless, not in any hope of escape but for the principle of the matter. He might have been captured, but he hadn't been cowed. He could always try telling the Admiral that any bruises he had were the result of abuse by his captor. That might scuttle Freeman's promotion, even if it didn't win Blaise a respite.

"HERE'S the pirate, as promised," Freeman reported with a salute, pushing Blaise into the room in front of him.

"Privateer," Blaise protested. "I just carry the cargo I'm given."

"Save it for...."

"Yes, I know," Blaise interrupted. "Save it for the Admiral. Well, unless I'm mistaken, this is the Admiral, so if you'll just run along like a good boy and leave the men to discuss business, we'll all be a lot happier."

Freeman frowned, but he backed out of the room at the Admiral's gesture of dismissal.

Blaise made a show of looking around the room. "Now that we're alone, Admiral, do you suppose we could dispense with these?" he asked, gesturing to his wrists. "They're a tad uncomfortable."

Keller allowed a chuckle for the other man's audacity. His eyes raked over the pirate's—*excuse me, privateer's*—body. He was tall, dark, and handsome, the perfect picture of a dashing rake. Fortunately for Peter, he was also a criminal. "They're supposed to be," he replied, not making a move to release his prisoner. "It's one more deterrent."

"One more punishment," Blaise muttered.

"Oh, no, Mr. Risner, the punishment hasn't started yet."

"Don't I even get a chance to defend myself?" Blaise protested.

Peter waved a magnanimous hand at the handsome pirate. "But if you waste my time, it will only add to your penalty."

Blaise opened his mouth to brazen it out, but then thought the better of it. "What am I accused of?" he asked cautiously.

"Piracy, smuggling, general mayhem." Peter ticked each one off on his fingers as he spoke. *And maybe more,* he added to himself, trying to imagine the man before him firing on a defenseless research station. Maybe it was time to cycle up the intimidation. He'd more than once wrested a confession through the judicious use of some very specific threats. If it meant finding the killer who'd wiped out two innocent research scientists, he'd live with his less-than-pure conscience.

"I didn't know what was in the containers," Blaise insisted automatically, "but I'll accept the smuggling since it was clearly contraband. If I plead guilty to that, can we forget the other charges?"

"Do you know the sentence for smuggling?" Peter asked.

"No idea," Blaise admitted.

"Three to five years' hard labor," the Admiral replied.

Blaise grimaced. "Well, I've never been much good at hard labor, but I don't have much ground to argue it."

Peter ran an appraising eye over Risner's lean physique. Those muscles had come from somewhere. He approached the pirate confidently. The man's wrists were bound, and it would take only a flip of the control in his pocket to send an electric shock through the cuffs, if necessary. "The report said you were alone on your ship," he commented. "It must get lonely, all those weeks with no one for company."

Eyes narrowing, Blaise searched for the trap in the words, but could find none. "Sometimes," he agreed slowly.

"You must miss having congenial companionship," Peter continued as he slowly circled the pirate.

"I can usually find what I need when I go planetside," Blaise replied warily. The Admiral was hinting at something, but Blaise didn't know what.

"Lucky for you," Peter said. "I don't have that luxury. My uniform keeps me from getting what I need planetside."

Blaise was getting a very bad feeling about this, but he had to ask. "What do you need that you can't get?"

Peter backhanded Blaise roughly, knocking him to the floor. "Someone to dominate," he replied, bending over the pirate and grabbing his hair. "I can't get it planetside," he repeated, "but I find I can get it occasionally aboard my ship."

Blaise looked up at the hard smile that contorted the handsome face. He read desire there, but he also saw more than a passing suggestion of cruelty. "What do you want?" he asked, rising to his knees as the Admiral pulled on his hair.

"I want to see what you have to offer me." Peter smirked. "I already know what you were carrying on your ship. Let's see what you're carrying on your person." He let go of Blaise and sat back in his desk chair, fixing the smuggler in his steely glare. "Strip."

Blaise looked down at his bound wrists. "I can't oblige you even if I wanted to," he pointed out reasonably, hiding the frisson of foreboding that went through him at the order. "So you're either going to have to undo these or strip me yourself."

The Admiral's hand strayed to the control for the restraints. "You look almost stupid enough to try something," he mused, fingering the selection of buttons. "I'd enjoy seeing you try to fight me." With a flick of his thumb, he let a jolt of current surge through the bonds; not enough to hurt—much—but enough to remind the pirate who was in charge here.

As soon as the tension left the dark-haired man's body, Keller pressed a second button releasing the charge that held the prisoner's wrists together. "Now, I believe I told you to strip," he repeated lazily.

Blaise flinched from the pain that radiated out from the manacles, biting his lip to stifle a cry. He might not be able to do anything about his situation—his options had just gone from few to none—but he wasn't about to let the Admiral wring a sound from him this soon. He'd been manhandled by worse than him before this. Rubbing his wrists painfully, he reached for the toggles on the sleeveless vest he wore, undoing them just slowly enough to convey his resistance.

Propping one leg on his desk, the Admiral made himself comfortable. It was obvious the pirate was going to try and draw this out. Not that Peter minded. He was enjoying the anticipation, even if his prisoner wasn't; and he was finding it increasingly difficult to imagine the rogue in front of him as a vicious killer. "Give me a good show, but don't think you're delaying anything," he cautioned, raising the control in warning. "I can still get your attention if I think you're wasting my time."

Blaise glared at the Admiral silently but did as he was told, slipping the vest from his shoulders in gross mockery of a striptease. He let it slide from his arms and fall to the floor. He paused for a moment, arms outstretched slightly to let the Admiral look his fill before bending to unlace his boots.

Peter hid a smile at the pirate's theatrics, though he had to admit the man was well worth staring at. His chest was broad and well-muscled, his arms corded with just the right amount of brawn. Instead of the pallor that so often marked spacers who spent too much time trapped on their ships, his skin was the warm color of Aldebaran honey. Now that the utilitarian vest was gone, Peter noticed a tattoo inked around the thief's meaty bicep, an abstract design of horses' heads, their manes twisting together in a swirling pattern. And the Admiral could see the glint of a small silver ring, half-hidden by the pelt of dark hair that coated the privateer's defined pecs.

Since it was obvious he was on stage, Blaise turned slightly as he worked the laces loose on his boots, giving Keller the opportunity to ogle his ass beneath his tight pants. Loosening the boots enough that he could toe them off, Blaise stood and turned back to face his captor. He had no problem with the Admiral's gender—he had often taken male lovers— but he did have an issue with being ordered about this way. He didn't know what he could do about it as long as the officer held that control device, but he had to do something. The other option was to accept being raped without even putting up a fight.

"Not bad," the Admiral admitted, not above letting his captive know he appreciated the view, especially when it looked this good from both sides. "Now the pants. I'm curious whether your skin's that color all over."

Blaise's face hardened, but he did as he was told, unfastening the fly of his trousers and pushing them off, letting them join his vest on the deck of the ship. He was not embarrassed by his nudity—he looked good and knew it—but he definitely felt the lack of covering in the chilly room. Goose flesh sprang up over his arms and legs, and he could feel his nipples tightening, much to his annoyance.

A flashing screen drew the Admiral's attention from the provocative display. Glancing down discreetly, he smiled at the message from Lieutenant Freeman that the prisoner's ship couldn't have been involved in the destruction of the space station. Its blasters weren't powerful enough, and the energy signature didn't match what they'd been able to glean from the wreckage. Hitting a key to acknowledge the information, he returned his gaze to the prisoner, the message transforming his interest from official to very personal.

Peter could feel himself starting to stir in appreciation of the really exceptional example of male flesh before him. Getting up from the desk, he circled the younger man, running a hand down one firm flank. The pirate glared at him, but Peter could see that his nipples had already hardened in their thicket of curls, and he felt the slight tremble of the skin beneath his fingertips that encouraged him to continue. He'd played this game with a few select prisoners before. This one was no different than the others, he thought. A bit mouthier, maybe, but he'd be begging for it before the end.

Blaise raised his hands as if to push the Admiral away, but he managed to stop himself before acting. "Can we make a deal?" he asked. "I do this willingly. I follow your every command, no matter what it is, without hesitation. And in return, you forget about the piracy and mayhem charges. I know you can make me do what you want. You've proven that already since I'm standing here with no clothes on, but I'm offering to do better than that. Is it a deal?" He held his breath as he waited for Keller's reply. Obviously, he would have no way of enforcing the bargain if the Admiral reneged later, but he had a reputation for being an honorable man. Blaise was banking on it now!

"Think highly of yourself, don't you?" Peter asked, though he'd been about to make a similar offer himself. "A few hours with you, against three to five years' hard labor for smuggling? Not to mention the penalty for general mayhem." He trailed his hand down the pirate's lean buttocks, resting the curve in his palm, as if weighing his options. His other hand went to the fastening of his uniform trousers, which were quickly becoming uncomfortably tight. Releasing the closure with a practiced flick of his wrist, Peter let his erection jut free of the restrictive material. He threaded his hand in the pirate's dark, spiky hair, yanking his head down abruptly. "Show me what you can do with that mouth of yours besides make smart comments," he growled, forcing the other man to his knees.

Blaise sank to his knees but pulled his head back. "You've got me cold for the smuggling," he replied. "I'm not arguing about that, not questioning the sentence. Just the piracy and mayhem." Without waiting for an answer or a punishment, he took a deep breath and licked his way around the head of the Admiral's thick cock even as he concentrated on giving the best blow job of his life.

Peter's breath caught as the pirate's hot tongue worked its way around his cock. By the Seven Suns, the man knew how to give head! His fist tightening in the dark strands, he pushed deeper into the moist cavern, impressed that the younger man took his considerable length without gagging. "Fuck, that's good," the Admiral gasped as the smuggler's tongue continued to circle him. "I think you've just done away with the general mayhem," he managed to force out, his hips rocking into the increasingly demanding suction.

A part of Blaise's brain informed him that he should be rejoicing at that statement, but that seemed trivial next to the sensations swamping him as Keller fucked his mouth. He consciously relaxed his throat, letting the thick shaft slide in and out of his mouth at the Admiral's pleasure. It had been a while since he'd last had sex, and it seemed his drought was about to end spectacularly. Lifting a hand, he cupped the heavy sac hanging between the Admiral's legs, rolling it in his palm as he swirled his tongue around the steadily leaking cock in his mouth.

Peter didn't usually come from being sucked, preferring to spend his energy buried inside some hot, tight ass—but in this case, he didn't doubt he'd be able to enjoy both pleasures. Giving in to a need he hadn't felt in longer than he could remember, he grasped the prisoner's dark head with both hands and thrust deep into the supremely talented mouth. With a low groan, he threw back his head as his orgasm seized him, pulsing a thick stream of come down the pirate's throat.

Blaise swallowed convulsively, accepting every last drop and milking the other man's balls for more. When the spasms eased, he pulled back, still lapping at the sated flesh to make sure he hadn't missed a drop. Finally, he rocked back on his heels and looked up at his captor. "What now?" he asked, his hand dropping to stroke his own aching cock lightly.

Peter leaned back against his desk, catching his breath, shocked at the intensity of the orgasm the smuggler had wrenched from him. When he trusted his voice enough to speak clearly, he considered the man below him with a sly smile. "You look good on your knees. Maybe I should just keep you there a while." He smirked when he noticed that the pirate was sporting his own impressive hard-on as a result of the blow job. "I see you enjoyed that, too," the Admiral purred. "You must have plenty of time to yourself during your smuggling runs. Show me what you do to pleasure yourself."

Blaise's eyes drifted shut and he leaned back on one hand so that his body was completely open to the Admiral's gaze. His free hand slid away from his cock and up his chest to his pierced nipple, toying with the ring. He pulled on it lightly, then with more force, as his body grew used to the stimulation. He couldn't stop the hiss of pleasure that escaped his lips as he worked the metal back and forth in his sensitive flesh. Peeking out from beneath his long lashes, he tried to judge Keller's engagement in his show. Seeing the man's eyes riveted on him, he looked up coyly. "If you gave me a hand with this, I could show you what else I do to make myself feel good."

Peter couldn't hold back a bark of laughter at his prisoner's boldness. "Oh, I'll give you a hand, all right," he husked, dragging the younger man up by his arm and laying a hard slap across his ass. "I give the orders around here, not you. You'd do well to remember it." He struck the firm cheeks again, then dropped into his chair and pulled the pirate onto his lap so that the hard length of his resurgent cock pressed into the reddened crease. Holding the limber hips down with one hand, his other found the worked silver ring on the spacer's chest and twisted it roughly. "Now, you were showing me how you pleasured yourself," he reminded.

Blaise yelped in surprise when the first blow landed, but his only reaction to the second one was to push his ass back for more. He didn't get more spanking, but the feeling of the Admiral's cock rubbing between his cheeks was more than enough sensation for the privateer. The cry that tore from his lips when Keller twisted the piercing in his nipple was one of pure pleasure. He'd often thought he could come just from having someone play with his ring, but he'd never actually had the patience to try it. Now didn't seem the opportune time to suggest it to the Admiral either, so he tried to focus on what he was supposed to be doing. One hand circled his cock while the other slid between his legs to cup his balls as he had recently cupped the commander's.

The Admiral didn't miss his captive's cry of pleasure at the rough tweak of his nipple ring or the way he pressed his ass back against Peter's thick cock. The signs that his prisoner welcomed his touch pleased the hardened spacer more than the capture itself. He might like a bit of rough play, but he prided himself that he'd never taken anyone against his will. Stirring his hips against the smooth leather of his desk seat, Peter slid the head of his revived cock up the pirate's crease, slickening it with the precome leaking from its tip as his fingers continued to worry the silver ring.

Blaise shifted, trying to change the angle of his hips so the Admiral's cock would bump his entrance instead of sliding teasingly along his cleft. The man's hands, though, kept him from his goal. With a moan of frustration, he lifted the hand that had been palming his balls to his lips, sucking his fingers into his mouth to get them wet. When they were coated with saliva, he reached back down, intending to stretch himself for the fucking he had been dreading but was now anticipating.

When the pirate squirmed against him, trying to force the Admiral's cock into the contact Peter knew he craved, Peter tightened his hand on the captive's hip. He had every intention of fucking Risner long and hard—especially now that he knew the younger man wanted it as much as he did—but it would be when he was ready and not before. So when the pirate sucked his fingers into his mouth and moved them toward his ass, Peter intercepted the wet digits. Lifting the hand to his own mouth, his closed his lips around the work-roughened fingers, stroking them with his tongue as sensuously as the smuggler had tongued his cock. When the digits were dripping with Peter's saliva, he guided them back down to the pirate's shadowed cleft. Leaving his own hand resting on the back of Blaise's, but no longer controlling its motion, he leaned back in the chair, giving the pirate room to move freely. "Now, show me how you prepare yourself," he rasped, his voice hoarse with desire. "Show me how much you want me to fuck you."

Blaise was long past caring about things like captive and captor. All he knew was how empty he felt and how he craved the cock that teased him. He pushed his wet fingers roughly into his body, moaning at the burn of muscles that hadn't been stretched this way in far too long, but he couldn't be bothered to slow down. The sooner he was stretched, the sooner he'd feel that thick, hard shaft inside him, filling him, stretching him wider and deeper than his fingers would ever be able to do. Shunting his fingers in and out a few times, he withdrew his hand. "I'm ready," he husked. "Fuck me."

"Still think you're the one giving the orders?" Peter growled hungrily. Watching Risner fuck himself on his fingers had set a fire burning inside him, a fire he would only be able to quench by burying himself in the pirate's body. Pushing the younger man to his feet, Peter spun him around so they faced each other and dragged him back down onto his lap, pressing the leaking head of his cock into the well-slicked entrance. "Ride me," he demanded, bending his head to capture the cool silver ring in his teeth, tugging at the hardened nipple while the smuggler's tight channel squeezed around him. "Fuck yourself on me. Ah, fuck, that feels good…."

The privateer didn't hesitate, shifting so he could get his knees on the chair to give him the leverage he needed. He posted up and down on the thick shaft splitting him, not giving either of them time to catch their breaths. His back arched against the Admiral's mouth when he felt the other man's lips on his chest, playing with the ring that made his nipple so amazingly sensitive. Feeling incredibly daring, he threaded his fingers into the short blond hair, holding Keller's head against him as he moved. He almost stifled the moans that welled in his throat, but there was no one to hear but the spacer, and the Admiral hadn't given him any indication that he should be quiet.

Peter nipped hungrily at the distended nipple while the smuggler's tight sheath enveloped him, again and again. "Ah, fuck, so good...." Risner's body moving against his, taking him deeper with each rough push of his hips, was turning the heat inside Peter into a conflagration, hot enough to warm the cold depths of space itself. The Admiral didn't protest when Risner held his head to his chest; he'd give the dark-haired man anything he wanted at that moment to keep those wild moans of pleasure coming from his lips. Peter bit down on the pierced nipple, pulling it into his mouth as he reached for the hard shaft nudging his belly. He wasn't going to be able to hold off much longer, and he was going to take the pirate with him when he crashed.

Blaise's moans morphed into a shout when the hot, hard hand closed over his cock. "More," he begged hoarsely, hips rocking between the fist around him and the erection inside him. He was teetering on the edge of release, and he knew he'd explode like a plasma bomb any second. If he could just get a little more friction... there!

"Ah, fuck," Peter moaned as Risner undulated around him, pleading for more. When the pirate shouted and clenched around his throbbing cock, the blond went off like a tank full of rocket fuel. Lights brighter than the Antares Nebula danced behind his tightly closed eyelids as he emptied himself into Risner's heat, the aftershocks of the smuggler's release milking every drop of fluid from his softening balls.

Blaise felt his climax surge up and out, splattering his chest and the front of the Admiral's uniform with creamy liquid. He collapsed backward against the edge of the desk, boneless from his orgasm. Several smart comments flitted around the edge of his mind, but he brushed them aside, content for the moment to wallow in the feeling of being filled. Reality would return soon enough.

Peter slumped back in his chair, his hands sliding down to cup Risner's taut buttocks, holding the younger man to him. Most times he'd pull out and fasten up as soon as he was spent, having no further use for his plaything once he'd found his release. But Risner.... Damned if he knew what it was about the cocky, brash, demanding, dark-haired scoundrel that had gotten under his skin so quickly, but he was in no hurry to push the pirate off his lap.

With a resigned sigh, Blaise looked up and met the Admiral's eyes. As incredible as the past hour had been for him, he had no illusions about his fate. The Admiral had the law to uphold, and while Blaise might have bargained his way out of the multiple charges, there was nothing to be done about the smuggling. "Where will I be sent for my hard labor?" he asked dully.

Peter slid reluctantly from Risner's warmth, fastening himself back into his splattered and wrinkled uniform. "You've more than worked off the lesser charges, but not even I can get the smuggling charge dismissed. You were caught red-handed, after all." At the spacer's woebegone expression, a glimmer of slyness lit the Admiral's viridian eyes. "But I can have some say in where you serve your sentence, and I can truthfully say that you have certain... *highly specialized* skills that could be put to good use right here on my ship."

Not daring to hope he understood correctly, Blaise searched the Admiral's face. "In what capacity?" he asked slowly. He didn't make a move toward his own clothes yet. If he interpreted the man's implication correctly, the last impression Blaise wanted to give was one of disinterest.

"I can always find a position for someone who's demonstrated the flexibility you have," Peter said smoothly. He nodded to the younger man's clothing. "As much as I hate to obscure the view, you might want to be dressed when the guard escorts you to your quarters."

Still unsure of exactly what the Admiral intended for him, Blaise let his guard down a little more as he dressed. "I wouldn't happen to be serving you in a... personal capacity?" he worked up the temerity to ask.

"A *very* personal capacity," the Admiral confirmed, swatting at the pirate's bare cheeks before the spacer covered them with his rather worn flight suit. "And if you give satisfaction, you might even earn time off for good behavior."

Blaise grinned. "If you're to be my punishment, I'm not sure I want time off."

As much as he would privately enjoy his prisoner's unfettered spirit, Peter knew discipline must be maintained, especially in public. Pulling the small control from his pocket, he reluctantly pressed the button that reactivated the bonds around the pirate's wrists. "Don't get too cocky, Risner," the Admiral warned, with a gleam of desire in his eyes. "I still have ways to keep you under control."

CHAPTER 2

HARD LABOR

THE High Court justice for the Sirius Quadrant of the Galactic Confederation glared from her bench at the figure standing in the docket before her. "Prisoner Risner, you have been charged with piracy, smuggling, and general mayhem, and I see from your record that this isn't the first time you've appeared before this court." She frowned at the data pad before her and then back at the dark-haired man dressed in an unadorned detention jumpsuit, his wrists and ankles restrained in energy cuffs. "How do you plead to these charges?"

Blaise had kept his face deliberately neutral as he waited for the trial to begin, letting his gaze wander over the courtroom to see if the Admiral had arrived. When the High Justice began speaking, he politely gave her his attention. She was not terribly different from every other Sirian he'd ever encountered—green skin, golden blond hair shot through with emerald strands—except for the slenderness of her form. Sirians tended toward stocky, but not this one. If he'd been interested in women, he'd have been eyeing her with serious interest. Even as it was, he could still see the allure she would have for the average male of any human and most other humanoid races.

Then the list of charges registered and he frowned deeply, his expression matching hers. He should have known Keller was full of shit when he offered to waive the charges for piracy and general mayhem. So much for the value of the Admiral's word. He'd known this might happen when he'd agreed to play at being the commander's slave in exchange for having the harder-to-prove charges dropped, but he'd let himself believe this time would be different.

"If it please the court, I would like to confer with Justice Perry," a deep voice interrupted before Blaise could respond. At a nod from the slender but imposing judge, the bailiff stepped aside to allow Admiral Keller to approach the bench. The Admiral's dark dress uniform set off his rugged good looks and hard physique to excellent advantage, a consideration which the presiding justice seemed to note with appreciation. "Peter," she said quietly when he neared, "how good to see you again! I didn't know the *North Star* was back in this part of the galaxy." Raising her voice to project through the courtroom, she continued, "What interest does the Admiralty have in a common pirate?"

Admiral Keller smiled warmly in return as he stood before the judge, his hands clasped behind him. "The *North Star* apprehended the prisoner, Your Honor, and in the course of transporting him to base I had the opportunity to... interrogate... him thoroughly. While he was clearly found with contraband goods in his vessel, I believe the charges of piracy and of mayhem may have been, shall we say, overzealousness on the part of the arresting officer? I would like to petition the court to vacate them at this time."

Relief surged through Blaise at the Admiral's words. It looked like Lieutenant Freeman wouldn't be getting that anticipated promotion after all! For once, amazingly, his trust hadn't been misplaced. He shifted against the restraints as best he could, well aware that the jumpsuit he was wearing would do nothing to hide his body's reaction to the memories of Keller's "interrogation." The time spent on his knees, bent completely to the older man's will, was etched into his memory as permanently as the space dust embedded in the hull of the *Golden Stallion*. Even if he never saw the other man again, he would never be totally free of him, the sensation of losing himself to Keller's control like nothing he had known before. His eyes closed as he let himself hope the Admiral would keep the rest of his bargain.

"The Court is always willing to take Admiral Keller's suggestions under consideration," High Justice Lapis Perry answered with a cool smile. "As I know you often extract classified information from your prisoners, I believe we should retire to the privacy of my chambers to discuss your suggestions in more depth."

"I serve at the Court's pleasure," Peter responded smoothly. Before turning to follow the High Justice, his eyes strayed to the prisoner for a moment, long enough to assure himself that Risner's condition hadn't changed materially since custody had transferred from the *North Star* to the galactic court system. He wasn't the only one to "play" with prisoners from time to time, and not everyone shared his scruples. Settling a familiar hand in the small of Lapis's back, he escorted her to her chambers, prepared to convince her that his suggestion could benefit them both.

Blaise's eyes darkened with an emotion he refused to label jealousy when he saw the familiar way the Admiral touched the High Justice. He reminded himself he should be grateful for Keller's assistance, and that any relationship that existed between the Admiral and Perry could only help in convincing her to release him to Keller to serve his sentence.

He knew the Admiral was interested in him—his mere presence was proof of that—but that didn't mean Keller was *only* interested in him. A little voice in Blaise's mind pointed out that he was a fool for wanting that interest focused solely on him, but he'd never been one to share his lovers. Then again, he'd never been one to submit to a Master the way he suspected he'd be submitting to Keller, so maybe what was typical of his attitude toward sex wasn't important anymore. Recent events had called a lot of his dearly held notions into question. What was one more?

When the two blond heads reappeared in the courtroom a few minutes later, satisfied smiles on their faces, Blaise studied them closely for any sign of a possible tryst, but neither's appearance had lost any of its professional polish. The High Justice reclaimed her seat behind the bench.

"Based on classified information provided by Admiral Peter Keller, the piracy and mayhem charges have been dropped, but there is still the allegation of smuggling to contend with. How do you plead to that charge, prisoner?"

Blaise swallowed the lump in his throat. "Guilty, Your Honor," he forced himself to say. "I didn't know what was in the containers, but it was undeniably contraband, and I won't fight the charges."

"The sentence for smuggling is three years at the penal colony on Delta Auriga." The judge motioned the bailiff to step forward. "Return the prisoner to custody until the next transport ship is ready to depart."

"Your Honor," Peter raised a hand to pause the proceedings, not missing the betrayed glance Risner threw at him. Of course he and Lapis had worked all this out in her chambers, but the formalities, such as they were, still needed to be maintained. "If I may ask another concession, I would like to recommend that the prisoner's sentence be served upon the *North Star* rather than the Auriga colony. He has certain talents that would prove useful, and I would be willing to take him under my personal recognizance. After all," he added with another smile, "I have had a certain success in… rehabilitation."

The Sirian's eyes sparkled at the Admiral's request. They had both benefited more than once from his successes. "It's true that the prisoners who have served time on the *North Star* have left as changed men," she mused. Her glance swept over the man in the dock from head to toe, a smile twitching the corners of her lips as she noted how the drab material stretched over the prisoner's body. "Obedient. Docile, even. Hardly recognizable as the men they had once been."

Blaise fought down the panic that rose in his throat at the judge's words. The way she was eyeing him and the smile that danced around the edges of her mouth clued him in. She knew exactly what Keller had done and what he planned to do. And it suited her just fine. He wondered for a moment if he should have held out for the Auriga colony, but he pushed the thought aside. He was strong and cunning. He could play the Admiral's game, pretend to give him what he wanted, while staying true to himself within. And when his time was done and he could reclaim his ship, he would show them "rehabilitation."

"The Court so orders," Justice Perry intoned, "that the prisoner shall serve three years on board the *North Star* under the personal custody of Admiral Keller. Have Mister," she glanced at the data pad, "Mister Risner delivered to the brig on board." Extending her hand to Peter, she added softly, "Perhaps the next time you're in port I can observe your efforts with the prisoner."

"You know you're always welcome to oversee my methods, Lapis," the Admiral agreed, raising her hand to his lips. "Feel free to join us any time your schedule permits."

THOUGHTS still all ajumble as he struggled to assimilate his change in status over the past twenty-four hours, Blaise stood quietly outside the closed door as the soldier escorting him buzzed their presence. He did not know where they were on the ship, but he knew they were not in front of the Admiral's office again. He would have recognized that spot from his earlier visit. The time he had spent in the brig waiting to be summoned and assigned his first duties had given him a chance to think, but he hadn't really made much sense of anything. Obviously, the judge and the Admiral had an agreement of some sort that allowed the Admiral to get his kicks with the occasional prisoner. He didn't know exactly what the judge got out of it, besides prisoners off her hands, but he couldn't help but wonder if he'd be summoned to attend the Admiral one day only to be ordered to attend Her Honor instead. He hoped not. She wasn't at all his type.

The rest of his thoughts had centered around what his duties would be. He was fairly sure he could satisfy Keller on a purely sexual level, but he wasn't sure what else the man would expect. He would just have to stay on his toes and one step ahead of his jailer. The door opened and the crewman pushed him inside, not bothering—not daring?—to enter himself.

Glancing up from the book he had been reading, Peter grinned as the prisoner stumbled into his quarters, his hands and feet still restrained by energy cuffs. "Ready to begin your sentence, pirate?" he asked cordially, setting the rare volume aside and rising to his feet.

"Privateer," Blaise retorted automatically. "The piracy charges were dropped."

"So they were," the Admiral agreed. "The charges for general mayhem, too. I hope you remember the rest of the bargain that led to that."

"I'm here, aren't I?" Blaise responded cheekily, his cavalier attitude not completely hiding his body's reaction. "I didn't lodge a complaint with the court for sexual harassment. I didn't question why I was getting special treatment." He met the Admiral's eyes boldly. "I keep my bargains."

"Harassment?" A flare of what might have been anger lit the Admiral's ice-green eyes for a moment before his shields raised and their gaze returned to cool disinterest. "Correct me if I'm wrong, but you seemed to enjoy our previous encounter." Rising from his chair, Peter crossed to a storage cabinet and retrieved something small from inside, holding it hidden in his palm.

"Not saying I didn't," Blaise agreed coolly, "but that doesn't mean I would have chosen it if I'd seen another way out of the situation. Somehow I doubt the court would officially sanction your actions, no matter how much of a blind eye the High Justice turns when it's just between you and her."

"No, Justice Perry is hardly one to turn a blind eye," Peter agreed with a sly smile. "Someday you may find out just how closely she likes to observe my charges." To his surprise, Peter found that as much as he enjoyed Lapis's participation in his games, he was in no hurry to share this one with her. He'd enjoy having the big "privateer" all to himself for a while. "So, you're anticipating special treatment, are you?"

"I'm here and not on the Auriga colony," Blaise pointed out reasonably. "I'd say that already qualifies as special treatment. And since I'm quite sure the talents you referred to in the courtroom didn't include my piloting or mechanic's skills, I'm assuming I'll be spending my sentence in your quarters."

"Oh, you'll have regular duties aboard the ship," the Admiral corrected. "Maintenance, mainly, until I learn what your other skills encompass." He grinned at the younger man, eyes raking over his toned physique. "Beyond the obvious ones, of course."

"You were easy enough to please the last time," Blaise observed. "If you want me to please you again, let me loose of these restraints. Unless you don't think you can handle me without them?"

Without warning, the Admiral turned and shoved his prisoner with enough force to drop the unsuspecting man to his knees. Grabbing him by the collar of his worksuit, he flung Risner against the wall of his cabin, the material tearing beneath his grasp to hang off one muscular shoulder. Thumbing the device he'd concealed in his palm, Peter activated the security field that snapped Risner's restraints against the contact points built into the smooth panel, spreading his arms and legs in a position that left him open to whatever correction Peter chose to indulge in.

"What the fuck?" Blaise shouted in surprise as he found himself suddenly spread-eagled with his chest against the wall, unable to move his arms or legs at all. The best he could do was crane his neck in an attempt to meet the Admiral's eyes. His knees hurt from hitting the floor so suddenly, and he began to wonder just exactly what he had let himself in for by agreeing to this bargain with the devil. Despite the pain, despite the trepidation he was feeling, his body was already tightening in anticipation of being as thoroughly fucked as the last time he'd been at the Admiral's mercy. He tried to tell himself it was fear of whatever pain Keller might inflict on him, but his inherent honesty made a lie of that illusion.

"You think this is all just some kind of a game, don't you?" Peter rasped, recognizing the unquestionable signs of arousal as Risner tried uselessly to pull away. There was no question that his struggles would be unavailing—the security system had been designed to the Admiral's exacting specifications—but he enjoyed watching the realization of his helplessness dawn on his captive. Meeting the spacer's wide-eyed stare, he approached until he could grasp the torn edge of the detention coverall, ripping it from Risner's back with one strong tug. Letting the fabric dangle from the pirate's wrists and ankles, Peter ran an appreciative hand down the powerful muscles of the man's back, thrilling at the slight tremble beneath his fingers.

"Life's one big game," Blaise insisted, though he was sure his captor would not appreciate the sentiment. "You play the hand you're dealt to the best of your ability. The best player wins." Despite himself, he could feel his body tensing at the touch of the Admiral's hand even as gooseflesh pimpled his skin. "You could keep it a little warmer if you intend to have me naked," he added.

"I'm sure I can think of something else to keep you warm," Peter countered, flicking another button on the control device. A crackling stream of energy snaked out and lashed against the pirate's back, leaving a thin red weal where it fell. Even as Risner hissed in pain at the contact, the line faded, leaving the tanned skin unmarked.

Blaise, though, felt no fading, no easing. The nerves where the energy had struck burned as surely as if he bore a much more serious welt. Reminding himself not to be cowed, not to give in on the inside where it counted, he schooled himself to stillness, waiting to see what Keller would do next.

Peter hadn't expected to wring a reaction from Risner at the first touch of the energy whip; in fact, he would have been disappointed if he'd broken so easily. Thumbing the scourge to the next level, he began to wield it in earnest, laying a cross-hatch of fast-fading welts on the big man's back. He kept the power low enough to avoid any real damage; he wanted to find his new plaything's limits, not incapacitate him.

The blows hurt like hell, always enough to make him jerk futilely in his bonds, but never quite enough to make him cry out. Before long, his back was burning like the volcanoes of Parsus, nerves aflame as the whip lay repeatedly over his skin. He could not feel any blood—a small consolation—but he was sure he would be in far too much pain to do any serious work the next day. He was beginning to doubt if that would matter to the Admiral, though. Closing his eyes and dropping his head in concentration, he reminded himself to breathe through the pain and simply endure. He had survived being tortured at the hands of the Gavenelians, the most sadistic race he had ever encountered. He could survive this.

After Risner had taken nearly a dozen lashes with no more than stiffening his posture and shortening his breath, Peter realized he wasn't going to hear the groans or pleas that most of his other prisoners had been reduced to by this point. That was intriguing, but Peter had other means at his disposal to get what he wanted. Flicking the control off and sliding it into the pocket of his uniform trousers, he stood behind the restrained smuggler, close enough that the growing bulge of his arousal could brush against the younger man's backside. He trailed a hand over the fast-fading lines of contact on Risner's broad back, knowing how his touch would flare along the excited nerves before the sensation faded.

The sudden cessation of pain made Blaise tense, wondering what the Admiral had planned next. Surely he was not satisfied with those few strikes. Then he felt Keller's cock nudging his bare backside and thought perhaps he understood. His captor didn't need his screams and groans, only his submission. At least today, their interaction was about power, not about pain. Remembering the pleasurable pounding he had already undergone at the commander's hands, he decided it would not be so terrible a thing to give Keller what he wanted. Moving as much as he was able with his ankles and wrists still bound, Blaise pushed back against the swelling in the blond's groin, his nerves still stinging from the whip but at a level that was fast becoming a counterpoint to the pleasure to be gained from the Admiral's hard cock.

Peter had expected Risner to tense or even recoil at his touch. The eagerness with which he pushed back, seeking more contact, sent a plasma bolt of arousal coursing through the Admiral's veins. Stepping even closer, he wrapped his arms around the smuggler's chest, the crisp fabric of his uniform rubbing against the sensitized flesh of Risner's back. He thrust a hand into the short, dark hair, pulling Risner's head back and biting down on the straining tendons of his neck, hard enough to bruise the skin but not break it. "You like that?" he challenged, pumping his hips once to grind in provocative counterpoint to the prisoner's movement.

Blaise hesitated a moment before answering, weighing the relative benefits of his possible responses. Admitting it would give Keller that much power over him far more quickly than the privateer would have preferred, but it seemed pointless to deny his body's reaction, not when he couldn't keep his hips from reacting to the Admiral's movement. On the other hand, denying it could well mean a return to pain and, while Blaise knew he could bear it, he certainly preferred not to. "What do you think?" he replied in the end, sure the refusal to give a clear answer would incense the Admiral, but his pride demanded he attempt to resist.

A satisfied smirk broke over the Admiral's face at Risner's admission. He was no different than all the others after all. "I think you're a slut for my cock," Peter answered, dropping his hand to the younger man's thickening erection. He squeezed and felt it pulse against his hand. "I think you're going to be begging me to fuck you before we're finished."

"Begging you to hurry up and finish so I can go back to my quarters," Blaise retorted even as his body reacted. He couldn't stop his erection from swelling, but he could still control his own mind, and he had no intention of folding like a house of cards when he already knew that challenging the Admiral would get him a much more satisfying reaming. "It's not like I have much choice anyway, bound the way I am. We both know you can do anything you want to me and I can't do a damn thing about it."

"That's right; you can't," Keller agreed. His hand slid lower to capture the smuggler's balls in his palm, tightening his grip as his other hand sought the silver ring that he remembered adorned one of the spacer's pectorals. Twisting and tugging at the cool metal, he sank his teeth into a firm shoulder muscle, his every action calculated to demonstrate his complete control.

Blaise hissed at the amalgam of sensations assaulting him. His back still burned from the beating, abraded constantly by the stiff uniform behind him. The grip on his balls was just this side of painful, reminding him it could become that way at any moment, yet still skirting the line between pleasure and pain. Attention paid to his piercing was always pleasurable, and his back bowed to seek more of that welcome pressure. The teeth in his shoulder hurt, but Keller had found the most sensitive spot, the spot that made Blaise thrash and moan every time. He clenched his teeth, trying to hold back the sound, but the vibrations in his throat escaped nonetheless.

The moan was low and quickly bitten off, but the way it made Peter's cock throb inside the constriction of his uniform made him all the more determined to elicit more of them. He ran his tongue over the marks he had left in Risner's shoulder before biting down again, dragging his palm roughly over the length of hard cock in his hand, a dribble of viscous fluid leaking out in response. "That's it; moan for me," Peter urged, grinding his hips into the pirate's ass. "Tell me how much you want it."

Blaise couldn't stop another moan from escaping, but he bit down firmly on the words that wanted to pour out of him. He wanted the Admiral just a little more forceful first.

"I said tell me how much you want it," the Admiral repeated, twisting the sac in his palm at the same time he pushed more firmly against the darker man's buttocks. As soon as he heard the pirate give him the admission he demanded, he was going to rip open his damn dress uniform and give the cocky bastard the fucking of his life. They'd hear his screams at the galactic core before he was done with him.

"Talk, talk, talk," Blaise goaded, pretty sure Keller had reached his limits. "All you do is talk. I'm starting to think that's all you can do."

His control snapping at Risner's taunt, Keller slammed his forearm into the back of the man's neck, pinning him even tighter to the cabin wall. Giving the balls in his palm a final vicious squeeze, Peter pulled his hand free, determined that would be the last time he'd touch the prisoner's tackle the rest of the night. His free hand tore open his uniform trousers, extricating his rampant erection. Spitting into his palm, he gave his cock a quick wetting before shoving roughly between the toned cheeks of the spacer's ass. *Maybe a nice big ball gag next time,* Peter thought. *That would keep him quiet, though it would be a shame not to be able to hear him scream when—* With a single powerful thrust, the Admiral buried his cock to the hilt in Risner's tight ass, the friction almost as painful to him as he was sure it was to his captive.

"Oh, fuck," Blaise moaned, half in pain, half in pleasure as he got what he'd been wanting since he saw the Admiral in the courtroom that morning. It hurt like hell to have his body invaded this way, with no preparation and only spit to smooth the way, and yet the thought that he had pushed the unflappable commander to this point kept him completely turned on. His range of motion limited by his bonds, he nonetheless pushed back against his captor as much as he could. He'd feel this still tomorrow, but for now, he wanted more.

Leaning against the smuggler's muscled back, Peter let the last vestiges of control slip and pounded into the sinfully tight channel, his fingers digging into one hip firmly enough to cut off circulation as he pulled the hard body even closer. He was making no effort to give pleasure, but the moans escaping from the pirate's throat as he fucked him seemed to hint that Risner was enjoying this too. Peter hadn't had a plaything this responsive in longer than he could remember. It was going to be a real treat to break him and train him up right.

Blaise burned beneath the heaving pounding, pain and pleasure mingling until it was all one morass of sensation. He continued to bite back the words of encouragement that threatened to spill from his lips, but he gave up trying to silence the gasps and grunts of pleasure as he was fucked harder than he'd been in recent memory. He wanted to shift, to change the angle so the thick cock splitting him would strike his prostate more steadily, but that was not an option. Instead, he had to simply hang there within his restraints and take whatever the Admiral chose to give him.

By this point, as Peter continued to work his cock mercilessly in and out of the clenching sheath, any other prisoner would have been pleading with him, to stop or to give him more. This one did neither, and that gave Peter pause in the small part of his brain that could still function. His standard routine of beating and fucking was obviously not going to be enough for this one, and that—along with the little grunts and groans that were the only sounds to escape his prisoner's lips—turned the Admiral on beyond belief. His cock got even harder, his thrusts even more savage as he imagined the fun he would have finding Risner's limits. The images and the frantic pounding built like a phaser on overload until he could feel the energy crawling all over his skin, suffusing every part of his body. His balls tightened almost painfully and his release screamed out of him, leaving him shaking and panting with the force of it as he slumped against Risner's sweaty back.

The sudden loss of friction even as the thrusts continued, hard and fast, let Blaise know his captor had found his release. The thick cream coated his insides, easing the way while stinging the abraded tissue. He hissed at the added sensation before groaning in frustration when the pounding stopped, leaving him teetering on the edge of his own glorious explosion without the final push he needed to go off like a supernova. He bit his lip as he pushed back, asking silently for just a little more.

As he slowly came back from his orgasmic high, Peter felt Risner squirming underneath him. The mouthy spacer hadn't come yet, and he wasn't going to until he told Peter what he wanted to hear. "A little uncomfortable?" he asked, his voice still raspy from his own release.

"Nothing I can't handle," Blaise retorted, though the rough voice sent a fresh bolt of lust dancing down his nerves. A part of him knew he could probably get what he wanted if he would simply ask for it, but his pride insisted he keep his silence.

"Hard to the end, eh?" Peter pulled back enough to look at his partner's face for the first time since he'd started fucking him. He could see the tension in the dark eyes, and also the resistance. Risner knew exactly what Keller wanted to hear, and he wasn't going to give it to him. "Well then, you can just stay that way the rest of the night, unless you tell me why I shouldn't just pull out and leave you hanging here."

"You'll do what you want regardless of what I say," Blaise argued, though his body stiffened at the thought of losing the contact with Keller.

"I know your type. You'll make me beg only to refuse me, just to watch me suffer."

"If I wanted to make you suffer, I'd do this," Peter retorted, working his hand into his uniform pocket to press another key on the control device. A low frequency of energy hummed through the restraints, sending tendrils of stimulation snaking along Risner's nerves to converge in his groin. "Like that?" he asked as the pirate twitched beneath him. "I can leave you on edge like this as long as I want. The charge is completely harmless, except for the frustration factor, of course." Still sheathed deep in Risner's ass, Peter could feel the overflow of current seeping into his own nerves, stirring his softened cock to renewing life.

Blaise's pride issued one last protest before he pushed it aside. He'd gotten what he wanted from the Admiral. Would it really be so terrible to give the older man what he wanted in return? He would try it this once, but if his cynical side was right and Keller was just trying to humiliate him, he would never give in again. "Please," he said softly. "Please make me come."

The quiet request should have made Peter feel triumphant, and he did, but he also felt a glow of satisfaction that none of his former pets had been able to draw from him. Still, it was time for this one to learn his place, which was under Peter's control, always. "You'll come, all right, but for being such a stubborn bastard, the only thing you're going to get is my cock." He shuttled the stiffening length in the come-slick channel, just enough to brush over the smuggler's sweet spot before drawing back. "Is that what you want, Blaise? You want more of my cock pounding into you?"

The admission that hovered on Blaise's lips at the Admiral's first statement died a sudden death at the taunting. He would have admitted that all he needed was Keller's cock to come, but the thought of begging for it turned his stomach. Feeling the movement stop, though, he forced himself to utter a minimum of encouragement. "Yes," he ground out.

Risner's recalcitrance only made Peter all the more determined to wring an admission from him. This was a battle of wills he needed to win if he expected to keep the other man under his control. "Say it," he demanded, upping the power to a higher level. The sonic stimulation couldn't make Risner come by itself, but it would increase his need until he'd do almost anything to find relief. The fact that it was having the same effect on Peter himself was something he'd just have to deal with. At least he'd already come once. "Tell me how badly you need my cock."

Shoulders slumping, Blaise realized there was no way out without giving the Admiral what he wanted. "Give me your cock," he said dully, not caring how insincere he sounded. He couldn't force himself to make it sound believable, not now when all his fears had come to pass. Keller didn't care about anything but humiliating him.

Blaise just wanted this over so he could go back to his quarters and lick his wounds. The energy pulse through the cuffs on his wrist kept his body on the edge of his release, but his mind and heart were no longer in it, recoiling from the mortification of being forced to beg. "Pound me into the wall," he added in a monotone.

Keller had been intending to do just that, but the dead note in Risner's admission stripped any sense of value from the victory. More from sheer stubbornness than anything else, Peter gentled his thrusts, finding a depth and rhythm that matched the ongoing hum of the stimulator wave. He wrapped both hands around Risner's hips, changing the angle so the head of his cock dragged over the knot of nerves deep in the smuggler's sheath with every roll of his hips, adding to his own pleasure as he manipulated Risner's.

The sudden shift in tone left Blaise as confused as he was aroused, the pounding easing up, the movement changing so that every pass of the thick head nudged his prostate, making his body hitch and jerk. No more taunting words followed, either—no more demands—and he felt himself warming again to the moment, beginning to move again within his bonds, to participate once more in their intercourse.

Feeling Risner begin to stir beneath him was even more satisfying than forcing the words from him had been. It was becoming a point of pride for Peter to make the spacer come, the harder the better. He'd vowed not to touch his prisoner's cock again, but he hadn't prohibited himself from anything else, so he let his hands roam over the pirate's body, familiarizing himself with its contours and noting the more sensitive spots, finally rubbing his thumbs over the peaked nipples and playing with the silver piercing until he had Risner moaning again. "Come," he urged forcefully, struggling to hold back his own climax until he could win Risner's.

The strange contrast between the tenderness of Keller's hands and the relentlessness of his cock left Blaise trembling, his body superstimulated, but the order had him stiffening again. He was not a trained lapdog to be ordered to come that way. He shook his head even as his body tried to react. He fought it, not wanting to set the precedent of coming on command like a circus animal, but his passion-saturated system could not take any more. With a shuddering gasp, he climaxed, his cock twitching violently as it gave up its load at last. He slumped forward against the wall, hanging lax in his restraints as he struggled to make sense of all the contradictions. His body hummed with contented satiation even as his mind rebelled against giving control of his body over to another.

Risner's muscles tightened involuntarily around Peter as he came, the added pressure just what the Admiral needed to trigger his second orgasm. Emptying himself inside the body that was suddenly not fighting him any longer, Peter groaned deeply, thumbing off the control pad and letting his weight press against Risner while his heartbeat slowly returned to normal.

It took a few minutes, but eventually, awareness returned to Blaise, awareness of the Admiral still leaning against him, softening inside him. The stimulation from his restraints had ceased, but Keller did not seem to be finished with him. The spacer wondered uncomfortably what else the man wanted from him. If the situation had been different, he might have said the Admiral was leaning against him, holding him like a lover, but there was nothing of that dynamic between them. They were jailer and prisoner. Master and slave. Nothing more. As perverse as that seemed, he needed the assurance that it was true. Squirming, he tried as best he could to dislodge the other man.

Peter floated in free-fall, letting himself drift mindlessly on the endorphin rush of his climax. Coming twice in such rapid succession was unusual for him, even with the added stimulation of the energy boost; usually he was content to find his release as quickly as possible and be done with it, but he felt no hurry to disengage from his current position.

Risner squirming beneath him broke him out of his reverie to the reality of the present situation.

Pulling out with no effort at gentleness, Peter took a step back and tucked himself into his trousers, settling his persona back in place along with his uniform. He needed to kick Risner out of his quarters and get some sleep; the *North Star* would be breaking orbit tomorrow, resuming its standard patrol, and he had more than enough responsibilities to see to before then. Still, something stopped him from just thumbing the release to disengage the energy restraints, knowing when he did that his prisoner would slump bonelessly to the floor. He'd usually be halfway to the 'fresher without a backward glance before any of his earlier toys had crawled out of his cabin. Come to think of it, he'd never given any concern to how they'd made their way back to their quarters in whatever tatters he'd left of their worksuits, but the idea of Risner being exposed to the scrutiny of whoever chanced to pass him in the corridors disturbed him in a way he was too exhausted to consider at the moment.

He powered off the restraints and held Risner against the wall to prevent him from falling. "There's a clean shipsuit in the closet you can put on," he grated, unsettled by his own uncharacteristic behavior with this tempting but infuriating man.

Blaise blinked in surprise as he was supported and allowed to retain what little dignity he had left. He had not expected such kindness from his captor. Certainly, he had not seen this side of the man before, and it left him completely nonplussed. Feeling steady enough finally to keep his own balance, he pulled away and started toward the closet, intending to dress and leave as quickly as possible. He needed to get away from the Admiral and try to make sense of everything that had happened. Maybe then, he could decide the best way forward. He refused to be just another statistic, another notch in the commander's belt. And that meant finding a way to stay true to himself while surviving whatever Keller threw at him.

Refusing to allow his eyes to linger on Risner's reddened backside or the bruises already developing on his hips as the pirate stepped carefully into the fresh worksuit, Peter made his way back to the chair he'd been reading in earlier. "Someone will collect you in the morning to show you your duties. Your *other* duties," he couldn't help but add curtly as he picked up his book, knowing he was too keyed up to fall asleep right away. "Don't expect any special consideration there just because I've fucked you. You'll work as hard as any other member of my crew."

"I know how to hold my own on a ship," Blaise retorted instantly, offended that Keller would think otherwise. "I probably know more about running a ship than any crewman under your command. I'll pull my weight on any task you give me." He finished dressing and pulled his tattered dignity around him as best he could. "If you're finished with me, Admiral, sir, I'd like to return to my quarters. I want to be well-rested for my first day on the job."

He wouldn't be able to rest, he knew. His back and his ass both burned, constant reminders of what he had experienced at the Admiral's hands, and he could smell the other man's release on him and feel it as it seeped from his battered hole. He couldn't stay here any longer, though, not without saying or doing something he would certainly regret.

"Dismissed," Peter threw out without looking up from his volume.

Blaise left as quickly as he could, his body protesting any sudden movements. As he made his way back to the quarters he'd been assigned, a little closet barely big enough for a bed, he tried to wrap his mind around the contradictions Keller embodied. One minute, the man was beating him and fucking him nearly dry, the next he was practically cajoling him into coming. So which one was the real Admiral Keller? Which one was the personality he needed to be prepared for? If it were only one or the other, he would know how to act, but he had no idea how to handle two disparate facets at the same time.

With a sigh, he let himself into his quarters and stripped off the worksuit. It was the only one he had at the moment, though he imagined he would be issued more. For now, though, he would have to go through the day tomorrow with the smell of Keller's come surrounding him. The thought had him hardening slightly. With a muttered curse, he cleaned himself up and climbed onto the narrow bunk, wondering what the penalty would be for murdering the infuriating bastard. Whatever it was, it might almost be worth the satisfaction.

Only when the cabin door whooshed shut did Peter throw his book onto the desktop, running his hands through his cropped hair as he stood to pace restlessly, replaying his second climax in his mind. He'd won the words his pride demanded from the stubborn smuggler, but it was a savorless victory, knowing the admission was all but forced by the irresistible urges of the stimulation wave. As he stripped off his uniform and readied himself for sleep, Peter turned his mind to considering a way he could win the admission from the dark-haired spacer unforced. *What the fuck makes this one so different?* he asked his reflection before waving off the lights and dropping onto his bunk. *He's a mouthy, unyielding bastard who's going to fight me tooth and nail.* He battered his pillow into shape and stared at the ceiling, a smile quirking the corners of his lips now that no one was there to see. He'd never admit it to Risner, but he was looking forward to it.

CHAPTER 3
SHIP'S DISCIPLINE

Blaise stormed through the corridors of the *North Star* toward the Admiral's ready room, incensed at the potential danger he had discovered just a few minutes ago. Never mind that he was a prisoner here. Any threat to the ship was a threat to him as well. Punching at the door sensor, he stomped inside as soon as it snapped open, eyes focused exclusively on the commander sitting at the far end of the table.

"Does your crew have any discipline at all?" he demanded, not even looking around the room. "I'd have sent any officer of mine to the brig for this kind of negligence. The insulation on that power cable is all but eaten through, and if it had gone completely, you would have had an outage and a fire at least, possibly an explosion big enough to tear a hole in the hull. A standard inspection should have caught this weeks ago!"

A muffled cough penetrated Blaise's tirade. Breaking his eye contact with Keller, he glanced around the room at the other faces at the table, some there in person, others there via hologram. He didn't recognize any of them, but he guessed they were the command crew for both the *North Star* and the rest of the fleet at the Admiral's command. "Sir," he added belatedly, fully aware the title would not make up for the way he had started the conversation.

Admiral Keller glared at the smuggler with barely controlled anger. His temper was already frayed at his squadron's failure to find any trace of the mysterious vessel that had destroyed the science outpost. There had been increasing reports of ships gone missing as well, and while some of those disappearances had doubtless been by choice, the increase was too large to dismiss as mere coincidence.

His frustration had a more immediate cause as well. After pulling strings and calling in favors to have the provocative piece of ass assigned to the *North Star,* he'd deliberately stayed away from his prisoner for the past week, trying to make sense of the unprecedented welter of emotions the dark-haired smuggler aroused in him. Right now, infuriation was definitely prevalent. His crew knew better than to interrupt the daily officer's briefing, and Risner's thinly veiled criticism rankled to a degree disproportionate to his admittedly perceptive discovery.

"Dmitrov!" he barked to the *North Star's* engineer and his second in command. "Why hasn't your staff seen a bad cable show up on your routine scans? Why does it take a maintenance worker—a correctional worker!—to do your job for you? If it's too much for you to handle, I can drop you off at our next stop and you can find your own way back to your homeworld!"

The Regulosian flushed to the roots of his pale hair, but at least had the intelligence not to make excuses to his commanding officer. "Let me get down to the engine room and get a crew on it right away, sir," he answered, rising to his feet. "In which corridor did you find the damaged cable?" he addressed Blaise.

"Deck C, corridor twelve," Blaise replied, aware of the tension in the room but not sure how to extricate himself from the situation now. "I was cleaning as assigned and smelled hot plasma. I opened one of the hatches and found the cable with the insulation almost eaten through. Another few days and it would have gone for sure." He deliberately kept his tone even and his eyes on the albino engineer rather than on the Admiral. While he'd felt Keller's rejection keenly the past few days and had plotted ways to recapture the man's attention, this was not at all what he'd planned.

Nodding his acknowledgment, Dmitrov all but raced from the ready room. The Admiral's gaze returned to his infuriating prisoner. It was time to remind Risner exactly what his place was on this ship. "Report to my private cabin. I'll deal with you once I've finished here," he snapped.

Blaise nodded once and retreated from the room. He'd left his cart in the corridor where he'd discovered the cable, but he didn't go back for it. It would serve the crew right to have to clean up after him. Slowly, he made his way to Keller's quarters and waited. Pacing the luxurious cabin, he wondered what the next few hours would hold, entirely sure not all of it would be good. He'd succeeded in getting the Admiral's attention, but quite possibly not the kind he wanted. He somehow doubted that he'd put the commander in the mood for an afternoon of energetic fucking with his unintentional show of disrespect.

The swoosh of the door sliding open drew Blaise's attention, and he turned to face the scowling Admiral who prowled into the room. Nope, definitely not fucking. If he was lucky, he'd get off with just a beating.

Peter kept his expression firmly rigid as he stalked into his cabin. He'd found it hard to concentrate on the remainder of the meeting after Risner's departure. Despite giving his officers a ferocious dressing-down for daring to allow system checks to become lax on his ship, and assuring them of the consequences if he discovered similar laxity in their sensor sweeps for the hostile vessel, his thoughts kept drifting to his cabin in anticipation. Risner looked suitably apprehensive after having been kept waiting, which Peter had counted on. Yes, he'd enjoy teaching the pirate the error of his ways. He had some toys he hadn't used in far too long that he'd certainly appreciate, even if Risner didn't.

"Just what did you think you were doing, interrupting a senior officers' meeting like that?" the Admiral demanded, pacing in front of the dark-haired spacer.

"I didn't actually know you were having a meeting," Blaise defended himself. "I asked where you were and was told your ready room. Regardless, would you really have wanted me to wait to let you know what I'd found? That few days I gave the power cable was probably generous. You could have had a potentially lethal situation on your hands." He didn't say he would have taken a different tack had he known about the meeting. He doubted Keller would believe him anyway.

As irritated—and to be honest, as embarrassed—as he was to have Risner discover anything slipshod, let alone potentially dangerous, on his ship, Peter's innate honesty forced him to say, "It was a good find, and bringing it to my attention was the right thing to do." He narrowed his eyes, their emerald depths glinting with intensity. "It's your manner of bringing it to me I have a problem with." Eying the smuggler's defensive stance, he gestured with one hand, the other delving into his pocket. "Come closer."

Blaise approached the Admiral warily. That hand in the commander's pocket never boded well for the subsequent few minutes. Whatever toy or control resided in the tight space would surely be used to torment him in a matter of moments.

"Right there." Peter stopped Risner when he was positioned where he wanted him. "Now, strip." He saw the flare of resistance in the pirate's eyes and added, "Or I can take it off you myself, but I expect you're running low on worksuits."

Blaise knew exactly how his clothes would come off if the Admiral took them off—in shreds—and he really didn't have very many to spare, much less with him. Deciding this was not a fight he could win, he efficiently pulled the coveralls from his spare frame, tossing them aside where hopefully they would survive whatever Keller had in store for him. Lifting his chin, he faced the commander with as much dignity as he could muster, clad only in the dormant restraints that still circled his wrists and ankles.

A bit surprised that Risner hadn't protested his order, Peter pressed the key on his pocket transmitter that activated the restraint system. Contact points in the floor forced Blaise's legs a precise distance apart, while a metal bar lowered from the ceiling to catch the wrist restraints, leaving him spread-eagled before his captor. Peter circled the pirate, admiring the well-defined musculature that enforced labor had only enhanced, but not touching. Not yet.

Blaise tensed as his arms and legs were forced into place by the cuffs that surrounded them. His head twisted as he tried to follow the Admiral, to guess what the other man had planned for him. Naked and thus displayed, he was once again completely at Keller's mercy, a feeling he could not help but detest, not when he had no say in the matter, no way out if things got too rough. No, the fleet officer hadn't tortured him yet the way the Gavenelians had done, but that didn't guarantee anything. "What are you going to do to me?"

Pausing in his anticipatory perusal, Peter ignored Risner's question. "I've been lax in your training," he said instead, his voice cool. "I wouldn't expect a pirate to understand military discipline, but on this ship I'm in command. I don't give a damn what your personal opinion is of me, or of your situation. You can try your defiance on me all you like when we're alone, but when we're in public, you will approach me with the respect to which I am entitled."

"Privateer," Blaise retorted automatically, "and respect wasn't very high on my priority list when faced with a potentially life-threatening situation. Leaks happen on any ship, but that one had been there for six weeks easily, to have damaged the cable that badly. You can be sure something like that wouldn't have gone unnoticed for so long on my ship!"

As much as Peter was grateful that the problem had been discovered, he'd already given the insolent "privateer" all the credit his pride would allow. He didn't need some criminal whose one-man smuggling ship was held together with spit and scavenged parts telling him how to command his vessel. "You're on *my* ship now, and in case you've forgotten, you will be for the next three years. And since you obviously need a lesson in discipline, that's exactly what you're going to get." Turning his back on the restrained pirate, Peter stepped behind the partition that separated the workspace from his sleeping quarters, returning with a flat metal box.

Blaise bit his tongue against repeating his question. The Admiral clearly wasn't going to give him an answer, and he refused to demean himself any more by seeming to plead.

Selecting the implements he'd decided on in his ready room, Peter set aside the container and turned back toward Risner. "I doubt you have enough self-discipline to keep from coming until I tell you to," he commented, weighing the contents of his palm.

"Try me," Blaise challenged. "I did it last time."

"Tempting," the Admiral considered, "but the purpose of this punishment is to teach you discipline." He couldn't help but notice the way Risner's cock thickened at his words. "You like that idea? You think you're going to enjoy this? You'll come when I'm ready to let you come, and not before." Grasping the hardening shaft, he closed an ornamented metal circlet around its base, flicking it shut with a tap of his control device. Immediately, a low level of power energized the ring, sending ribbons of stimulation up and down Blaise's length and tingling into his groin.

Biting his lip against a moan that wanted to escape, Blaise felt his shaft swell to full hardness immediately, constrained by the ring even as he was stimulated by it. His hips jerked forward of their own accord, reaching for contact, for relief. It seemed his captor had a taste for torture after all, albeit of a very different kind.

"You definitely need to learn discipline," Peter chuckled, noting Risner's instinctual response to the stimulus field. "We haven't even gotten started yet." Picking up the matching silver ornaments he'd placed to one side, he dangled the elegantly decorative toy before Blaise's eyes. "Nipple clamps," he explained, spreading the first clip to squeeze around a brown nub. "Got them as a matched set with the ring from a trader in the pleasure bazaar on Regulus." He could feel the sensuous vibrations affecting him just from handling the clamps; affixed to his captive's chest, they'd provide the most exquisite torment. "Given your penchant for self-adornment, perhaps you'll appreciate them." He carefully affixed the second clamp around the pirate's piercing, aligning it so that it would vibrate the ring for even more stimulation.

Ah, shit! Blaise's back arched and his head fell back as he struggled to assimilate the steady pulses from the clamps and ring. When he trusted his voice to be steady, he looked at the Admiral again, challenge plain in his eyes. "I get it," he spat. "You can't make me beg fast enough yourself so you resort to something like this to break me. Nice try, Admiral, but it won't work."

"You wound me with your suspicions, Blaise," Peter murmured solicitously. "I don't want to hear you beg. In fact, I have no doubt you'll be begging so soon and so often that it will become tiresome. That's why I have this." He held up a small ball, less than an inch in diameter, which looked like some sort of translucent bead or marble. "Open your mouth—that never seems to be a problem for you."

"That's supposed to keep me quiet?" Blaise asked suspiciously, eyeing the small object. Even if Keller did force it into his mouth, it wouldn't keep him from talking if he wanted to. He could just slip it into his cheek. "Tell me another one."

"It looks innocuous, doesn't it?" Peter agreed, popping the bead past Risner's full lips without resistance. "Don't let the size fool you. That's a Canopian ball gag. It's activated by heat. The warmth of your mouth is already making it swell, isn't it? The hotter you get, the bigger it gets." His leering gaze left Blaise with no question that he'd be getting him plenty hot. "Don't worry; its internal sensors will stop its growth before there's any danger of it choking you."

Blaise's eyes widened as he felt the object reacting exactly as Keller said it would, pressing his tongue down, forcing his jaw open, not far yet, but enough that he already could not talk. Even if the Admiral didn't touch him again, the oscillations from the nipple clamps and cock ring had already jump-started his passions, and the privateer was sure they were on the lowest setting, not the highest. A deep-throated groan escaped him, the only sound he could now make.

"Comfortable?" Peter asked, trailing a hand down Blaise's ribs and setting the filigree between the nipple clamps swaying with a flick of one long finger, knowing it would send the vibrations dancing through Blaise's body. "I hope so, because I have some work to do before I can give you the attention you require." Crossing the room to his small desk, Peter powered on the vidscreen and began reviewing the daily department heads' reports.

Blaise groaned again, as much in frustration this time as in passion. Trussed up as he was, he could do nothing but hang in his bonds and let the toys work their spell on his body. He had no way even of enticing the Admiral back to his side, no way to draw the other man's attention. Resigning himself to the wait, he closed his eyes and tried to send his mind elsewhere, a trick he had learned well at the hands of the Gavenelians. It seemed, though, that pleasure was much harder to escape than pain and he found himself unable to retreat, to distance himself from the intimate, arousing sensations. Head falling forward, he relaxed as much as he was able and endured.

The Admiral had every intention of completing some of the work Risner had interrupted when he burst into the daily officers' meeting, but after reading the same screen of text three times without comprehending a word of it, Peter admitted to himself that he was much more interested in the man behind him than the status of the hydroponic gardens. *Discipline,* he thought wryly as the sound of muffled moans and the limited movement Blaise was capable of tempted him. He forced himself to focus on ship's business until the chronometer showed that thirty minutes had elapsed before shutting off the monitor and spinning his chair around to survey the prisoner again.

Hearing the squeak of the chair, Blaise lifted his head, his gaze hot as he regarded his captor. His body thrummed with unassuaged lust, his nerves tingling all over, the vibrations spreading out from the points of contact until every inch of his skin felt exquisitely sensitive. He was almost glad for the ball in his mouth. Without it, he would surely be begging for the Admiral's attention, and that was more power than he was willing to give the other man.

Judging by the need simmering in the smuggler's eyes as he stared pleadingly at Peter, the stimulant devices had done their work well. The Admiral rested his chin in his palm and returned the stare. "Need something?" he asked calmly, stretching his legs in front of him, the bulge in his uniform trousers readily apparent.

Blaise whimpered against the gag, feeling a fresh wave of lust hit him as he stared at what he craved. Immediately, the gag in his mouth swelled again, almost choking him, but as the Admiral had promised, it stopped just short of cutting off his breath. Twisting his wrists within the cuffs that held them immobile, he beckoned with his fingers, the only part of his body he could move freely.

His eyebrows crawling upward, Peter leaned forward, resting his elbows on his knees as he regarded his prisoner. He spread his legs to relieve the press of his arousal as he took in the sight of Blaise's cock straining against the decorative metal of the ring, the delicate filigree swinging from his distended nipples, the tremors that shook through his powerful frame as each movement sent another pulse of stimulation wavering through him. "Feeling a bit uncomfortable?" he asked, letting one hand drift down to ghost over his own swelling cock.

How Keller expected him to answer, Blaise had no idea. Instead, he glared at the arrogant Admiral and beckoned again. At least if the commander was touching him, there was some chance of the vibrations passing to him as well and moving this torture along.

"Cocky bastard, aren't you?" Peter commented, staring pointedly at Blaise's crotch, which was leaking a spider's silk of pale fluid down to the cabin floor. "Rather literally, at the moment. But you don't deserve my cock after the lack of respect you showed to me and my position."

He rose and strolled over to the pirate, breaking the strand of pre-come with his finger and raising it to Blaise's lips. "Oh, you can't, can you?" he purred, licking the fluid from his finger with a show of enjoyment, his tongue lingering over the long digit before returning to lick his lips.

Sadistic bastard! Blaise snarled in the silence of his thoughts. He was sure his frustration showed clearly on his face, but he could do nothing more than stand there at the Admiral's whim. His cock strained futilely against the ring surrounding it, his orgasm threatening but powerless against the constriction. He wondered how he was supposed to make reparations for his lack of respect earlier when he couldn't even move, but of course, he had no way of even asking the question.

Even with his mouth gagged, Risner's emotions were clear on his face, and it was all Peter could do to keep from grinning at the darker man's blatant frustration. "I could leave you like that all night. They say it's quite safe to leave the stimulators on, for days even," he continued, ignoring the choking sound coming from Blaise's throat, "but I suppose that could be considered cruel and unusual punishment. No, I suppose I'll just have to find some other way to finish you off." His viridian gaze swept the built-in shelves along the wall to his left, though he already knew exactly what he planned to use to bring the arrogant smuggler to his knees. Figuratively, at least.

Blaise nodded his head vehemently, not even caring what Keller might come up with. Anything that got him off would be better than being left in limbo like this.

Crossing to the display case, Peter picked up what appeared to be a sculpture made of some translucent, veined material. It was thick and sinuously twisted, a rib of darker material spiraling around its length. "Pretty, isn't it?" he asked Blaise, stroking the serpentine curves. "The Orion trader I got it from swears it was once used in the pleasure harems of the Emperor himself, before the revolution that led to their joining the Confederation."

Blaise's eyes widened as he took in the lines of the sculpture, realizing that it was far more than just a piece of art. His ass clenched reflexively at the thought of the ribbed length sliding inside him even as his hips tilted forward as if inviting the touch.

"Slut," Peter grinned as he squeezed a generous portion of lubrication over the cool stone of the exotic dildo. "You wouldn't care what I shoved up your ass at this point, would you? All you care about is getting off." Circling behind the pirate, he grabbed a handful of one cheek and pressed the head of the artifact against the puckered muscle, smearing it with lube but not pushing inside.

Blaise whimpered through the gag, pressing back against the restraining hand and the teasing toy. He couldn't even bring himself to care about the Admiral's taunts, not when he couldn't do anything about them and his body was so very, very hungry for the attention.

"You need this, don't you?" Peter rasped, letting the blunt head of the dildo stretch the entrance and twisting it slowly. "If it weren't for that gag in your mouth, you'd be begging me to fuck you with it, promising me anything if I just put it inside you and reamed you fast and hard, wouldn't you?" Blaise pushed back against him and Peter smacked the cheek he'd been holding, hard enough to redden it, the impact letting the tip of the stone phallus push past the straining ring of muscle.

Blaise's head dropped forward in defeat as he nodded. The Gavenelians couldn't break him with pain, but it seemed the Admiral had already done it with pleasure.

The pirate's seeming docility didn't fool Peter for a minute, and he'd wager a bottle of hundred-year-old Cornixian brandy that it wouldn't last once he gave him what Blaise's entire body was begging for. With a twist of his wrist, Peter worked the ridged dildo deep into Blaise's channel, corkscrewing it in a way that would ensure the smuggler felt every rib spiraling inside him.

The gag in his mouth couldn't silence Blaise's scream of pleasure as he finally felt himself filled, the alien dildo rubbing against every sensitive spot in his passage. His back arched as his body tried to climax, held back only by the still-pulsing ring around his cock. Every muscle in his body stood out in sharp definition as the various sensations warred within him, leaving him trembling even as he pushed back into the Admiral's touch, begging silently for more.

A backwash of lust coursed through Peter at the sudden tension in Blaise's body as he tried to take the dildo even deeper inside him. He wanted it to be his cock buried inside that clenching channel, pounding into the dark-haired spacer the way he was working the dildo, deep and fast and hard while Blaise writhed and groaned against him. *Discipline,* he reminded himself, gritting his teeth as he twirled the veined phallus until he was sure he was hitting Blaise's prostate with every stroke. His free hand groped around Blaise's body until it found his cock, the head slick with fluid as it fought the stimulus ring in an effort to climax.

Blaise thrashed against his bonds, the hand on his cock more than his shattered self-control could stand. He needed to be free, needed to come, needed Keller to fuck him into the next galaxy, not with the dildo but with his own hard erection. Tears thickened his lashes as he struggled to find his release through the ring holding him back.

His own cock throbbing with need, Peter slid his hand down the length of Blaise's shaft to the root, fingering through the wiry curls until he found the release catch of the stimulus ring. Twisting the thick dildo so that its head scraped roughly over Blaise's prostate, he thumbed the release, letting the ring fall to the floor and wrapping his palm around Blaise's spasming cock. "You can come now," he purred, fighting to retain his own control as a flood of thick, hot seed splashed over his hand.

Blaise was far beyond conscious control, his body reacting even before the Admiral's words registered in his head, his cock spewing fluid all over Keller's hand and his own belly. His back arched as he screamed through the gag, the force of his release leaving him hanging limply from the bonds around his wrists.

The gag prevented Peter from demanding that Blaise clean up the mess he'd made of his hand, but his cock was doing some demanding of its own. Tearing the dildo gracelessly from Blaise's still-twitching ass and dropping it to the floor, Peter fumbled his uniform trousers open with his clean hand. Smearing the still-hot come over his cock, he grabbed Blaise's shoulder for leverage and plunged into the pirate's passage, burying himself to the hilt in a single stroke. The walls tightened around him as he rutted ferally, not caring what the power of his thrusts was doing to Blaise, intent on nothing but finding his own relief from the lust that rode him.

Blaise whimpered softly, head falling forward as the Admiral pounded into him, using him callously for his own pleasure. He suspected he should have felt dirtied by it, but he only felt desired. In the back of his head, a voice whispered that he—his body—had pushed the Admiral beyond the limits of his control just as surely as Keller had pushed him. His body reacted predictably to the pummeling, his shaft hardening again as the clamps around his nipples continued to send arousing vibrations to add to the sensation of the commander's cock stretching him perfectly. The dildo had rubbed places Keller's erection did not, but Keller fit him in a way nothing else, no one else, ever had.

Hot tongues of fire danced across Peter's nerves as Blaise's aftershocks squeezed him, each clench of the spasming passage driving him closer to his own release. He wrapped his free hand around the spacer's hips to push in even deeper, his hand brushing the evidence of Blaise's resurgent arousal. Was it only the stimulant field, Peter wondered, or was it him, his cock reaming into the pirate, that was making Blaise react this way? A thrill of pride and possessiveness filled him and he grasped the thickening shaft again, fisting it in time with his thrusts. "Come for me again," he growled, his teeth worrying the skin of the other man's throat, marking him. "Come for *me* this time."

Blaise strained back against the shaft driving relentlessly into him, reaching for the release that hovered just out of his grasp. He was so close, wanted so badly to come and end the sensual torment, even knowing it would be giving in to the Admiral. *Please,* he begged silently. *Make me come.*

He had Blaise right where he'd imagined, writhing against him as he pounded into the hard flesh. The spacer encouraged his assault in silence, his body pushing back against him thrust for thrust. Suddenly Peter wanted nothing so much as to hear Blaise scream as he forced a second climax from him. Lifting his hand from the spacer's broad shoulder, he worked a finger between Blaise's lips, wedging it under the swelling gag ball and tearing it from his mouth. "Scream for me," he rasped hoarsely, his fist speeding on Blaise's cock as he felt himself losing his own battle for control.

Mouth freed from the constriction, the sounds that had been muffled tore from Blaise's throat, screams and cries and pleading. Blaise had no idea what he even said, but the rhythmic pounding didn't cease, instead increasing in intensity.

The sounds of need and entreaty he wrung from Blaise were the catalyst Peter needed to trigger his own orgasm, his release flaring with the power of a rocket's ignition as he shuddered and pumped into Blaise's abused channel. The blaze of pleasure lifted him into orbit, his body continuing to rock as he chased the waning sensation, his hand never slowing on Blaise's leaking shaft.

Feeling the thick fluid flooding his passage pushed Blaise over the edge, sending him spinning out of control. With a shout, he came again, his knees giving out so that only the cuffs around his wrists and Keller's body behind him kept him from collapsing to the floor. His vision grayed around the edges as he fought not to lose consciousness, not wanting to show weakness in front of his captor.

Peter let himself drift in a nebulous haze, leaning against Blaise's restrained body. The warm sweaty skin against the stiffness of his uniform almost made him want to be naked too. Just for a moment he let himself imagine stripping off his confining garments and taking Blaise again, without the artificial stimulus this time, to see if he could make him scream as loudly and come as hard from his own efforts alone, but there were still too many reports to get through, too many duties to be completed. Biting back a sigh, he disengaged his softening shaft from Blaise's channel, adjusting his uniform and knowing he'd have to step in the 'fresher after Blaise left or he'd be distracted by the scent and the memories of their sex for the rest of the ship's day.

Eying Blaise in consideration, he decided the younger man would be able to stand on his own before pressing the control to release the restraint field. "In the future, you will extend me all due respect in public," he ordered, nodding toward Blaise's discarded shipsuit. "You can consider this only a taste of what to expect if your defiance continues."

Blaise stumbled a little when his hands were released, his muscles screaming in protest as he could move again. He rubbed at his shoulders even as he bristled at the words. "You'll get the respect you deserve," he muttered, though he knew he would not intentionally provoke the Admiral in public. He was coming to enjoy their games. He could admit to himself at least that he craved Keller's attention, but the stimulant devices, the dildo, were not what he wanted. He wanted the commander's hands, the commander's cock in his body, and flaunting his independence in public didn't seem likely to get him that privilege. Reaching for the nipple clamps that still stimulated his abused flesh, he pulled off one, then the other, handing them silently to the Admiral before walking stiffly toward his clothes.

Sinking back into his desk chair, Peter curled his fingers around the nipple clamps as he watched Blaise dress, nodding a silent dismissal once the last fastening was sealed. He wasn't sure whether he hoped Blaise would learn to follow ship's discipline or not. He had a feeling that dealing with the pirate's rebellious nature would be a lot more rewarding.

CHAPTER 4
BOUND AND DETERMINED

PETER ran a hand through his cropped hair and glared at the vidscreen, willing it to display information that just wasn't there. After months of tracking down reports of ships gone missing in the sparsely colonized sector where the science outpost had been destroyed, he'd begun to feel the *North Star* was chasing after ghosts. His bridge crew had started to cringe at his reaction when each trail went cold without any trace of the vanished vessels. He'd overheard his navigator, Lieutenant Bhaskar, complain to his executive officer, Sasha Dmitrov, that she'd rather shave her hair off than admit one more time that she couldn't find anything on her sensors. Since despite keeping it intricately braided while on duty, the Altarian probably hadn't cut her long silver hair since before she'd entered the Academy, he judged his officers were getting as frustrated as he was.

Then, two days ago, they'd finally found one of the ships that had been reported missing. Unfortunately, the scraps of wreckage that were all that remained of the *Scheherazade* hadn't been able to tell them much. The small freighter had been hit by heavy blaster fire, judging from the scarring on the hunks of metal they'd been able to scavenge. Half his science staff was poring over sensor scans of the remaining hull fragments, while the other half was searching the starfield for parsecs in every direction, hunting for any trace of the vessel responsible for the *Scheherazade*'s destruction. Peter had spent hours since the ship's identification studying the freighter's specifications and flight plans for the months prior to its disappearance, in a vain attempt to find anything that might explain its fate.

The comm panel beeped, the screen changing to the image of his chief science officer, Aiko Hiroyuki. "Anything?" he growled irritably.

"We've been able to get enough of a reading to match the energy signature of the blasters," the petite scientist reported. "They're definitely the same class of weapons that destroyed ConSci 2114."

The impact of Peter's fist on the desk was enough to make Lieutenant Hiroyuki flinch. Throttling his anger, the Admiral nodded curtly. "Good work, Aiko. Put a report together to notify Fleet HQ as soon as possible." At least now they had proof that the station's destruction and the disappearing vessels were related.

Blaise paused outside the Admiral's quarters, debating the wisdom of entering. He needed to report that they were getting low on supplies for routine maintenance, but he could easily report that to Commander Dmitrov or one of the other senior staff. He didn't really need to disturb the Admiral, except that he hadn't seen Keller in almost a week and this seemed like the perfect excuse. He might not always like the man, but his body definitely craved his touch. Deciding that being sent away was the worst that could happen, he buzzed at the door.

Peter's brow knit in renewed concentration when the vidscreen flipped from Aiko's somber features to the mocking image of the *Scheherezade*'s twisted hull. He scowled at the wreckage, balked at the little they'd been able to learn from it, until a buzz from the corridor drew his attention. "Come," he called without looking up, the cabin door sliding open in response to his voice command. Turning in his chair, his expression unconsciously lightened when he spotted Risner lounging in the doorway. "I don't remember sending for you," he drawled, though in truth, the interruption was welcome. His crew might not realize it, but they'd have found him even more short-tempered if he hadn't occasionally been able to work off some of his frustrations after duty hours with the dark-haired pirate.

"You didn't," Blaise admitted, "but we're running a little low on plasma refills and I thought you'd want to know right away. Since we're pretty far out and all."

Lips twitching at the flimsy justification, Peter waved his prisoner inside. "I'll be sure to get right on that. Any other requests while you're at it?"

Blaise shrugged, unwilling to admit to his true desires. "Is everything all right?" he asked instead, seeing the tension obvious in the set of Keller's shoulders and the tightness around his eyes.

An automatic denial turned into a grimace when Peter stood, muscles protesting the hours he'd spent hunched over his comp screen. On impulse, he nodded toward the image of the scarred metal hulk. Risner'd spent plenty of time in space; maybe he could spot something Peter had missed. "What do you make of that?"

Surprised—Keller had never expressed interest in anything except his body before now—Blaise crossed the room to peer at the vidscreen. His eyes widened even further as he took in the destruction. "That had to hurt," he replied, automatically flippant in his usual defense against anything that hit too close to home. "I take it since we're sitting here and not headed out after someone that you don't know who the culprits are." He looked closer, a low whistle escaping his lips. "It looks like they took direct hits, like the weapons went straight through the shields."

"Tore through them like tissue." He'd still be after the attackers in a heartbeat if he had the first idea where to look. Whatever shields a tramp freighter had couldn't possibly be as strong as the *North Star*'s. Peter snapped off the viewer in frustration. "Unfortunately, the only thing we know about them is that they like to blow things up."

"I'm not sure that's a recommendation," Blaise quipped, trying to lighten the Admiral's mood a little. He told himself it was self-protection, because otherwise the blond would take his mood out on Blaise's ass.

"I wasn't planning on inviting them over for drinks." Peter briefly considered pouring himself something, but Blaise's sarcastic remarks were doing a better job of easing his stress than a bottle of Centaurian cognac. "Am I to assume that you've finished your duties for the day?"

"Yes," Blaise acknowledged. "I was just about to head back to my quarters to clean up and see if I had any orders for the evening."

"Orders? I didn't think you knew what those are." Deciding he'd done all he could for the day himself, Peter indulged in a slow perusal of the smuggler's lean, toned body. He knew what Risner was insinuating, knew he could simply order the prisoner to see to his needs, but he'd admitted to himself by now that he enjoyed the added spice of their confrontations. Judging by how often the pirate continued to goad him, he was beginning to suspect Blaise enjoyed it, too.

"Just because I choose not to follow them doesn't mean I don't understand the concept," Blaise retorted with a smirk. He took immense pleasure in bucking the Admiral's authority just enough to unleash the other man's temper.

"What about tonight?" Peter asked in a deceptively soft voice, meeting Risner's cocky gaze with his own unyielding stare. "Were you planning to choose to consider my orders?"

"I haven't heard any yet," Blaise retorted. "I can't consider a hypothetical." He crossed his arms easily over his chest, leaning against the wall as he grinned. "So what orders am I considering obeying tonight, Admiral?"

"Let's start with an easy one. Strip."

That *was* an easy one. Pushing away from the wall, Blaise unfastened his worksuit, peeling it off his shoulders to reveal first his pierced nipple, then the tattoo adorning his upper arm. Letting the suit fall to the floor, he stepped out of the puddle of fabric. "I'll need something to wear back to my quarters," he commented by means of justification for his easy obedience.

"Not necessarily, but it's good to know you respond to self-interest, if nothing else." His erection hardening enough for his uniform to feel constrictive, Peter tweaked the ring glinting through Risner's dusky hair. "Now me."

Blaise's chest arched into the touch. He'd almost immediately stopped trying to hide his reaction to tugs on his piercing. Keller spent far too much time playing with it for him to have any hope of succeeding. Better to let his captor see that weak spot and hide others. He could feel his cock swelling, but given his nudity, he had even less chance of success at hiding that. He slid his hands over the Admiral's chest, finding the closures at his shoulders, undoing them and revealing Keller's hard body. A man who spent all his time on a ship should *not* look so good!

Shrugging out of the sleeves of his uniform, Peter traced the wing of Blaise's hip bone backward, sliding down to cup a curved cheek and squeeze possessively. "Do you leave your other chores half-done too?" he goaded when Risner made no move to continue.

"Only the ones I might enjoy redoing," Blaise replied, pushing Keller's uniform the rest of the way off. "The others, I make sure to do right the first time."

"And which classification does this fall under?" Peter asked, catching Blaise's other hip and pulling him forward to grind against him demandingly, the immediate surge of the pirate's erection its own answer.

"Have I disappointed you yet?" Blaise answered, deliberately vague. His body's reaction was telling enough without giving the Admiral any more power.

The Admiral's grip on Blaise's ass tightened enough that he was probably leaving bruises. The thought of Blaise feeling his finger marks beneath his shipsuit as he worked the next day appealed to Peter, and he used the grasp to drag his cock roughly against the pirate's. "Let's just say you don't always respond with alacrity to every suggestion."

"I wouldn't want you getting bored with me before my sentence is up," Blaise quipped, a slight gasp escaping his lips as the Admiral's fingers dug into his cheeks and his cock teased Blaise's. "What would I do without you to keep me entertained in the evenings?"

"I think you have that backward," Peter countered, connecting a swat to Blaise's rear that won a groan from each of them when the impact slid their cocks together with raw friction. "You're the prisoner here; you're supposed to be entertaining me."

Blaise smirked, his skin smarting lightly from the slap. "So how shall I entertain you tonight, O Mighty One? I'm not wearing manacles, so you'll have to find some other way to tie me down. Or up. Or whatever suits your fancy."

Admitting silently that he preferred Blaise without manacles, at least in public—unless a prisoner had tried to escape, on a ship in deep space their only purpose was demeaning—Peter still had to smile at the smuggler's response. "Are you asking to be restrained, Risner? Because I'm more than happy to comply." Stepping back, he aimed another swat at the reddened cheeks that, sure enough, displayed a clear set of finger-spaced marks. "Get in the bedroom. I'm sure I can find something to accommodate you in there."

Blaise's eyebrows shot up. This was the first time he'd been invited—okay, ordered—into the Admiral's bedroom. "Going to show me all your secrets now?" he asked lightly, walking toward the screen that shielded the sleeping alcove from view. "I can't wait to see what you have in store for me tonight."

"Do I look like a fool?" Peter asked, lingering to enjoy the view of Risner's really exceptional ass before following into the private half of his quarters. "You already think you can give me orders. If I showed you all my secrets, you'd be trying to take over the ship." He paused, watching as Blaise looked around the rather utilitarian space. "Or the fleet."

"You know me so well," Blaise joked, looking back over his shoulder at the fine form of a man following behind him. "My ambitions have always been bigger than my good sense."

"Is that what led you to smuggling?" Peter asked, surprising himself with the question. He'd never had any interest in a prisoner's history before, but Risner's comment made him realize how little he knew about the dark-haired spacer beyond the scant information in his court record.

Blaise shrugged. "You've got me in your bedroom naked. You don't really want to talk about my past, do you?" he replied evasively. He didn't want to talk about his attempts at legitimate shipping, the huge debts he'd accrued and how the only way to pay them off had been to take illegal runs. Hoping to distract Keller, he stretched out on the Admiral's bed as if he had every right to be there. "Surely you can think of more interesting things to do with me."

And that's why I never ask my prisoners questions, Peter thought wryly. Dismissing his curiosity about Blaise's background as irrelevant, he turned his mind instead to the pleasurable task of deciding which restraint to use on his provoking pirate. "Make yourself at home," he murmured sardonically, though he had a feeling he'd be picturing Risner's decadent sprawl over his bedcover long after the smuggler had returned to his own cabin. Turning away from the arousing tableau, he bent to retrieve a box from a recessed cabinet that opened only to his retina scan.

"Oh, I plan to," Blaise drawled easily, enjoying the view of Keller's ass as he bent over to get something out of a cabinet. With another lover at another time, he'd have taken that as an invitation and pounced, but he suspected the Admiral would not be impressed, so he limited himself to ogling the finely toned flesh, filing the image away for fantasies on the nights Keller didn't have time for him. "So what delights do you have in store for me tonight?"

Rising, Peter dangled an unimpressive ball of tangled string from his finger. "As comfortable as you look, I'm afraid I'll have to ask you to stand again. You need to be erect for this to work." Glancing at the definitely impressive cock curving up from its nest of dark curls, Peter lifted an eyebrow. "That doesn't appear to be something you have a problem with."

Blaise snickered. "Not when you're around, no." Languidly, he pushed to his feet, wondering what fiendish torture the ball of thread would inflict on him. He remembered the Canopian ball gag and had resolved never to underestimate Keller's toys again.

Finding an end on the dark skein, Peter draped it across Risner's shoulder, letting the rest drop free. At a touch to the accompanying control, the strands began to work their way around the pirate's body, twisting across his chest and lower, slithering between his legs and up again to encircle him in an intricate pattern of knots. To his credit, Peter noted, Blaise controlled his instinctive reaction, not flinching until the ropes wove around his cock and balls, the constriction making them harden even more.

"Interesting gadget," Blaise commented evenly, controlling the gasp that wanted to escape as the ropes moved over him, binding him in an intricate design that reminded him of shibari, an art he had seen on Earth but never experienced. He shifted experimentally. The ropes moved with him, adjusting to his position without chafing or pulling, but never letting up on the pressure on his groin. "So what happens now?"

Peter didn't answer, his eyes raking over the enflaming image of the dark ropes against the smuggler's honey-hued skin. He'd bought the device from a sex bazaar on Spica Virginus, but the opportunity to try it out hadn't arisen until now. He had to admit it lived up to every one of the vendor's claims. Dropping the control on the bed, he reached forward, adjusting the cords to better frame the ring on Risner's chest. The adornment glittered in contrast, goading him to twist it until Blaise groaned. "Now I do anything I want to you, of course. Unless you have another suggestion?"

"Far be it from me to presume," Blaise groaned as Keller played with his piercing. "Although this isn't going to keep me here if I wanted to leave. It moves with me too easily."

"Are you planning to leave?" Peter retrieved the control, tweaking it until the ropes tightened, tendrils trailing around the pirate's limbs to hold him immobilized. "You can try, though you'd give quite a display to any of the crew you might pass in the corridors."

"They know why I'm here," Blaise replied easily. He would have shrugged, but the suddenly tight ropes made that impossible.

Sudden, inexplicable anger at the careless response flared through Peter's blood. A fist curled around the knots defining Blaise's cock, squeezing just short of the point of pain; long fingers traced the vein throbbing against the constriction, smudging the creamy droplet that oozed from the tip. "You didn't answer my question. Do you want to leave?" he demanded.

"Does it look like I want to leave?" Blaise asked incredulously. His entire body ached to be touched, to be fucked. The last thing he wanted was to leave!

Breaking past Risner's infuriatingly perpetual cockiness to win an honest answer had just become of paramount importance to Peter. Ignoring the mental voice that asked why it was so important with this one—granted, he was an exceptional piece of ass, but still just a piece of ass, wasn't he?—Peter spread his palms over the bound man's chest, lingering over the warm, smooth skin and the pulse throbbing beneath its surface. Without warning, he shoved hard, knocking Blaise off his feet. The smuggler hit the bed with enough force to bounce once before landing on his back, staring up at Peter with a startled expression quickly replaced by his habitual insouciance. "You still didn't answer my question."

"Why does it matter?" Blaise retorted. "I'm here, naked in your bed, completely at your mercy. What more do you want?" He couldn't possibly want Blaise to admit he wanted to be there, could he? Their entire interaction was predicated on their roles as captive and captor.

"I'm glad you at least recognize you're at my mercy." Peter moved onto the bed himself, crouching between Risner's splayed legs, a predatory gleam kindling in his eyes. His fingers settled on the arabesque of slender ropes defining the hard muscles of the smuggler's thighs, tracing the bindings' path. A tremor shook his captive and Peter smiled. "And you won't come until I get the courtesy of an answer."

The challenge appealed to Blaise's competitive nature. He knew Keller would win in the end, but Blaise would take as much pleasure from their interaction as he could before finally giving in and saying the words the Admiral apparently wanted to hear. "Do your worst," he goaded.

"You're nowhere near ready for my worst." Peter's expression hardened for an instant before he consciously threw off the memories that impinged on the pleasures of the moment. Those pleasures included leaning closer to the decadent offering in his bed, breathing in the spicy masculine tang of his prisoner's unmistakable arousal, and using his fingers, lips, and tongue to tease at the golden skin beneath the elegant restraints. No inch of the smuggler's toned body was off limits to his torments, save for the rampant erection and equally engorged balls set off so wantonly by the constraining knots.

Blaise squirmed on the smooth surface of the bed, unable to do anything but accept Keller's teasing caresses, the restraints still too tight on his limbs for him to move enough to encourage, much less reciprocate the provocative touches. He gasped and moaned and gave all manner of nonverbal praise, but he bit back the words the Admiral wanted to hear. His body already ached to come, but he knew as soon as they'd found their release, Keller would send him on his way, and Blaise wasn't ready to be sent back to his empty cabin.

"Stubborn fuck," Peter muttered, his own cock as hard as the monoliths of Maraven thanks to his sensual inventory of his prisoner's really magnificent body. Too irritated to grope for the remote, he pushed at Risner's legs until he could pull him over and up onto his knees, digging the ropes more deeply into Blaise's skin but rewarding him with an eye-level view of his target. Peter's tongue danced a relentless path that swept closer to the furled portal with each pass.

"Oh, fuck, please!" Blaise begged when he felt Keller's tongue so close to his entrance without ever penetrating. His eyes rolled back in his head at the thought of the Admiral rimming him.

As much as he itched to delve into the tantalizingly musky pucker, Peter wasn't sure he could restrain his own need much longer. Rolling away reluctantly, he reached blindly into his bedside drawer for a container of lube.

The seductive touch disappeared. Without thinking of what he was giving away, Blaise looked back over his shoulder, his eyes desperate. "No, please!"

"Please, what?" There were more free atoms in space than between Peter's lube-coated fingers and the heat of Blaise's skin as he tutored in an uneven rasp, "Please, don't stop? Please, fuck me? Please, I don't want to leave?"

"Yes," Blaise pleaded. "All of them. Just…." As desperate as he was, he couldn't quite force the words out. Not quite yet.

Deciding that was probably as close an admission as he was going to get, Peter thrust two fingers into Blaise, too impatient for more than a cursory preparation. The groans muffled by Risner's head buried in the mattress demanded more, as did the wanton arch of his back, pressing into Peter's touch as best he could within the tight restraints.

The ropes cut deeply into his skin, making Blaise feel like he'd never be free to move again, but he wasn't about to complain, not when Keller's fingers were finally preparing him. He wanted to rock into the touch, to encourage them to go deeper, stretch him wider, but he didn't have even that much range of motion. "More," he gasped, hoping that would get him what he wanted.

Peter was more than happy to give in to that demand, scissoring his fingers until he won the gasp that told him he'd found just the right spot to continue his torment. Working in a third finger, he dragged them in and out of the tight hole, careful to rub over the bump of nerves only enough to keep Blaise constantly on edge—until he remembered the cleverly placed knots were not only aesthetically pleasing, but served as an effective cock ring as well. Blaise's sudden groan suggested he'd just realized it, too. "Something you wanted to say?" Peter prodded, a well-paced twist of his fingers reminding Blaise of what was at stake. "You don't come until I get your answer."

It took Blaise's mind a minute to process the words and understand what the Admiral wanted. "No, I don't want to leave," he groaned, hoping that would be all his demanding captor needed. At this point, he'd say anything, though, if it would end the sensual torment. "Fuck me!"

"Remember who gives the orders around here," Peter demanded, pulling his fingers free of the constrictive sheathe. Fortunately for Blaise, his own body was issuing the same command. Slicking himself quickly, he drove into the hot channel with enough force to nearly flatten Blaise to the mattress. As incredible as the clenching heat felt, it wasn't enough. He didn't want to fuck an immobilized captive. He wanted to feel Blaise thrusting back against him, wanted to know his partner was with him. Freeing one of the hands that was holding Blaise up, he scrabbled blindly on the bedding until he found the remote, notching it down until it gave Blaise back the use of his limbs.

The moment the bindings eased, Blaise pushed up on his elbows, bracing his hands against the headboard as he rocked back against Keller, trying to get the other man's cock deeper inside his aching passage. It took only an embarrassingly few seconds for his orgasm to slam into him, the constriction on his balls loosening enough for his come to spurt out hard over the Admiral's bed. "Fuck," he groaned in repletion as Keller continued to ride him hard.

The sudden spasms of Blaise's climax were too tantalizing for Peter to hold out any longer. After a few more stuttering thrusts, his release shook him with the power of the *North Star*'s engines, though he continued to slide in and out until the last aftershocks faded. Slipping free lazily, he dropped to the bed beside Risner, thumbing the control to release the bindings before dropping it to the floor. When their panting had quieted to more even breathing, he rolled onto his back, thinking that he could probably manage a few hours of sleep before resuming his scrutiny of the *Scheherazade*'s attack. "You can leave now," he announced to Risner, smothering a yawn.

Blaise shouldn't have been surprised at the abrupt dismissal. Keller always sent him away as soon as they'd finished fucking, but it didn't make it any more pleasant to drag himself up and get dressed again when all he wanted was to fall asleep himself. It was a good reminder, though, of exactly what position he held in the Admiral's world. "Don't forget the plasma refills," he said as he stood and went back into the main room to dress. "I'd hate to have wasted the trip up here."

"Oh, it wasn't a wasted trip at all," Peter murmured sleepily as he watched Blaise dress and leave. *Not for either of them.*

CHAPTER 5
COURT SUPERVISION

BLAISE paced the confines of his quarters, waiting for the summons. The Admiral had made it very clear that tonight would be different and that he was to be on his best behavior, all fun and games aside. What he didn't know was why. And that made him antsy. And when he was antsy, he paced. Back and forth, back and forth, as if by wearing a hole in the floor plates, he could somehow release the nervousness skittering up and down his spine. He wasn't in trouble, as far as he knew. Since he'd discovered the plasma leak six months ago, Keller had slowly entrusted him with more responsibility. Nothing like he'd had on his own ship, of course, but more than just sweeping the decks. And they'd found a balance on a more intimate level, too. Keller fucked him through the mattress or the wall or any available flat surface on a regular basis, and Blaise pretended to hate it just enough to get them both good and worked up. Everyone was happy. Except this didn't feel like their usual games. Thus the nerves. And the pacing.

Peter paced the confines outside the docking bay, waiting for the shuttle to deliver Justice Perry for her "inspection" visit. As soon as the *North Star* returned to the Sirius quadrant from their recent patrol, the High Justice had contacted him, asking when it would be convenient for her to schedule a visit to monitor the progress of his prisoner's rehabilitation. Peter wasn't foolish enough to believe it was truly a request. He and Lapis had played this game with several prisoners before Risner, to their mutual pleasure, even if the prisoner involved hadn't always felt the same. Risner should be no different—*was* no different, he told himself. True, he'd found the privateer more capable, more intelligent than his previous charges. More stubborn, too, though the Admiral had to admit that wasn't necessarily a bad thing. He enjoyed their clashes as much as, he'd begun to suspect, Blaise did. Still, he itched to be back on patrol. They'd recently found several derelict ships in the fringes of the sector, blasted hulls clearly bearing the same energy signature of the vessel that had destroyed the science station. He should be hunting the attacker, not pandering to the High Justice's prurient interests.

Stepping lightly off the shuttle into the drab docking bay of the *North Star*, Justice Perry couldn't help but smile when she saw the dashing Admiral waiting to greet her. She crossed the grey metal floor to his side, bussing his cheek lightly. "So, Peter," she purred, "what delights do you have in store for me today?"

Knowing better than to let his impatience show, Peter inclined his head with a matching smile and offered Lapis his arm, an old-fashioned gesture he knew the petite blonde considered her due. Leading her through the flagship's corridors toward his quarters, he waited until they had left the docking bay crew behind before answering. "You remember the prisoner remanded to me at the last session we were in-quadrant," he replied, though he knew perfectly well she remembered. It was all part of the game.

"Of course," Lapis replied with a hard smile. "Risner: smuggling, tall, dark, handsome, arrogant. I expect he's still tall, dark, and handsome since your tastes never ran to disfigurement, but I hope he's lost some of that arrogance. There's nothing quite like seeing a strong man crawl."

Peter's equally hard smile felt a bit forced as he considered his answer. "I'm trying something a bit different with this one," he countered, pausing at the doorway to his cabin. If he were honest with himself, the difference was in Risner rather than any change in Peter's routine; treatment that had left his earlier playthings cowering seemed to roll off the privateer's broad back. "Break them too quickly and the spice is gone. I find this one's attitude a refreshing challenge."

Lapis looked at the Admiral in surprise. "It's your ship," she allowed slowly. "As long as he's well and truly broken before the end of his sentence, the court will be satisfied. I would hate to have to reconsider our... arrangement."

Had Lapis always been this much of a bitch, or was he just beginning to notice it? "It is, of course, to both our interests that the court be satisfied," Peter agreed tightly, palming the control that snapped open the cabin door. Blaise had damn well better toe the line while the High Justice was on board, or he'd find himself learning a whole new definition of discipline. Though he was sure Lapis's threat was an empty one, Peter would take a demotion back to ensign before he'd let her win this round. "May I offer you some refreshment, or would you prefer to... inspect... the prisoner at once?"

"Oh, by all means, let's be civilized," Lapis replied. "Do you have any of the single malt whisky you served the last time I visited you?" She would enjoy sipping it while she watched Peter put the prisoner through his paces.

"I keep some just for you. I know how hard it is to find this far from Earth," Peter answered smoothly, opening a concealed panel to extract a cut-crystal decanter and two glasses. Pouring them each several fingers of the smoky liquor, he handed a glass to his companion and toasted her with his own, the ritual helping to settle his disposition. "To the loveliest woman ever to grace my vessel with her presence."

"That would mean more if I could persuade you to appreciate my charms," she teased, savoring the bite of the drink as it slid down her throat. "Now, shall we see about the prisoner?"

"Certainly," Peter agreed, crossing to the comm link to order Risner escorted to his cabin. He emptied his glass as he crossed back to Lapis's side, pouring himself another splash of whisky before joining her on the cushioned seating area.

The door to Blaise's quarters swished open to reveal one of the crewmen, energy manacles hanging from his hand. Blaise's eyebrows shot up as he saw the restraints the Admiral hadn't insisted he wear in months. He didn't fight them. There was no point. They did add to his nerves, though, as he walked docilely through the corridor toward the Admiral's quarters. As soon as the door shut behind him, he looked for Keller. "What...?" he began.

"I can always gag you if you can't mind your tongue in front of our guest," Peter broke in, sending a glance over his shoulder to where Lapis sat at her ease. "Justice Perry may have questions for you. See that you offer her the respect her position deserves."

Blaise froze, his eyes glancing back and forth between the Admiral and the green-skinned judge he recognized from his trial. She had mentioned she might come to observe. It looked like that time had come. He nodded silently, not sure what Keller expected of him, but he'd been in and out of enough sticky situations to fly by the seat of his pants if he had to. Not, judging by the lascivious once-over the woman was giving him, that he expected to be wearing his pants for very long.

"How long have you been on the *North Star*?" the High Justice asked blandly.

"Six months, ma'am," Blaise replied politely, not sure where the trap was, but quite sure the judge was leading somewhere with her questions.

"And has the Admiral been treating you well?"

There it was. "I've no cause for complaint," he said neutrally. He was quite sure Perry knew exactly how the Admiral had been treating him, but complaining about it would see him punished for sure. He doubted eagerness would be well viewed either, and he had no desire to suddenly find himself on the Auriga colony.

"And will you be returning to your smuggling ways after you've served your sentence?" she pressed.

"That will be a little difficult without my ship," Blaise pointed out, unable to force himself to give the answer he knew she wanted to hear.

Peter had bitten his tongue against interrupting several times during Lapis's interrogation, knowing the High Justice would be quick to jump on anything she interpreted as a weakness, but he couldn't let an insolent remark like that pass unchallenged. Backhanding Blaise hard enough to make him stagger, he fixed the prisoner with a glare colder than the ice moons of Xanidii. "Enough backtalk," he growled, hoping Risner was intelligent enough to grasp the undercurrents of the justice's questioning.

Blaise went to his knees under the blow and stayed there, eyes downcast to hide the temper that sparked at Keller's harsh treatment. They'd gotten past this, he'd thought, except when the pain added to their pleasure.

Lapis tsk'ed in her seat. "I see you still have progress to make," she commented to Peter, "but it's early days yet. Show me what he can do."

As if he were a *vithr*-jockey putting his mount through its paces, Peter thought, bristling at the unspoken order. Lapis's arrogant tone of command had never troubled him before, but it rankled now. "On your feet," he snapped to Blaise, his voice harsh as he released the energy manacles. "Strip, and be quick about it."

Deciding there was nothing to be gained in fighting, especially since Keller had already showed himself willing to tear the clothes from Blaise's body if the mood struck him, Blaise rose and shed his shipsuit, letting it lay where it fell, and stepped forward proudly naked. He looked good and he knew it, and the Admiral had expressed his appreciation more than once, albeit silently. If they wanted him cowed, they'd have to work a lot harder than this.

Circling Risner without speaking, Peter approved the quick obedience and confident posture. Blaise looked damn good, and they both knew it. A corner of his mouth quirked as he noted the smuggler beginning to stiffen at his appraisal. Though he could end this quickly by bringing Blaise to a rapid climax, judging by Lapis's mood, that would be far too tame for her taste, and only keeping her happy would ensure she'd uphold her part of their bargain. Reactivating the energy bindings around Blaise's wrists, Peter accessed his toy cabinet to retrieve the appliance he'd obtained at the sex market on Eta Eridanus and saved for just this purpose. Returning to Blaise's side, he kicked the smuggler's legs farther apart, making it easier to fit the device: the ring around his cock, the plug up his ass.

"A restrictor field," he explained to Lapis, thumbing on the power. A pale glow illuminated Risner's groin, and he watched the spacer's hands clench into fists as the stimulus hardened him to full stiffness while preventing him from succumbing to its tantalizing provocation.

"Impressive," the blonde commented, referring to both the man and the device. "I've heard of those before, but I've never seen one. Have you used it on him before? He took it quite well. Didn't fight you at all."

Did she think he was deaf as well as stupid? Blaise wondered irreverently as his body reacted to the ring squeezing his cock and the plug vibrating gently in his ass. Once he'd figured out that Keller's games could be pleasurable if he didn't fight too much, he'd stopped struggling except for form. Why deny himself the mind-blowing climaxes the Admiral could wring from him? That would be cutting his nose off to spite his face.

"He's responded quite well to the stimulus restraints and the energy whip, but I've never used this on him yet. I thought you'd appreciate seeing him react to a new toy," Keller smirked, nudging up the power a bit to increase the constriction—and the vibrations. His own cock was responding to the swell of Blaise's purpling erection jutting upward. A light coating of sweat glistened over the smuggler's impressive musculature, but the Admiral noted with appreciation that Blaise didn't flinch, withstanding the added stimulus in silence. Months of experience with the fractious spacer had taught Peter that the silence probably wouldn't last much longer, and he considered gagging Risner again, finally deciding against what Lapis would undoubtedly see as a weakness. He'd just have to gamble on Blaise's innate intelligence to grasp that nothing good would come from antagonizing the High Justice.

Lapis rose from her seat, setting the glass aside as she circled the prisoner. "Well, look at this," she crowed, seeing the piercing in his nipple. "Did you do this, Peter? Or did he come so nicely decorated?" As she spoke, she reached out and tugged forcefully on the ring. The prisoner winced as she twisted a little, abusing his sensitive flesh.

Blaise bit his lip to keep from crying out at the rough pull. Keller used his nipple ring to toy with him frequently, but the Admiral had never been so harsh. With his hands bound, he couldn't do much to stop the High Justice from doing what she pleased, but he didn't know how long he'd be able to keep his mouth shut if she continued. Keller's toy would make sure he stayed physically aroused, but the pleasure he usually took in their battles was waning quickly at the unwelcome touch.

"The ring and the tattoo are both his," Peter answered, his lips thinning into a frown at Lapis's actions. His voice must have sounded more clipped than usual too, because she swung her head around to glance at him before returning her attention to Risner. "I've been thinking of adding a second, though," Peter continued, crossing to Blaise's side and running a hand down his chest, tweaking the unadorned nipple and casually moving between the smuggler and Lapis. "Like clamps, I prefer them in pairs."

"What are you waiting for?" Lapis asked curiously. "An invitation?"

Blaise tensed, ready to fight them if they tried to force another piercing on him. Not that he was opposed to having a second one. He wasn't even particularly opposed to Keller doing the work, but he didn't want the memory of the High Justice branded permanently into his skin.

"Just waiting for the right occasion," Peter countered smoothly, wondering how strongly Blaise would fight a second piercing. Presumably the ring, like the tattoo, was a voluntary adornment. "Give him something to remember his time on my ship."

"A parting gift," Lapis agreed with a chuckle. "I like that. Perhaps I'll come early enough to watch when it's time to release him. Just to make sure he's well broken."

Masking his nagging annoyance at Lapis's presumptive attitude, Peter decided the preliminaries had gone on long enough. He knew what Lapis was here to see, and the sooner he gave it to her, the sooner he could escort her off his ship for another cycle. "Perhaps I can save you a trip by demonstrating how far he's already come," Peter suggested. Turning back to face Blaise, he let his gaze rake over the spacer's sculpted body. Catering to the High Justice's voyeuristic tendencies had never been a hardship, and it would be pure pleasure to show her what Blaise could take... and give. Widening his stance, he met Blaise's eyes with a glittering stare. "On your knees," he ordered. "Suck me."

Blaise smothered a sigh of relief. This he could do and willingly, a fact he was sure swayed the Admiral's choice of commands. Dropping to his knees awkwardly because of his bound hands, he shuffled forward until he could find the fastener that held closed the front flap of Keller's uniform trousers. Grabbing the tab with his teeth, he worked it down, nuzzling his way inside to find the hard column of flesh that awaited his attentions. He could hear the High Justice's heightened breathing as he began his assigned task, but he pushed all thoughts of her away and concentrated on blowing the Admiral as thoroughly as possible. The sooner he got Keller off, the sooner *she* would be off the ship.

Peter didn't have to turn his head to know that Lapis was impressed by Blaise's ingenuity, and even more impressed with the way he swallowed Peter's sizeable cock. Arching his hips, he rocked into the wet suction until his balls slapped Blaise's chin. Who needed the pleasure gardens on Gamma Arietis when he had this on his own ship, any time he chose to claim it?

The pirate was impressive, Lapis had to admit silently, and not just for his physique. He was clearly resourceful as well, but while that was a good trait in a pirate, she wasn't sure she approved of it in a prisoner. Deciding to see just how docile he'd become, she slid a Protean laser out of the pocket of her loose robes, flicking the switch to its lowest setting. On high, it could leave a small burn if pointed too long on any one patch of skin, but she rarely used it for punishment. On this particular setting, it would set Risner's nerves to tingling nicely. Aiming it carefully at the tattoo on his upper arm, she traced the inked lines and waited for him to notice.

At first, Blaise thought he was imagining things, the sensation of something crawling over his skin, but it persisted, until he could no longer ignore it. It didn't quite hurt—certainly nothing like what the Gavenelians had subjected him to—but it wasn't really comfortable either. Trying to glance out of the corner of his eye without neglecting Keller's cock, he caught sight of a red beam. Instinctively, he jerked away from the laser.

"He's still sensitive," Lapis observed. "That's good. Too many people inure their toys to pain so quickly that there's no fun left to be had without damaging them."

Hissing a Denebian curse, Peter managed to extract his dripping cock from Blaise's mouth as he flinched away from the laser, just before the spacer's teeth reflexively snapped closed. "It's polite to ask before playing with someone else's toy," he reminded her, "and I'd as soon not be gelded in the process. Besides," he added, holding her gaze until she snapped off the ruby beam, "if you break him, you'll have to get me a new one." And he seriously doubted Lapis would be able to find Blaise's match.

Blaise wanted to laugh and tell them both that it would take far more than the Justice's laser to break him, but he decided playing least in sight was definitely wise at this point. After all, he didn't want them to decide to break him in earnest. He was pretty sure they wouldn't succeed, but that was no reason to tempt fate.

"Oh, very well," Lapis conceded, resigning herself to watching and wondering what was different about Risner that Peter wouldn't let her play, even a little. "Carry on."

"Play with this instead," Peter offered, tossing her the control for the Eridani device. At least she couldn't hurt anyone with that, though she could definitely make Blaise squirm. "Now I believe you were in the middle of something?" he reminded his prisoner.

Relieved that the Admiral had intervened on his behalf, Blaise sent him a grateful look and returned to fellating the blond commander. He studiously ignored the High Justice, even when she suddenly upped the power on the restrictor field, sending jolts of lust through him as the plug vibrated rapidly against his prostate.

Peter felt Risner jump when Lapis raised the restrictor setting, the vibrations transmitting through the wet suction of Blaise's mouth to his cock. The phantom tingling tightened his balls, adding to the impeding urgency to empty them down Blaise's throat. While that would be personally satisfying for Peter, he knew their observer would prefer a more energetic climax. Thrusting a hand into Blaise's spiky dark hair, he pushed back reluctantly, earning a surprised grunt from his prisoner. "Enough," he muttered thickly, as much to the High Justice as to Blaise.

Though surprised, Blaise released the Admiral's cock. After all, as hard as he was, Keller was bound to give him an enthusiastic fucking at this point. He rocked back on his heels and waited for his new orders.

"He's mastered that skill, I see," Lapis drawled, fiddling with the controls so the pirate's body jerked erratically. It wasn't her Protean laser, but it still provided amusing results. "What else can he do?"

"I've found he has unexpected talents," Peter admitted, easing open the front of his uniform tunic and hiding a smug grin as Lapis's eyes sparkled in appreciation. He might not be as young as Blaise, but his daily regimen of zero-gravity workouts kept him fit. Shrugging the dark material off his shoulders, he let the shipsuit fall to his hips, baring his chest. It fed his not-inconsiderable ego that both his companions seemed to find the sight equally gratifying. By the rings of Regulus, if he had to perform like a trained concubine for Lapis, he might as well enjoy it. "Did you have a request?"

"Bring him over here," she ordered. "The arm of the couch will support him nicely while you fuck him. What with the toy stretching him, he shouldn't need any more preparation."

"You heard the High Justice." Peter nodded Blaise in the direction of the seating alcove, diverting to retrieve a flask of lubricant from his toy cabinet. The Eridani plug might have left Blaise stretched, but Peter didn't see the need for either of them to suffer the discomfort of taking him dry.

Blaise frowned slightly at the order, not sure he really wanted to be within the woman's reach, but he didn't argue. He didn't want to know what his punishment would be if he did. Keller didn't seem inclined to let her hurt him, so at the worst, she'd cop a feel. He didn't care for a woman's soft grip, but he figured he could put up with her groping him if it came to that. It would be far better than getting sent to hard labor. Stopping at the edge of the couch, he waited for the Admiral to come up behind him, keeping his gaze fixed carefully on the wall beyond the High Justice. He didn't want to encourage her!

He was too calm by far, Lapis decided, turning the restrictor field up as far as it would go. The prisoner's knees buckled and he had to lean on the arm of the couch to support himself. Her smile turned feral. That was what she liked to see.

Blaise's sudden lurch caught Peter by surprise and he reached out reflexively to keep the pirate from falling, the tremors shaking him and Lapis's gleeful smile making it clear what happened. Scowling, Peter yanked the plug free with less than his usual finesse, letting it dangle as he quickly slicked his cock and plunged into Blaise before Lapis could protest. He could still feel the vibrations from the ring at the base of Blaise's cock, and he debated removing it as well, but the quivering walls of the clinging passage provided a unique massage for his own shaft. Promising himself he'd make it up to the pirate, he thrust powerfully enough to keep Blaise bent over the arm of the couch. His hands splayed around the spacer's ribs, fingers coasting over the flexed pectoral muscles.

Blaise couldn't stifle a groan when Keller's cock pierced him forcefully. The plug had stretched him just enough that it wasn't painful, but not enough for the Admiral's girth to be truly comfortable. He bit his lip, rightly guessing that the High Justice would enjoy thinking him in pain. Then the commander's hands started moving, covering his chest and pressing into his nipples, and he forgot about the observer and everything else except what Keller was doing to him. The rough tug on his nipple ring only added to his pleasure until the pinch of sharp fingernails made him realize who was touching him. He didn't protest—he doubted he had the right to do so—but he froze momentarily as he fought the impulse to pull away.

His palms enjoying the play of hard muscles beneath them, Peter let his fingers grope in search of the nipples he'd learned made Blaise writhe when he tweaked at them, his motions freezing when a third set of fingers joined the game. Swallowing his annoyance, he teased at the hardened points a little longer, then let his hands slip lower, following the curves of Blaise's torso. Grasping his hips tightly, he hammered into the pulsing passage, the shiver of the Eridani enhancer and Blaise's own clenching around him driving him close to losing control. The artificial stimulus grated, and it suddenly became important that he feel only Blaise pulling him into climax. Dropping his grip even lower, he worked the release with one hand and wrapped the other around the pirate's cock, fisting it in time with his increasingly hurried thrusts.

The sudden cessation of the mechanical stimulation shocked Blaise almost as much as the release of the constriction around the base of his cock. With a muffled gasp, he began climaxing, his seed darkening the leather beneath him. He jerked back reflexively when he felt the same sharp fingernails raking the tip of his erection, unable to stop his reaction as he had when the High Justice touched his piercing. As ridiculous as it should have been, he realized he didn't want anyone but the Admiral touching him that way.

Beyond rational thought as Blaise spasmed around him, forcing his orgasm with the sudden fierce constriction, Peter batted away the trespassing hand that would interfere with his granting Blaise pleasure. Flooding the tightened sheath with his come, Peter still worked Blaise's softening shaft, drawing out the blissful shudders that wracked them both. He could hear the Eridani device chattering away forgotten on the floor, accompanied by Lapis's silvery laughter, but neither had the power to disrupt this moment.

"Very well done," Lapis applauded after a moment's enjoyment of the sight of two replete faces. She couldn't help but notice a softness in Peter's features as he climaxed that was so rarely visible, and it made her wonder. "You're making excellent progress with him, Peter. I can't wait to see what he's like the next time you come into the quadrant. Unfortunately, duty calls. Walk me back to my ship?"

Duty over pleasure, Peter thought wryly as he withdrew, tucking himself back into his uniform before offering the diminutive blonde his arm. Wondering whether he would find Blaise in his quarters when he returned, he kept his voice blank as he spoke over his shoulder. "Clean up the mess you made before I get back."

Taking the Admiral's words as permission to remain in the cabin until he returned, Blaise didn't move until he heard the door close behind them, his wrists falling free just as it shut. Standing up slowly, he moved his hands from behind his back, stretching to relieve the tension of muscles pulled too long in unusual ways. Going to the 'fresher, he found a towel and set about cleaning up his mess.

Out in the hall, Lapis smiled up at Peter. "He might find cleaning difficult with his hands still bound."

"Oh, Blaise is quite ingenious," he purred, the control that had released the energy shackles hidden in his pocket. "The room will be clean if he has to lick it up."

"So tell me what is different about this one," she demanded as they walked. "Despite your comment on the way in, you have obviously made considerable progress with him. Have you been neglecting your duties to play with your new toy?"

"You know me better than that," Peter growled. He didn't understand why everything Lapis said seemed to rub him the wrong way this visit. Forcing himself to answer more civilly, he smiled at the blonde. "After all, if I did that, you wouldn't let me keep them."

She laughed in earnest this time. "So true, unfortunately," she agreed. "Life would be so much more enjoyable if we didn't have duty to drag us away from our pleasures. But you didn't answer my question. What's different about him?"

Peter pondered the question, his honest answer slipping out before he could censor it. "I don't know. He's cocky, abrasive, and despite what you saw just now, he's not above fighting me when it suits him." He shook his head, wondering if he was being a fool admitting the truth. "And I'm not sure I'd have him any other way."

Lapis didn't say anything, letting her enigmatic smile answer for her. Peter could interpret that however he pleased. Leaning up, she kissed his cheek gently. "Let me know the next time you're back in my sector," she insisted, "even if it's only so I can have another glass of your whisky."

Despite his unsettled reaction to his admission, Peter's smile at the brush of Lapis's lips was genuine. "You're still the only woman I'll accept that from," he reminded her. "You know you're always welcome on the *North Star*."

"I know," she agreed, laughing up at him lightly, "but I figure once every six months is as often as you can stand to have me kiss you."

Still chuckling, Peter watched the High Justice board her ship before turning back to his cabin, wondering what kind of reception to expect from his irrepressible prisoner. One thing was sure: Blaise had yet to bore him as too many of his previous toys had already done by this point in their sentences.

"So how often can we expect visits from Her Majesty the Bitch Queen?" Blaise asked irreverently when the Admiral walked back into his quarters. He'd get one of two reactions depending on the commander's mood. Either Keller would laugh or backhand him again like he'd done earlier. Blaise really hoped he'd get a laugh to put things back on even footing between them. The entire evening had been... off.

"You'd do well to give the High Justice the respect she deserves, considering your presence here depends on her pleasure," Peter snapped, more sharply than he intended, but the entire encounter had left him feeling as if he were trying to navigate the Mintakan asteroid belt without sensors. It irritated him that he'd been unable to keep Lapis from sensing that Blaise was different than his former sub-toys when he couldn't even define the difference to himself. It was more than just Blaise's sexual attractiveness, despite the fact that Peter's arousal was already returning just at finding the spacer still naked in his quarters.

"It would be easier to do if she hadn't treated me like some animal," Blaise pointed out reasonably. "She talked about me like I wasn't even there. Or like I was too stupid to understand her."

Because most of your predecessors were, Peter thought, running a hand through his close-cropped hair. "You did well," he admitted, recognizing how difficult it had been to hold his own tongue at some of Lapis's actions. "I don't expect we'll hear from her again until your sentence is up." The thought of Blaise's release did little to restore his equilibrium.

"I wasn't sure," Blaise replied, pretty sure the unusual compliment had cost the Admiral as much as his own admission was costing him. "It wasn't as... intense as it usually is."

Raising an eyebrow in amusement, Peter chuckled. "Is that a complaint?" He bent to retrieve the Eridani restraint device, weighing it consideringly in his palm. "Maybe I don't like performing for an audience any more than you do," he offered, though it had never bothered him before. "I'll have to come up with something more... interesting... for you next time, then, won't I?"

"It wasn't the device," Blaise said softly. "She doesn't have your finesse in wielding it. You might have brought me to my knees, but you would have made me wait a lot longer for it. You would have kept me on the edge for hours, until I was ready to beg you for release."

"Is that what you want?" Peter asked, eyes glittering dangerously as his cock jumped at the image Blaise's words painted. This desire, this hunger... *this* he understood. That he'd just asked a prisoner what he wanted never occurred to him as he unfastened the front of his shipsuit. "Because I'm more than happy to oblige."

Without his conscious volition, Blaise's hands moved behind his back again as if bound by the energy manacles. His eyes sparked with a matching hunger, a smile crossing his face as he drawled, "You can try to make me beg."

Peter bounced the restrictor in his palm, a wide smile creasing his face. "Oh, believe me, it will be my pleasure."

CHAPTER 6
A VERY PRIVATE CELEBRATION

ADMIRAL KELLER scowled at the vidscreen, even though the woman speaking couldn't see him. The *North Star* had headed into deep patrol after leaving the Sirius starbase, so High Justice Perry had recorded her message until it could catch up with him. Probably as well, or he would have found it hard to hide his annoyance at Lapis's meddling. Their long-standing friendship notwithstanding, Peter didn't take well to being manipulated, and Lapis's message, innocent on the surface, carried an undercurrent of gleeful needling. Scowling again, the Admiral hit a button to replay the transmission, wondering if he'd really been that transparent during the High Justice's "inspection" visit.

"I took the liberty of doing a little checking for you, Peter. Your pirate's birthday is coming up on June third. You said you were waiting for a special occasion. You only get one chance at some things in life. Don't waste this one."

Peter wondered what the High Justice would consider a suitable activity to make *his pirate's* birthday a special occasion. The question of why she assumed he would want to make it special was one he preferred to ignore completely, the same way he avoided looking ahead to the cocky smuggler's eventual release. He'd suggested marking Blaise with a second piercing as a spur of the moment comment during Lapis's visit, knowing it would titillate her, but the more he thought about it, the more the idea pleased him. A ring to mark Blaise as his.... He shook his head, rejecting the all-too-seductive image. He didn't have anything suitable on board, and in any case, he doubted that permanent body modification of his prisoner fell within the limits of his admittedly wide-ranging discretionary latitude. Unless Blaise wanted it too, of course....

Peter's uniform trousers were becoming uncomfortably tight, and he rubbed the insistent bulge absently as he pondered. Still, why not plan a birthday celebration for his pirate? A very private celebration, one he was sure to enjoy at least as much as Blaise?

Clearing the screen of Lapis's image and his mind of her presumptuous innuendo, Peter settled back into his chair, amusing himself with plans for a very special occasion indeed.

BLAISE didn't know quite what to expect of the summons to the Admiral's quarters. He'd seen Keller only rarely since the night the High Justice had visited two months earlier. It had been... memorable. After she left, the Admiral had ravished him thoroughly, keeping him hard and begging for hours before finally fucking him through the wall. Then Confederation business had come up and the Admiral had been too busy for his prisoner, calling him only once every couple of weeks, leaving Blaise horny and frustrated between times. His body had gone from getting no sex to getting mind-blowing sex and it didn't appreciate the times of deprivation in between. Blaise rather hoped Keller intended to make it up to him. Taking a deep breath to settle himself, he buzzed at the door to the Admiral's quarters.

"Come," Peter called, his voice activating the release to the cabin door. Reports of another unprovoked assault, on a still remote but more populated outpost, had occupied nearly all his time for the past weeks. Like the first attack, the assailants had struck without warning, leaving no survivors. His squadron had combed the sector and followed up on every lead and rumor, no matter how nebulous, but they were still no closer to identifying the attackers. Even though a part of him begrudged any time not spent hunting for their unknown enemy, Peter had forced himself to go forward with his plans for the night, recognizing he needed the respite of this time with Blaise. Time he wasn't going to spoil, for either of them, with talk about the mysterious attacks.

Blaise stepped inside, balancing restlessly on the balls of his feet as he waited to see what orders would greet him this time. A quick glance revealed the room to be empty of unexpected guests, much to his relief. "You rang?" he quipped when the Admiral didn't immediately react to his presence.

"Something you meant to tell me about today?" the Admiral asked, leaning back in the chair at his work desk.

Blaise shrugged. "It's a day," he commented blandly. "Tuesday, to be exact. The first Tuesday in June, the one hundred fifty-fourth day of the year. Shall I go on or was that what you wanted to know?"

"So there's nothing special about this day? Or have you really forgotten?"

Blaise shrugged again. "So it's my birthday," he replied self-consciously. "That makes me thirty-three instead of thirty-two. Birthday parties are for kids. I stopped celebrating it a long time ago."

Something in the tone of Blaise's response made Peter suspect his smuggler missed having someone to commemorate his birthday more than he let on. "That's rather unfortunate, then, since I'd planned a private party for just the two of us." He glanced at the younger man from beneath hooded lids, his expression bland. "Perhaps you'd prefer to return to your quarters?"

"Have I ever complained about spending an evening with you?" Blaise countered quickly. Too quickly, probably, but if his choices were spending an evening with the sexy Admiral and spending it alone in his quarters, he'd definitely take the Admiral. Any way he could get him.

"I seem to remember some remarks," Peter commented dryly.

"I'd like to stay," Blaise said quietly. His birthday didn't have the best of memories associated with it, but maybe that was about to change.

The admission warmed something inside Peter, and he fought to keep his relief from showing on his face. It felt good to know Blaise was staying by choice, even if the alternative was a night alone in his quarters. "I've ordered a special dinner to be delivered," he commented, crossing to the recessed cabinet where he kept his liquor. Moving aside the decanter of whisky and the memories of Lapis's visit associated with it, he extracted a tall ruby bottle. "I thought you might care for a drink before we eat."

Blaise arched an eyebrow in surprise, but didn't mention that he doubted Keller was supposed to be plying his prisoners with alcohol. "Depends on what we're drinking."

"You'll have to tell me," Peter replied, popping the seal off the bottle. "Since it's something you were carrying on your ship when we seized it."

"Betelgeusian wine," Blaise marveled. "You managed to keep it?"

"A few bottles," Peter shrugged. "Rank does have its privileges, after all."

"I'll say," Blaise agreed. "This is so potent it's not even legal on most Confederation planets. Pour me a glass, Admiral."

Splashing a generous amount of the blood-red liquid into a pair of tumblers, Peter handed one to his companion. "Happy birthday," he toasted, taking a sip and lifting an eyebrow in surprise. "Potent indeed," he agreed, raising the glass to drink more deeply.

"The merchant I got this from told me a single glass of Betelgeusian wine is as strong as a full bottle of most Earth vintages," Blaise commented as he sipped the rich beverage. "I don't know if that's true or just spaceflot, but that's what he said."

"Are you saying you never sampled your own wares?" Peter asked, moving to the seating area and stretching his legs, enjoying the slow burn of the heady vintage.

"I'm a smuggler, not a thief," Blaise protested, following Keller to the couch. "I only get paid for the cargo I deliver. I wouldn't have much of a reputation if I didn't deliver the goods."

"An honorable smuggler, then," Peter mused. "I suspect that makes you a rarity among your cohorts." A buzz sounded at the door, and he paused to admit a member of the ship's commissary staff, steering an anti-grav cart laden with delicacies. He glanced over the dishes before nodding his acceptance. "Ah, dinner. I wasn't sure about your tastes, so I ordered a variety of entrées," he explained as the door slid shut behind the departing crewman. "Hopefully you'll find something you enjoy."

"I'm easy," Blaise replied, glancing at the wide array of tidbits on the cart. He had to give the Admiral credit for trying to make the evening special. "If it's edible, I pretty much eat it, but it was kind of you to make such an effort for me." He took another sip of the wine before adding softly, "It's been a long time since anyone has."

"It's been a long time since anyone's accused me of being kind," Peter retorted. "This is as much of a treat for me as it is for you," he confessed. "I spend too many dinners at my computer console, not even noticing what I eat." He sat again, rather abruptly, surprised at his own admission.

"You need someone to take care of you," Blaise admonished, his eyes widening as he realized what he'd said. Carefully, he set aside the wine he'd been drinking. If his words were this unguarded after only a few sips, he was afraid to see what he'd say after finishing the glass! Deciding wisdom was the better part of valor in this case, he studied the contents of the cart with great interest, finally selecting a purplish vegetable in a creamy white sauce. He took a bite and smiled in delight. "Regulosian barszcz," he sighed as he took another bite. "My grandmother used to make this. I don't think I've had it since she died."

"Try some of this," Peter suggested, sliding a wedge of a rather virulent orange hue onto Blaise's plate before adding the rest to his own. "Nekkarian paté—try it with the Sukafat flatbread." He chewed a bite thoughtfully before asking, "You're from the Regulus system, then? You're obviously not native."

"No, I'm from Earth," Blaise replied, taking a taste of the dish Keller proposed. "My grandmother just claimed she was adventurous, although I wonder if there wasn't more to it than that. She had this picture—she'd never show it to anyone—but I caught a glimpse of it once, and the man in the picture was albino. From what my mother told me, though, my grandmother's parents were pretty xenophobic. They wouldn't have approved of her marrying an off-worlder, much less one of a different race."

Taking another sip of wine, Peter shook his head. "You'd think that kind of close-mindedness would have disappeared by the time we reached the stars," he said, adding a few more of the items from the cart's variety to each of their plates. "So was your becoming a smuggler a way of rebelling against your family?"

Blaise chuckled. "I never thought of it that way, no. My grandmother married to please her parents, but she didn't tolerate any kind of prejudice from her kids or grandkids. She was quite the matriarch. None of us wanted to cross her, that's for sure. No, it was more a matter of not being able to make a living in shipping. I don't know if you see it, here on your Confederation ship, but the tariffs on interplanetary freight take almost all the profit out of the fees we can reasonably charge. What about you? How did you end up in the Admiralty?"

"Without those tariffs, there'd be no ships like this to protect the shipping lanes from the real pirates," Peter retorted, emptying the bottle of wine into Blaise's glass. He snorted softly as he raised his own drink to his lips. "Listen to me, defending Confederation policies to a smuggler! Not that I can claim I entered the service for the noble cause of defending the space-lanes. I was simply mad to get off Earth and making it into the Academy was the only means I had to do it."

Blaise tipped his glass in Keller's direction. "Good for you," he complimented the other man sincerely. "I tried to do it that way, but I didn't have the discipline to make it in the Academy. I don't take orders well," he explained with a self-deprecatory smile. "I hired on with one of the big shipping companies, but the pay was barely enough to make ends meet. Then my grandmother died. I used the money she left me to buy the *Golden Stallion*. I guess that's money out the airlock now." He tried to keep his words light, but the bitterness came through despite his efforts. *What the hell*, he decided. It wasn't like the Admiral could expect him to be happy about losing his ship.

The spacer's emotion was so palpable that Peter opened his mouth to speak, only to bite back the words before they could escape. He could imagine he'd feel equally bitter if he had to turn control of the *North Star* over to someone else. Rising to his feet, he retrieved a second bottle of the rich Betelgeusian wine and topped off both their glasses, realizing he had no idea how to reply to Blaise's remark without sounding smug or callous. He watched the younger man's head tilt back as he raised the glass to his lips, his throat working as he swallowed, seeing him for the first time not as a smuggler, not as a prisoner, but simply as a man. A very desirable man. A flare of heated arousal lit inside him, and for a moment, he wondered what Blaise saw when he looked at him.

"I think I've had enough," Blaise declared, setting the wine aside. "It's making me maudlin. I knew the chances I was taking when I started running contraband. I just didn't think it would happen to me." He stood with a forced smile. "I really appreciate you thinking of me tonight, but

I'm not very good company, I'm afraid. I have a bad track record with birthdays."

"Stay," Peter urged, reaching for Blaise's arm and pulling him back down, the word a request, not an order. He could blame it on the wine, but he didn't want Blaise to go back to his quarters, even when it seemed obvious he wasn't feeling the same desire Peter was. Of course, what did he expect? He'd wrangled Blaise here as his prisoner, used him to assuage his own loneliness and lust—why should he expect Blaise to spend time with him of his own choice?

The request surprised Blaise enough that he sat back down without thinking. Keller had never even pretended to do anything but give orders before today. He lifted curious eyes to the commander and found himself getting lost in the serious green gaze. His breath caught in his throat and his pulse stuttered at the intent look on the Admiral's face.

The silence stretched between them as Peter held Blaise's gaze. He'd never really noticed his eyes before, hazel edged with a ring of darker color, brightened by a spark of golden highlights. Peter tried to decipher Blaise's emotions from those eyes, but the fire growing inside him was licking at the edges of his self-control, and with a low growl he pulled the younger man to him, crushing his lips in a demanding, hungry kiss.

Blaise gasped beneath the onslaught, his mouth opening to the Admiral's, letting the blond ravage him. His passion ignited instantly, flaring out of his control like the twin suns of Gamma Cephei. He thought about struggling, for form if nothing else, but the wine had lowered his inhibitions and he had no fight left in him—not to get away. Instead, he sucked roughly on Keller's tongue, urging him on.

The sharp Betelgeusian wine was even more potent when Peter tasted it in Blaise's mouth, heating his blood, urging him to probe deeper. A hand worked behind Blaise's head, threading into the dark hair, holding him still as he plundered the hot, wet cavern. The other hand roamed blindly over whatever it could reach of the hard-muscled body, his breath hitching when his fingers traced the outline of the silver ring adorning one side of the firm chest.

Blaise moaned when Keller's hand lingered over his piercing, evoking the memory of the High Justice suggesting the Admiral pierce the other side. "Damn, that feels good," he groaned, breaking the kiss to gasp for breath, arching toward the wandering fingers.

Peter dropped his hand from Blaise's hair to work impatiently at the fastener of his shipsuit, the other burrowing beneath it to seek warm skin and cool metal. His fingers closed around the ring and tugged it until the pierced nub pulled away from Blaise's body, the deep groan that rumbled beneath his palm signaling his partner's enjoyment. "Fuck, I love hearing that," Peter admitted, pushing aside fabric to bare all of Blaise's chest to his attentions. "This should have a mate... right here...," he rasped, rubbing both nipples beneath his thumbs.

Blaise's entire body went tense at the suggestion, eyes rolling back in his head as he fought the urge to beg. "Fuck," he groaned, cock swelling to diamond hardness at the thought of having the Admiral mark him, of carrying that with him even after his sentence ended. He opened his eyes, heedless of the desperate need he was sure the Admiral would read on his face. "Do it."

A bolt of pure heat stronger than the storms on Lambda Ophiuchi electrified Peter at Blaise's words. "I don't have a ring to pierce you with," he said regretfully, pulling Blaise forward to latch his lips roughly around the dark flesh. "Some day," he vowed, mouthing the nub before dragging his teeth over it in response to Blaise's shuddering intake of breath. "Some day...."

Blaise trembled at the thought. "Some day," he agreed, hoping Keller would keep this promise. In the meantime, he bucked up against the commander, wanting the struggle of body against body that so aroused him.

Letting himself push against Blaise until the smuggler lay on his back against the seating cushions, Peter explored the broad chest spread out like a feast before him. His teeth closed around a patch of dark hair, pulling at it while his hands coasted over firm pecs, his thumbs rubbing across ribs and down the concavity below them, following the dip of the iliac crease to the thicker hair that surrounded Blaise's cock. His hips rocked as he straddled Blaise's thighs, seeking friction against his own aching arousal.

"Fuck...," Blaise groaned again, angling his hips to try to get those fingers on his straining cock. The stray thought that he was giving in too easily crossed his mind, but between the wine and the lust coursing through him, he had no hope of holding back. Intent instead on encouraging his ravishment, he spread his hands over the Admiral's chest, parting the fabric of his uniform and running his hands over the strong body beneath.

Blaise's fingers awoke sparks everywhere they touched, and suddenly Peter wasn't satisfied with cramped grappling amid the remains of their meal. He pushed up and rolled to his feet, dragging Blaise behind him as he headed for the more spacious expanse of his bed, leaving pieces of his uniform behind him on the way.

Another time, without the wine as an excuse, Blaise might have struggled, but the sight of the body appearing ahead of him as the Admiral shed his clothes drew him like a lodestone. Stripping out of his own shipsuit, Blaise dared to reach out and caress the smooth skin of Keller's ass, hoping to incite the commander to fuck him hard.

Peter's cock jumped at Blaise's caress, and he pushed the pirate—*his pirate*—down onto the bed, his body settling over him, cocks rubbing together in a predatory dance. "Tell me what you want, Blaise," he offered, nipping at the curve from shoulder blade to throat, leaving small red marks in his wake. "Since it's your birthday, any toy you like." Peter's mind was already imagining Blaise writhing beneath him as he tormented him, playing with him until he was wild and begging for Peter's cock to split him apart, begging for Peter to claim him, make him his.

"No toys," Blaise requested softly. "Just you. Don't need anything but you." Any other night, he would have bitten back the admission. He certainly would have cursed himself for letting it slip out now, but he was warm and hard and more than a little drunk, and Keller had just given him carte blanche.

The thought had teased Peter at times, wondering what it would feel like to make Blaise come just for him, without toys or energy fields or any other kind of artificial enhancement. It looked like he was about to find out. "Just me," he repeated. No one had wanted just him since he was a child back on Earth. Everything came at a price, even Blaise in his bed, but for now he was going to enjoy what was offered and worry about repayment later. He knelt over Blaise's body, hands clutching the spacer's lean hips to lift them into contact while he bent forward to claim Blaise's mouth.

Blaise let the Admiral move his body as he pleased. Keller had agreed to his request; he would not press for more. Returning the kiss voraciously, he let his body convey his ever-increasing urgency.

Their cocks clung together as they moved, a fine trail of clear fluid binding them. Peter gasped for breath when he finally raised his head, leaning toward the bedside console to reach for lubricant. The increased contact drew a moan from them both, and Peter pulled back, not willing to have his time with Blaise end this quickly. "Roll over," he urged, spreading a coat of gel over his fingers.

Blaise complied immediately, moving to his hands and knees, offering himself to the dominating commander. Always before when Keller fucked him, he was already so on edge from the games they played that he didn't last long. He hoped tonight would be different and the Admiral would keep him on edge for hours.

Peter let his gaze rake over the spacer's sculpted body, the alacrity with which he'd moved almost enough to make the jaded Admiral believe Blaise really wanted him. *He's just glad he managed to escape any toys tonight*, the cynical side of his brain told him, but the wine and the eager way Blaise was looking at him over his shoulder, pushing his pert ass up in the air, were overriding his better sense. He ran his palm over a bronzed flank and Blaise groaned and arched into the touch, sending the last of Peter's reservations blowing away on the solar winds. He spread the honey-colored globes and ran his slicked fingers down the path where they joined, dropping back on his heels and leaning in to nip at the firm cheeks while he fingered the tight, hot pucker.

Blaise groaned again, eager for more of Keller's attentions. His body relaxed the instant he felt the Admiral's fingers, welcoming them inside him as he hoped to soon welcome the blond's cock. He dropped his head onto his clasped arms, every line of his body submissively begging for the commander to ravish him. He only hoped Keller was in the mood to be accommodating.

Twisting his fingers in the clinging channel only made Peter ache all the more to sink his cock into the same tight heat. He'd meant to take this slow, to string Blaise along until he was desperate for Peter to fuck him, but his plans were unraveling as quickly as his self-control. In fact, it was Peter who was starting to feel desperate, the musky scent of Blaise's sweat and the hungry sounds he made as Peter stretched him making the Admiral's cock surge and leak against his belly. Leaning forward, Peter dragged his lips up the curve of Blaise's spine, biting at the nape of his neck, and his body instinctively molded itself to the younger man's warmth, his cock nudging insistently at the taut buttocks his fingers reamed with increasing urgency.

The pinch of pain from Keller's teeth silenced the last of the pirate's inhibitions. "Just fuck me already," Blaise pleaded as the Admiral continued to tease him with his fingers.

"You always forget who gives the orders here," Peter chided, but his voice was softer than its normal cadence. He bit at the smuggler's ear, his tongue darting out to trace its whorls, the knowledge that it made Blaise tremble feeding not his sense of power, but of satisfaction. "I'll fuck you when I'm sure you're good and ready."

"Birthday boy," Blaise retorted, shivering in delight as Keller lavished attention on his ear. "Aren't you supposed to give in to my every whim?"

"And what is your whim?" Peter asked, amused, his mouth sliding down the stubble of Blaise's cheek to nip at his full lips.

"I want you to fuck me," Blaise enunciated clearly and slowly so there could be no confusion, turning his head to meet the kiss. "Just you and me and your hard cock."

He knew he ought to wait, make it last longer, but Peter couldn't resist the demands of both Blaise and his own body. Spiraling the three fingers he had buried in Blaise's ass, he spread them as far as he could, stretching the smuggler as best as his waning patience would allow. The pad of his index finger found the spongy bump of nerves and stroked it firmly, the weight of his body holding Blaise pinned to the bed as he jerked wildly at the contact.

Blaise's scream sounded loud in the stillness of the cabin, his body fighting frantically for more stimulation. "Please," he begged, pushing back shamelessly against Keller. "Please!"

The cries aroused him wildly, but this wasn't about making Blaise beg, not this time, not when Peter wanted it every bit as badly. Pulling his fingers out roughly, he smeared a coating of gel over his cock and slammed into the welcoming sheath, throwing his head back as his body froze, a nimbus of elemental passion swirling through him.

"Yes," Blaise moaned as Keller filled him, the Admiral's heavy cock rubbing in just the right places. He rocked back against the invading member, trying to draw it deeper into his body as if he could fill all the empty places inside with this moment of physical joining.

As if Blaise's moan was the permission he'd been waiting for, Peter drew back and plunged in even farther. One hand clutched Blaise's hip tightly enough to bruise while he pulled him closer, trying to bury himself in the younger man deeper than anyone else had ever been, so deep that no one but Peter would ever touch him there. His other hand moved forward to encircle Blaise's cock, fingers still slick from stretching him sliding easily over the silken flesh.

Blaise's cry might have been mistaken for one of pain if he hadn't been participating so eagerly in his own reaming, aching to be filled again and again and again. Harder, deeper, better than ever before. He wanted this to last forever, but his body had other ideas. "Close," he gasped, sliding a hand toward his cock, intending to squeeze the base to stave off his release as long as possible.

"No," Peter protested, his hand never slowing on Blaise's shaft as he nudged the smuggler's hand away. His own climax was growing imminent, swelling inside him like an expanding gas giant, and he wasn't going to be able to hold it back much longer. "Let it happen," he gasped, dragging his thumb over the leaking slit when he felt the first flashes of his own explosion sparking along his nerves. "Come... for me...," he groaned, the words dissolving into a hoarse cry as he shook and then stiffened, his release jetting from him to fill Blaise with his essence.

The feeling of thick, hot come flooding his ass melted Blaise's remaining control. He climaxed hard, clenching around the spearing cock still inside him. The force of his orgasm narrowed his focus to the point between his arms, braced on the mattress, and then even that faded as he lost consciousness momentarily, collapsing limply onto the bed.

It ended far more quickly than Peter had wanted, and the blond rolled to his side to keep from crushing Blaise beneath him. The pirate lay motionless, and Peter reached for him without conscious thought, feeling for the pulse still racing in the base of his throat. Pulling the lax body closer, Peter ran a hand through the tousled spikes of dark hair, his other arm circling sweat-damp skin to rest at the small of Blaise's back, more content now than he'd felt for longer than he could remember.

Rousing slowly, Blaise came to the uncomfortable realization that he was resting placidly in the Admiral's arms. Reminding himself that they were not lovers, not that kind of lovers anyway, he pushed himself to sit up. "You sure know how to show a guy a good time," he quipped, eyes searching for his shipsuit so he could dress and leave while he still retained some of his dignity.

Peter's hand reached out to grasp Blaise's arm before he realized he'd done it. He could blame the potency of the Betelgeusian wine for making him act and speak without thinking; he was going to have to be damn careful about its effects in the future. Tonight, though, he decided it was too late to do more than give in and enjoy it. "Going so soon?" he protested. "It's still your birthday for—" he craned around Blaise's body to check the chronograph— "another four hours. Are you sure you don't have any more whims you want indulged?"

"Well," Blaise drawled, surprised at being invited, but not about to look a gift horse in the mouth, "now that you mention it...."

CHAPTER 7
ZERO G

BLAISE switched out the light bulb, the third on that corridor, and wondered how such a high-tech ship didn't have a more reliable lighting mechanism. He'd certainly managed a better system on the *Golden Stallion*, and his ship, honey that she was, couldn't begin to compare to the *North Star*. He shouldn't complain, though. He could have been on some godforsaken planet working in a dank mine. Here, at least, he was on a ship, doing only light maintenance and custodial duties during the day. And at night—if he was lucky at night—he spent the evening with the Admiral, enjoying the benefits of Keller's demanding, creative sex drive. Unfortunately, he hadn't seen much of that lately. Whatever business was taking the *North Star* out of its usual quadrant, it was something serious enough to distract Keller almost completely. Blaise counted himself lucky these days if he saw his jailer *cum* lover once a week.

A sound at the end of the corridor brought Blaise out of his daydreams. Schooling his face to the slightly rebellious, slightly bored demeanor he cultivated except when he was alone with Keller, he glanced toward the noise to see what had caused it. He caught sight of an unfamiliar Regulosian officer wearing the uniform of a fleet captain walking toward him.

Captain Arkady Petrov hated having to report to the Admiral's flagship. Keller was a martinet at the best of times, and Arkady wasn't looking forward to having to explain the attack on a colony outpost near Orion. It wasn't as if he hadn't been doing his best to protect the sector. He hadn't even made it to a base for shore leave in months, leaving him uncomfortably unsatisfied. Lost in his thoughts, he nearly collided with the figure standing in the corridor before he caught himself.

"Beg pardon, Captain," Blaise said deferentially, stepping out of the way. The man probably would have been considered handsome in most quarters, but enough of the smuggler remained to make it hard for Blaise to see past the uniform. Only his Admiral's uniform didn't have that effect on him.

Arkady transferred his attention to the darkly handsome and really quite well-built man before him, apparently some type of maintenance worker. *Now this was more like it!* "Not at all," Arkady replied smoothly. "The fault was mine for not watching where I was walking. Why, if you hadn't stepped aside, I might have wound up on top of you!"

Despite his satisfaction with Keller, Blaise remained enough of a rogue to recognize and respond to the flirtation he sensed in the words. "That could have been quite... interesting," he commented. "I almost regret missing out."

Encouraged by the response, Arkady's gaze flickered appreciatively over the other man's muscular physique, laughing eyes, and dark, shaggy hair. He looked a bit too rakish to be regular service. In fact, the more the Captain considered him, the more he was sure he wasn't military at all. That could make things even easier. "I'd hate to disappoint you," Arkady answered silkily. "Are you off duty? Perhaps I could buy you some refreshment, and we could discuss... mutual interests?"

"Now that would be a real pleasure, Captain," Blaise drawled, mind racing as he debated whether he should accept the obvious—and the less obvious—invitations. "But I have a few more things I have to finish up before I could consider your offer. These lights won't change themselves, and the Admiral gets a bit... put out when things aren't maintained to his demanding standards."

Hearing a different note in his quarry's voice when he mentioned the Admiral, Arkady narrowed his eyes in consideration. He'd heard the salacious rumors that Keller sometimes took a particular interest in certain prisoners held on his ship. It would be just his luck to be hitting on one of the Admiral's "special projects."

"And would it trouble you to put the Admiral out?" he asked.

Blaise snickered as he considered the possible reactions Keller might have to his dereliction of duty. "Not especially," he admitted, since it would almost certainly result in a workout of a different kind, ending in a stupendous orgasm. "I try not to make a habit of it, though." If he did, the Admiral might change his method of punishment, and he certainly didn't want that to happen.

"I'm sorry to hear that," Keller growled, rounding the curve in the corridor. He knew Petrov would seduce anything in pants, but the *Pleides*'s captain had information he needed about the third attack, this one on a planet closer to the quadrant's populous central core. Petrov's ship had been one of the first to respond to the distress signal and had firsthand data readings of the aftermath. "What exactly do you think you're doing, Captain Petrov? This man is a prisoner. He's in enough trouble without your encouraging him to dereliction of his duties." He focused the full glare of his blistering gaze on the junior officer, turning his back—for the moment—on the incorrigible space pirate. "Don't you have more critical obligations to attend to?"

Behind Keller's back, Blaise smothered a grin. He hadn't intended to get caught flirting with the captain or neglecting his assigned tasks, but the Admiral had only himself to blame. If he'd spent more time seeing to his prisoner, Blaise wouldn't have been feeling lonely and horny and possibly amenable to Petrov's seductions.

"I—ah—that is—I was—," Arkady stammered, trying to come up with an explanation that wouldn't get him banished to permanent patrol in the most remote corner of the galaxy. "I heard this man was a smuggler. I was hoping he could give me some information about the activities in my sector."

"I'm sure your interrogation techniques aren't nearly as... rigorous... as mine," Keller smirked. "Besides, he's been out of action for months now. I doubt he'd have anything new to show you, even if he were willing." *Which he'd damn well better not be,* Peter added to himself.

"Nope," Blaise agreed cheekily, "nothing new to add. Sorry I couldn't help you, Captain. It would have been my pleasure, though."

"I doubt it," Peter muttered, sparing a steely glance at the former pirate. "Now, Captain, don't let us detain you from your duties, especially since your performance makes it clear they require all your attention." Knowing that subtle threat would be enough to send Petrov scrambling back to his ship at light speed as soon as he finished dumping his data, the Admiral turned his attention to the snickering prisoner. "And just what do you think you were doing?" he purred dangerously.

"Changing the light bulbs," Blaise replied facetiously. "That's what I was told to do today." He held up a burnt-out bulb as proof. "He all but ran into me and struck up a conversation," he added. "I didn't realize I wasn't supposed to speak when spoken to."

"There's only one way you can open your mouth without getting into trouble," Peter rasped. "Maybe I need to remind you of that, since you seem to have forgotten whose pleasure you serve here." He eyed the dark-haired rogue, pondering what activity would best reinforce that point, as well as take his own mind off the frustration of being unable to prevent yet another attack. "I'd say you're overdue for your mandatory zero-gravity training."

That sounded promising! "Mustn't miss that," Blaise agreed, leaning subtly closer to the Admiral. "Will you be seeing to my training personally, sir?" he asked.

"Don't I always?" Peter answered, grabbing a handful of Blaise's shipsuit and pulling him forward until their faces were only inches apart. "You don't seem to respond to correction very well, though. I keep having to teach you the same lessons over and over."

Blaise forbore to reply. He could hardly tell the Admiral that he didn't learn his lessons precisely so the other man would have to teach him again. He enjoyed his "punishments" far too much to deprive himself of them by being a good student.

"Report to the zero-g chamber in ninety minutes," Peter ordered, walking away without a backward glance. He knew Blaise wouldn't dare disobey him. The ex-smuggler might push his limits every chance he got, but the Admiral knew they both enjoyed the consequences of those actions. In the meantime, he'd ensure he learned everything Petrov had to disclose about the most recent attack.

"Yes, sir," Blaise replied to Keller's retreating back. He finished changing out the last light bulb quickly and returned his cart of supplies to the maintenance closet. Deciding he had enough time for a shower, Blaise returned to his quarters and turned the 'fresher on high, letting the hot water wash away the grease and grime of the day. Relaxed afterward, body humming in anticipation, he grabbed a quick bite to eat before reporting as ordered to the zero-g training room, figuring he might not be free again for quite some time.

It hadn't taken Peter as long as he'd thought to grill Petrov. Unfortunately, the *Pleides*'s captain didn't have as much information as he'd hoped, the attackers once again leaving frustratingly little evidence in the wake of their destruction. He'd pumped Arkady for everything he could remember, but other than the now-familiar energy signature, there'd been nothing but smoking ruins left behind. Peter had cursed as he looked over the vid-scans after Petrov left. The small mining facility hadn't had much of value to attract pirates, and it didn't appear the attackers had made any attempt to claim any of the ore from the storage silos before blasting them—and the planetoid's dozen miners—into ions. Scowling at the images of senseless devastation, he keyed off the display and stalked toward the zero-g chamber, determined to work off some of his aggression.

He was finishing up his preparations when the door swished open and Blaise entered, his attitude as unconsciously arrogant as ever. The Admiral was sure that Blaise's rebellious attitude was one reason he had yet to tire of the younger man as he had all his earlier subs; that, and the fact that the smuggler made him hotter than the surface of a supernova. As soon as the door closed behind Blaise's tight ass, Keller tapped the controls to lock the door and kill the chamber's gravity. "Show me how well you can maneuver in freefall," Peter ordered. "Strip."

Blaise was no rank beginner. He had worked more ships than probably most of the sailors under the Admiral's command, and many of them had been little more than junkyard scrap. He'd had plenty of experience with freefall, mostly when the gravity generators failed. With confident ease, he moved slowly to keep himself from spinning out of control, releasing the fastenings on his shipsuit and sliding it off his shoulders and down over his hips.

Peter watched the smuggler appreciatively as Blaise gracefully wriggled his way out of his work uniform, revealing his bare skin and the fact that his cock didn't require gravity to get hard. "Very good," he acknowledged, completely comfortable after decades of zero-g experience. "But in your former line of work, you were alone on your ship most of the time. What would you do if you had a shipmate who needed your… assistance?"

"Do you need my assistance, Admiral?" Blaise asked teasingly, though he was also following protocol. He would never approach a shipmate in zero-g conditions without alerting the other person to his intentions.

"One of these days, Blaise, that mouth of yours is going to get you into real trouble," Peter warned. "Let's see if you can make it over here without knocking me into orbit, for a start."

Blaise pushed off gently, floating smoothly across the room, aiming for a spot a little to Keller's left. "Would you have preferred I come sailing over here with no warning whatsoever?" he countered as he caught himself smoothly on the railing next to the Admiral's elbow. "I would have thought that against shipboard procedure. It certainly was against mine."

"You had shipboard procedures?" Peter scoffed in disbelief. "Hard to believe, since you're so obviously ignorant of proper discipline." Using just enough motion to slam into Blaise forcefully, he spun the younger man around and pressed his chest firmly against the chamber wall. "You know what kind of assistance I'm looking for, Blaise," he hissed, holding the pirate's hip with one hand and rubbing the evidence of his arousal against the taut cheeks. His other hand caught Blaise's thick hair, pulling the younger man's head back into his kiss.

Blaise returned the kiss eagerly, far beyond caring that the Admiral knew of his willingness and desire. They had finished with those games for the most part after his birthday, the effects of the wine having broken down barriers they'd chosen not to restore. Instead, he reached behind him and used his grip on the commander's hips to give him enough leverage to push back into the cock that pressed against him so invitingly. "I'm always happy to serve, Admiral," he replied when his lips were released.

"You seemed eager enough to serve Petrov earlier, too, so that's not saying much," Peter retorted. He slid his lips down the strong curve of Blaise's neck, biting down hard when he reached the junction of his shoulder, marking the skin with his teeth. The bruise wouldn't show beneath Blaise's worksuit, but it would remind him of who he belonged to, for a day or so at least.

"A change is as good as a rest," Blaise quipped, though he would never have submitted to the captain the way he submitted to the Admiral. Only Keller could elicit this response from him. The older man didn't need to know that, though. Blaise knew the Admiral enjoyed his rebellion as much as the smuggler enjoyed the consequences.

At Blaise's flippant answer, the Admiral felt a surge of jealousy that surprised him with its intensity. Wrenching the grinning smuggler around by his hair, he towed him across the room to the opposite wall, where he'd secured a pair of leather straps. Removing one, he ran it over his palm, nodding to the other. "Grab that and hold on," he ordered the pirate. "And don't let go. If I have to restrain you, it will only make things worse for you."

Blaise obeyed the Admiral's orders immediately. His innate sense of self-preservation told him he'd pushed the commander as far as he safely could. Now, it was just a matter of holding on for the ride. A thrill shot through him as he imagined all the possibilities presented by their current situation.

Peter hooked a foot under the rail that circled the training room walls, knowing he'd need some way to brace himself. Otherwise, the first time he brought the strap down against Blaise's ass—*like that!*— would send him spinning across the room in reaction.

Even in zero-g, the strap moved with enough force to smart when it hit Blaise's skin. His hips jerked forward, a motion that would have sent him spinning helplessly through the room if not for his grip on the leather cuffs. As it was, his body twisted around, leaving his vulnerable belly facing the Admiral.

Reaching out to the younger man, Peter spun Blaise back around to face the wall again. He wanted to teach his brash lover a lesson, not leave him incapacitated. Holding Blaise's shoulder secure with his free hand, Peter brought the strap down a second time, raising a bright red welt on the honeyed skin.

"Ah, shit!" The second blow was enough to pull the muttered curse from Blaise's lips. Rarely did their games cross over the line to true pain.

The energy whip the first night he'd been on board was just about it. His usual punishments involved being denied release. While relatively minor compared to what he'd endured while aboard the Gavenelian ships, it was still enough to leave him tense against the next blow, and none too happy about the situation either.

Peter hardened himself against Blaise's exclamation of pain. Six blows in all, he told himself. That should be enough to get the cocky bastard's attention. "Maybe you won't be quite so eager for a change after this," he growled, laying a series of quick blows across the spacer's backside.

Blaise bit his lip to stifle his cries as four more blows fell. He was panting by the time it was done, his body tense and braced for more. His relief when the Admiral released the strap and let it float away was palpable. Still trembling, he tried to steady his breathing, using meditation techniques he had perfected during his imprisonment to push aside the adrenaline coursing through him.

Peter dropped the strap and positioned himself behind his shaking partner. He ground his cloth-covered erection against Blaise's reddened ass, letting the younger man feel his unabated arousal. "Now, I believe you were going to show me how eager you were to serve me," he husked against the pirate's ear. Letting go of Blaise's hips, he pushed off gently, letting himself float freely.

Blaise took a deep breath and started to release the strap he held when he remembered the earlier order. "I can't do much if you're over there and I'm over here," he said softly. He'd had his fill of punishment for the day.

Impressed that Blaise had remembered his order not to let go of the strap, Peter grinned. "Very good," he acknowledged. "But I think you're going to need both hands now. Get over here and take care of what you started."

Blaise released the leather he was holding and pushed himself in Keller's direction, letting their bodies bump and the momentum push them toward the far wall. Catching the railing with one hand, he used the other to keep the Admiral from crashing into the wall. As quickly as he dared in the zero-g conditions, he undid the uniform and bared the commander's body to his gaze. Nudging the Admiral upward, he steadied them both when the thick arousal was at the height of his mouth. Lowering his head, he inhaled the swollen shaft, swallowing around the mushroomed head.

Peter didn't bother to hold back his moan of pleasure as Blaise's talented mouth closed around his cock. Holding the dark head in place with one hand, he pried Blaise's hand away from the railing with the other, letting their bodies drift weightlessly.

Unattached now as they were to anything grounded, Blaise had no choice but to use his grip on the Admiral to provide the leverage he needed to bob his head up and down over the hard cock. One thing, though, didn't require gravity to be effective. Grinning as best he could around his mouthful, he hummed in his throat, letting the vibrations tease Keller's erection.

Blaise's oral prowess never failed to arouse Peter's admiration—among other things—and at first the Admiral simply enjoyed the delicious suction on his rigid shaft. He watched as a string of saliva escaped the privateer's lips, breaking into tiny glittering globules that floated past Peter's face. As he felt his control beginning to slip, he grasped Blaise's bicep around the stylized horse tattoo, flipping gracefully end over end until he faced the younger man's well-striped ass. Unable to lay hands on the mysterious attackers, he'd taken out his anger and frustration on his smuggler. He owed him something in recompense.

Blaise had let Keller's cock slip from his mouth in surprise at the maneuver, and the Admiral grasped the spacer's lean hips and twisted him around, thrusting the neglected organ back in his face. "Didn't tell you to stop," he ordered, lowering his head to lap at the droplets of fluid beginning to escape from Blaise's swollen erection.

The howl that tore from Blaise's throat at the feeling of the Admiral's tongue on his cock was muffled by the shaft in his mouth, but nothing short of the void of space could silence it, not when he was feeling Keller's mouth on him for the first time.

Blaise's uninhibited reaction made the Admiral wonder why he hadn't given in to this particular temptation before. True, he'd never been tempted to taste another prisoner's cock before Blaise's, but the salty taste and silky texture of the pirate's thick shaft felt damn good in his mouth. Not as good as his cock would feel buried in Blaise's ass, though. With that thought in mind, Peter slid two fingers into his mouth alongside the slick column, coating them thoroughly with saliva and Blaise's pre-come.

Blaise tried to focus his attention on his ministrations to the Admiral, not wanting to be rebuked for neglecting his duties, but he could feel Keller's fingers sliding alongside his shaft in the other man's mouth. He knew where those fingers were going, and the thought alone had him trembling with desire.

Peter tightened his thighs around Blaise's shaggy head, forcing himself into the smuggler's mouth until his balls pressed against the man's sensuous lips. Keeping a firm grip on one hip, he pushed his wet fingers into Blaise's hole with more urgency than care. He'd make sure the younger man was stretched enough to receive him, but he needed to be inside him the way he needed oxygen to breathe in the void of space.

Blaise's back arched under the rough penetration, not to fight it, but to draw Keller's fingers deeper. The sharp movement sent them spinning gently through the room, but he paid no attention to that. His mind was on the thick flesh in his mouth and the callused fingers stretching his ass. Everything else had lost all meaning for him.

Feeling Blaise arch and clench around him, the Admiral worked his fingers deeper, spreading them until he could feel the tight muscle start to relax. When their entwined bodies bumped gently against the chamber wall, he groped for the rail to steady them. Reluctantly abandoning his efforts to work his cock down Blaise's throat, he pulled the dark-haired captive up to face him. Taken by a sudden impulse, he pulled the younger man's mouth to his, savoring the taste of his own essence on Blaise's tongue.

Blaise offered his mouth as willingly as he offered his body, though they still kept to the pretense that the Admiral was forcing his submission. He wondered fleetingly if they would ever move beyond these games, but there was no time for such considerations now. All that mattered was that Keller was fucking his mouth with his tongue like Blaise hoped he would soon be fucking his ass with his cock. He sucked hard on the invading muscle, welcoming it eagerly.

Peter groaned at the ferocity of Blaise's kiss. He sucked at the smuggler's tongue until every atom of his own taste was gone, leaving only the addicting spice that was Blaise's own flavor. Moving his lips over the smuggler's throat, he effortlessly turned Blaise's body until he could rub his leaking cock over the still-reddened crease, trying to work the fluid into it before it could float away.

Blaise grasped the rail when he was spun around, using it as leverage to push back against the hard shaft that teased him so mercilessly. "Damn it," he cursed. "Fuck me already!"

If the Admiral had even thought of taking Blaise slowly, the smuggler's fierce demand—for Peter had yet to break his prisoner of thinking he could give the orders—sent that idea flying out the airlock. Pulling the straining hips against his, he filled Blaise with one strong thrust. The reaction bounced Blaise off the wall and sent them spiraling across the empty room. Peter wrapped his legs around Blaise's and rocked his hips in an urgent rhythm, each stroke sending them tumbling in a new direction.

Moans and shouts poured from Blaise's lips at the burn when the Admiral finally fitted their bodies together. Saliva was a poor substitute for the slippery lube they usually used, but even without it, he wanted this, craved this, and fought to push back against Keller's thrusts. The lack of leverage limited his movements' effectiveness, but no one could fault him for lack of effort. Finally, in desperation, he reached behind him, using his hands to pull the Admiral closer, hoping that would provide the extra depth of penetration he desired.

Blaise's hands cupping around Peter's ass, pushing him even deeper into the maddening friction, snapped what little control the Admiral had managed to retain. Peter knew they both enjoyed the pretense of Blaise's resistance, but in moments like this he could believe the other man wanted him as desperately as Peter needed to claim him as his own. Clutching Blaise's spiky hair with one hand and groping with the other until it closed around the smuggler's straining shaft, he bit into the flesh of Blaise's shoulder and pumped without restraint, each drag of his fist bringing him closer to his own release.

Blaise could feel his climax building, tingling along his lower back and radiating out from his ass where the Admiral completed him. With a hoarse shout, he gave in, letting it spool out of him, his muscles contracting rhythmically with each spurt of his eager cock.

When Blaise shuddered and spurted around him, Peter felt as if he'd been caught in a tractor beam of raw sexual power. Pulling the pirate's hips roughly against his, he threw back his head and cried out wordlessly as his orgasm overwhelmed him, filling Blaise's tight channel until it overflowed with his hot juices.

Replete from his own release and the warmth of the Admiral's come, Blaise's muscles went completely limp, leaving him to float without direction in the weightless space of the room, his only connection with the man behind and inside him.

Peter let their entangled bodies drift aimlessly, content to let his breathing slow and his pulse return to a normal rate still joined with his rebellious lover. Soon enough, he knew, Blaise would need to make some show of resistance, but for these brief moments he could allow himself to imagine a day when Blaise might come to him unforced.

Unsure how to interpret the uncharacteristic quiet from the Admiral, Blaise took refuge, as was his wont, in cheekiness. "If this is your reaction to me talking with the fleet captains, I may have to talk to every one I see," he joked.

Smothering a sigh at the cocky remark he had known was coming, Peter pushed away from Blaise, using the momentum to aim for the nearest wall. Grasping the rail with one hand to steady himself, he refastened his uniform and leaned back into a comfortable slouch. "If you enjoy having your ass whipped, by all means," the Admiral agreed cordially. "In the meantime, though, I have a better use for your mouth than talking." He gestured at the globules of pearly fluid that floated lazily throughout the room. "You're not leaving until you clean up the mess you made."

CHAPTER 8
UNEXPLORED TERRITORY

WHISTLING tunelessly to himself, Blaise worked his way around the Admiral's quarters, straightening, dusting, and generally tidying up. He could hardly complain about the "hard labor" he was forced to serve when this was pretty much the worst of it. He did some maintenance on the ship as well, but he'd done worse than that on the *Golden Stallion* without blinking an eye. And on the upside of it, he had gotten to fuck the Admiral—well, be fucked by him, anyway—somewhat regularly for the past ten months. His pride continued to insist on making it a battle between them, but he had started wondering recently whether it was worth the effort to maintain the façade when all he really wanted to do was sink into Keller's arms and beg for his attention.

With his mind wandering, he didn't see the bottle of lube sitting on the edge of the table by the bed. His elbow clipped it, knocking it onto the floor. He lunged for it, but it rolled under the bed before he could grab it. Muttering a curse, he dropped to his hands and knees, lowering his shoulders as he reached under the bunk, trying to retrieve the tube. He didn't want to think what the Admiral would do to him if the lube was missing. Keller might be rough, but he'd rarely taken Blaise dry, and even then, not in some time. The privateer didn't want *that* to start again!

A dull ache was throbbing in Admiral Keller's temples as he palmed the sensor to enter his quarters. Viewing and re-viewing the vid-scans of the latest attack for any possible clues that could lead to the perpetrators had left him with a pounding headache. He'd tried to put himself in the attackers' place, to understand what could be motivating them, with damn little success. They'd made no attempts to communicate, and didn't seem interested in plundering their targets before blowing them to their component atoms. The Admiral suspected the enemy, whoever they were, was testing them, assessing their defenses with a series of escalating assaults. When he'd suggested that to his superiors at the Admiralty, though, he'd been quickly shot down as an alarmist. Recognizing he'd need hard evidence to convince them, Peter tried to dismiss the problem from his mind, at least for the rest of the evening. He was looking forward to kicking off his boots and relaxing with a cool drink. As the door *thwock*ed shut behind him, he stopped short, bemused by the sight that met his eyes: a tight ass thrust up into the air from beneath his bed, what he could see of the trimly muscular body attached to it leaving no question to whom it belonged. The immediate thickening of his shaft in response was enough to remove any lingering doubt. Only one man had ever won such a consistent response from Peter, a response that showed no sign of abating nearly a year after the smuggler's capture. "Blaise," the Admiral drawled appreciatively. "Are you asking to be spanked?"

Blaise jerked back from under the bed, hitting his head in the process, though he did manage to maintain his grip on the lube. "It seems to be a bad habit of mine," he drawled, moving to standing, his eyes taking in the sight of the handsome man in front of him. He could see the stress in the set of the Admiral's eyes and decided a round of rough, domineering sex was just what the doctor ordered. Now all he had to do was provoke Keller into giving it to them. "I figured you'd be far more upset if I lost this," he added, holding up the tube with a cocky grin.

"You'd be the one who'd feel the lack," the blond countered, though in truth it had been some time since he'd taken Blaise dry. He found it much more stimulating to make the dark-haired sub cry out in pleasure than in pain, though he'd been careful not to make that obvious to his partner. Blaise had worked his way under the Admiral's skin far enough as it was; he didn't need the younger man to realize how much power he really had over his nominal jailer. Peter's gaze raked over the smuggler's lean body, wondering how he managed to make even a standard shipsuit look somehow disreputable. "Do you consider that proper attire for the Admiral's quarters?" he asked silkily.

"This is the only uniform I was issued," Blaise retorted cheekily, feeling the weight of the older man's gaze. *Let the games begin.* "If you want me in a dress uniform, you'll have to give me one."

"That isn't what I meant, and you know it," Peter purred, stalking to the bed and dropping into a lounging pose. "Strip," he commanded, his headache beginning to recede already at the prospect of the encounter to come.

Jauntily, Blaise lifted his hands to the fastenings on his shipsuit, undoing them slowly, taking his time and giving the Admiral a good show as he went. This was part of their game, the feigned reluctance that fired their blood. At least Blaise hoped it fired Keller's blood as much as it fired his own.

The crotch of Peter's uniform was growing uncomfortably tight as he watched Blaise's leisurely striptease, but he made no effort to relieve himself of the constriction—yet. When Blaise dropped the worksuit to the floor, he rose and circled the smuggler slowly. The younger man's strong, honey-colored body never failed to set his senses humming with arousal. He trailed a languid hand over the dark thatch that covered Blaise's chest, giving a rough tweak to the silver ring that pierced his nipple and grinning at the appreciative moan he wrung from the pirate. "Now," he ordered, coming to a stop in front of the bed, "undress me."

As always, attention paid to his piercing drove Blaise crazy with lust, a fact it was useless to deny when his cock jumped so visibly. The Admiral's order aroused him even more, but he had to maintain the charade that allowed this to work. "And how else shall I serve my captain this evening?" he asked obsequiously, dropping to his knees in front of Keller to remove his boots.

Having Blaise on his knees before him was not a new sight, but something about the way his lover—Peter admitted, to himself at least, that he thought of Blaise that way now—caressed the smooth leather of his boots awoke a raw hunger in his gut. He briefly contemplated ordering Blaise to fetch his restraints and some other toys, but the service he really craved didn't require any special equipment. Unusually hesitant to ask for what he wanted, Peter reminded himself as he hadn't needed to in years that he was in command now. The Admiral licked his lips as Blaise set the footwear aside and ran large hands up his legs, skimming his groin teasingly before unfastening his uniform. As soon as the younger man had eased it over his shoulders and knelt again to help Peter step out of the clinging material, he kicked it aside and caught

Blaise's chin, meeting the sparkling hazel eyes with a ravenous gaze. "Rim me."

Blaise's eyes grew wide at the order, one his commander had never given him before. Nodding slowly, he shifted around so he knelt behind the Admiral. "Here?" he asked, not sure if Keller would want to sit or stand or recline on the bed.

Peter knelt on the edge of the bunk, leaning forward on his elbows to bare his ass to the pirate. The position was an unusually vulnerable one for him, bringing back memories of a time he'd put behind him forever when he left Earth and making his voice harsh as he twisted his head to gaze over his shoulder at the dark-haired man. "What the fuck are you waiting for?" he grated. "Don't tell me this is the first time you've ever tongued someone's ass."

Feeling far more chastised than the words alone merited, Blaise shuffled closer, his hands closing over the muscular backside, spreading the cheeks to allow him access to the Admiral's tight hole. They still maintained their charade, yes, but it had been months since the Admiral had taken that particular tone with him. He was surprised by how much it stung. Reminding himself that Keller was his warden, not truly his lover, and that he should not anger the man unduly, he bent his head and began to lick up and down the slightly sweaty crease, teasing a little before settling to his primary task.

Clenching his fingers in the bedcover at the first swipe of the pirate's wet tongue over his most private spot, Peter let his legs spread further apart, opening himself more fully to the decadent attentions. He fought not to push backward as Blaise's lips played around his hole, craving this touch as he never had before.

He wondered for a moment what it would feel like to let Blaise fuck him, to feel the other man's thick, hard cock impale him and stroke over his prostate until he was writhing with need. It had shocked him the first time he'd brought himself to climax that way, on a rare night when for some unremembered infraction he'd banned Blaise from his bed, reaming himself with his fingers as he imagined the pirate forcing himself roughly into his tight sheath, fucking him with almost feral intensity, until he'd sprayed his release over his stomach and chest, screaming Blaise's name. He could never allow himself to appear that needy, that weak, to his prisoner, not as long as Blaise continued to require at least the pretense of Keller's authority to initiate their every encounter. At least, Peter hoped it was only pretense; he'd hate to think that after all this time he still had to force Blaise to accept him.

Determined to bring his Admiral as much pleasure as possible, Blaise applied himself to his task with great diligence, working his tongue in and out of the tight hole, then circling the exterior, before diving inside again, reaching for Keller's prostate. It was so rare that he was allowed any control in their interactions. The Admiral would order him to suck him, but other than that, Blaise knew he was the one who received the vast majority of the pleasure as Keller teased and tormented him with all manner of devilish implements intended to send him soaring among the stars before he exploded with his release. For once, he hoped he would be allowed to lavish that degree of release on his master.

Peter couldn't control the low growl of pleasure as Blaise's tongue stabbed into him repeatedly, its probing depth just tantalizingly short of the spot that would send him flaring like a comet hitting the atmosphere. Unable to stop himself, he clenched around the hot muscle, trying to draw it deeper inside. His cock leaked a string of fluid onto the slick surface of the bedding below him, denying him the friction he needed. Scrabbling behind him with one hand, he grabbed at Blaise's hair, trying to pull the pirate close enough to bring him the release that floated just out of reach.

Blaise moaned when he felt Keller pushing back into his mouth. He rolled his tongue, spearing it into the Admiral as far as he could. Daringly, he reached forward, his hand closing around the older man's cock, not even thinking that bringing the commander to climax would deny him the rough fucking he craved.

The touch of Blaise's hand on his cock was all Peter needed to send him into orbit. He thrust between the channel of Blaise's fingers and the fierce pistoning of his tongue until the sensation built to overload, short-circuiting all his nerve endings in a blaze of spectacular pleasure. Tossing back his head with a hoarse cry, he shuddered as his release shot from him, coating Blaise's hand with thick hot liquid.

Feeling the contractions of the Admiral's release, Blaise continued to pump Keller's cock until the aftershocks faded, lifting his sticky hand to his mouth and licking it clean. The taste never ceased to arouse him. His whole body ached with pent-up passion, but he held himself in check, waiting for some sign from the older man to indicate what he should do. He hoped Keller would grant him release one way or another rather than sending him back to his quarters to deal with his erection alone.

Leaning into the mattress until his rasping breath returned to a more normal rate, Peter bit back a moan when Blaise's tongue slipped from between his cheeks. Rolling to his side, he watched his dark-haired lover clean every droplet of come from his hand, the sight itself erotic enough to keep the roil of arousal churning in his gut. Blaise's own cock thrust up stiffly from a riot of dark curls, hard and red and leaking a trail of its own sticky fluid against the spacer's taut stomach. "That looks uncomfortable," Peter husked, the image of taking that powerful shaft into himself flashing again through his lustful thoughts. The reaction shocked him into silence. A climax as fierce as the one Blaise had just wrung from him would usually have left him sated for at least a short while, but he was just as hungry for the other man as he had been when he first walked into the room and spotted his ass poking out from beneath his bunk.

Such a comment from the Admiral usually led to an order to do something about his erection or else to get a cock ring and make it worse. The silence that followed this time chilled Blaise more than the darkest reaches of space. "Please," he begged, "don't leave me like this. Just touch me. That's all I need."

Peter had never heard Blaise ask for something for himself with such a pleading note in his voice. He'd been demanding before, rebellious, forgetting or choosing to deny the Admiral's control, but he'd seldom asked—begged—like this before. Peter could almost believe that Blaise really wanted this—wanted *him*—and just as Blaise had given him a release like none they had experienced before, he wanted to grant his lover something unique as well.

Rolling upright, he knelt at the edge of the bed and caught Blaise by the hips, pulling him forward until the younger man's straining erection bobbed in front of his face. Leaning forward, Peter took the thick shaft into his mouth, savoring the salty tang of pre-come that coated the silky head.

Totally surprised by the feeling of the Admiral's mouth closing around his cock, Blaise nearly came right then. Keller had tasted him once before, when they were updating his zero-g training, but it hadn't been like this. Then, it had been a few licks to tease him before fucking him through the wall. This was different. This was... for real. He tried not to thrust into the wet heat, tried to hold himself back until his lover gave him permission, but his climax was bubbling through him, approaching the critical mass to explode. Unable to stop himself, he threaded his fingers into the short blond hair, gasps and moans falling freely from his lips.

Blaise's untempered reaction sparked an even greater hunger in Peter to see the dark-haired spacer lose control completely, to prove that his need was as great as Peter's own. The blond took the heavy cock deeper into his mouth, relaxing his throat until he could swallow around the head, milking the ropy veins with his tongue. It had been decades since he'd done this last, but the lessons once forced had never been forgotten. He cupped Blaise's swollen balls in one palm, his other hand squeezing the firm buttocks that undulated beneath his grasp, sucking harder and groaning as he felt the shaft beginning to jerk against his palate.

Pushed beyond his control by the heat of Keller's mouth, Blaise's grip tightened as he felt his orgasm begin. "Peter!" he wailed as it spilled out of him, completely unaware that in his passion, he had spoken the Admiral's name aloud for the first time. He knew only the heat of the man's mouth, the caress of his tongue, the squeeze of his throat, and that was enough to leave him shuddering with pleasure, only his lover's grip on his hips keeping him upright.

Hearing Blaise's ragged voice shouting his name was more delicious to Keller than the salty tang that poured down his throat, and he spurred the shudders that wracked through the younger man as he swallowed and squeezed and lapped, not letting the softened organ slide from his lips until he had drained it as dry as the moons of Cerberus. Lying back on the bed, he pulled Blaise down beside him, ignoring the demands of his resurgent erection in favor of wrapping an arm around Blaise's slackened frame, combing the dark, sweat-damp hair from the smuggler's brow with uncharacteristic tenderness.

"I... Forgive me," Blaise stuttered, realizing what had escaped his lips. "I didn't mean to overstep myself." His head was still swimming from the Admiral's attentions, enough that he had trouble forming coherent thought, much less anything else. He knew, though, that he was in his lover's arms, being cradled with a gentleness Keller had never before employed. *Could it mean...?* He dared not let himself hope.

His partner's unusual docility made Peter uneasy, unsure how to respond. He was used to Blaise's defiance, not this quiet submission that sparked hope even as it left him feeling adrift in space, as if he had floated away from the moorings of everything comfortable and familiar. Falling back on habit, he gave Blaise's ass a swat, and if his hand lingered afterward, cupping the firm globe with a soothing touch, Blaise certainly wasn't complaining. He pulled the pirate closer, wrapping his legs around him until the hard length of his cock mated against Blaise's sated one. "You'll make it up to me later," he replied, closing his eyes as he let himself imagine what form that repayment might take.

"Any way you want," Blaise promised rashly, simply relieved at not being booted from bed or ordered to fetch a belt or paddle. He would willingly—eagerly even—offer the Admiral whatever sexual favors he demanded if it meant he avoided an actual punishment. He had never refused one, and never would, but he by far preferred Keller's other means of forcing his submission.

The acquiescent response made the Admiral's head snap up in suspicion. As much as he fantasized about Blaise submitting to him willingly, he couldn't believe the sudden change in attitude was anything but a ploy of some kind. "What new devilry are you plotting?" he growled, eyeing the dark-haired rogue warily. "Whatever it is, it won't work. You're mine for another two years, Risner, and I'm not about to let you forget that," he added. The idea that Blaise had hatched some scheme to try and escape took possession of him so forcefully that he dug his fingers into the younger man's shoulders, pinning him to the bed. He wouldn't even let himself think beyond the end of Blaise's sentence; he'd deal with that, find some other way to keep Blaise bound to him, when that time came.

The Admiral's words were so at odds with what Blaise was thinking and feeling that he pulled away sharply in anger. "You just don't get it, do you?" he demanded angrily. "You can't get past the way we met and the fact that you're in charge. You made up your mind about me that day, and you haven't looked again since then. All you see is the criminal

scum your lieutenant dragged in instead of seeing the man I really am."
Barely pausing for breath, he barged on, "Did it ever occur to you that I
might enjoy the time we spend together, that I might get as much
pleasure out of it as you do, that I might lo...." He froze as he realized
what had almost come out of his mouth. "Just let me go back to my
quarters," he finished, his voice defeated.

Throughout Blaise's rant, Peter maintained his grip on the spacer's
broad shoulders, holding him in place when he tried to wrench away.
The sudden lack of resistance caused him to slam the other man back to
the mattress. Blaise blinked up at him for a moment, his hazel eyes
dulled, and then Peter pounced on him ravenously, his teeth cutting into
Blaise's lip as he forced his way into the younger man's mouth, doing
his best to ram his tongue down Blaise's throat in a ferocious kiss that
staked an unmistakable claim. "Mine," Peter insisted, breaking away just
long enough to drag a gasping breath into his lungs before seizing his
lover's mouth again.

Blaise's body responded automatically to the powerful claiming far
sooner than his mind, lips parting, tongue wrapping around the one that
invaded his mouth, body arching to meet the one that covered his. Then
his mind caught up and he melted beneath the sensations, arms coming
to encircle his lover, pulling him tighter, inciting the Admiral to finish
staking his claim. Never mind that he had just come. The argument and
the near miss in his admissions fueled his desire again, in a way only
Keller could assuage.

Grinding his hips against Blaise's to force him back onto the bunk,
Peter could feel the younger man's cock swelling against his, despite
having come just a few minutes before. That was fine with Peter; he was
going to make Blaise come again, and again, until the pirate was
delirious with pleasure, too drained and replete to even consider leaving
Peter's bed, or his life.

He eased his crushing grip on Blaise's shoulders, burying one hand
in the smuggler's short dark hair, holding his head still as he continued to
plunder his mouth. The other hand followed the curve of Blaise's spine
down his sweat-coated back, slipping between the cheeks of his ass to
prod at his tightness. "Hope you held onto that lube," the blond rumbled,
working a thick finger into the opening. "I'm going to fuck you into the
next galaxy."

Blaise didn't even hesitate, rolling immediately onto his stomach and presenting his ass to the Admiral. He wanted this, wanted to be claimed so badly the emptiness inside him hurt. Maybe this way he could pretend this wouldn't end with his sentence in two years. He scrambled for the lube still within easy reach, pressing it into Keller's hand. "Yes," he pleaded. "Take me."

Squeezing a dollop of gel onto his fingers, Peter spread the tawny cheeks and then paused. Before he could stop himself, he bent down and dragged his tongue up the musky crease, tasting sweat and the remainder of Blaise's earlier climax. When the younger man squirmed beneath him in shock, he nipped at the rounded flesh and flipped Blaise onto his back, pushing his thighs apart with an impatient knee. "Like this," he demanded, coating his cock with the handful of lube and sliding into Blaise's channel with one firm thrust.

"Adm... Peter!" The cry of surprise at the feeling of the Admiral's tongue on him was replaced by one of absolute fulfillment as he was flipped and taken forcefully. Keller had bent him over every available surface, but never like this, face to face like lovers. His body arched into the penetration, pulling his ravisher deeper, completing the bond that joined their bodies. In that moment, he stopped trying to deny it, giving himself totally over to the blond's control. He tried to speak, to offer encouragement, but no words came out, only a string of incoherent groans, punctuated by the Admiral's given name.

The utterly carnal way Blaise moaned his name made Peter vow never to let him go back to calling him "Admiral." He wanted to hear Blaise whisper it, groan it, scream it as he exploded in a nova of ecstasy. Sliding both hands under Blaise's ass, he pulled his lover closer with every snap of his hips, trying to fuse their very atoms together.

The need to come was building like a chain reaction, but this time he was going to take Blaise with him. He worked a hand between their bodies to grasp Blaise's cock, fisting it as he bit at the straining tendons of the pirate's neck. "Now," he gasped brokenly. "Ah, fuck, Blaise, come now...."

Helpless to refuse or deny his lover anything, Blaise climaxed, a second smaller load shooting from his aching cock to coat the Admiral's hand, his passage clenching tightly around the thick organ filling it, hoping to drive Peter to the same mind-blowing release. "Peter!"

That cry was Peter's undoing. A cluster of stars exploded behind his closed eyes as he clutched Blaise to him, rocking in short hard thrusts as his seed poured out of him, filling the pulsing channel and spilling out to streak Blaise's ass as they shuddered with aftershocks.

Shivering with the afterglow of his orgasm but more than a little unnerved by the rest of what he was feeling, Blaise rolled from beneath the Admiral almost immediately, reaching for his shipsuit so he could return to the safety of his quarters and reflect on what he had admitted and almost admitted to his lover. And to himself.

Peter wasn't ready to slide out of Blaise's body when the younger man moved away, wasn't ready to go back to an empty bed and an empty heart. Holding the other man's arm, he kept him from rising, his lids dropping to shield the expression in his eyes. "Stay," he said quietly.

Blaise's head turned in surprise, the word far too gentle for the Admiral's usual orders. He studied the familiar face, hoping to see something there to give him a clue, but Keller's gaze was hooded, his thoughts shuttered. He had occasionally refused an order, just to provoke the older man, but he found he did not want to refuse this... request, almost the first he had heard from the blond's lips.

Nodding slowly, completely unsure in this suddenly new starscape they had entered, he lay back down next to his lover, not curling against Peter as he wanted to do, unsure if he would be welcome, but not with any resistance either. He would take his cue from the Admiral. As he lay there, he finally allowed himself to hope that perhaps, just perhaps, Peter was coming to care for him a little, in his own way. Closing his eyes, he told himself not to get his hopes up, but he could not douse the flame that burned in his heart any more than he could quench the fires of the Horsehead Nebula.

Passing his hand over the sensor beside the bed, Peter dimmed the cabin light, finding it easier to draw Blaise to him in the darkness. Threading their legs together, he shifted until Blaise's head rested against his shoulder. He slipped a hand behind his head and let the other coast over damp skin until it rested on Blaise's hip, rising and falling with the younger man's soft breaths. There were no star charts to guide him in the place they were now, but at least for tonight, Peter was content to drift peacefully. They were explorers. They'd find their way.

CHAPTER 9
AND SO IT BEGINS

BLAISE paused in repairing a broken air duct when he heard footsteps coming down the corridor. He told himself to stop being ridiculous, but he swore he recognized the Admiral's footsteps. In the past week, he had learned more about the blond commander than he had in the ten months since he'd arrived on the *North Star*. That's what happened, he supposed, when you lived with someone. He still wasn't quite sure how it had happened, but Keller had asked him to stay a week ago, and he had. The next night, he fully expected to be sent away, but so far, the Admiral hadn't shown any signs of wanting to be rid of his new bunkmate. Blaise certainly wasn't about to complain.

He hid a smile and made a point of working diligently when the Admiral came into view with a group of officers Blaise didn't know. He kept his gaze fixed firmly on his task, not wanting to compromise the commander's authority in any way. As they walked by, he heard Keller murmur, "Good work. Carry on."

The smile that elicited couldn't be hidden and didn't fade until several minutes after the group passed out of his sight. Then a frown marred his features as something tugged at his senses, filling him with the same nameless dread that had awakened him from a nightmare three weeks ago.

Chancing upon Blaise working in a corridor as he escorted the crew of the Confederation scoutship to his officers' briefing was the only part of the morning that Peter wouldn't cheerfully have blown out the airlock without a spacesuit. Suspicions of an unknown alien presence infringing on Confederation space had been growing with each escalating attack— on the science station, various small ships, and the mining colony near Orion—but top brass consistently dismissed the speculations as baseless rumors, insisting the attacks were the work of pirates. The "rumors" had been proven suddenly and gruesomely true with the destruction of a small agricultural colony on Merope Gamma. Unlike previous attacks, where the outposts had simply been blasted from space, this time the invaders, an alien race of unknown origin, actually landed on the planet before wreaking their destruction. The scout had just returned from the ruins of the devastated colony, and as the closest ship of any size in the quadrant, the *North Star* had been ordered to rendezvous and evaluate any information from the scout ship's crew that might provide a clue about the attackers.

What little the crew had been able to tell them set Peter's blood boiling. The colonists had been wiped out to the last man, woman, and child. It didn't appear they'd had any chance to defend themselves, the attackers leaving the bodies lying where they fell in their houses and fields—except for the few corpses they'd found in one of the barns, which appeared to have been tortured. Other than a tantalizingly short glimpse of the approaching ship from the planet's comm station video— a ship that bore more than a passing resemblance to the one captured by CX-2114's final transmission—the scout's crew hadn't found a thing that pointed to who the attackers were, where they'd come from, or what they wanted. They'd buried the colonists' bodies on the planet, except for two they'd placed in stasis to bring back to the nearest starbase, in hopes the research facilities there could discover something from examining them.

The *North Star*'s officers were ready to head off in search of the attackers then and there, especially second engineering officer Lieutenant Royce, who'd grown up on a similar small farming colony and had taken the massacre hard. Keller might have agreed with them, if he'd had the first idea where to look.

He hadn't allowed himself more than a nod and a murmured word of acknowledgment to Risner, though just the sight of him had helped ease some of the impotent rage simmering in Peter's veins. He'd slept better in the past week since inviting Blaise to share his bed every night than he had in longer than he could remember. Their coupling had lost none of its power or urgency, though since the night of Blaise's birthday celebration Peter had returned to making full use of his collection of sexual enhancers. But afterward, Blaise stayed beside him until the slow cadence of his breathing evened out to sleep, the warmth of his presence bringing Peter his own measure of peacefulness. He suspected he would particularly need the combination of adrenaline and release to find any sleep tonight.

Finished with his duties, Blaise headed back to his quarters to use the 'fresher and change into a clean shipsuit. He had no doubt where he would be spending the night, but at least so far, the Admiral had not suggested sharing any more of his personal quarters than his bed. Blaise didn't mind. It gave him a place to retreat when he needed a few minutes to himself. He took a quick spin in the shower, getting off the worst of the sweat and grime from the day's work before pulling on tomorrow's uniform and heading back toward Keller's rooms, whistling to himself as he walked, anticipation humming in his veins as he wondered what delights his lover had in store for them tonight.

Much to his surprise, the quarters were empty when he arrived. He let himself in, not entirely sure he had the right to be there without Peter. The Admiral never locked his quarters—who would dare disturb them on his own ship?—but even having been told he could come as he pleased, he felt like he was intruding without Keller there to welcome him. Glancing back at the door, he stepped past the screen to the sleeping area, approaching the cabinet where the commander kept all the devices he used on Blaise to such devastating effect. It was locked, but the frosted glass door allowed Blaise to glimpse inside. He examined the various implements, cock starting to swell as he remembered how good most of them could make him feel when employed by his lover's talented hands.

Unconsciously rubbing at the tension in the back of his neck, Peter allowed himself a moment of anticipation as he neared his cabin. He'd lost track of time, going over the scout crew's reports and the vidclip of the unknown ship with his own staff, yet he'd seldom spent such a frustrating afternoon. They hadn't been able to find anything that would help them identify the murderers who'd wiped out the colony. He'd have to be careful not to let his emotions carry over too forcefully into his interaction with Blaise. As much as they both enjoyed playing rough, he'd taken out his frustrations on Blaise after the last attack and regretted it afterward. He wasn't going to make the same mistake again.

Entering his cabin, the Admiral was pleasantly surprised to find Blaise already there, peering through the swirled glass at the contents of his toy cabinet. "See something you like?" he asked dryly, though he didn't think there was anything left he hadn't tried on his pirate at least once by now.

"All of it," Blaise replied huskily, turning to face the owner of the collection he'd just admired. "Or none of it. As much as I've learned to enjoy them all, I don't need any of them."

I think I will, tonight, Peter acknowledged to himself, though he wasn't ready to admit that out loud. The ugliness was still too raw to share, but he knew he had to work off some of the emotions still roiling inside. "Pick something," he ordered abruptly, the need to take charge of something he could control flaring at Blaise's words.

"The anal beads from Orion," Blaise requested immediately. They'd played with those before to devastating effect. The composite beads stayed cold even after they had been inserted for a time, adding an additional layer of stimulation to the way they stretched him open, the smallest bead pushed deep inside while the largest one stretched him wide for whatever else the Admiral had planned.

"Fuck, I need a shower," Peter muttered as he palmed open the cabinet to extract the strand of variegated beads. "Strip, and have them inside you by the time I get back," he instructed, knowing he'd spend the whole of his time in the 'fresher imagining Blaise working the beads into himself.

Blaise frowned at Keller's retreating back, but he wasn't confident enough yet to disobey a direct order. Stripping out of his shipsuit, he picked up the beads and went in search of the tube of gel to ease their entrance. The first one was so small he barely felt it going in except for the shock of its iciness. He shivered as he pushed the next two inside easily, feeling the first one nudge against his prostate as he did. The fourth one was a bit of a stretch and he lifted his leg onto the edge of the bed to help alleviate the burn. Without the fire of Peter's touch, the next one hurt. Blaise forced it past his guardian muscle, panting through the pain as he contemplated the three remaining beads. He knew he could take them—he'd had the entire string inside him before—but when the Admiral had first used them on him, he'd teased Blaise with them until he would have borne any amount of pain just to be filled completely. Putting them in himself didn't have anywhere near the same effect.

Having tantalized himself with the anticipation of stirring the beads in Blaise's slick channel, Peter was surprised to find the smuggler standing with one foot on his bunk, the three largest beads still dangling outside his body. His temper snapped at being balked in even so simple a command as this. "I thought we'd gotten past your flouting me just for the pleasure of the fight," he growled dangerously.

Blaise turned sharply to face the Admiral, his body contorting with the mixture of pleasure and pain. "I wasn't...," he gasped as he reacted to the movement of the beads. "Just give me another minute or two and I'll get them in. The big ones hurt if I force them in too quickly."

"Can't handle it on your own?" Peter smirked, stepping forward to grab Blaise by the shoulder. "I'd have thought you'd have plenty of experience getting yourself off, all alone on that ship of yours." Squeezing a healthy portion of lube onto his fingers, he let his other hand slide down Blaise's back and pushed him off balance, forcing the pirate's arms to snap forward to keep from landing face-first on the bed. As soon as his ass was pointing upward, Peter held his shoulders down and shoved the next largest bead into Blaise's passage with slick fingers.

"Shit! Fuck! That stings," Blaise shouted as the next bead stretched him wide. This time, though, it was Peter's hands touching him, Peter's hands pressing the bead inside him, and that made all the difference. He could feel his body relaxing into the pressure in a way it hadn't when he was doing it. He took a deep breath, exhaled slowly, and consciously relaxed his ass, waiting for the penultimate bead. A part of him insisted he shouldn't settle so readily into this submissive headspace when the Admiral touched him, but he couldn't fight both himself and the commander, especially not when giving in netted him such mind-blowing pleasure.

Despite his cry of pain, Blaise didn't fight as Peter played his fingers around the distended opening, guilt at his unnecessary roughness driving him to ease the burn. Blaise wasn't the cause of his anger and didn't deserve to take its brunt; it was up to Peter to ensure he worked off the fierce need to do *something* in ways that proved gratifying to them both. Letting his free hand glide over the tensed muscle of Blaise's shoulder,

Peter ruffled the light mat of hair that covered his pecs until he found the small arc of his partner's nipple ring. Closing his blunt nails around the pierced skin, he tugged, winning a soft moan as at the same time he scissored two fingers at the entry to Blaise's body, stretching it to accept the next largest bead.

Given the way the evening had started, Blaise fully expected the Admiral to shove the rest of the beads inside him, regardless of the pain. The confrontational mood seemed to have disappeared suddenly, though, the lover taking the place of the master. Not that the touches were any less firm. Not that the demands placed on his body were any less taxing. But the feeling behind it changed, bringing a smile to Blaise's lips even as he moaned again at the insistent play of Keller's fingers around his hole. His breath still caught when the commander pressed the next bead inside him, but it didn't hurt like the previous few had. He dropped his head against his forearms and pushed back needily against the fingers that continued to stretch him for the last bead on the string. He could feel the others deep inside him, icy cold, a stark contrast to the heat radiating off him and his lover. "Go ahead," he murmured. "Give me the last one."

"Still think you give the orders," Peter rumbled, but even he could hear the harsh edge was gone from his voice. With a last twist of his fingers, he pulled his hand free of Blaise's seductive heat and brought it down in a sharp clap on the spacer's backside. The cheek flared pink and Blaise bucked and then froze—Peter could only imagine the blow had stirred the beads that already filled his passage. Wincing in sympathy at the same time his cock jerked fiercely in anticipation, the Admiral slammed the last bead home.

The slap on his ass wasn't hard enough to hurt, just to make his skin tingle seductively, but the rebound caused the beads to press hard against his prostate, wringing a deep groan from his throat. Before he could recover from that, Keller worked the biggest bead inside, stretching him just beyond the point of comfort. He knew, given time, he'd grow used to it, but it would take a few minutes, time the commander hadn't given him last time they'd played with this particular toy. He sucked in a deep breath and prepared to endure until his hole grew accustomed to the burn.

Blaise's lusty groan tempted Peter to give him a matching slap on the other cheek, but the image his pirate presented, his ass sticking up at just the right height on his bed, was more provocation than Peter wanted to resist. Stepping forward and kicking aside Blaise's discarded worksuit, he grabbed Blaise's hips, then slid his hands down over the bronzed globes of his firm cheeks. His cock slid into the crease between, the tip nudging the dilated opening, the contrast of the beads' iciness and Blaise's natural heat rocketing his arousal to the stratosphere.

"Oh, fuck!" Blaise groaned again when he felt the Admiral's cock sliding between his cheeks. There was no way he could accommodate his lover's girth and the beads, but he wanted to. Oh, how he wanted to! Sometime in the past few months, he'd become a total slut for Keller's attention, but he couldn't bring himself to regret it. He squirmed beneath the lash of sensation, senses spinning out of control like a runaway shuttle on a collision course with his climax. "Close," he managed to gasp so that Keller could stop him from coming if he wanted.

"Not yet," Keller ordered, wishing he'd thought to put a cock ring on Blaise—fuck, and one on himself!—before they'd started. This was going to be over all too soon, but he wrapped a tight hand around the base of Blaise's shaft, squeezing it and as much of his heavy sac as he could capture in his fist. The tip of his cock burned with cold fire, but he bit his lip and worked it inside until just the head breached the tight ring of muscle, touching the largest bead. The icy tingle spread up his shaft, freezing his balls until they tightened, the pleasure-pain so fierce it made his knees buckle. He could only imagine what it was doing to Blaise. He rocked his hips, more a shudder than any controlled movement, shifting the beads in their sheath. "Ahhh, fuck," Peter gasped, his grip tightening involuntarily as he fought his own urgent need to come.

"Please, Peter!" Blaise pleaded, the thought that the Admiral was fucking him with the beads enough to shatter what little control he had left. His hips bucked wildly, fighting to get more sensation as the heat of Keller's cock burned his entrance after the frozen beads. "Need... to come."

If his own need wasn't so desperate, Peter would have taken his time, sliding each bead out with excruciating slowness, each rub over Blaise's prostate driving him higher and higher, until his pirate was too delirious with lust to speak. This wasn't that day, though. Peter needed to come just as badly as Blaise did, maybe even more. Promising himself that pleasure on another occasion, Peter pulled back until the head of his cock slipped free. Grabbing the largest bead with fingers that immediately went numb, he yanked the entire string out in one sharp motion. Blaise howled, but before he could do more than flinch, Peter thrust inside, burying his cock in the hot/cold channel. His hands slid up Blaise's sides to encircle his chest, pulling him up to his knees, locking them together back-to-chest.

The sudden contrast of the heat of Peter's cock with the lingering chill from the beads dragged a hoarse, wordless scream from Blaise's chest. He struggled against the arms holding him, trying to get Keller to move, to fuck him with the urgency that invested both their bodies. The Admiral released his hold on Blaise's cock to steady his hips, and without the restraining constriction Blaise could no longer hold back his release. His climax tore from him, spattering the duvet on the commander's bunk with his spunk.

The sudden clench of Blaise's sphincter around his shaft as the pirate shook through his orgasm was the spark that triggered Peter's own conflagration. He thrust fiercely through the insistent contractions, heat and cold and pressure combining to set him off with the raw burn of rocket fuel. His balls pumped until he felt drained dry, his frustration jetting out of him along with his seed. With a final muscular shudder, he unlocked his knees and sagged toward the bed, carrying Blaise's limp body with him.

The familiar weight of Keller's body provided the last bit of relaxation Blaise needed to drift off to sleep, not even bothering to move under the covers. His Admiral had worn him out in the best possible way.

Glad someone could sleep, Peter slid to his back and tucked a hand beneath his head, staring blindly at the ceiling. Blaise's warmth anchored his body, but his mind continued to examine and reexamine the little bit of knowledge the scout ship had brought them, looking for anything they'd missed that could identify the attackers.

The dream started benignly enough: the sensation of warmth surrounding him, even cradling him. Blaise had grown used to that feeling in the week since he'd started sharing the Admiral's bed for sleeping as well as for recreation. The first flash of fear caught him off guard, making him twist restlessly in his sleep. He couldn't see the source of his anxiety, but he knew he had to run, as far and as fast as he could. He thrashed on the bed, trying to break free of the restraints that held him as nightmarish images assaulted his senses: screams and the smell of blood and fear and death.

Blaise's first uneasy stirring surprised Peter. The smuggler had been a sound and quiet sleeper, in the Admiral's limited experience, but he hitched himself closer, restoring the warm contact of Blaise's back to his side almost without thinking. When Blaise started to move more roughly, Peter sat up, waving on the dim bedside light. In the shadows, his pirate's face was contorted in pain or… fear? It was an expression Peter had never seen on Blaise's waking face, and it disturbed him to see it now. He reached out a hand, hesitated a moment before touching, then grasped Blaise's shoulder firmly, holding him still. "Blaise?" he asked, his voice low with concern.

The familiar voice startled Blaise awake. His eyes opened to meet the safe, reassuring gaze of the Admiral. He lifted a shaking hand to his forehead, wiping away the cold sweat as he forced down the bile rising in his throat. "Peter?" he croaked, hating the way his voice trembled.

"I'm here," Peter answered, wondering what could have possibly shaken Blaise so badly. He worked his free arm under the smuggler's shoulder, helping him sit up, then left it there, loosely draped, when he felt the trembling. "You're cold?"

"Nightmare," Blaise gasped, pulling his knees up and putting his head down between them as the nausea worsened.

Peter stared, unsure what to do. He shook his head and rose, padding first to pull a robe from his closet to drape over Blaise's shivering shoulders, then into the head, bringing back a glass of cool water. "Try drinking this," he suggested, standing at the side of the bed, feeling helpless for the second time that day. It was a feeling he'd left behind when he left Earth, and he hated it.

Blaise tried to take the glass, but the water sloshed over the edge, splashing both of them. "Damn it," the privateer cursed, trying to get the weakness under control. He hadn't dreamed like this since a few months after he'd escaped from the Gavenelians.

Sitting on the edge of the bed, Peter wrapped an arm around Blaise's shoulders again, the other closing over Blaise's hand to guide the water to his lips. After a few sips, Blaise nodded and Peter placed the glass on the bedside cabinet. Feeling the shivering lessen, Peter looked at Blaise's ashen face and took a deep breath, wondering again what had the power to affect his cocksure lover so viscerally. "Want to talk about it?"

"Not really," Blaise replied honestly. There wasn't really anything to talk about, just a series of flashes, feelings almost, and that sick-to-his-stomach dread that only the sadistic aliens could inspire. He certainly didn't want to tell the Admiral about them!

"Let me rephrase that," Peter said dryly. There was no way he was letting Blaise off without an explanation for such aberrant behavior. "Something obviously affected you very strongly. I want to know what it is."

Blaise grimaced, but accepted the decree. He didn't really have much other choice. "It's a recurring nightmare," he began slowly, trying to put into words the amorphous terror that struck him. "I hear screaming—my first mate, Garrett, who was killed in an attack on my ship a few years ago. I didn't see him killed. I just heard these hideous screams." Blaise never did see Garrett's body, but he could guess what had been done to him. The Gavenelians were experts at inflicting pain on their victims. "In the dream, I'm trying to get to him, to save him, but I can't see anything. There's just the sickening smell of death and his never-ending screams."

Peter's lips tightened at Blaise's description. The death of a shipmate, especially a violent death, was never easy to take, but the intensity of Blaise's reaction suggested this Garrett might have been more than just a member of his crew. Peter's own reaction to that thought was one he didn't particularly care to explore. "Is that why you were working alone?" he asked, his voice sounding neutral—he hoped.

Blaise shrugged. "I didn't ever find anyone else to replace him," he explained. "On a small ship, on long runs, you've got to get along with your crew or you'll end up killing each other. I guess I'm particular." The fact that he was never completely convinced the Gavenelians had stopped searching for their favorite toy was additional incentive to work alone. He wouldn't put anyone else through what he'd suffered if he could help it.

Something in the tone of Blaise's response grated on Peter's already ragged nerves. "Sorry you don't have that luxury on this ship," he snapped, wondering if the remark was Blaise's way of letting him know he didn't measure up to his former lover.

"What?" Blaise asked, confused, his mind so lost in memories and nightmares that he couldn't even connect the Admiral's comment to anything relevant.

"Being particular," Peter muttered. Waving off the light, he settled on his back again, speaking into the darkness. "I'm… sorry you lost your lover."

"My…. Oh, you mean Garrett?" Blaise asked, even more confused now than before. He sat up and turned the light back on. "He was my first mate and my friend, but he wasn't my lover," he insisted. "Not that it made losing him any easier."

"I expect not," Peter answered, not sure if he believed Blaise's denial but deciding not to press the point. Lover or not, the man had clearly meant a lot to Blaise, to judge by the violence of his reaction to the memory of his death. The Admiral wondered if something had happened during the day to trigger the nightmare. Maybe one of the scout ship crew resembled Blaise's first mate? A sudden yawn escaped him, and he realized he was too tired to worry about it. Besides, he had more important things to think about, like the attack on Merope. Dimming the light again, he settled back on the bed. "Think you can sleep now?"

"I don't know," Blaise replied honestly, curling back into his place at Peter's side. "I used to get these a lot more often, and they'd leave me wrung out for the rest of the night, sometimes for days. I haven't had one in a while, though." He didn't mention the nightmare a couple of weeks ago; he didn't want Peter pressing for more details. "And I'm not alone this time, so maybe that'll help. If I keep you awake, just tell me to go back to my quarters. I don't want to be a nuisance."

"You won't keep me awake." Other things might do that, but Peter was shocked at how much the thought of spending the night without Blaise's warmth at his side bothered him. He extended an arm to rest lightly on the smuggler's shoulder. "Get some sleep."

CHAPTER 10
nIGHTMARE

ADMIRAL KELLER'S frown deepened as he wandered through the remains of what looked to have been a prosperous, if small, marketplace before the attack. While a few buildings were still little more than rubble, recovery crews were beginning to cart away the wreckage and salvage anything that could be reclaimed. A number of merchants had already reopened for business, displaying their wares under colorful tents or even the open sky.

The attack had come without warning. Zaniah was a small planet in a sparsely populated sector, its inhabitants making their living from farming, some mining, and trading with the other equally isolated colonies in its quiet backwater arm of the galaxy. They had no defense against the ships that had swept into their skies without warning, blasting energy weapons at every sign of habitation, then disappearing as quickly as they'd appeared. It bore the same signs as the attack a month earlier on the Merope outpost, though Peter couldn't see anything to tie the two together. Of course, he couldn't see any reason behind any of the attacks.

As one of the largest ships in the sector, the *North Star* had been ordered to pick up a cargo of supplies and relief workers and render all aid it could offer to Zaniah's survivors, the first the attackers had left at any of their targets. These were a resilient people, Peter noted as he passed a stall selling clothing, the proprietor sewing as he exchanged news with the vendor beside him, who was testing what looked to be comp-mech components. At the far end of the marketplace, relief workers had set up a registry to record survivors and distribute food and supplies to those who needed it. As Peter watched, a father learned that his son had survived the destruction of the village school; a much more pleasant sight than the one Peter had left at the opposite side of the ruined settlement: the hospital and morgue.

The familiar frustration at not being able to do more to help settled in Peter's chest. The Confederation provided all the aid it could, but until they knew who was behind the random attacks, there was no way to predict where the aggressors would strike next. Frowning, Peter paused in front of a table of skillfully crafted jewelry and decorative baubles. Surely the proprietor would find small demand for such fripperies when most of the townsfolk had little if anything left. Still, he supposed the man had no choice but to resume his livelihood as best he could.

"Look at this," the man muttered under his breath as he sorted his wares. "It'll be months before I have anything to sell again. Pieces damaged, pieces missing." Looking up to see the Confederation officer watching him, he added, "Most of these earrings only have one of the set now. How am I supposed to make a living with those?"

Drawn to the jumbled tray of wares, Peter's eyes were caught by a cleverly twisted ring of fine metallic wire. A stone was threaded on it, the variegated hues reminding him of the changing colors of Blaise's eyes. "I'll take this one from you," he said, already imagining it glinting in the dark hair of his pirate's chest.

"I haven't found its mate yet," the jeweler stuttered, surprised. "I was just blowing off steam. You don't have to buy something just to make me feel better."

"I don't need its mate," Peter chuckled at the vendor's bewildered expression. "Offer them as they are," he suggested, handing over a credit voucher and waving away the shopkeeper's offer of change. "You might find there's more of a market for them than you think."

"If you say so, sir," the man replied skeptically as he pocketed the voucher and returned to his sorting.

The first smile since he set down on the devastated planet crossed Peter's face. His frustration became a little easier to bear when he thought of what he had to look forward to that night.

THE peculiar scent of fear and death penetrated the fog of sleep surrounding Blaise as he tossed restlessly on Peter's bunk, catapulting him back into the nightmares that had flitted around the edge of his sleep for the past several months. He fought the bonds that held him against the wall, refusing to give in to the pain he knew would follow. His back arched as the energy whip cracked over already flayed skin, tearing a scream from his throat. His mind recoiled from the pain, seeking refuge in the depths of unconsciousness. His torturers weren't masters for nothing, though, pulling him back from the darkness before resuming their work. He had escaped this, he tried to tell himself. This was just a dream, but the smell would not leave him alone.

Blaise's restlessness gradually woke Peter from a sound sleep. He'd returned to the *North Star* far later than he'd planned, after the rescue teams' registration process determined that a number of the planet's residents were still missing. It was possible some bodies were still trapped under rubble or had fled in terror, but the discovery of a large patch of scorched earth in the fields some distance from town had made Peter suspect a ship may have landed there. They'd searched and scanned the area for any clues, until darkness and exhaustion had led him to call a halt for the night.

He'd been too tired to do more than throw his uniform in a corner and fall into bed, working off his remaining energy in a quick, heated fuck with Blaise before dropping unconscious. His partner's growing grunts and moans finally penetrating, Peter pushed up to one elbow, trying to make out Risner's form in the darkness. "Blaise? What's wrong?"

"No! Don't!" Blaise had learned that pleading with the sadistic aliens did no good; but, his defenses down in sleep, he couldn't stop the words from escaping as he thrashed on the bed. "Why are you doing this?"

"Blaise!" Peter snapped, seizing the flailing smuggler by the shoulders and holding him still. "Blaise, it's all right. I'm here. No one's hurting you." He tightened his grip as Blaise continued to struggle against him, lowering his voice and running a hand through the dark hair. "Blaise, you're safe. Come back now."

Blaise's eyes flew open, wild with fear and remembered pain as he met the green gaze of his Admiral. Bile rose in his throat as the scent of the Gavenelians followed him out of his nightmares. He pushed away, stumbling into the head where he retched violently, emptying the contents of his stomach. Leaning his head against the cool wall, he realized he was going to have to tell his lover everything he knew, and that meant revealing the most closely guarded secret from his past. The thought was nearly enough to make him sick again. Delaying the inevitable, he pushed to his feet and rinsed his mouth out before stepping into the 'fresher, letting the hot water beat away the smell of his own sweat and fear.

Still shaking off his own grogginess, Peter was unprepared for the pang he felt when Blaise shoved him away and stumbled to the bathroom. He waited impatiently, offering some privacy while he heard Blaise retching, but when the sound of the 'fresher reached him he rose and entered the head, watching Blaise's body for a moment through the frosted plasglas before sliding open the 'fresher door and joining him in the narrow cubicle.

Blaise froze when the door opened and Peter stepped inside, the sickening smell hitting him again, but at least this way, the Admiral would be clean and the odor gone. He leaned his head against the cool wall, waiting for the interrogation to begin.

The tense set of Blaise's shoulders practically broadcast his distress, and rather than questioning him immediately as his impulse demanded, Peter dispensed a palmful of cleanser and began to lather Blaise's back. He worked his thumbs into the tight muscles, following the corded tendons across Blaise's shoulders and back before starting down his spine. Resisting the urge to either swat or caress the globes of his ass, he gave them a cursory cleaning and then leaned forward to murmur in Blaise's ear. "Turn around, so I can do your front."

Not sure where this side of Keller had come from, Blaise turned around as directed, eyes still closed against the memories assailing him. He knew he needed to tell Peter what he knew, but he didn't want to relive those months even in words and so he let the moment stretch out between them as the commander cleaned him carefully. He suspected the lover would disappear as soon as he revealed his past. He only hoped he wouldn't lose the other man completely.

His hands skating over Blaise's honey-toned torso, Peter tried to catch the younger man's eyes, but the smuggler kept them closed, even when Peter slid lower, moving carefully to his knees to wash down the strong thighs and calves. Leaning back to let the 'fresher rinse the soap away, he was surprised to find Blaise still soft. He'd never touched Blaise without the pirate reacting immediately. Pride stung as much as he was worried about Blaise, he moved back, lifting the quiescent cock to rinse beneath it and then taking the lightly furred balls in his mouth. Blaise jumped and began to stiffen in his hand. Smiling around the load in his mouth, Peter swirled his tongue over the sensitive contents and then let them slip free, only to take in the hardening cock in their place.

"Peter," Blaise gasped, his body's reaction to his lover's touch pulling him out of his nightmares and back to the present. His eyes flew open, meeting the glittering green gaze, lust beginning to soften the lines of tension around his mouth and eyes. His knees trembling, he braced himself on the Admiral's strong shoulders and wondered if they were broad enough to help him bear the burden of his past. Maybe... maybe it was time to trust again. Then Peter's tongue prodded at the slit and all coherent thought flew out of his mind. "Please...."

Sucking harder at the hot shaft filling his mouth, Peter returned one hand to surround the heavy sac, rolling the testes in his hand. He had all kinds of questions for Blaise, but he'd learned enough to know that if he pressed, the smuggler would only turn stubborn. Maybe softening him up first would prove more effective. Then Blaise groaned, "Please..." and Peter lost any thought but wringing that sound from him again. His free hand drove into the spacer's crease, following the streaming water until he brushed the puckered hole.

The combined touch of the Admiral's mouth and hands stole what little sanity Blaise had left. His head fell back against the wall of the 'fresher as he came hard down Peter's throat, a long, low moan tearing from his chest as he climaxed. His knees gave out then, and he slid bonelessly toward the floor next to his lover. Turning his head blindly, he sought the lips that had brought him such pleasure.

The shock of Blaise's lips against his startled Peter so much that his mouth opened reflexively, granting access inside. He didn't think Blaise had ever initiated a kiss before, and as the smuggler's tongue twined around Peter's, a flare of arousal flashed through his veins. For a minute more he let Blaise control the kiss, then he slowly reclaimed the mastery, following Blaise's tongue back into his lover's mouth, plundering the wet cavern and wrapping an arm behind Blaise's head to pull him closer.

The kiss was so antithetical to Blaise's nightmares that he felt the last of them slip away as Peter ravished his mouth. Reaching for his lover, he stroked the hard cock. "Why don't we go back to bed and see if I can take care of this for you?" he suggested.

The Admiral had every intention of finding his release buried deep in Blaise's body, but he was going to get some answers first. Since collapsed in the bottom of the 'fresher wasn't the most conducive spot for his interrogation, he let Blaise help him up and flashed them both dry before heading back to their bed. As soon as Blaise slid under the sheets beside him, he flipped them both, pinning the dark-haired spacer beneath him. "Now," he purred, grinding his arousal into Blaise's groin, "suppose you tell me what that was all about?"

Feeling the nausea roiling in his stomach again, Blaise turned his head as he gulped in air, fighting the renewed urge to retch. "I will," he gasped, "but something in here still smells of them, and it's making me sick again."

"Them?" Peter repeated, not understanding what Blaise meant, though it was obvious the other man was truly ill.

"I'll tell you everything I know," Blaise promised, struggling to sit up. "Just help me figure out what stinks or I'm going to make a mess of the bed." His eyes searched the room for the source of the foul odor. "Your uniform! You wore it planetside today. That's what I smell."

"Something on the planet is making you sick?" Peter asked, rising to toss the offending garment into the recycler. He hadn't noticed an unpleasant odor himself, though there was a hint of acrid scent from the scorched ground of the landing site. "Some kind of allergic reaction?"

With the uniform gone, the odor began to clear. Blaise took a couple of deep breaths to settle his stomach. "Nothing that pleasant, unfortunately," he said slowly. "I didn't realize it until tonight, but the Gavenelians must be behind the attacks, at least the one today and the one on Merope. I've had... dealings with them in the past. They're a nasty bit of work." Just saying it was enough to bring the woozy feeling back, but he fought it down. Peter needed what little knowledge he had, and that meant keeping his fears under control.

"Gavenelians?" Peter shook his head, frowning. "Never heard of them...," he trailed off as the implications of what Blaise was saying hit him. "You had knowledge of these attacks that you didn't tell me about?" His voice sharpened in anger. If Blaise thought sharing his bed would give him protected status if he'd been concealing information.... Peter's teeth clenched as he fought to control his anger. The games they'd played would be nothing to the real hurt he'd lay on Blaise if he found the younger man had been deceiving him. Using him.

Blaise's eyes flashed. "You always think the worst of me!" He rose from the bed to pace restlessly, the hurt of Peter's accusations cutting far deeper than any torture the Gavenelians had inflicted on him. "They kept me locked in a cell no bigger than an arm-length wide and tortured me for six months! They're sadistic, vicious creatures who take great pleasure in torturing prisoners for no reason other than to hear them scream, and I didn't realize it was them until I smelled them on you tonight. I don't know what else I can tell you, but I can't talk about it now. I'll come to the briefing room tomorrow." Head down, he started toward the door, unable to contemplate spending the night in Peter's arms now.

Peter's hand snapped out to stop Blaise's progress, his other running through his short hair, trying to hold back the incipient headache he could feel building behind his eyes. "You didn't see it down there," he grated, shaking his head. "The senseless destruction, the bodies... they were peaceful farmers and miners, all but defenseless. I felt so fucking useless, bringing them food when the monsters that did this had vanished without a trace." He took a step closer, wrapping his arms around Blaise from behind, drinking in his warmth. "The thought that you might have known something that could have stopped them before this happened...."

Sighing heavily, he rested his head beside Blaise's. "I should have realized from how violently you reacted that it wasn't a conscious response. Come back to bed, and tell me whatever you can remember."

Letting himself be soothed, Blaise rejoined Peter on the bed, his mind casting back, trying to separate the bone-deep fear he still felt from the facts he had gleaned during his captivity. "We were deep in the Beta quadrant when they attacked," he began dully, the memories assailing him. "The ships came seemingly out of nowhere, two of them, heavily armed and with shields our weapons couldn't penetrate. The *Golden Stallion* isn't a war ship, but it was armed to fend off anyone who might think a privateer was fair game. And their weapons tore through our shields like they weren't even there. We fought, but it was obvious we weren't going to win that fight. They killed Garrett soon after boarding; I could hear his screams, but I never saw his body so I don't know what they did to him. Whatever it was, they learned from it because they tortured me for six months after they took me prisoner. All I saw once they got me on their ship was the inside of my cell and the torture chamber. When I escaped, we were at the edges of the Delta quadrant. I swore I'd kill myself before I'd let them get their hands on me again."

"How did you escape?" Peter asked, sensing more from Blaise's tone of voice than from his words not to probe too deeply about the specifics of his captivity. A part of him marveled that Blaise would endure—and even seem to enjoy—his discipline games after surviving real torture, but he pushed that aside for another time. Right now his focus was on finding something, anything he could use to find these Gavenelians.

"They attacked another ship, one that actually fought back," Blaise replied. "In the confusion—I don't think they're used to targets fighting back successfully—they didn't lock the door to my cell. Their ship was big enough they'd kept my ship in their hold. When they brought the new ship in, I flew out. If I'd had the good sense to run when they first attacked, they wouldn't have caught me. They couldn't catch me then, even with the *Golden Stallion* at less than her best."

"Sloppy," Peter mused. "That could be a weakness we can exploit, but we have to find them first. Did you see anything that might give you a clue where their home base was?"

"No," Blaise answered honestly, "but...." He hesitated for a moment as he considered what he was about to do. "I know somebody who might have more information. I don't know whether he'll tell me—he sure as hell won't tell the Admiralty—but I have no way of contacting him from here."

Somebody as in a former smuggling contact, Peter was sure. A nagging voice asked whether it was also a former lover, but he dismissed the thought as unimportant compared with a chance to find the murderous aliens. "One of the perks of being an Admiral is having fairly wide discretionary latitude," he murmured. "I think I can come up with a way to approach your contact without scaring him away." A yawn escaped along with the last word, some of his tension easing as it seemed they finally had at least a chance of finding the attackers.

"Perks," Blaise snorted, trying unsuccessfully to control the instinctive shudder that went through him at the thought of coming into contact with the Gavenelians again. "Do you really understand what we're going up against?" he asked painfully. "Do you have any idea what they would do to us, to any of us, if they get their hands on us? I won't survive a second time."

"I have a fair idea," Peter countered, picturing again the devastation the aliens had left in their wake. "But this time you won't be facing them alone. We'll have the power of a Confederation flagship backing us up, and once we find those bastards, they won't be able to hide from the might of the entire Galactic Confederation of Planets."

Blaise hoped to all the powers in the pantheon that Peter was right because he wouldn't be around to say "I told you so" if the Admiral was wrong. "Figure out a way for me to meet with Harry without involving the Confederation, and I'll see what he knows," he agreed. "But please, Peter, by all that's holy, don't underestimate them. You've seen what they can do. You've seen what they *choose* to do. I haven't asked about any of the specifications on your ship, and I'm not going to ask now, but unless you're using completely different shields and weapons than what's on a ship like mine—and I don't mean more powerful, I mean different—then all the Confederation will be able to do is delay their victory, not stop them. I don't want to imagine you in their hands."

Any more than Peter liked imagining what they'd done to Blaise, he realized. "I won't underestimate them," he pledged. Anyone who could inspire such alarm in his cocky, stubborn pirate was definitely a force to be reckoned with. Pulling his lover down beside him, he tucked an arm under his head and the other around Blaise's chest, deciding everything else could wait until tomorrow. "Sleep now," he said, his eyes drifting closed, his last coherent thought the realization that he hadn't given Blaise his ring.

It wasn't the promise Blaise wanted, but he didn't imagine it was realistic to ask an admiral to promise to avoid all danger in a situation of open war. He'd have to be satisfied with what he could get. He was almost asleep when he remembered his offer to take care of Peter, but his lover was clearly out for the night. He'd just have to wake the Admiral in the morning.

CHAPTER 11
SHOT THROUGH THE HEART

HIS internal clock waking him a few minutes before the Admiral's alarm, Blaise rolled over quietly, silencing the buzzer so it would not disturb them. Peter always set the clock for well in advance of the time he needed to rise, often using the time for a rough-and-tumble morning fuck before beginning his day. As much as Blaise enjoyed the games they played in the evenings, he cherished the mornings because it was just him and Peter without the elaborate devices the commander used at night to spice up their interactions.

Sliding down beneath the light duvet that covered them, Blaise found his way by feel alone to his lover's cock, half-hard against his thigh. Smiling in the darkness, he angled his head until he could suck the tip between his lips.

Peter gradually awoke to the rhythmic pull of hot, wet satin over his cock. Such erotic dreams were not infrequent since bringing Blaise on board, and now that the smuggler shared his bed for sleeping as well as fucking, it was much easier to make those morning fantasies reality. This felt too damn real for any wet dream, though, and Peter cracked open an eyelid and pulled back the bedding to the provocative sight of Blaise's dark head bobbing between his thighs. The spacer grinned around the hardening cock in his mouth and winked at Peter before turning all his attention to the matter at hand.

Peter's breath caught in his chest, as much from the realization that Blaise had initiated this without his having to order it as from the debauched slide of the smuggler's fingers over the skin behind his balls. "Fuck, yeah," Peter hissed, spreading his legs wider and threading a hand into the spiky hair. "Gods, what you can do with that mouth…."

Blaise just hummed in reply, knowing the vibrations would only add to the stimulation Peter was feeling. Feeling daring since the blond hadn't slapped him down for taking the lead, he slid one finger in his mouth next to his lover's cock, wetting it thoroughly before dipping it into the crease of Peter's ass and bumping questioningly against the ring of tight muscle. Peter had occasionally ordered Blaise to rim him, once even letting him tongue-fuck him, but the privateer hadn't dared take those liberties uninvited before today. Even now, he fully expected to be slapped down.

Rocking into the increasing suction, sparks flaring up and down his nerve endings, Peter let Blaise man the controls until tantalizing fingers started probing at his hole. That was a contact he wasn't ready for yet. He wasn't sure he'd ever be ready. Even now, memories of the abuse he'd suffered as a youth awakened at the touch. Denying their power to disturb him, he grasped the intruding hand, leaning forward until he could bring it to his mouth, sucking on the blunt digits until they were dripping with his saliva. Releasing Blaise's wrist, he fell back to the pillows. "Touch yourself," he rasped, fighting to hold on long enough for Blaise to prep himself. "Make yourself ready for me."

It was a far better reaction than Blaise had expected. Pulling up onto his knees, he kept up the pressure on Peter's cock as he reached awkwardly between his legs in search of his own hole, stretching it as best he could from that angle. Unless Peter took pity on him, it would be rough going when the Admiral first slid home, but Blaise knew from experience that it would be worth it.

The shift in angle took a bit of the pressure off the suction on Peter's cock, but that was more than made up for by the sight of Blaise's fingers sinking between his firm cheeks. Wondering why he hadn't thought to order Blaise to stretch himself more often, Peter enjoyed the show until the growing tightness in his groin started demanding relief. Stretching for the lube would take more energy than he had left, so he tugged at Blaise's hair until the younger man raised his head, a thin bead of saliva dripping back down his shaft.

"Come up here," Peter directed, guiding Blaise to straddle his widespread legs. He positioned the pirate until the head of his cock nudged eagerly at the wet hole. "Ride me," he insisted, letting Blaise take him in at his own pace until the darkly furred balls were flush against his pubic bone.

Slowly but deliberately, Blaise did as Peter directed, savoring each inch as it slid in and out of his barely stretched passage. It burned, in that delicious way nothing but Peter's cock ever did. Some of his lover's toys stretched him wider or penetrated deeper, but nothing filled him the way Peter did. Biting his lip to hold back a declaration that would surely be unwelcome, he increased the pace, taking advantage of the position to explore the Admiral's body in a way he wasn't usually allowed, his hands sliding over the strong, hard chest and tweaking the taut pink nipples against their palate of golden skin. In moments like this, he could almost believe they were lovers in truth.

Peter's hands rode up Blaise's hips, spreading over the bronzed skin to span his rib cage on each side until his thumbs brushed the dark peaks of his nipples. He flicked the small gold ring with his thumbnail, grinning in anticipation of piercing the other side of his lover's broad chest with the bauble he'd picked up on planet. Tugging the twin nubs, he rolled them between his fingers, his grip tightening as Blaise's undulations on his cock became more frantic. Peter canted his hips upward, driving deeper into the clinging channel, chasing the explosive release that remained just out of range.

Peter's fingers on his nipples and the change in angle were enough to send Blaise's senses spinning out of control. He gasped needily, bearing down hard on Peter's cock, trying to take his lover with him as ecstasy exploded over him.

The rippling waves of pressure as Blaise came around him were nearly enough to set Peter off, needing just one stimulus more to set the trigger. With a guttural curse, he dragged Blaise down to claim his mouth in a fierce kiss, his tongue plundering his partner's mouth, the change in angle letting him slide in just that millimeter more he needed to erupt. Ever-expanding waves of pleasure shook him, grinding against Blaise as if by joining them closer together he could envelop them both in the crackling nimbus of ecstasy.

Moaning into the kiss, Blaise collapsed on top of Peter, letting repletion fill him with contentment. It wouldn't last, he knew. The rest of the galaxy would intrude on their heated cocoon far too soon, but he clung to it for as long as he could.

Eventually, Blaise's weight and the need to breathe forced Peter to break the kiss. Rolling to one side, he worked a hand between their bodies, sliding through the slick fluid that coated their bellies to anoint Blaise's unadorned nipple. "I bought something while I was planetside," he rumbled, too indolent to move more than his fingers as he tweaked the dark bud.

Blaise chuckled. Even in the middle of a war zone, it seemed, the Admiral collected sex toys. "Am I going to like this something you bought?" he asked lazily. He was pretty sure he knew the answer to his own question. He'd liked just about everything in Peter's collection.

"You seemed to like the idea on your birthday," Peter answered, shifting just enough that he could lick the cooling come from Blaise's chest. He closed his teeth over the nubbin he planned to mark as his own, teasing it until it stood proudly erect. "A second ring, right here."

"Fuck," Blaise groaned, hardening again from the combination of Peter's lips on his nipple and the thought of getting a second piercing. "You bought a ring?"

"Mmmnnn," Peter hummed, letting the slick bud slide from his mouth. Rolling away reluctantly, he padded to the head for a steri-wipe, then detoured to the cabinet where he'd stored the merchant's package before stripping off his uniform the night before. Returning to the bed, he knelt beside Blaise's still recumbent form, his eyes raking appreciatively over the long, strong body. "Thought I'd support the local economy," he said, masking an unaccustomed feeling of awkwardness as he tossed the small box to the smuggler.

Blaise opened the box, curious to see what Peter's gift looked like. The ring was fashioned of thin, artfully twisted wire surrounding a small stone, perhaps a carnelian, an elegant contrast to the thin circle Blaise already wore. It was more decorative, but Blaise decided he liked it. A more decorative tribute to a much more welcome captivity. He'd pierced the first one when he escaped the Gavenelians, a first step to reclaiming his body as his own. "Nice," he said with a smile, handing it back to Peter.

"Still want it?" Peter asked casually, tossing it lightly in his palm.

"Yeah," Blaise replied huskily, leaning back against the bolster and offering his chest. He didn't need to look down to know his cock was fully hard and leaking again.

Peter swung one leg over Blaise's torso, straddling the younger man, his own cock filling at Blaise's obvious excitement. He swiped the steri-wipe over Blaise's chest, capturing the nipple between the folds of soft cloth and rubbing until it peaked again, standing free of the light mat of hair. Opening the ring's pointed catch, he cleaned it as well and then caught the very tip of the nub with his fingertips, pulling it taut. "Ready?" he asked, meeting Blaise's eyes, his own darkened with lust and possessiveness.

Blaise nodded, not sure he could put his feelings into words without giving away more than he wanted Peter to know. Then again, the fact that he was letting Peter mark him permanently, as opposed to the occasional bruises and welts left by the Admiral's collection of toys, probably gave the commander some idea of the depth of his emotions.

Moving quickly, Peter thrust the point of the ring through Blaise's skin in one sharp jab, sealing the clasp and wiping away the single drop of blood with the steri-wipe. *Mine*, his blood whispered in response, his lips closing over the site before his mouth could utter the word aloud.

Blaise hissed slightly as the sharp metal penetrated his skin, eyes closing against the expected bite of pain. For a time after his escape from the Gavenelians, he hadn't been able to feel anything but pain. He'd despaired of ever having a normal sex life again, until an old acquaintance had suggested the first piercing as a way of combining the two and introducing his body to softer sensations again. It had been the first step in a long recovery that had, in many ways, culminated in his experiences here aboard the *North Star* at Peter's hands. As the Admiral closed his lips over the new piercing, Blaise wondered what that presaged about his future. He certainly knew what he hoped it signified.

Peter knew the piercing had to be sensitive, but he couldn't stop playing with it, even when he leaned upward to claim Blaise's mouth again. His hands went to the twin rings, twisting them in counterpoint to his tongue fucking Blaise's mouth, his hips pulsing so that their cocks slid in the slickness that leaked from them both. A steady chant echoed in his head—*mine, mine, marked you now, never let you go*—that he refused to give voice, other than with the hunger of his kiss. That Blaise had agreed to the ring was enough. It had to be enough, since it was all he was going to get.

"Fuck," Blaise groaned again, breaking the kiss to catch his breath as his lover used the rings to drive him wild. "I need you. Please... fuck me."

Knowing Blaise was still stretched and full of his come, Peter didn't hesitate to agree. "Spread your legs," he groaned, moving between them and pulling Blaise's hips up as the spacer's legs wrapped around him, impaling Blaise in a single long thrust. His balls were already tightening, and he knew there was no way he was going to make this last. Reaching for Blaise's dripping cock, he fisted it roughly, the other hand returning to the ring like a magnet pointing to galactic center. "Now," he growled, hips shunting roughly as he fought for a last vestige of control. "Now, damn it! Come for me now!"

The rough fucking alone probably would have done it, but the low, deep growl and the sharp pull on his exquisitely sensitive new piercing guaranteed that Blaise had no problem following Peter's order, his release spurting out to cover his belly and chest, splashing even as far as his nipples, covering Peter's ring with the evidence of his desire. His shout of pleasure grew louder as the Admiral bent his head and licked away the sticky cream while shuddering inside him.

Collapsing in satiation on Blaise's chest, Peter let his eyes drift closed for a moment, lulled by the slowly steadying beat of Blaise's pulse. "I could sleep for another watch," he murmured, though even as he spoke, the memory of what he'd learned the night before nagged at him. "But we ought to make contact with your friend, the one who can tell us more about the Gavenelians." He forced himself to sit up, rubbing at his hair as he tried to reengage his higher brain functions.

Blaise shuddered, all the pleasure in the new ornament and the tender feelings its bestowing had evoked fading at the thought of what he'd offered to do and what that could well mean. "We can't contact him on a Confederation frequency, and we'll have to be in civvies and on a private ship. Harry's the suspicious type. He'll notice those kinds of details." He sighed. "This would be a snap if I still had access to my ship, but we're going to have to come up with an explanation he'll accept for me not being on the *Golden Stallion*."

"That shouldn't be a problem," Peter answered. "I'm not stupid enough to think we can rendezvous with your smuggler friend in the *North Star* and have him tell us everything he knows." Rising to his feet, Peter stretched, walking toward the head. "I can get us a ship your friend will never question."

"An upstanding Admiral like you?" Blaise teased, following Peter toward the 'fresher. After their morning exertions and the piercing, he needed a shower or the entire crew would know what they'd been doing that morning.

"Discretionary latitude," Peter repeated, stepping into the 'fresher and closing the seal behind Blaise before waving it on. The hot spray eased muscles he hadn't realized were tense, and he rinsed through his hair before stepping aside to let the stream reach Blaise. "Once we're done, I want you to contact your smuggler friend. My comm officer can mask the signal so he won't be able to tell it's coming from a Confederation ship."

"I'll talk to him, but I can tell you now, the best we'll get out of him is an agreement to meet. And that's if we're lucky. I need to know what I can offer him in exchange for whatever he knows, because he isn't going to talk out of generosity alone. And if he sees me consulting with someone offscreen, he's going to get suspicious. He knows I work alone." Harry'd been the first person Blaise had gone to after his escape. The other smuggler knew the worst of what he'd endured and the reasons he'd made the decision to stay alone on his ship.

"Offer him whatever it takes, within reason," Peter answered, his eyes narrowing. "But only if the information leads us to the Gavenelians."

Blaise nodded. This wasn't his first negotiation with Harry or others of his breed. It was more a matter of knowing what latitude Peter would allow him. Finishing his shower, he waited for Peter to turn off the water before turning on the automatic dryer, a ghost of a smile dancing over his lips as the blast of warm air on his new piercing sent fresh desire through him. They couldn't indulge it now, but he knew he'd be walking around half hard all day long just from the brush of his shipsuit against the delicate ring. "I'll see what I can do," he promised, taking another steri-wipe from the dispenser and cleaning around his nipple carefully. The last thing he wanted was for it to get infected.

Peter watched with hooded eyes as Blaise tended the new piercing, just the sight of those agile fingers manipulating the ring making him start to stiffen again. Turning to pull a clean uniform from his wardrobe, he paused. "You can't wear a shipsuit on screen or your contact might get suspicious," he observed. "Here." Opening a drawer, he tossed Blaise the sleeveless vest he'd worn the day of his capture.

Blaise looked at the garment in confusion for a moment before looking back up at Peter. "This is mine," he said slowly, his confusion clear in his voice. "Why do you have this?"

"Prisoners' personal effects are stored until their release," Peter said, refusing to allow his thoughts to dwell on that inevitability. "Since you're here rather than a labor colony, your effects are here."

In your drawer? Blaise thought in surprise, but he didn't want to disrupt the harmony between them by pushing for a declaration Peter wasn't ready to give. He simply pulled the leather on, making sure it concealed the new piercing. Harry understood the significance of the first one. He'd surely demand an explanation for the new one as well, and Blaise didn't feel like lying to his old friend or diminishing the meaning of the new ornament in any way. "I'll need something to wear on my legs unless you're planning on giving your staff a peep show," he joked, waggling his eyebrows at Peter.

If the stakes weren't so critical, Peter would be tempted to keep the smuggler in his cabin and see how coherent he'd be with his "old friend" with an Aldebaran plug stretching his ass, but finding the Gavenelians was far more important than his own personal pleasure. Retrieving the rest of Blaise's garments, he held them out to the other man with a premonition that they were taking a step that would change things between them forever.

Pulling his pants on, Blaise remarked how odd they felt after months of wearing nothing but shipsuits. They didn't seem to fit him anymore, though no one looking at him would have noticed anything wrong. They just didn't seem a part of who he was at the moment. Pushing aside that uncomfortable thought, he turned to Peter. "Let's see if I can roust Harry from whatever hellhole he's settled in."

"You can use one of the small conference rooms. They're plain enough that they could be any ship," Peter suggested as they started down the corridor. "I'll have Lieutenant Yebra open a masked channel for you. Just give him the contact information," he continued, not adding that he would of course be monitoring the entire conversation.

Blaise hesitated. "You won't go after Harry based on anything he says to me while we're bargaining, will you?" he verified.

"He'll have complete immunity," Peter agreed. "But he'd better have something substantive to tell us. If he tries to play games, I'll be on him faster than a Tularian on a death watch."

"I can't promise he knows anything," Blaise cautioned, "but he's a techno dweeb. He collects all kinds of alien technology. If there's anything out there about their technology, he'll know about it."

"Let's hope so," Peter answered, waving open the door to a small meeting room and following Blaise inside. Activating the comm port, he held a brief conversation with his communications officer, who was well-trained enough not to question why his commander needed an untraceable channel, or why the Admiral's pet prisoner would be giving him the contact coordinates.

"I'm going to get some coffee," Peter said. "Meet me back in my quarters when you're finished."

Blaise didn't imagine for a moment that Peter would let him speak with Harry alone without listening in, but at least the Admiral wouldn't be hovering just out of sight of the vid feed making Blaise nervous. He keyed in the coordinates for Harry's private link and hoped his friend was somewhere safe. Within moments, the other smuggler's voice came across the channel, video blocked as usual.

"Blaise, great timing. I've been trying to get in touch with you. I've got news for you."

"Good news, I hope?"

"The best, man. I've been playing with that piece of equipment you gave me. Learned all kinds of interesting things, especially since it looks like your old friends have been leaving calling cards in Confederation space. What do you think the Admiralty would give me for my little toy?"

"Probably just about anything you want," Blaise replied honestly, trying not to flinch at the mention of the device Harry'd found implanted into the *Golden Stallion's* hull. Harry wouldn't understand about the domineering commander in the next room who would want an explanation as soon as the transmission ended.

"That sounds promising. They're probably so desperate they wouldn't even bother to make sure it worked."

"Don't underestimate them, Harry. They mean business, especially where these attacks are concerned."

"In the Admiralty's head now, are you?"

"No, of course not," Blaise hastened to reassure his friend. He'd lost the knack for this kind of subtle wordplay while he'd been serving time. "But I happened to be near Zaniah and saw the Confederation response. They want those bastards almost as much as I do. Have you found a weakness?"

"Have I found a weakness?" Harry scoffed. "You wound me with your doubts."

"What is it?"

"Uh-uh. You know I never share information in a space transmission. Meet me at our old hangout on Nicodemus Vector and we'll see."

Blaise did some quick calculations in his head. "It'll take me a few days to get there," he warned. "Probably a week, maybe even a little longer. Keep yourself safe while you're waiting for me."

"Nobody gets anywhere near me there unless I let them. Keep yourself safe. Nobody's looking for me."

Before Blaise could reply to that the comm channel went dead. With a sigh, he rose and headed back to Peter's quarters as directed, sure he was about to get grilled.

"You don't honestly expect me to trust that con artist, do you?" Peter flared as soon as Blaise entered his quarters.

"Not really," Blaise replied honestly, taking a seat on the couch and marshaling his arguments in Harry's favor, "but I had rather hoped you'd trust me. Harry might sell the Admiralty a dud. He might even give me a dud if it were something else. But not with the Gavenelians. Not to me."

Frowning, Peter paced the cabin as he considered that. "What's this 'equipment' you gave him? You didn't mention anything about that."

Blaise sighed. He'd known this would lead to another interrogation. "When I escaped, I went to the safest place I knew, Nicodemus Vector. Harry took me in, nursed me back to health, and while I was there, he found a homing beacon on the *Stallion*. He disabled it and kept it, to see what he could learn about their technology. He's obviously discovered something, even if he won't tell us what over the space waves."

Peter kept his questions about exactly what kind of care "Harry" had given Blaise to himself. "Where is this Nicodemus Vector?" he asked instead.

"Algol V," Blaise elucidated. "It's a code name he developed years ago for his hideout. Fred Nicodemus was a twentieth-century physicist who discovered the bidirectional reflectance distribution function that allowed for... do you really want to know why he calls it that?" Peter shook his head. "Anyway, it's his stronghold. Every time he comes across a new piece of technology, he takes it there and figures it out. When he does, he updates his own defenses. If there's a safe place in the universe, it's his compound on Algol V."

Mentally calculating from the *North Star*'s present position, Peter nodded. "It's a good thing we're still in the Sirius quadrant, even if it is the spiral arm of nowhere. We'll need to make a slight detour on the way, but we should be able to better that week you estimated."

"Detour?" Blaise asked. "Oh, to get a ship. As long as we don't get there faster than would be believable for the ship you find for us from here. Untraceable signal or not, I don't doubt for a minute Harry knows where we are right now. And his comment about me being in the Admiralty's head probably means he knows this was a Confederation frequency."

"You'd know better than I would how long it would take to reach your friend from here," Peter countered, even more determined to keep a close eye on that "friend" when they met. "After all, we'll be flying your ship."

"What?!" Blaise demanded, surging to his feet in the Admiral's face. "You have my ship? How the hell do you have my ship and why are you just now telling me?"

"Don't take that tone with me," Peter growled, meeting Blaise's glare with an icy stare of his own. "Your ship was impounded when you were found guilty of smuggling. Normal procedure would be to dispose of it at auction, but as I'd think you'd have learned by now, I have the means to bypass normal procedures."

"Oh, you must have been laughing," Blaise grated. "Poor little Blaise, crying into his Betelgeusian wine over his lost ship. Well, fuck you, Admiral Keller, you and your sadistic submissive games. I don't want your sympathy. I expect my cooperation in the war effort against the Gavenelians to be noted in my file, along with a request for early parole based on said efforts. Otherwise, you'll never get anywhere near Harry's stronghold."

"You're not in any position to be making demands," Peter snapped back. He hadn't expected Blaise to fall over himself thanking him for saving his ship, but he hadn't expected to be attacked for it, either. "Maybe you'd prefer to be spending your sentence at hard labor in a penal colony, your ship sold for scrap to the highest bidder? You don't want sympathy? Good, because you're not getting any. I don't give a fuck if you're angry. I expect you to help me find these murderous alien bastards. I thought you had a personal stake in stopping them, but maybe I was wrong about that, too."

"I have a personal stake in making sure they don't get anywhere near me again," Blaise agreed, heart clenching painfully as he turned away. If only Peter had really cared.... His hand brushed over the new piercing, making him bite his lip to hold back the anguish that threatened to break free. Peter was obviously no different than anyone else who wanted him for what he could do rather than who he was. "But the rest of the galaxy's on its own. Nobody cared about me when they were torturing me. Why should I care about them?"

"Then help me for your own selfish reasons, but *help me*," Peter demanded, only years of discipline allowing him to mask the pain he felt at Blaise's words. He'd thought that accepting the ring was a sign that Blaise had started to care, but obviously he was wrong. He was just another torturer in Blaise's eyes.

Blaise's shoulders slumped. A few hours ago, he would have done anything Peter asked, but the lover he thought he'd had was clearly a figment of his imagination. "When I see a note in my file about my cooperation in the war effort," he replied dully. "Until then, I'll just return to my duties, Admiral, sir."

"Sure you don't want to dictate it to me?" Peter retorted, his eyes hard. "You'll get your damn commendation. Now until we get to the impound yard to pick up your vessel, you can return to your own quarters." He turned away before his expression could reveal the emptiness clawing at him. "I don't want to see you before then."

"I don't want to see you ever again," Blaise muttered as he started slowly for the door. He expected a hand on his shoulder or arm, longed for Peter to spin him around and remind him who gave the orders here. It would all be different if Peter actually cared. If Peter actually cared, Blaise would have moved heaven and earth to get him what he needed to win this war, but he needed to know he was more than just another plaything. The touch never came, the door opening to let him leave. He stepped across the threshold, praying for an order to stop. Even if it meant more fighting. But silence followed him into the corridor, only the swish of the closing door breaking its deafening stillness.

Peter wanted to stop him, to grab him, throw him against the bulkhead and kiss him senseless, rip off his clothes and fuck him blind and remind him that he wore Peter's ring now, that he belonged to him. But doing any of that would only reinforce that he was no better than the Gavenelians in Blaise's eyes. The silence echoed Blaise's final words in his head, the door hissed closed against the bulkhead, and Admiral Keller was alone.

CHAPTER 12

SOMETHING ABOUT HARRY

THE ship hadn't changed. It had been almost twelve months since he'd last stepped foot inside his baby, but she hadn't changed a bit, except to smell a little stale. He figured that was because nobody'd done any maintenance on her climate control. He'd get them in route to Algol V and then he'd take care of her. She was all he had, and if he didn't take care of her, how could he expect her to take care of him?

The stray thought hit him that Peter probably felt the same way—that Blaise wasn't taking care of him—but Blaise pushed it away. He refused to acknowledge that he'd missed his surly Admiral the last two days… the last two nights. If he'd had his way, he wouldn't have left, but Keller had made that impossible with his betrayal. His body protested, though, not understanding why it suddenly wasn't getting the incredible loving— *scratch that, the predictable fucking*—it had grown accustomed to since his arrival on the *North Star*. It would just have to get used to celibacy again because while Blaise couldn't imagine letting anyone else take him the way Keller had, he also couldn't imagine how they could repair the rift between them. He refused to take the first step. After all, he was the wronged party, and he knew better than to think the Admiral would unbend far enough to apologize, which left them in a stalemate.

And that left him with nothing but his ship, assuming he could reclaim it once his sentence was up. With a stifled sigh, he set the coordinates and sent the ship hurtling through space before turning his attention to all the little repairs that inevitably built up over time. He'd start with the ventilation system, to see if he couldn't get the stale smell out of the air. From there, well, he'd see what came up as he worked. Either way, he'd be avoiding the captain's cabin unless he had no other choice, quite sure Keller would set himself up in there as if this were his ship and those quarters were his right. Well, fuck him. Blaise didn't need him.

Peter prowled the narrow passageways of the *Golden Stallion*, familiarizing himself as much as he could with its layout and design. It had been a long time since he'd piloted a ship this size—not that he expected Blaise to ever let him get his hands on the controls—and he found to his surprise that he'd missed it. Commanding a starship was a far cry from really flying, but since that wasn't an option, he'd learn all he could about the ship's systems instead. That knowledge might be a matter of life and death some day—and it wasn't as if he had anything else to do in the meantime, until they reached the planet where Blaise's contact had agreed to meet.

From the moment Peter had reclaimed the smuggler's ship from the impound spacedock, Blaise headed straight to the bridge and hadn't left it since. Peter had explored the rest of the small interior: two cabins, a central kitchen/dining/common area, the head, and a hatch that led below deck to the engines—and a number of obvious and not-so-obvious storage compartments. He'd dropped off his single bag in the cabin that seemed to be unoccupied—there were no clothes or other possessions there, anyway—and then started pacing. And thinking.

Flying his own ship wasn't all he missed. He missed Blaise—which he expected, his body having gotten used to the release of almost daily sex—but more than that, he missed the warmth of Blaise's body next to him as he slept, missed waking up to a bed that wasn't empty in the morning, missed the conversations as they ate and the way Blaise's eyes changed color when they.... Peter smacked his hand against the bulkhead where he'd been examining an atmospheric control vent and cursed the three more days until they'd reach their rendezvous. Once he had the information he needed to find the Gavenelians, he'd be able to *do* something, to take action. He'd never been good at waiting—especially waiting in enforced idleness on a two-man ship with a man who hated him.

Well, that was just too damn bad, Peter decided. He wasn't going to spend the whole trip hiding in his cabin. If Blaise didn't want to be around him, he'd just have to put up with it, the same as Peter did. Slamming the hatch closed, he stalked forward to the small bridge, dropping into the mate's chair and staring out the viewscreen at the starfield ahead of them.

"What do you want, Admiral?" Blaise asked shortly, his tone clearly turning the title into an insult. He couldn't order the man off his bridge, but he could do his damnedest to make it uncomfortable for the commander to stay.

That was a question he'd asked himself since ordering Blaise from his quarters two days before. Obviously, from Blaise's sneering response, it wouldn't matter what he answered; he wasn't going to get it. "Can I help with anything?" he asked instead, his own voice level. They couldn't spend the next three days at each other's throats.

The lack of response disheartened Blaise. At least if they were shouting, he knew he still had the power to rouse something in his former lover. The neutrality in Keller's voice cut far deeper than any angry words. "No," he said softly. "Nothing you'd want to, anyway. I'm plenty used to running my ship by myself. Just...." He waved vaguely in the direction of the cabins.

"You might be surprised what I'd want," Peter answered, encouraged that Blaise hadn't snapped at him again. "I'm not used to having nothing to do."

"You mean no one to do?" Blaise asked sarcastically. "Sorry I can't oblige you, but this is *my* ship. I'm not yours to order about here."

His hope that they might reach some type of detente shattered, Peter's anger flared to the surface. "Enjoy it while it lasts," he snapped. "Just remember you're still a prisoner—*my* prisoner. And if you have any ideas about trying to escape now that you have your ship back, you can forget them right now." He leaned back in the chair, raking his eyes over Blaise's torso. "If you're tempted to forget, just remember whose ring is under that vest. I marked you, and I'm not letting you go." A sneer twisted his face. "Until you've served out the rest of your sentence, you're mine."

"What, my ring?" Blaise retorted, forcibly keeping his hands in place on the controls instead of letting one reach up to cover the new piercing. He'd thought about taking it out, but it wouldn't matter since Keller wouldn't see it again anyway. Stupid though it was, he wanted that gift, that illusion that for a few hours, it had actually meant something. Of course, he wasn't about to tell the Admiral that. "And why the hell would you care what happens to me? You obviously don't want me anymore."

"It wouldn't look very good on my record to let a prisoner escape," Peter retorted, refusing to be baited by the taunt. He wasn't about to admit how much he still wanted Blaise, only to be treated as if he were no better than the torturers the pirate had escaped. "I might not get another one if I did," he added, though he already knew he'd never bring another prisoner on board the *North Star*. Blaise was the last.

"Fuck you," Blaise spat, rising from his seat and leaving the pilot's seat. "Don't touch anything. You'd probably break it." *Just like you're breaking me.* The Gavenelians couldn't do it with all their exotic torture devices, but the man in front of him had without even trying. Turning on his heel, he left the cockpit for the engine room. Surrounded by the familiar hum of his baby's drives, he grabbed a wrench and beat futilely on a bulkhead, trying to let out the painful tearing in his chest.

Peter stared blindly out the viewscreen, cursing himself and Blaise equally and wondering how the fuck he was going to survive three more days of this.

"WE'LL be in the Algol system in about twelve hours," Blaise informed Keller evenly. Things hadn't gotten any easier between them in the past two days, to the point they'd started avoiding whatever space the other was in. "I've sent a transmission to Harry telling him when to expect me."

"You mean us," Peter shot back. "No way in hell I'm letting you meet with him alone."

"Why not?" Blaise snapped. "He's not the one with a history of hurting people for the pleasure of it. It'll be nice not to have to worry about every word I say. He'll just be glad to see an old familiar face again."

"An old familiar lover, you mean?" Peter sneered. "I intend to make sure you get the information we came for and nothing more." *Like help with an escape attempt, or another fuck for old time's sake*, Peter thought, not sure which would be more painful. "Besides, I seem to remember you enjoyed it when I hurt you." As soon as the angry words slipped out, he regretted them, but it was too late to call them back.

"I enjoyed the sex," Blaise disagreed, knowing it would be pointless to deny that anyway when he'd come hard at Keller's hands too many times to count. "I didn't enjoy the lies or the betrayal."

"Lies and betrayal? What the hell are you talking about? You're the one who's been hiding secrets about your past." Peter leaned closer, fists on the wall on either side of Blaise's shoulders, pinning him to the bulkhead. "Do you think I don't know you haven't told me everything about this 'Harry' we're meeting? Enjoy fucking him while you can. When this is over, you're still coming back with me."

"You didn't care about my past until it could be useful to you," Blaise shouted, ignoring his body's reaction to Keller's proximity. He wanted to arch into the seductive heat, but he couldn't let himself react that way. "So don't accuse me of keeping secrets. You knew far more about me, even before last week, than I know, even now, about you. And yes, lies and betrayal. You could have told me—should have told me—the night of my birthday that you'd kept my ship from going to the junkyard. As for Harry, at least I know to expect it when he fucks me over. I thought you were different, though."

"I thought…. Ah, fuck it. I don't have to justify myself to you," Peter snarled. He'd honestly thought it would be harder for Blaise to know about the ship while he was still serving his sentence, but obviously the smuggler was going to see everything he said or did in the worst possible light. "And believe me, when I'm going to fuck you over, you'll be in no doubt what's happening."

"Oh, I'm not in any doubt," Blaise agreed bitterly. "You've obviously had plenty of experience at it."

"You never had any complaints about it before," Peter retorted. He meant to leave it at that. He meant to push away from the bulkhead and head back to the first mate's seat, or better still back to his cabin, even though he already knew his own hand wasn't enough to deal with his frustration. What he didn't intend to do was lean forward, his eyes locked with Blaise's sparking hazel stare until they were sharing the same heated breath. And he surely didn't intend to lock his mouth to

Blaise's, while his hands groped under the sleeveless vest to prove to himself that the thin strand of Zanian metal still pierced Blaise's left nipple.

Blaise knew he should push Peter away, but he couldn't. His arms had no strength for that gesture, especially when the Admiral's fingers slid over skin and found the piercing he hadn't been able to remove. He moaned into the kiss, lips parting eagerly and welcoming the hot thrust of Peter's tongue. His chest lifted into the seeking caress, offering himself in a way the Admiral would have to be stupid not to understand. Keller was many things, but he wasn't stupid.

Peter didn't know whether Blaise's sudden and surprising reaction was the spacer's version of an apology, or if the other man was just as horny and frustrated as he was, but at the moment he couldn't be bothered to care. He had Blaise's body pressed against him, Blaise kissing him back, and he'd be stupider than a Zirilian slug if he didn't take advantage of the moment. *Especially when it might be the last one you have*, an irritating voice in his head muttered, but he silenced it ruthlessly, turning all his attention to burying his tongue down Blaise's throat and tearing away as much clothing as he could to bare skin to his ravaging hands.

It was hot and raw and fast, everything Blaise needed it to be, but it wasn't cruel. However angry with him Peter was—and Blaise didn't believe for a second this frantic fucking would fix anything—he wasn't motivated by hatred, and that gave Blaise hope. He'd take what he could get at this point, and when they were back on the *North Star*, they'd have it out once and for all. For now, he'd be satisfied with feeling the Admiral inside him again. Working blindly, his hands wormed their way beneath layers of clothing, quite a change from Peter's usual uniform, seeking the smooth, golden skin and hard muscle he had come to think of as his own.

They'd be able to take it slow next time, Peter decided, Blaise's willing assistance in shoving aside the bare minimum of clothing giving him hope that there would be a next time. He'd take his time, lavishing pleasure on every tanned millimeter of Blaise's body, leaving him no doubt who he belonged to... and maybe, just maybe, asking him to stay after his sentence was up. But all that needed to wait, because right now Peter's body and mind were insisting on only one thing: sinking into

Blaise's intoxicating heat, as hard and as fast as the laws of physics would allow. Even though both their cocks were leaking, there wasn't enough slickness to ease his way, so Peter wet his fingers with his own saliva and worked them into the tight passage, stretching Blaise as fully as his limited patience would allow.

Blaise lifted his leg to circle Peter's hip, giving the blond easier access to his body. He needed this. That thought pulsed through him with every rapid thud of his heart. He sucked on the tongue currently fucking his mouth, hoping it wouldn't be long before Peter's cock followed suit. The fingers stretching him roughly weren't enough. He needed Peter's cock. "Inside me," he gasped, pulling away just long enough to speak. "Need you... now."

Since he couldn't agree more, Peter gave his fingers one last twist, pulled them out and ran them over the head of his cock to spread the wetness, and drove inside Blaise in a single strong thrust. It felt fucking fantastic—it felt like coming home. Hitching Blaise's leg higher on his hip, he pulled back and sank in again, finding the perfect angle to bury himself to the root. It was the perfect angle for Blaise too, if his gasps of ecstasy were anything to go by. Peter dipped his head to reclaim Blaise's mouth, rolling his hips in a staccato tempo driven purely by his body's instincts.

Peter's cock rubbed over Blaise's sweet spot in just the right way, setting off explosions behind his closed eyes with each thrust. With one leg around his lover and his weight balanced precariously on the other, Blaise could do little more than take the welcome pounding. He thought for a moment about trying to turn around, but that would mean pulling away and after the tension of the past five days, that was impossible. Instead, he clasped his fingers around Peter's head, keeping their lips firmly joined as he rocked as best he could into the powerful thrusts.

Sparks of energy crackled along Peter's synapses, colliding and growing stronger until he couldn't hear, couldn't see. He could only feel the exquisite friction of Blaise's body embracing his. He groaned deeply into Blaise's mouth as the charge exploded through him, his grip tightening as he fought to keep to his feet through the powerful shudders that wracked his muscles.

The hot wash of Peter's release inside him triggered Blaise's, sending him into orbit. He sagged against the other man, unable to support his weight at all. His breath still rasping in and out, he opened his mouth to apologize, to say anything at all to end the hostilities between them, but before he could get the words out, his comm beeped insistently. "Fuck," he muttered against Peter's shoulder. "Harry's spotted us."

As much as he wanted the information the smuggler could offer, Peter cursed the execrable timing. He'd hoped, in the atmosphere of something like intimacy that lingered after their climax, to say something to make Blaise understand his feelings, if he could clarify them to himself first. "Blaise, I...," he started, then shook his head when the comm sounded again. He'd already seen what could happen when he spoke without thinking. He needed to work through his own emotions and figure out how to explain them, and that would take time they just didn't have at the moment. "You'd better answer him," he muttered, easing away from the bulkhead.

Blaise paused a moment longer, leaning in to kiss Peter quickly. He wanted to believe he'd been wrong. He wanted to believe there'd been more to this round of sex than just fucking, but he'd thought that before and had been wrong. Maybe after they'd finished with Harry, there would be time to talk. "Just remember," he warned Peter, "I'm the captain and you're my first mate. You can be my jealous lover first mate, but you can't be the Admiral or we'll never learn anything from him."

"I think I can manage that," Peter countered wryly. At least Blaise didn't seem inclined to protest Peter's near-mauling of him. Maybe that was a positive sign. He just hoped Blaise didn't plan to get his own back by flaunting his relationship with his former lover. He might see more jealousy than he'd anticipated.

Smiling slightly, hoping that meant Peter wouldn't mind being his lover, Blaise settled in the captain's chair, making sure his vest was back in place enough that Harry wouldn't see anything amiss on the vid screen. He glanced at Peter as he took the first mate's seat, making sure he was presentable as well. Blaise didn't mind Harry knowing they were lovers, but he didn't want to shock the other man, either.

He flipped the switch for the vid screen and Harry's familiar blue face popped onto the screen. "You're not alone," he accused before Blaise could even say hello.

"I have a new first mate," Blaise lied easily. "I got tired of flying alone. Long hauls get lonely sometimes."

Harry huffed but nodded. "The outside code hasn't changed," he told Blaise. "I'll meet you at the landing port and take you inside."

The screen went blank before Blaise could reply.

"You didn't tell me he was one of the...." Peter bit off his words at the challenging lift of Blaise's eyebrows. He probably wouldn't take kindly to referring to his ex-lover as one of the "fish people," even if that was the common name around the galaxy for his race. "One of the Andromedites," Peter finished blandly.

"Does it matter?" Blaise asked sharply. "Harry's been called every insult you can imagine and probably some you can't by narrow-minded idiots with no compassion. The last person to say something about it is minus an arm right now. Personally, I think he has beautiful skin."

Personally, Peter didn't give a Regulosian's rear end whether Harry was blue, green, or purple with orange stripes. He'd been Blaise's lover, and that was reason enough to object to him on principle. "I'm not some small-minded bigot to care about that," Peter protested. "Just something else you failed to tell me about."

Blaise's temper rose in his throat, but he bit it back. It would be bad enough walking into Harry's compound smelling of sex. Going in there smelling of sex and angry would set off warning bells in his friend's mind for sure. "I honestly didn't think about it," he replied evenly. "I think of him as Harry, not as an Andromedite, and since he blocks video unless he knows the channel he's using, I didn't see him from the *North Star* to be reminded of it."

Peter could understand that—he'd long since stopped thinking of Lapis as a Sirian, thoughts of her focusing on her sharp wit and acerbic tongue far more than her green skin—but they'd already spent more than enough time discussing Blaise's former lover, as far as Peter was concerned, so he remained silent.

Skillfully, Blaise flew the ship through the narrow passage that was Harry's outer line of defense. He entered the code to get past the first set of shields and into the more spacious landing field. Seeing Harry near one entrance to the compound, he piloted the ship to the nearest landing pad and set it down delicately. Damn, but he'd missed his ship!

Making sure his clothes were all fastened properly, Blaise lowered the gangplank and stepped out onto the surface of the planet. "Good to see you, Harry," he said with a smile and an embrace for his old friend. "This is Peter."

Fluidly, Peter performed the intricate series of gestures that served as a formal greeting on the Andromedite home world—at least, as best he could without a few sets of extra tentacles. "Harry," he acknowledged, deciding that for the present, the less he said, the better.

"This one is better than the last one you brought here," Harry told Blaise, charmed by the compliment of being greeted appropriately for his homeworld rather than in the far more casual way of most spacers.

"Garrett was a hell of a pilot," Blaise defended his former first mate.

"He was," Harry agreed, "and I know you miss him, but I'm glad to see you aren't flying alone anymore. It's a dangerous universe out there."

"Don't I know it!" Blaise replied. "So what do you have for us? Could you make anything out of that gadget?"

"Not out here," Harry insisted, leading them inside, making sure his body blocked the pad as he entered the code. Once the door shut behind them, leaving them in a small, cluttered lab, Harry picked up the device Blaise recognized. "Interesting piece of hardware, this," he said, his tentacles curling around it. "It almost certainly was intended as a homing beacon. I managed to disable that early on, but that's not what makes it so interesting."

"So what makes it interesting?" Blaise pressed.

"The fact that it can't recognize very high frequencies of light," Harry explained. "You told me your weapons bounced off the Gavenelian shields like they were nothing, but a high-frequency beam—

far higher than anything we normally use now, upward of one Zettahertz—will go straight through their shields."

"That would mean using gamma radiation," Peter interjected. "It could be as dangerous to us as to the Gavenelians."

Harry glanced over at Peter in surprise. "Not as dangerous as what the Gavenelians will do to you if they capture you," he replied calmly. "Or has Blaise not told you what they did to him?"

"I told him enough," Blaise insisted flatly, not wanting Harry to reveal what shape he'd been in when he'd found his way here. "Anything else we need to know? Anything that might help us shield against their weapons?"

Harry shook his head. "Nothing yet, but I'm not convinced I've learned all the secrets this little goody has for me yet. If I find anything else out, I'll let you know. I'd rather wait until I know more before this goes on the market, but I don't mind telling you. I don't want you facing them again without better weapons."

"Thanks," Blaise answered genuinely. "We should go. I've got a meeting with a supplier who doesn't like to be kept waiting."

"Good to see you as always," Harry said with a smile. "Come back some time when you aren't in a rush, though. I want to get to know your mate better. I think this one might be a keeper."

Peter glanced at the Andromedite in surprise at the comment, wondering if he was reading something into his choice of words—*mate*, as opposed to first mate—that wasn't there. In his experience, Andromedites were usually reticent about personal comments, though Harry was apparently atypical in many ways. Peter decided he'd like to get to know him better as well, if only to learn more about Blaise's past. Harry might prove easier to get answers from than Blaise himself. A question nagged at him, though, from something Harry had mentioned earlier. "You said it was designed as a homing beacon," he recalled. "Is there any way of reversing that to trace back to the Gavenelians?"

"Definitely a keeper," Harry crowed, looking at Blaise. "He actually has a thought in his head besides getting in your pants."

Blaise flushed. "Just because he wanted to doesn't mean I let him, as you well know," he retorted, not daring to look at Peter. "It's a good question, though. So is there?"

Harry stared down at the gadget in his grasp. "I don't know. Haven't tried it, but I can. It'll take some time, though. It hasn't given up any of its secrets easily."

"Time. That's the one thing we don't have," Blaise replied slowly. "I'll check back with you in a week or two and you can tell me if you've figured anything else out. I can always come back later." He hoped he could anyway, but even if he couldn't, it was what Harry would expect to hear.

Harry shrugged. "It's your credit, not mine, paying to get you here."

Blaise nodded. "Thanks," he added one more time. "Take care of yourself."

"Always have, always will," Harry joked with a grin as he walked them back to the landing site.

Blaise waved one last time as he climbed back into the ship and waited for Peter to strap in next to him before steering the ship back out into space.

"'*Doesn't mean I let him*'?" Peter queried as soon as they were alone on the ship.

"I told you Garrett and I weren't lovers," Blaise reminded Peter. "And it was true, but not from lack of interest on Garrett's part. Just lack of interest on mine."

Whatever Peter might have said in reply was lost in the explosion that rocked the ship.

CHAPTER 13
BURNOUT

"WHAT the fuck?" Blaise demanded immediately, hitting the console to show the exterior view. His stomach sank as he recognized the shape of the two ships bearing down on them.

"More friends of yours?" Peter asked, though the expression on Blaise's face was its own answer. "Apparently not," he answered himself, as a second energy bolt narrowly missed the ship. "I presume you have weapons of some kind? I'll fly, you man them," he directed, the command instincts of long years taking over.

Blaise almost argued, but he had a better chance of finessing the weapons system to let him use the new information from Harry than Peter did. "The weapons will be useless until I can reconfigure them to fire gamma beams," he warned, "and the shields won't hold out for long. I don't know how in the hell they found us, but those are Gavenelian vessels."

"Probably missed one of their homing beacons," Peter grunted, studying the flight controls. Luckily they were fairly standard, with a few customizations he suspected Blaise's friend Harry had a hand—or a tentacle—in designing. Leaning over to Blaise's position, he flipped a switch to transfer control to the mate's console. Before moving back, he clasped Blaise's shoulder briefly. "Get to reconfiguring. I'll try to keep us from getting fried in the meantime, but there's two of them and only one of us. I don't much like those odds."

"Hail the planet," Blaise suggested, his fingers flying over the weapons control panel as he bypassed safeguards, trying to get the codes from Harry entered. "It's the last frequency on the comm. Warn Harry. And if I know that sneaky old fish, he'll have the base's weapons updated already." The computer beeped at him in protest and kicked him back out. "Damn it!" he cursed, starting again from the beginning. "We don't have to destroy them. We just have to hold them off long enough to get free of the planetary system. Once we do, they can't catch us. The *Stallion* is faster than anything they have."

"Nicodemus Vector," Peter hailed after finding the comm link. "This is *Golden Stallion*, do you copy? You have some unwelcome guests looking to visit. We're holding them off but could use some help, copy?" As he spoke, he slung the *Stallion* into a hard vector, trying to get behind the attacking vessels' guns, at least until they could escape the planet's gravity well. The ship veered as responsively as Peter could have hoped, buying them a few seconds before the Gavenelians could turn to follow. "Sweet ship," he murmured under his breath as he jagged to another heading. No wonder Blaise was so attached to it.

"They're not all that unexpected," Harry's voice came back over the comm, "but they are in for a surprise. Get Blaise out of here. I'll take care of our guests."

"Now you see why I was so upset when I thought I'd lost her," Blaise replied absentmindedly as he fiddled with the weapons control again. "There, I think I've got it! Can you get me a clear shot at their bridge?"

Even as he spoke, the planet's weapons came to life, firing volley after volley of gamma rays at the Gavenelian ships, tearing holes the size of asteroids in the nearest one's shields and hull. "Or, on second thought, we can let Harry rip them to shreds and get out of here while we can."

Peter had already swung the *Stallion* around to face the larger of the two ships, but he quickly plotted a heading to take them out of the planetary elliptic. He didn't like running from a fight or leaving the Andromedite to face their attackers alone, but the planet was definitely better armed than they were. "Aye, Captain," he agreed, sparing a quick glance at Blaise while pouring all the power he could into making their escape.

Keeping an eye on the receding battle, Blaise breathed a sigh of relief when he saw one of the two ships disintegrate beneath Harry's fire. He took his hands off the weapons controls and slumped back into his seat. "That's two times too many I've come face to face with those bastards," he complained as the second ship veered away from the planet. "Shit," he spat, "they're coming after us." He leaned forward again, angling the weapons behind them so he could fire on the pursuing ship. "Come on, baby," he urged his ship. "Just a little bit more, and we'll be out of their range."

"She'll do it," Peter assured him, nodding at the acceleration curve as the planet's gravitational pull lessened. "Been too long since I've had my hands on such a responsive beauty," he crooned, flashing a grin at his partner. "Once we—fuck!" he broke off as a wave of energy seared from the remaining Gavenelian ship. He skewed away wildly, but the bolt just clipped the *Stallion*, rocking it violently and setting a flare of plasma erupting from the panel in front of him. He raised an arm instinctively while the other fought to keep them accelerating away from the attackers. The pain was blinding as the burning plasma energy raced along his nerves, and with a strangled gasp he slumped forward onto the arcing panel.

Blaise cursed a blue streak as he hit the button for autopilot, hoping to hell Harry took care of the last ship. Grabbing Peter's shoulders, he pulled him away from the panel, taking in the extent of the damage caused by the plasma explosion. The hand that had protected his eyes was badly seared, the bone showing in a couple of places. His chest and arm were also scored with sizzling plasma, as well as a lesser burn on the left side of his jaw and neck.

He fumbled with the medi-kit, pulling out the bottle of sani-wash. Lips moving in a silent prayer, he sprayed the contents over the still-sizzling plasma, trying to keep it from burning Peter any more than it already had. When he had emptied the entire bottle, he dug in the kit for bandages and burn cream. Hands trembling, he applied them as best he could to the red scores covering most of Peter's left arm and the side of his chest.

As soon as the Admiral was as comfortable as Blaise could make him, the smuggler turned his attention to the ship's heading. He scanned the star charts for the closest Confederation outpost. He'd have some explaining to do and more, but that didn't matter. Peter needed better medical treatment than Blaise could give him, and he doubted the commander could wait the three days it would take them to return to the *North Star*. Even if he pushed his ship to her absolute limits, he couldn't cut more than about twelve hours off that time, and that was still forty-eight hours too many.

Eudorae Prime was fifteen hours away if he pushed it. "Come on, baby," he urged the ship. "We've got the most precious cargo we'll ever carry, and he's not going to make it if we don't fly like we've never flown before."

The *Golden Stallion* surged beneath his hands as if she'd heard him. Blaise took every noncritical system offline, channeling the power saved to the engines, trying to coax that much more speed out of the ship.

Searing agony flamed through Peter's senses, tempting him to sink back into blissful darkness. His eyelids twitched when he drew in a ragged breath, the rise and fall of his chest raw torment to the scorched tissue. "Blaise?" he rasped, forcing an eye open and fighting to focus through the haze of pain. "Safe?"

"We're fine," Blaise assured him. "You got us out of the Algol system. We're on our way to Eudorae Prime so we can get your burns treated. Unless you know some place closer?" he added hopefully.

Peter shook his head, the movement causing a wave of nausea. Forcing back the bile that threatened to choke him, he had to clear his throat to speak, feeling as if he were breathing in fire. "Not fast enough," he muttered hoarsely. "Should have—" A bout of harsh coughs shook him, stealing his voice. So many things he wanted to say jostled in his thoughts, and he couldn't find words or voice for any of them. "Sorry," he husked through another rale of coughing, his eyes locking onto his lover's face, hoping Blaise understood he meant more than just the damage to the ship.

"Don't try to talk now," Blaise insisted, voice catching on the emotions clogging his throat. "Just rest. We'll talk when you're on the mend." To seal the promise in his words, he leaned forward and kissed the Admiral's soft lips. He might have said more, but the green eyes closed once more, Peter's breath growing raspier with each breath. More scared than he had been since he realized the depth of cruelty the Gavenelians possessed, he turned to the control panel again, trying to figure out where he could find more power for the engines. He was already running on the barest of life support. Glancing back to the emergency gear, he made a decision. He fitted a breathing mask over

Peter's face and placed a second mask over his own, then cut the gravity and life support systems as well.

Moving carefully and trying not to remember the Admiral yanking his cord about helping a crewmate in need of assistance during his zero-g training, Blaise grabbed Peter's uninjured arm with one hand and the waist-high struts lining the walls with the other, pulling them cautiously out of the cockpit and down the corridor to his cabin. He secured Peter to the bed with the leg straps, arranging him on his uninjured side to avoid pressure on any of the burns, then angled himself down behind the Admiral. He spooned around Peter, fastening the chest strap across his own torso and pulling the one space blanket over them both. It would get pretty damn chilly before they reached Eudorae Prime, but not enough to kill them.

WHY did prison cells have to be so damn small? Blaise growled silently as he paced the confines of the brig where he'd been summarily thrown upon his arrival on Eudorae Prime. The Confederation personnel had whisked Peter away to be treated for his burns. They'd checked Blaise as well, but as soon as they ascertained he was unharmed, he'd been locked up without so much as a thank-you for saving their precious Admiral. He wouldn't have minded that so much if someone would just tell him how Peter was doing.

"Hey!" he shouted, pounding on the cell door. "Somebody answer me!"

He was beside himself with worry. It had been hours. Surely there was some news by now. He'd told the authorities that he and Peter were on a Confederation mission, but nobody seemed to believe him, particularly since he wouldn't elaborate beyond that. He couldn't, not without talking to Peter and Harry first.

He knew Peter intended to use the information they got from Harry in the war effort, but he didn't know who Peter wanted to tell. Likewise, he could hardly give up Harry's discovery for nothing. He owed it to his old friend to make sure the Andromedite got credit for his work—and preferably payment as well. On the other hand, Harry had used the word *mate* when he referred to Peter. Not first mate, as he was always careful to say when talking about Garrett. Just mate. He'd understand.

"What do you want, pirate?" the prison guard demanded, answering Blaise's shout.

"I just want to know how the Admiral's doing," Blaise replied pleadingly. "Is he all right?"

"What do you care?" the guard retorted.

But he did care. That was the realization he'd come to while locked up in here. The *Golden Stallion* had been impounded again, no surprise there, but Blaise had discovered the thought didn't even bother him next to his worry for Peter. They could have the ship. Just give him his Admiral back.

"Let me talk to the base commander," Blaise insisted.

"Why?" the guard demanded.

"I have some information he might find useful," Blaise offered cagily, "but in return I want to see the Admiral."

IT had taken some fast talking with the base commander, but the man had finally ordered Blaise escorted to the Admiral's bedside. The soldier wouldn't leave Blaise alone with Peter, so there wouldn't be any chance to touch the beloved face, to see if his touch would rouse his lover from his unconscious state, but at least he could look, could see for himself that Peter was alive.

He was so swathed in bandages that Blaise wouldn't have recognized him except for the golden hair above the dressings. The hand that had shielded his face was so thickly wrapped that Blaise couldn't even identify the individual fingers. "Will he lose the use of his hand?" he asked the medic who came in at that moment to check the Admiral's vitals.

"It's too soon to tell," she answered honestly. "I've seen worse burns, but not often."

Blaise nodded his thanks, face falling at the thought of Peter's injuries. The Admiral would surely hate him now since it was his ship that had caused the wounds. "When he wakes up, tell him…."

Tell him what? There wasn't anything to say that he'd entrust to a stranger except platitudes, and Blaise didn't want to pass on any of those. "Never mind. I'll tell him myself the next time I see him."

The medic looked at him strangely, but shrugged. She didn't have the time or energy to get involved in every patient's private life.

Turning to the soldier, Blaise squared his shoulders. "Let's go talk to the base commander. He kept his part of the bargain. I'll keep mine."

GENTLE but relentless hands probed at Peter, sending spikes of pain lancing through him, though not the raw agony he remembered. Everything around him was darkened, deadened; a low, steady hum filled his ears, an acrid scent he recognized but couldn't identify irritating his chest as he breathed. He vaguely remembered flashes of blinding light, of noise, of pain. Sickbay, he realized slowly through dulled senses; likely drugged. Had they made it back to the *North Star*? He strained to pick out voices from the buzz around him, sure for a moment he'd heard Blaise, but then it was gone. Fear suddenly gnawed him. *Is Blaise hurt too?* He tried to open his eyes, but wasn't sure if he had. It was all still dark. "Blaise?" he called, the name coming out a strangled whisper.

"Easy," a female voice said, touching his arm, and then the darkness expanded and Peter didn't remember any more for a long while.

The next time he struggled to consciousness, the pain was still there, but muted; either they'd eased back the drugs or his body had recovered enough to function despite them. The sickbay definitely wasn't the *North Star*'s, though. He was looking around for some sign of Blaise when a white-clad medic paused at his bed. "Where am I?" Peter asked, his voice still rasping.

"Eudorae Prime," the medic replied easily. "And if you're awake enough to be asking, then you're finally on the mend. How do you feel?"

It took a moment for Peter to place the planet, proof to himself that his mental processes were still dulled. "Like hell," he admitted. "How long have I been out?"

"Three days," the medic replied. "I can give you something for the pain if you want, but the chief medical officer really wants us to start weaning you off of it before you get addicted. Think you can stand to wait another hour before I give you more?"

Three days, and Blaise wasn't here with him? "I'll manage." He frowned. "The other man on the ship—Blaise Risner—was he hurt?"

"The pirate?" the medic asked. "No, he's fine. They have him safely locked in the brig awaiting your orders in his regard."

"The brig?" Peter snapped. "He saved my life. He—" Peter broke off, knowing the medic didn't have the authority to order Blaise released. He needed to report their findings about the Gavenelians, too. "Who's the commanding officer here? I need to speak with him at once."

"Commander Rigatelli," the medic answered. "I'll let him know you'd like to speak with him, but he's a very busy man, especially these days."

"Maybe I didn't make myself clear," Peter responded in a voice his crew had learned meant trouble. "Tell *Commander* Rigatelli that *Admiral* Keller expects to see him within thirty minutes. Unless you'd like me to set off all your alarms by tracking him down myself?"

The medic frowned. He doubted the Admiral was actually strong enough to carry out his threats, but he didn't want to see his hard work undone. "I'll pass on the message, but the rest is up to the commander."

"Unless he wants to get broken back to ensign, he'll get his ass down here on the double," Peter muttered, leaning back against the sickbed as the medic scuttled off. Despite his assurance, the pain was building again, making him wonder how bad his injuries really were. Bad enough to keep him unconscious for three days had to be pretty damn bad. His left hand was swallowed in bandages that continued up his arm and around his chest. Peter touched his sternum lightly with his unbandaged hand, just the brush of his fingertips sending pangs slicing along his rib cage. He traced the sterile dressing up his neck and along the side of his face and skull, pain flaring beneath his touch. He'd really managed to fuck himself up, hadn't he? No wonder Blaise hadn't tried to see him. Fairness made him reject the thought as soon as it occurred. The man was in the brig, after all; what did Peter expect him to do—break out just to visit him? Still, Peter knew he couldn't fool himself. Blaise might have put up with his attentions, even started to enjoy them, but that was before Peter had nearly gotten his precious ship blown up and, it seemed, burned half his face off in the process. He could no longer expect things to go forward the way he'd begun to hope; but he owed Blaise his life, and Peter always paid his debts.

"You rang, Your Excellency?" Commander Rigatelli drawled, walking into Sickbay, more than a little put out at being summoned like a foot soldier.

Ignoring the pain, Peter pulled himself erect, clenching a fist to keep from clutching at the bed to stop himself from swaying. His gaze raked over the base commander from head to toe and back again, a glare that had reduced stronger men than Rigatelli to quivering subservience. *But not Blaise*, Peter's thoughts intruded. The smuggler had never been afraid of him, even when coerced into submission. Peter forced his mind back to the task at hand, his silence only unnerving the commander more.

"Get rid of the attitude, Commander," he demanded, his voice low since he wasn't sure how long it would hold out. "In case you've forgotten, in the event of an act of war, I have authority to take command of this station and everyone on it. That includes you," he reminded the younger officer. "So instead of mouthing off, I suggest you work with me. We'll both be much happier that way."

"What act of war?" the commander demanded. "A bunch of rogue pirates hardly counts as a hostile force."

"The raid on Zaniah wasn't the work of pirates, and neither were any of the earlier attacks," Peter retorted. "The only reason the Confederation isn't already at war is that we didn't know the identity of our enemy—until now. Captain Risner has identified the attackers as a race calling themselves Gavenelians. Based on his prior experience with them, we not only know who they are, but how to hit them back. Now, do you want my report to Galactic Command to include your obstruction of my orders? Or are you more intelligent than you look?"

"Sir," the commander said, snapping to attention. "As you say, sir. The prisoner already gave us the information you obtained on your mission, although we didn't realize how serious the threat was. We'll get busy outfitting the base with the new weapons. I hope that meets with your approval."

Blaise had been busy, Peter mused, impressed but not really surprised. His pirate had as much concern in stopping the Gavenelians as anyone. Maybe that was why he hadn't had time to stop in Sickbay.... "I'm sure Captain Risner has been a great help in that effort," he observed.

Rigatelli frowned. "He's been confined to the brig where he belongs, Admiral," he explained defensively. "He's a prisoner. What was he even doing off your ship?"

"Is that any of your concern, Commander?" Peter exploded. "The man brought you information to counter a galactic threat to the Confederation, not to mention saving the life of one of its Admirals, and you keep him locked in the brig like some common criminal?" His skull was beginning to throb, and as much as he wanted to tear this petty bureaucrat's head off his shoulders and shove it up his ass, he didn't have the strength to keep fighting, especially since he suspected he'd face the same argument with his superiors at Galactic Command. Reaching a quick decision, he turned on the spluttering officer. "I want the fastest shuttle on this base to return Captain Risner to my ship at once," he ordered. "I want the ship we arrived on searched from stem to stern—I suspect there's some sort of homing device that let the Gavenelians find us, and unless you want a fleet of them arriving on your doorstep, I suggest you find it and deactivate it as soon as possible. And I want a secure comm link at my disposal immediately. Do I make myself clear?"

"Yes, sir, Admiral," Rigatelli answered with a sharp salute, glad of an excuse to get out of Sickbay and away from this dressing down. He'd followed regulations! How was he supposed to know the Admiral expected the prisoner to get special treatment? "I'll get my comm officer to establish the link here in Sickbay and get on the rest of your orders immediately."

"Dismissed," Peter nodded, waiting until the sickbay door hissed shut before sinking back to his bed with a muffled groan.

BLAISE looked up in surprise when an ensign released the energy shield that kept him confined in his cell. It wasn't time for him to eat, which was the only time he'd seen anyone since he'd been returned to his cell following his visit to Sickbay.

"On your feet, Risner," the ensign ordered. "You're leaving."

"What?" Blaise asked, confused. "Where am I going?"

"Back to the *North Star*," the ensign replied. "Admiral's orders."

Blaise relaxed immediately. Peter. The Admiral must not have been hurt as badly as everyone thought. "Let's go, then."

As he'd come to expect on Eudorae Prime, the energy manacles on his wrists snapped into place, forcing his arms behind his back before he was allowed to leave the cell, but he didn't protest. They'd be back on the *Golden Stallion* soon, on their way home, and Peter would take the ridiculous devices off again. He followed the ensign through the corridors to the shuttle bay.

"That's not my ship!" he exclaimed when he saw the Confederation shuttle waiting for him.

"Of course not," the ensign replied. "Your ship's being torn apart so they can find the homing beacon on it. We don't want the creepies using it to track us down."

"No!" Blaise roared, pain slicing through him at the thought of anything happening to the *Stallion*. "You can't do that."

"Admiral's orders."

"Where is he?" Blaise insisted. "I know he wouldn't order that. Is he already on the shuttle?"

"The Admiral's still in Sickbay, pirate. It'll be weeks before he's well enough to go anywhere," the ensign replied, pushing the prisoner toward the ship. "Go on. The shuttle's waiting."

Peter wasn't going with him. Blaise's stomach clenched. "No," he spat, beginning to struggle in earnest. "I'm in the Admiral's personal custody. I have to stay here with him."

"Admiral's orders," the ensign said again, hitting the surge button on the remote for the manacles. A burst of energy shot through the bracelets, stunning Risner enough to take the fight out of him for a moment. The ensign pushed him a few more steps toward the ship before Blaise shook off the effects and started struggling again. With a frown, the ensign increased the shockwave, stunning him a second time. When even that only fazed him for a minute, he turned it on constant. "I'll turn it off when you're on that shuttle," he ground out in Risner's ear. "Now walk or I'll increase the power again."

Shoulders slumping, Blaise gave in. He couldn't get away, even if he managed to break free from the ensign. He still refused to believe Peter had ordered this, but what could he do? At least on the *North Star*, he knew the officers. Maybe they'd help him get to the bottom of this. And get the Admiral back where he belonged. Unless....

As the door to the shuttle closed behind him and the ship took off, a sickening thought took root. Was this Peter's way of getting rid of him, of saying he'd outlived his usefulness now that he'd gotten the information from Harry? Surely not. They'd made love that last time on the *Stallion,* no matter that it was up against the bulkhead rather than in bed. Hadn't they? Had he completely misread the look on Peter's face, the lightness of his tone as they landed at Harry's base? Even more importantly, had Harry, with his instinctive grasp of emotions that defied explanation, misread Peter's intentions? His friend had referred to Peter as Blaise's mate. That had to mean something. Didn't it?

He'd been so sure they'd have time to work everything out. *Fuck!* He should have waited for Peter to wake up before telling what he knew. At least that way, he could have seen for himself if Peter was done with him. He sighed, biting his lip to hold back a frustrated shout. He'd just have to wait for the Admiral to return to his ship and demand answers then.

PETER waited impatiently for his call to navigate the morass of protocol and identity checks required to gain access to the Admiralty High Command. As soon as he was done with this call, he'd contact Commander Dmitrov on the *North Star*, forward him the information Harry had provided, and let him know Blaise would be heading back soon. He'd be safer on board Peter's ship, in his own quarters, until Peter could make all the necessary arrangements and get back to the *North Star* himself.

A bleep sounded on the comm unit and Peter's superior officer, High Admiral Orell Hendershott, appeared on the vidscreen. "As I'm sure you heard by now, we've uncovered information about the perpetrators of the attacks," Peter began, when the senior officer interrupted.

"What in the name of the Seven Suns did you think you were doing, Keller?" Hendershott shouted. "Taking off on some half-baked scheme without authorization? Bringing a prisoner with you, in a private vessel? Are you out of your mind? Do you have any idea what the news outlets are saying about this?"

Stunned, Peter swallowed his indignation, knowing that losing his temper with his superior would only make things worse. "With all due respect, sir, I had a lead on a source of information that was reluctant to deal with Confederation bureaucracy. Approaching him in an official capacity would only have frightened him away. And if we'd been on a Confederation vessel, even one operating without markings, we'd be dead by now. Without that private vessel's speed, the Gavenelians would have caught up with us before we could report our information."

"This isn't the first time you've pulled this kind of rogue stunt, but by the galactic core, it's going to be the last!" Hendershott countered. "The Admiralty's turned a blind eye to your antics in the past, Keller, but you've gone too far this time! Consorting with criminals, ignoring the chain of command—"

"*Vithr* shit!" Peter protested, his own anger getting the best of him. "You're just too embarrassed to admit that a pair of smugglers uncovered more information about these attacks than the Admiralty's been able to find since they started!"

Hendershott's image visibly gritted his teeth. "If it were up to me, Keller, you'd be broken back to ensign on supply runs to the scrapyards of Ephicuus," the High Admiral complained. "Unfortunately, you and that pair of pirates are all over the galactic newsgrids. I don't know how those muckrakers got their information, but they knew about the Gavenelians almost as soon as we did. There's been a public outcry for the Confederation to take immediate action. We can't afford the black eye we'd get from disciplining you the way you deserve. In fact," he paused, and it was obvious to Peter that whatever his commanding officer was about to say was being dragged from him with the utmost reluctance, "in fact, I've been authorized to promote you, effective immediately, to Fleet Admiral. You're to report to Galactic Command as soon as you're fit to travel."

"Galactic Command?" Peter objected. "Stuck planetside pushing papers when there's a war going on? There's no way I'd agree to that. You need me on the *North Star*, fighting the Gavenelians."

"I can have you declared unfit for duty faster than that pirate vessel you commandeered can hit light speed," Hendershott interjected. "You don't seem to understand, Keller; you don't have a choice in the matter. You've made your own rules for the last time. You're grounded."

Hendershott's vindictive smile as he signed off set Peter's stomach to roiling. More thankful than ever that he was sending Blaise to the *North Star* before Galactic Command could get their hands on him, he punched the comm link to hail the base commander. "Rigatelli, have your men send Captain Risner up to see me," he ordered, rubbing at the pounding pulse at the base of his skull.

"He's already on his way back to your ship," the base commander answered, his voice faltering at the Admiral's incensed glare. "You did say you wanted him returned at once," he offered in justification. "We've already started tearing the pirate vessel apart, as well. We won't leave two bolts joined together until we find that homing device."

"I didn't say to rip the ship apart, you imbecile!" Peter shouted, pain lancing through his head and his heart. Blaise was gone, without his having had a chance to talk with him, to thank him, to…. There was nothing Peter could do about that now, but at least he could keep Blaise's ship from being destroyed by the base crew's overzealousness. "If there's a knob out of place by the time you're done with it, I'll have your commission. Now get me the specs you received from Captain Risner and then find that homing beacon." He was going to have a long talk with Commander Dmitrov; at least on the *North Star*, he could still be sure his orders would be obeyed.

For a little while longer, anyway.

CHAPTER 14
FALLOUT

THE two-day trip back to the *North Star* seemed even longer, if possible, than the trip out. Blaise hadn't been happy with Peter, but at least he'd known where the Admiral was and where he stood with him. As it was now, he had only his persistent doubts to keep him company since the soldiers on board the shuttle refused to have anything to do with a prisoner.

He spent his time mentally reviewing his options. Peter had ordered him returned to the *North Star*, not sent to the Delta Auriga penal colony, which gave Blaise hope that the Admiral intended to return to him eventually. So maybe he was being sent back so he could help prepare the flagship for battle with the Gavenelians. Blaise wasn't under any illusions that Peter would wait for the aliens to come to them. His question to Harry about the homing beacon had been quite clear. With the new, functional weapons, he intended to take the war to them rather than waiting for them to prey upon helpless settlements again, a sentiment Blaise heartily approved.

He could do that. He could help Commander Dmitrov and the rest of the *North Star's* crew outfit the ship with the new weapons, and he could get back in contact with Harry and hope the Andromedite would be willing to tell him any new information over the comm link instead of requiring another visit. That would be impossible now, since the *Golden Stallion* was still on Eudorae Prime (hopefully in one piece) and since Peter wasn't there to go with him even on another ship.

The change in the sound of the ship's engines alerted him to their arrival at their destination. He couldn't see the *North Star* from his cabin on the shuttle since it had no windows, but he monitored the approach in the speed of the ship. Eventually, a soldier came for him, locking the energy manacles back in place as he was escorted through the shuttle to the docking bay.

"Commander Dmitrov," he said with a nod of his head when he saw Peter's albino second-in-command.

"Risner," the commander acknowledged, frowning at the halting pace Blaise moved forward, restricted by the energy manacles. "I think we can do without those," he addressed the courier from the shuttle, the soft tone of his voice belying its underlying command. The soldier shrugged and thumbed off the power, leaving Blaise to catch his footing as the shuttle hatch snapped shut in preparation for departure.

"Admiral Keller forwarded the specs of the weapons enhancements," Dmitrov continued as he escorted Blaise from the shuttle deck. "I've got the engineering crew studying them right now. Lieutenant Royce would like to speak with you once you're settled in. He had a few questions he wanted clarified before tearing into the main power array."

Blaise breathed a quiet sigh of relief. Whatever else was going on, Peter hadn't cut him off completely or else he'd have been thrown in the brig here as well. "I don't have anything to settle," he assured the commander, "although something to drink wouldn't go amiss."

"The mess, then, or do you just want to catch something from the cabin before we head down to Engineering?" Dmitrov asked, pausing when Blaise didn't immediately follow him down the turn in the corridor to the Admiral's quarters. "You'd make Royce a happy man if you see him sooner rather than later," he added with a smile. That was putting it mildly. His assistant had been wearing him out with demands to know when they could start on the reconfiguration.

Blaise's brows raised when he realized where Dmitrov was leading him. "I'll just grab something from the cabin," he decided, reminding himself that he'd been coming and going from these rooms for over a month and that he didn't need to feel awkward about it when it was Peter's decision in the first place. "I've been up against those bastards twice now. I don't want to face them unprepared again."

Dmitrov nodded; he'd heard enough from the scout ship crew and seen enough from the surface of Zaniah to want a piece of the perpetrators of those atrocities himself. "Admiral Keller made it very clear that without your help, and your friend's, we'd still be in the dark about who we're up against," he said. "I want you to know that the crew of this ship appreciates it, even if Galactic Command doesn't. That, and for saving the Admiral's life. He might be a right bastard at times, but he's our bastard," Sasha grinned, offering Blaise his hand.

Blaise chuckled, taking the outstretched hand. "He is that," he agreed, letting the commander decide how to interpret the comment. He grabbed a bottle of something cold and fizzy from the mini-fridge and cracked it open, taking a long swig. "Let's go see what Royce needs to get started."

THREE days in the base sickbay had Peter close to climbing out of his skin at the inactivity, but it had given him plenty of time to think. By the time he'd confirmed with Dmitrov that Blaise was back on the *North Star*, working alongside the engineering crew to retrofit the cruiser's weapons systems to Harry's designs, he'd made some decisions, and took advantage of the private comm link (which the base commander had been too intimidated—or too determined to avoid further contact with the Admiral—to remove) to begin making arrangements. Galactic Command would discover that he wasn't a mindless robot drone they could program to suit their orders. After several commcalls that were definitely non-regulation, his next contact was strictly official: to the High Court of the Sirius quadrant.

"Peter," Lapis's warm voice came over the comm as the vid capabilities kicked in. "What can I.... Great heavens, what have you done to yourself? You look awful!" she exclaimed, interrupting herself as she got a good look at the burns on the Admiral's face, now uncovered to let the air encourage healing.

"And all this time I thought it was my vibrant personality that attracted you, not my looks," Peter countered dryly.

"Well, it certainly wasn't your prowess in bed," she sniped tartly, since despite her attempts, she hadn't even gotten anywhere near the Admiral's bunk.

"If I thought either of us would have appreciated it, I would have invited you before now, but I doubt you'd care to share my bed at the moment," Peter replied. "We took some damage from the ships that have been attacking our outposts, but what we've learned is more than worth it. It could be the edge we need, if the Admiralty isn't too blind to use it."

"That is good news," Lapis agreed. "You know I trust you implicitly," she went on seriously, "but as High Justice, I have to ask. Who has custody of your prisoner while you're in a sickbed on... Eudorae Prime?"

"He's back on the *North Star*," Peter answered, ignoring the ache of emptiness the words engendered. "My second-in-command has him in hand." Gritting his teeth against Lapis's smirk at the innuendo, he shifted to a marginally more comfortable position. "Though I'd like to make you aware of some information that could change that."

"What information?" Lapis demanded sharply, sitting forward at the idea that something might disrupt her bargain with Peter. Nothing they did was strictly illegal, but neither was it completely within the bounds of the law either.

"Everything the Admiralty has learned about the Gavenelians, the race behind the attacks, is a direct result of information provided by Blaise Risner," Peter stated. "Given the value of that information to the Confederation, I propose that the remainder of Risner's sentence be commuted."

"You don't ask for much, do you?" Lapis asked in surprise. "You know this is highly unusual."

"Our entire relationship has been highly unusual," Peter snorted. "This is hardly the time to start standing on principles now." He squeezed the back of his neck, resisting the temptation to rub the healing skin. "Risner and his contacts have already given the Confederation their first advantage in this war. Throwing him back in a brig is hardly the way to incent him to share any more information."

"You didn't promise him early parole for his information, I hope," Lapis warned, "because that's not a promise you can keep. And if this information is so vital, why are you the one calling me and not Galactic Command?"

"Galactic Command couldn't find the Triangulum Nebula with both hands and an emission spectrometer," Peter growled. "Besides, are you telling me you'd let the Admiralty give you orders on sentencing and parole?"

"I don't take orders from anyone," Lapis snapped immediately, "including you, so drop the attitude and tell me what's really behind this request. Given what I saw when I visited the *North Star*, I'd have thought you'd want me to extend his sentence so you could keep him longer. Now, tell me what's going on, or I'll send him to the Auriga Colony like I should have when he was first sentenced."

"Damn it, Lapis, he's the one who should be rewarded as a hero, not me," Peter snapped. "All I did was damn near get us caught because I'm as out of practice at flying a real ship as the rawest Academy plebe. The Admiralty want to 'promote' me to a desk job where I can't embarrass them by my—'rogue stunts', I think Hendershott called them." Scowling, Peter leaned forward to meet Lapis's eyes through the parsecs of space between them. "I can't—won't—leave Blaise unprotected for the rest of his sentence. He doesn't deserve that."

"It's not a crime to admit you love him," Lapis pointed out softly.

"I never thought you were a romantic, Lapis," Peter sneered, the pull at his scars accounting for the pain that lanced through him. "He was a—" Peter glanced away from the screen at the dressing still coating his hand, unable to make himself dismiss Blaise as just a good fuck. "He went beyond the conditions of his sentence," he said finally. "He deserves consideration for that."

"Then you won't mind scheduling another inspection visit and letting me put him through his paces this time," she gambled. "After all, I can hardly justify releasing him without making sure he's rehabilitated first."

"There will be no more damned inspection visits!" Peter erupted. "The Confederation is at war, or will be as soon as we find the Gavenelians' home base, and the *North Star* will be leading the attack, not ferrying you about to play your games! Either agree to commute his sentence, or I'll go above your head to someone who will!"

Lapis's face hardened, but she'd done all she could. The rest was up to Keller and his pirate. "The orders will be waiting for you when you return to the *North Star*," she told him coldly. "You'll have to return there to access them. What you do after that is up to you, but don't come asking for my assistance again."

"You won't have to worry about that," Peter assured her, ready to cut the connection when his anger died as suddenly as it had flared. "Thank you, Lapis," he added softly. "Whatever you think of me, it's the right thing to do."

"I hope you're right," she agreed. He was a stubborn bastard, but she thought maybe the pirate was stubborn enough to match him. Now if only they'd take the chance she was giving them.

THE two weeks since his return to the *North Star* had passed far more quickly than Blaise would have expected without Peter there, but they were preparing the ship for battle, and that meant far more than just jury-rigging a system here and there like Blaise had done on the *Golden Stallion*. He'd earned a new respect for Sasha Dmitrov and Billy Royce, for the entire crew, honestly, in that time. They'd asked questions—detailed, intelligent questions—but they hadn't doubted his experience once he shared it with them.

The ship was as battle-ready as his current knowledge could make it at this point. All that remained was to wait for the Admiral's return so they could go in search of the enemy. Blaise wished they knew a little better how to shield against the Gavenelian weapons, but at least they now had a weapons system of their own that could take out the enemy vessels.

With a sigh, he tossed restlessly on the Admiral's bed. Dmitrov had been so confident in returning Blaise to these quarters that he'd stayed even though he wasn't completely comfortable with the idea of being here without Peter. That explained why he'd had so much trouble sleeping. And if he said it often enough, he might even believe it.

The truth of the matter was, he missed the other man's warmth, the comfort of his presence. The nightmares had returned full force, leaving him sweating and trembling in the middle of the night, curled tightly around Peter's pillow in the hope of replacing the images of torture with images of his lover. Sometimes, it worked.

PETER fired the braking thrusters, maneuvering the *Golden Stallion* into the docking slip of the *North Star* with careful precision. Blaise would never forgive him if he damaged his precious ship a second time! It really was a sweet-handling beauty; Peter had enjoyed the flight back, even if the lingering pain from his injuries made sleeping difficult. The medics on Eudorae Prime had wanted to keep him longer, but Peter needed to get back to the *North Star*, back to check on the progress of the modifications... back to Blaise. Being on Blaise's ship, surrounded by constant reminders of the man, had only made Peter all the more conscious of what he was returning to. He was ready to swear he could smell Blaise's scent in the recycled air; thoughts of him filled Peter's mind whenever he let it wander, which seemed to be more and more often as the *Stallion*'s powerful engines closed the distance between them.

Once he stepped aboard the *North Star,* though, duty and responsibility seemed to settle back over Peter like an unseen uniform. He glanced around quickly when he stepped out of the docking hatch onto his ship, but only Sasha Dmitrov was waiting to greet him.

"Welcome home, Admiral," the commander greeted him, though privately Dmitrov was horrified by the extent of his senior officer's injuries. "It's good to have you back on board."

"How are the weapons modifications coming?" Peter asked, dismissing the welcome with a nod. He might once have thought of the *North Star* as home, but he was disturbed to find to find his concern was less for the ship than for one specific passenger. Still, he couldn't bring himself to ask Dmitrov about Blaise; at least, not yet. He hadn't missed the slight narrowing of his chief engineer's eyes at his appearance; Sasha's poker face served him well at the command staff's weekly games, but Peter wasn't fooled. He'd been thinking of Blaise the entire flight back to the *North Star*, but now he wasn't sure he was ready to face him.

"You must be tired of civvies," Dmitrov commented discreetly. "I'm sure you'd like to change back into your uniform before we begin the inspection of the new weapons system, fully functional thanks to Risner's assistance."

"I'll swing by my quarters on the way to Engineering," Peter agreed. Pausing as Dmitrov started to turn away, Peter added, "Thank you, Sasha—for everything. The *North Star* couldn't be in better hands."

"She's back in your hands now, where she belongs, sir," Dmitrov demurred. "I just kept her running for you."

Glancing down at his hands, still scarred from the plasma burns, Peter frowned. He needed to talk to Blaise before saying anything more to his executive officer. "I'll meet you in Engineering," he repeated before heading down the corridor to his quarters.

He'd hoped he might find Blaise there, but there was no sign of the other man. Peter pulled on his uniform as quickly as he could, the fastenings awkward to his stiff fingers. Well, he wouldn't need to worry about that much longer. As he sat on the bunk to struggle with his boots, he thought he caught a hint of Blaise's scent in the bedding; he wondered if he was imagining it, the same way he thought he'd sensed Blaise's essence aboard the *Stallion*. Finally dressed, Peter examined himself in the mirror. The long uniform sleeves hid the worst of the scarring on his arms, but nothing could hide the disfigurement of his face and throat. The medics on Eudorae Prime had talked about the possibility of skin grafts and cloning in time, but Peter didn't have the luxury or the patience to wait the months they counseled. Squaring his shoulders against the pull of half-healed tissue, he headed out the door toward Engineering.

The news of the Admiral's return spread through the ship at light-speed. Blaise cursed his timing silently. A few minutes sooner and he would still have been in Peter's cabin, giving them the privacy they needed for the conversation that would surely follow. As it was, they'd have to enact their reunion under the watchful eyes of the entire engineering team. He'd just have to refrain from flinging himself at the Admiral the moment he walked through the door.

"Admiral on deck!"

The call brought every member of the crew in the room to attention and a smile to Blaise's face as he turned to greet his lover. He'd known the burns were bad, but he couldn't stop the sympathetic wince when he saw the extent of the scarring on Peter's face. Knowing any comment to that effect would be unwelcome in public, he held back, letting the crew greet the Admiral first. This was one more score he had to settle with the Gavenelians.

His crew's reaction as they realized the extent of their Admiral's injuries was no more than Peter expected. Not all of them were as adept at hiding their shock as Dmitrov had been. He met each greeting with a short nod, eyes sweeping the large room until he caught sight of Blaise in conversation with Lieutenant Royce. Holding in his own response to the first sight of his lover in more than a week, Peter watched Blaise glance up and smile, the expression freezing when the younger man got a good look at Peter's face. He actually flinched back, turning his head away to listen to something the assistant engineer was saying.

Peter's gut clenched at Blaise's revealing reaction. He'd let himself hope, during the flight back to the *North Star*, that he might be able to share his plans for the future with Blaise, but now he knew that would never happen. Blaise hadn't expected to see him, and hadn't been able to disguise his instinctive repugnance at Peter's appearance. Peter cursed himself for a fool for expecting anything else.

He completed his inspection of the adaptations Royce had made to the weapons systems, nodding silently at the engineer's praise of Blaise's assistance. By the time the Lieutenant had described in painstaking detail every modification and test they'd performed, Peter's head was throbbing and his arm and chest ached. Commending the engineering team for their efforts, he was tempted to return to his quarters, but knew he needed to tour the rest of the ship first, make the rounds and let himself be seen by the rest of the crew. It would give him that much more time before he'd have to speak with Blaise.

Blaise could see the pain and fatigue on Peter's face, despite the Admiral's best attempts at hiding it. Making his excuses to Royce, he slipped out of the Engineering room, sure Peter would head for his quarters to rest. He'd meet his lover there and show him how much he'd missed him. It bothered him that the Admiral hadn't spoken to him, had barely acknowledged him in front of the others, but he reminded himself that to them, he was just Peter's prisoner. Nobody else knew the true extent of their relationship. He'd waited this long; he could bide his time a little longer.

Impatiently, Blaise paced the room, waiting for Peter to arrive. Had he been so discreet in his exit that Peter didn't realize he was leaving to meet him? As minutes passed and the door still didn't open, Blaise's stomach sank. Maybe Sasha had been wrong all along. Maybe the Admiral didn't want him still. Maybe.... As the minutes stretched on, the dread grew, and with it, his anger at himself for falling under the Admiral's spell and at the Admiral for making him think this might be more than just a diversion. By the time the door finally opened, Blaise was spoiling for a fight.

"What the hell took you so long?"

The pain in his skull rocketed upward at the harsh tone of Blaise's greeting. "Nice to see you, too," Peter snarled, letting the cabin door snap shut behind him and doing his utmost not to sag back against it. "Been making yourself at home while I was gone?" He didn't give a damn if Blaise had been staying in his quarters, but as the pounding in his head grew, all he wanted was to get this over with as quickly as possible so he could collapse on his bunk. Drinking himself into insensibility sounded like a damn fine idea, too. Anything to stop the pain, if only for the moment.

"I don't issue the orders around here, as you're quick to remind me," Blaise snapped back, all his fears coalescing when Peter greeted him in such a surly tone. "I just go where I'm told and try to make myself useful."

"According to Lieutenant Royce, you made yourself damn near indispensable," Peter countered. That was what he'd wanted, wasn't it? There was no reason that seeing Blaise standing next to the junior officer should set his pulse pounding. No reason at all.

"Was I supposed to withhold information?" Blaise demanded, the tone of Peter's voice grating on his nerves. Could he do no right? "We went to all the trouble to get it from Harry so your crew, your Confederation, would be able to stop the Gavenelians. Or did I misunderstand?"

Peter shook his head, the rasp of skin beneath his uniform collar adding another layer to the agony engulfing him. "No, you didn't misunderstand," he grated. "You did exactly what I ordered. That's all you've ever done, isn't it?"

"That's all you've ever let me do," Blaise pointed out harshly. "Every time I try to do more—or less—you shoot me down for it. You've made it very clear you want a mindless automaton who bends over when you need a hole to fuck and keeps his mouth shut any other time. Well, I'm sorry, but I'm more than just a robot to serve at your pleasure. If you'll excuse me, I'll return to my quarters."

Your pleasure. Blaise was making it perfectly clear he didn't find any pleasure in their time together—and that he couldn't wait to get away now. "Fine," Peter snapped, taking the pouch of papers from his desk and tossing it at the smuggler. "You can pack your things to take with you when you leave. You've been granted a full pardon for the remainder of your sentence in recognition of your contributions toward identifying the Gavenelians." He turned away, his voice muffled. "You're free to go."

"Whole hell of a lot of good that does me with my ship in pieces on Eudorae Prime," Blaise snarled, his mind reeling at the sight of his remission papers. Free to go? What the hell did that mean? Peter just wanted him to walk away from whatever had been building between them? Fine. Fuck him. He'd take the papers and see if he could snag a ride back to the Algol system. Harry would let him crash there until he could find a new ship.

"Your ship is waiting for you in the docking bay. You'll find the paperwork in there along with your pardon." Of course, the only thing that mattered to Blaise was his precious ship. "The techs on Eudorae managed to find the second homing device your friends left on board, so you should be able to stay out of any more trouble." Peter gripped the edge of his desk, locking his knees to keep himself upright. He'd walk out of the docking port without a spacesuit before he'd let Blaise see his weakness. "Of course, if you break Confederation law again, I won't be around to intercede for you a second time."

"Then I'll just have to make sure I don't get caught, won't I?" Blaise asked jauntily, grabbing the papers before Peter could change his mind. "It's been... interesting, Admiral," he added from the door. He paused for a moment, the feelings nothing had been able to extinguish welling up more strongly than he'd expected. "Take care of yourself," he murmured softly, wishing he had the right to be the one taking care of the other man, but that clearly wasn't meant to be. They couldn't even be in the same room without arguing. With a final nod in Peter's general direction, he left the cabin and headed for the docking bay and his freedom. He had the rest of his life before him, so why did it feel like his dreams were coming to an end?

As soon as the door closed behind Blaise, Peter slid to his knees, still clinging to the edge of the desk. His head fell forward against his forearm, tears of pain springing to his eyes. For just a moment he knelt there, the wave of agony nearly overwhelming him, and then he pushed himself to his feet. He needed to talk to Dmitrov, to hand over command of the *North Star* and submit his formal resignation to the Admiralty. Sasha could drop him off at the next planet they made orbit around. It didn't much matter to Peter where that was. All he wanted right now was to get the fuck out of uniform for the last time and do something—anything—to make the pain stop.

CHAPTER 15

AFTERBURN

FOR the past thirteen months, he'd wanted nothing more than to get back aboard the *Golden Stallion* and as far away from the Admiralty and the Confederation as she could take him. And now that he had his wish, Blaise wanted more than anything to be back on the *North Star* in Peter's arms. Except that the Peter he thought he knew, the Peter he wanted to be with, was a figment of his imagination. That much had been clear from the moment the Admiral stepped foot on his ship again.

Fuck him, then. Blaise had been fine before he'd gotten tangled up with the two-faced lying son of a bitch. He'd be fine again. Setting a heading for the Algol system, he put his ship on autopilot and headed for the captain's quarters, intending to take a long, hot shower to wash the last of the Confederation taint off his skin. He got three steps into the small room when he froze, the sight of the unmade bed drawing him up short. He was sure he'd straightened the covers on his bunk the last time he'd slept there, before they docked on Eudorae Prime, with Peter tucked up against him to share their warmth in the frigid temperature—but the blankets were bunched at the end of the bed, the pillows tossed every which way. He took another step and Peter's scent wrapped around his senses. His heart clenched, every muscle in his body tense with longing.

You've really got it bad, Risner, he scolded himself. *Of course he slept here. This is the captain's cabin and he's always the one in fucking charge.*

Angrily, he pulled the sheets off the bed and shoved them in the recycler. He'd deal with them later, but he knew he'd never get any rest at all on a bunk that smelled like his lover. Ex-lover. Grunting at his own stupidity, he stepped into the 'fresher and let it wash away the last of his foolish dreams.

It took five hellishly long days to reach the Algol system, days which Blaise tried to spend thinking about his future. He had his ship, his freedom, his health. All his contacts were still in the logs undisturbed. He could pick up his life right where it was interrupted when he was arrested. All he had to do was make that first call. It would be so easy. He had yet to do it, even to call Harry, because despite his best attempts to think about the future, his mind seemed determined to dwell on the past. On Peter.

The Admiral had looked awful the last time Blaise saw him, gaunt and in pain. It made him want to tuck Peter into his bunk and feed him painkillers and stew until he looked like himself again. The scars would fade in time, but that didn't even matter to Blaise. He just wanted to ease the lines of tension around Peter's mouth, creases that came, he was sure, from refusing to show weakness to anyone.

Blaise didn't know who would have the task of easing that pain, but it wouldn't be him, a fact that haunted his dreams, images of some faceless man soothing Peter's hurts, stroking his hair tenderly, folding him in a loving embrace, keeping him from sleeping well. By the time he steered the *Stallion* back into the Algol system, he looked nearly as exhausted as Peter had.

"Nicodemus Vector," he hailed, hoping Harry would let him lick his wounds for a few days, "do you copy?"

"Back so soon?" Harry's voice spoke over the comm link. "I thought you'd be busy reaping the rewards of being a galactic hero."

"Sorry about that," Blaise apologized, knowing he should have asked before using Harry's information, although he'd been quite insistent on giving credit where it was due, as had Peter, "but they wouldn't let me see Peter. It was the only bargaining chip I had."

"You don't have to apologize. It's been very good for business," the Andromedite answered smugly. "But you'll have to explain why you needed to cut a bargain to be with your mate."

"I will," Blaise promised. He owed Harry the whole story. "But I'd rather do it face to face, if you've got room for me for a few days."

"For you, always. I'll clear a landing vector for you."

"Thanks, Harry. It's nice to have someone I can always count on." He'd hoped, maybe, he might find that with Peter as well, but that clearly wasn't to be.

Harry's eyes examined Blaise keenly when the smuggler stepped off the *Golden Stallion*'s gangplank. His friend was clearly distressed, from more than just another close contact with the Gavenelians. Extending his tactile senses as Blaise caught him in his customary hug, he discerned an intriguing range of emotional emissions. "Let's take some refreshment and then you can tell me what brings you back without your mate."

Blaise nodded, clinging to anything that let him delay the inevitable rehashing of his life. He had no illusions that he'd get away with keeping any secrets this time, not with his emotions in such turmoil. If Harry hadn't sensed them already, he certainly would when Blaise began his tale. He took the drink the Andromedite offered and gulped it down, letting the slow burn of exotic liquor relax him. Pouring another shot, he downed it as well and then smiled sadly. "My 'mate' doesn't want me," he said dully in answer to Harry's last statement.

"That's not the impression I got when he was here."

"He told me to leave, Harry, not the other way around. I was a convenient body for him to fuck, nothing more," Blaise assured his friend starkly. "I just need a little time to get used to that idea, that's all. Then I'll leave you to your research again."

"I don't think you really believe that." Harry sipped his own drink, watching Blaise's aura darken. "I've known you too long to think you'd just fly away from someone who means that much to you."

"I didn't want to believe it. I didn't believe it, when we were here, but he sent me away, Harry," Blaise repeated, fighting the angry tears that threatened. "He handed me my papers and told me to go. What else am I supposed to believe?"

"Your papers?"

"You don't watch the newsgrids much, do you?" Blaise quipped. "Peter isn't my first mate. He's Admiral Peter Keller of the Confederation, and until a week ago, he was also my jailer. Instead of serving the smuggling sentence on a penal colony, I was serving it on his ship. Apparently, your genius bought me my freedom."

It had also brought Harry a large honorarium, with the promise of more to come if he was able to discover additional weaknesses the Confederation could exploit in its war against the Gavenelians. Judging it more important to deal with Blaise's emotional state at the moment, he continued probing. He could mention the reward later. Maybe.

"How do you think the newsgrids found out?" Harry asked instead. "I wasn't about to let the Confederation take all the credit for your discoveries and my hard work. So your sentence was commuted? I'd expect you to leave a flaming ion trail getting out of there before they changed their minds."

"I'd have stayed, if he'd asked," Blaise murmured, barely above a whisper, "but he all but threw the papers in my face. So I left, and here I am." *Alone. Again.*

"And did you offer?" Harry asked, just as softly.

"I didn't get the chance," Blaise admitted. "He threw me out before I could. You should have seen him, Harry. He was hurt so bad, hurting so bad, but he wouldn't even let me close. When I thought he was going to die, I didn't care about anything but being with him again, but he made it very clear he doesn't want me anymore. I'd have been anything he wanted, done anything he wanted, if he only cared a little, but I won't be his fucktoy for nothing."

"Maybe he didn't want you to see him hurting," Harry suggested. "On my homeworld, the bloodsharks are drawn to the slightest sign of weakness. I think your mate understands that dynamic."

"Within the Admiralty, maybe," Blaise allowed, "but I don't fit into that power structure, or if I do, I'm on the bottom. Why should it matter if I see his pain? All I wanted to do was ease it, not prey on it!"

"But why should he see you as any different?"

"Because he spent the past thirteen months making me fall in love with him, that's why!" Blaise snapped. "Of course I'm different."

One long tentacle snaked out and caught Blaise's chin, forcing him to meet the piscine gaze. "Did you tell him that?"

"Of course not," Blaise replied immediately. "He had enough power over me as it was."

Harry just stared at him piercingly.

"Oh, fuck. I'm an idiot, aren't I?" Blaise groaned.

"I'm sure you gave him your best 'I'm the hottest smuggler from here to the galactic rim, nothing matters to me but my next cargo run' act." Harry shrugged. "I know there's more to you than that, but how could he be expected to know it if you never showed him?"

"But I did show him," Blaise protested. "I told him about my grandmother, about the *Stallion*, about the Gavenelians. Oh, not the first night, obviously, but I did let him in. I let him hold me through the nightmares, through the retching and heaving. I let him see my weakness, Harry, and it wasn't enough. I didn't say the words, but I didn't keep the façade in place the whole time."

"Then maybe he's as stubborn as you are," Harry retorted, waving an irritated tentacle. "Or as big an idiot. You're perfect for each other."

How he'd longed for that to be true! "If this is perfection, I think I'm better off alone," Blaise sighed, downing another shot of whatever Harry was serving. "I'm going to sleep in a bed that doesn't reek of him. Maybe I'll actually be able to rest instead of tossing and turning all night long."

Harry had his own suspicions about that, but wisely decided to keep them to himself. "I'll give you one day to wallow in self-pity, but after that you'd better haul your weight around here or I'll kick your ass back out into space. I could use another set of hands de-engineering those Gavenelian toys your new friends sent me."

"What, you don't have enough arms of your own?" Blaise joked, pretending to count the tentacles that spread out from Harry's torso. Sobering, he added, "Let me get one good night's sleep, and you can have my hands and any other part of me that would be useful. I just need one night's rest and I'll be fine."

"Just your hands will be fine, thanks." Harry didn't think Blaise's mate would appreciate his making use of any other part of his friend's anatomy.

Hours later, Blaise's screams rent the air. He had finally fallen into a fitful sleep, only to be haunted by the nightmares he'd put to rest while he shared Peter's bed. Opening his eyes to Harry's concerned face, he scrubbed his hands over his stubbled cheeks. "I'm fine," he rasped, pulling away from the offer of a comforting embrace that came from the wrong man. "It was just a nightmare." He shuddered. "I thought they were gone. Will I never be free of them?"

"Seems to me you were free," Harry answered, ignoring the glare Blaise shot at him. "Let me ask you something. What do you think your Peter is doing right now?"

"Fighting the Gavenelians," Blaise replied immediately. "That's what we went to all this trouble so he could do. Or if he isn't fighting them yet, he's searching for them, with the *North Star* and a Confederation fleet at his beck and call."

"Assuming that's true, are you willing to let him face them alone? Without knowing how you really feel?" Harry didn't have to describe what the Gavenelians would do to Blaise's mate, if he fell into their clutches. The continuing nightmares were proof that Blaise remembered all too well.

"He isn't alone," Blaise protested, gut clenching at the thought of Peter in the hands of his erstwhile torturers. "He has the entire Confederation on his side."

"I'm sure that will make you both feel much better if he's captured," Harry observed. "I'm going to get some sleep. I have a Gavenelian shield generator to tear apart in the morning."

Blaise didn't even ask how Harry had come by a new piece of Gavenelian technology. He couldn't get past the image of Peter at their mercy. Even his proud Admiral would beg before long, and when they realized who he was, they'd kill him, and Peter would die thinking Blaise didn't care.

"Send me the specs when you learn anything new," he called to Harry as he grabbed his flight bag and strode toward his ship, his heart pounding. "I'll need all the help I can get, evading them and finding one Admiralty ship among thousands."

Blaise didn't see the affectionate smile Harry directed toward his back as he hurried toward the *Stallion*. At least now he wouldn't have to listen to his whining anymore.

PETER shifted uncomfortably in the narrow pilot seat of the small skiff. It wasn't as large or as fast as the *Golden Stallion*... against his will his thoughts turned to Blaise, wondering where he was and whether he'd returned to smuggling now that he'd regained his freedom. Angry at the direction of his thoughts, he stabbed at the nav screen, willing it to show him closer to Petarus. What the hell did he care what Blaise was doing now? It would serve the arrogant prick right if he got picked up again for piracy. If he wasn't caught first by the Gavenelians instead....

Cursing at falling into the same cycle of concern, Peter reminded himself that Blaise would surely have installed his friend Harry's weapons upgrades on his beloved ship. His own engineering staff had insisted on fitting the small personal skiff he'd acquired with the latest modifications before he'd left the *North Star*.

The crew's reaction when he'd announced his resignation had surprised him. He'd frankly expected most of them to cheer him on his way out the airlock, but a surprising number had stopped by his cabin as he packed his personal effects to offer their best wishes. He didn't have to worry about the *North Star*. Dmitrov would make a fine captain; he'd left them in good hands.

The hum of a proximity alert broke into his reflections. He'd reached comm range of his destination. Keying in a personal access code, he swung his chair around so the worst of his scars would be hidden from the vidscreen. He knew he wouldn't be able to hide them once he landed, but explaining what had happened wasn't a conversation he wanted to have until he was planetside.

"Peter Keller hailing Ryan Nelson. Hey Ryan, anybody home?"

"Peter, you old space dog, what are you doing in my attic?" Ryan's voice asked, crackling over the comm channel. "It's a good thing you didn't get here two days ago or you'd have found nothing but the spiders to keep you company."

"You mean to tell me you finally crawled out of your hole to see some of the galaxy again?" Peter felt his face relaxing into a smile for the first time since before the Gavenelian attack. Just hearing Ryan's voice was a balm for his wounded spirit. "Did you take your oversized canary with you?"

Ryan snorted. "Oversized canary… that's a new one. I'll have to tell Juo. Did you spend the whole trip here thinking it up?"

He'd spent the whole trip trying, uselessly, to forget, but that wasn't something he was ready to share yet, even with his oldest friend. "You know I love Juo. He's the closest either one of us will ever get to an angel," Peter said. Personally he felt like he'd been spending the past few weeks in hell.

"He's certainly my angel," Ryan agreed. "The landing pad's clear. You can set your ship down right outside the door."

"Race you there," Peter said, as they'd done since they were children together. "Loser has to buy the first drink."

"First drink's on me," Ryan countered, "just like it always is when you come to visit, but I'll still race you." His face disappeared from the vidscreen as he ran out the door toward the landing pad.

Peter inhaled deeply as he stepped off the landing ramp, ignoring the pang of stretching scar tissue as he filled his lungs with fresh, clean air. After a week of breathing his own recycled exhalations, any real air would be welcome, but the atmosphere on Petarus always carried a special crispness despite the hot tropical climate. Maybe it was all the plants, flowers in every color imaginable and soaring fernlike trees that shaded the pale stone buildings. He took another deep breath and turned toward the tall arched doorway where his friend stood waiting.

Ryan gasped in shock when he saw the livid scars covering one side of Peter's face and disappearing beneath the collar of his shirt. "Why didn't you tell me you were hurt? Juo's at the hospital, but I could have called for him to come home sooner. Come on; let's get you inside out of the sun and I'll call him right now. He may want you to come there, but your ship couldn't land there anyway. We'll use my speeder if he wants to see you there rather than here."

"Calm down, Ryan. This happened weeks ago. They're nearly healed, as much as they're going to, anyway." Peter shrugged. "I should have warned you, but I've gotten to where I forget they're there." That was a lie. The scars were still painful, though nowhere near the agony of the early days after the attack. At least he'd gotten most of the use of his hand back, even if the exercises the medics had prescribed to improve his range of motion felt like some kind of medieval torture.

"Almost healed?" Ryan repeated incredulously, counting himself fortunate once again to have stumbled across the Petari when he had. He wouldn't be alive if he hadn't. "If that's the best the Confederation can do for you, I'd hate to see what passes for average results. At least let Juo look at you. Even I can still see inflammation in places. He ought to be able to bring that down, even if he can't get rid of all the scars."

"Maybe, later." He didn't really think the Petari could do much for him, but right now he didn't feel like arguing. *Not when the only person who never backed down from him wasn't around anymore.* He pushed the thought away resolutely. "You promised me a drink first."

"Come inside. I'll get some parberry juice. I remember how much you liked that the last time you were here," Ryan suggested with a grin. At Peter's nod, he disappeared into the kitchen, using the link there to call Juo to come home as quickly as possible.

The cold, tart liquid soothed his parched throat and Peter found himself emptying the glass, holding it out for a refill with a smile. "I'd forgotten how good that is. I think I'll spend the next few days just lying under a tree in your garden with a glass of parberry juice."

"You'll be drunk as a skunk if you do that," Ryan reminded him as he filled the glass again, sipping his own portion far more respectfully. "Unless, of course, that's what you want."

The memory of the last time he'd indulged—in Betelgeusian wine, on Blaise's birthday—turned the parberry juice to bile in Peter's mouth. Setting the glass down, he tried to smile, though it came out more as a grimace. "Thanks for the reminder."

"Peter, what's...." Before Ryan could finish his question, Juo arrived in a flutter of heavy, dark wings, alighting in the doorway and walking inside with the grace of years of practice.

"What butcher has been practicing medicine on you?" the Petari snapped as soon as he got a good look at the burns on the Admiral's face. "How old are those burns? I don't know if I'll be able to heal all the scarring now that someone else has worked on them so incompetently."

His wings rustled in agitation as he grabbed Peter's chin and tipped it back so he could examine the marks better. "Why didn't you come here directly?"

"I wasn't exactly in any condition to dictate where I was taken after it happened," Peter admitted. "Though I'd love to see the chief medic of the starbase where I was treated hear you call him incompetent."

"Give me his comm signal," Juo spat. "I'll tell him gladly. I have first-year students who can heal plasma burns better than this. Without using their wings," he added before Ryan could remind him that not everyone was blessed with the Petari healing gifts. "These are plasma burns, aren't they?"

Peter nodded. "Control panel blew up on me." The pain of that moment—and of knowing he'd lost Blaise because of it—was for an instant as vicious as the day it happened.

"I'll do what I can," Juo declared. "How extensive are the burns, besides on your face? Your uniform should have protected your chest and arm somewhat. Let me look at the rest of them." Totally oblivious to the human notion of personal space, he reached for the closure of Peter's shirt so he could see the extent of the scarring.

"Is he this domineering with you, too?" Peter asked, arching an eyebrow at Ryan as he slipped out of his shirt to give Juo access to the rest of his injuries.

"Only when I don't do what he wants," Ryan replied with a matching grin. "Otherwise, he's as docile as a kitten."

"This 'kitten' is trying to concentrate," Juo interrupted tartly, "so unless you'd like me to leave Peter in pain, I suggest you let me work."

"I thought you said it didn't hurt anymore," Ryan accused Peter with a frown. "Stop being noble and let Juo take care of you."

"Fine!" Spreading his arms wide, Peter bit back a hiss as the movement pulled at puckered flesh. "Both of you can have at me. I'm too weak to resist two of you at once."

"I'll have at you all right," Ryan threatened, "just as soon as you're well enough to give me a good fight."

Juo just shook his head, well inured to the teasing camaraderie the two men shared from Peter's previous visits to the planet. Urging Peter to lower his arms, he knelt at the blond's side and extended one long, silky wing, draping it across the Admiral's chest and shoulder. He could feel the heat pulsing beneath the skin where the man's body tried to heal the wounds. Focusing on that, he drew it to the surface and out, taking with it the swelling and the pain.

Peter held his breath when Juo's wing enfolded him. The feathers felt surprisingly soft, caressing his chest in a touch that under other circumstances could have been almost erotic. A warm flush arose on his skin wherever Juo's wing brushed, peaking his nipples and leaving him feeling lightheaded. Ryan had tried to explain the Petari healing process, which involved a transfer of renewing energies through the healer's wings, but Peter had never expected to experience it himself. Small wonder a bond had formed between Ryan and Juo through such intimate contact. The kind of bond he'd thought he was forging with Blaise.... His balance wavered and his good arm groped out for something to stabilize himself.

"Easy," Ryan said, catching Peter's arm and steadying him. "Just sit still and let Juo help you."

"This isn't something I can heal in one afternoon," Juo warned them. "How much leave do you have, Peter?"

"As long as I want. I've resigned my commission."

"You did what?" both men exclaimed. "With a war starting?" Ryan added, moving so he could meet Peter's eyes. "You want to tell me what the hell happened? Despite the land you bought here for when you retired, you always said you'd die in uniform."

"I wasn't going to be let anywhere near the fighting. The Admiralty wanted me chained to a desk where I couldn't do anything to embarrass them. Fuck that. I told them to go to hell."

"What did you do to piss them off this time?" Ryan asked drolly as Juo dropped his wing and stepped back.

"That's all I can do for a first round of treatment," he interrupted, "but we'll do another round later. I have to go back to the hospital, but

I'll see you both tonight." He kissed Ryan swiftly and then stepped back outside, powerful wings lifting him into the air and out of sight.

"Now," Ryan said, pulling his chair so he sat directly in front of Peter, "tell me what's going on."

Feeling unaccustomedly exposed under his friend's stare, Peter reached for his shirt, his fingers still stiff on the fasteners. "We... I identified the race that's been attacking Confederation outposts, and gave the Admiralty a weapon to use against them. They just didn't like the means I used to find them."

"Who's 'we' and what means did you use?" Ryan pressed when Peter didn't elaborate further. He knew his friend. Getting information was like pulling teeth. Long and slow and painful, but he was pretty sure it was equally necessary.

Peter scrubbed a hand through his short hair before fortifying himself with another sip of juice. "You know I sometimes have—had—prisoners serving on my ship. The last one was...." Peter paused, unable to sum up Blaise in a few pat words. "He'd been captured by the Gavenelians before his arrest. When I came back from inspecting one of the outposts they'd attacked, he was able to identify them. With the help of one of his contacts, we found a change in weaponry that could penetrate their shields." He gestured toward his scars with a shrug. "Coming back from that meet, the Gavenelians caught up with us. Turns out they'd left a homing device on Blaise's... on the ship we were using. We were able to outrun them, barely. That's when I got the burns."

"And the Admiralty objected because?" Ryan probed, hearing a multitude of layers in Peter's words, not the least the fact that he used the prisoner's first name. Over the years, Peter had shared bits and pieces about the prisoner rehabilitation program, enough for Ryan to know it was an arrangement that allowed his friend to release his pent-up sexual needs in any way he saw fit. Especially since falling in love with Juo, Ryan had hoped Peter would move beyond that utilitarian relationship, but he understood the scars Peter's past had left well enough to give his friend the time he needed. It sounded now like maybe his wish had come true, except that Peter was here alone. "You'd think they'd be glad to have the information."

"Blaise was a smuggler. His friend had enough safeguards around his base of operations to make it clear he wasn't strictly legitimate either. Galactic Command didn't want it to become public knowledge that it owed its information to a couple of pirates."

"I assume you made sure it was public knowledge after they gave you a hassle about it," Ryan verified. At Peter's nod, he went on. "So tell me about this smuggler. You obviously trusted him if you went with him to get this information."

"He's arrogant and demanding and he fought me from the minute he came aboard my ship," Peter said, his throat thickening. He downed the last of the juice, the empty glass hitting the counter harder than he intended. "His sentence was commuted in recognition of his contributions, and he couldn't get away from me fast enough."

"Just because you're in love with him isn't a reason to break my glassware," Ryan chided gently, taking the glass from Peter's hand. "Where is he now?"

"How the fuck should I know? Or care?"

"You'd have to tell me why you care, but it's painfully obvious that you do," Ryan informed him. "You're welcome here with Juo and me as long as you want to stay, and we can start work on your house as soon as the permits are approved and you settle on a design, but that isn't going to make you forget about him. You can't go looking for him until after Juo's done with you, but that doesn't mean you can't start asking questions. He isn't the only one with contacts."

"I...." Peter met Ryan's eyes, filled with understanding and acceptance. "I thought there was something starting between us, something more than just physical." He shook his head grimly. "The first time he saw these," he waved toward his scars, "I saw his disgust in his face. He was gone as soon as he had the release order in his hand. Even if Juo's people can do something to help, that isn't going to change."

"Then he isn't worth your time," Ryan declared firmly, loyalty to his friend hardening his heart against the absent smuggler as his usually dormant temper flared to life in Peter's defense. "We'll just have to find you someone to help you forget him. Think you might want an oversized canary of your own?"

Peter forced a smile at having his words tossed back at him, but he couldn't find a clever retort. He'd love to have someone care for him the way Juo loved Ryan, but only if that someone was Blaise. And since that wasn't going to happen, he'd just have to hope that eventually he could forget.

CHAPTER 16
HERE, GOOSEY, GOOSEY

THE week back to where he'd last seen the *North Star* was longer, as far as Blaise was concerned, than the week it had taken him to get to Algol V in the first place, even though he pushed the *Stallion* harder than at any time other than when Peter was injured. He didn't hold out a whole lot of hope that the vessel would still be where he'd last seen it, but he hadn't heard news of any big battles—and he'd kept a constant feed of all the major newsgrids just in case—so he gambled on the Admiralty taking its time getting its battle plans in place and outfitting the whole armada with Harry's new weapons system rather than just the *North Star*. As powerful a ship as she was, she couldn't fight the war alone against the whole Gavenelian fleet.

When he found another ship in the dock where he'd last seen the *North Star,* he consoled himself with the thought that at least Peter wouldn't be facing the Gavenelians alone. The Confederation clearly intended to update its entire flotilla. Unfortunately, no one at the shipyards was able or willing to give Blaise information about the *North Star*'s current location or intended destination. With a frustrated sigh, he returned to his ship and sent a transmission to Harry.

"Any luck?" he asked when Harry's blue face appeared on screen.

"Seemingly more than you're having," Harry answered, frustration apparent on Blaise's drawn features. "Your mate had a good idea; I was able to subvert the tracking systems on a Gavenelian homing beacon so that it should be possible to follow its energy signature backward when it's activated. Of course I can't test it without turning it on, and I'm not about to lead them here. Think someone in the Admiralty might want to beta it for us?"

"I think I can find someone," Blaise replied with a grin, the first to cross his face in weeks. "Now I just have to convince them to tell me where he is. Send me the specs. We'll test it on the device they took off the *Golden Stallion* while Peter was recuperating."

Harry's smile was nearly as broad as Blaise's. "Good. I wasn't looking forward to someone else picking up the one I have. Who knows, I might find another market for it someday. In the meantime, get a good price for yours."

"I didn't forget how to negotiate while I was serving time," Blaise scolded. "I'm pretty sure they'll be far more interested in your information than they will be in protecting Peter's location. After all, I'm offering to help them win the war, not hinder them. I'll make sure you get your cut of the profits. I know how much I owe you."

"Just worry about finding your Admiral," Harry replied. "He might have some other good ideas to share. Fly safe."

"Thanks, Harry." Blaise cut the transmission as soon as the computer beeped that it had the specs for the tracking device. Setting a heading for Confederation Fleet Headquarters, he framed his arguments in his head, determined to drive as hard a bargain as he would if his heart weren't involved. Despite what Harry said, he owed it to the Andromedite to make sure he got the credit that was his due.

Three days later, his ship hovered over Admiralty headquarters and he sat at the comm, tapping his fingers as he waited for someone with enough authority to negotiate with him. Finally, an older man with a pinched face appeared on the screen.

"Risner?" he scowled, leaning forward as if it would help him see Blaise better through the vidscreen. "Risner? Aren't you the pirate that incited my best admiral to run amok? What are you doing out of custody? I don't care what the newsgrids say: you belong on a penal colony, where Keller should have left you in the first place!"

Blaise's face hardened. So it was all his fault, was it? "High Justice Perry doesn't share your opinion," he declared tightly. "She seemed to think my contribution to the war effort deserved a remission of my sentence and the restoration of my ship. You're welcome to take it up with her if you disagree. Now, Admiral... Hindspot, was it? Are you interested in my information or shall I sell it on the open market to the highest bidder?"

"High Admiral Hendershott, and if you have information that can help in the war against the Gavenelians, I demand you turn it over immediately! The Confederation will not be blackmailed by a damned pirate!" he blustered.

"It's not blackmail, Hipposlot," Blaise retorted. "It's called negotiation. Now, are you interested in talking or not?"

"How do I know you even have anything worth negotiating over? This could all be a trick to extort more money from the Fleet coffers."

"Extort?" Blaise repeated. "Are you suggesting the last pieces of information I supplied were less than reliable? And for your information, I didn't see a credit for discovering the identity of the attackers or for the weapons technology to penetrate their shields. Now, Handgrot, this is the deal. In return for the specs for turning the homing beacon that was found on my ship into a tracking device to locate Gavenelian vessels, I want Admiral Keller's current location and fifty thousand credits transferred to Nicodemus Vector."

"Fifty thousand...." Hendershott's eyes narrowed as Blaise's earlier words sunk in. "You have a way to locate Gavenelian ships? If this is some trick, you'll wish I'd sent you to a penal planet when I'm done with you. Do you hear me, Risner?"

"I have every reason to want to see those bastards wiped from the face of the universe," Blaise replied coldly. "If I could do it myself, I would, but since I can't, I'm perfectly willing to let the Confederation do it for me. Now, Admiral, do we have a deal?"

"Send me the specs and I'll arrange for the credits to be transferred. But if they don't work, I'm warning you, you'll wish the Gavenelians were after you instead of my ships."

Blaise scoffed. "You obviously don't know what the Gavenelians are capable of if you think that's a threat I'm likely to take seriously," he informed Hendershott. "Before I send the specs, I need the *North Star*'s location. I have unfinished business with Admiral Keller."

"Oh, I'll be happy to give you the *North Star*'s location," Hendershott smiled. "Though I'd be careful if I were you. They were rather in the thick of things the last I heard from them." He motioned to someone outside the range of the vidscreen. "Send me the specs, and we'll send you the *North Star*'s current coordinates in return."

"Done," Blaise replied, pushing the transmit button to send the files Harry had sent him. His heart clenched at the idea of Peter in danger, but at least he'd be able to fight at his lover's side. And he'd kept a copy of Harry's specs. He'd seen what Billy Royce could do with them. Surely the engineer could find a way to duplicate the effect even without a Gavenelian homing device. "I expect to see those credits in the right account by the end of the day, or I'll make you the laughingstock of the entire Confederation." He waited only to make sure he'd received the coordinates before turning back to the Admiral. "Nice doing business with you, Headsnot. Hopefully, I'll never have to see you again."

"Oh, I think that's mutual," Hendershott muttered. "Give my regards to Keller when you find him," he added before the screen went dark.

Fucker, Blaise thought as he entered the coordinates and sent the *Stallion* hurtling through space toward his destination. Twelve hours later, he came out of hyperdrive to see the *North Star* on his vidscreen. With a sigh of relief, he hailed her.

"*Golden Stallion, North Star* acknowledges. Back so soon, Captain Risner?"

"Commander Dmitrov?" Blaise asked in surprise, hoping the engineer's presence on the bridge didn't mean that Peter had suffered a relapse from returning to work too soon. "I expected Admiral Keller to be at the helm. I have some information for him."

"Actually, it's Captain now," Dmitrov replied, not bothering to mask the puzzlement in his voice. He'd privately thought the Admiral's decision had a lot to do with the man on the other end of the comm link; but if Risner didn't know what had happened.... "Hasn't he notified you? The Admiral is no longer in command of the *North Star*. He submitted his resignation from the Fleet two weeks ago."

"What?" Blaise exclaimed. "No, he didn't say anything...." Of course he hadn't said anything. He hadn't had the chance before they started arguing again. "Do you know where he went? I need to talk to him. It's important."

"I'm sorry. The Admiral didn't tell us his future plans," Dmitrov said regretfully. "Perhaps HQ knows."

Blaise snorted. "How do you think I found out where you were? Hendershott's laughing his ass off still, I'm sure, knowing he sent me all the way out here on a wild goose chase." He sighed. "He can't have disappeared completely. Somebody'll know where he is. I just have to keep looking, but if you hear from him, tell him I'm looking for him and that Nicodemus will always know where I am. If you don't mind, that is."

"I'll pass that along if I hear from him," the Captain said. "When you find him, tell him... tell him the *North Star* misses him, and that I respect him more than ever." Dmitrov smiled wryly. "And Blaise.... Good luck," he added softly.

Blaise smiled for the first time since he'd left Harry's lair on Nicodemus Vector. "I'll pass on the message. Oh, and I'm sending you something for your engineering team to play with. It's experimental, and I don't have the hardware it was developed on, but if you can make it work, it'll let you trace the Gavenelian ships. Hendersnot has it, but I don't expect him to get it to the ships in the field any time soon. I recognized his bureaucratic ass the second I saw him. Anyway, I hope it'll be of some use to you." He hit the transmit button and shot Dmitrov the same specs he'd given Galactic Command.

"You've just made Lieutenant Royce's day," Dmitrov grinned. "And if this really lets us track the Gavenelians, I'll buy you the best dinner we can find the next time we're in port together."

Blaise laughed. "It's a deal. Billy'll recognize the handiwork of the same guy who figured out the weapons frequency. He hasn't tested it because he didn't want to risk attracting them to his home base, but it works on paper. And even if all it does is let you set a trap for them, it's still more than you've got now. If I learn anything else, I'll send it along to you whenever I can."

"Our comm officer is sending you the frequency of a secure channel to contact us," Dmitrov said. "You'll be able to get through to me on it anytime. I wish there was more I could do to help you find Admiral Keller...." He paused for a moment and then added uncertainly, "You might try to contact Justice Perry. She's visited the Admiral on board several times, the only person I know who's done so. I got the impression they were personal friends in addition to the... prisoner rehabilitation program."

Blaise frowned. "Thanks, Sasha," he said honestly, but he didn't know if he wanted to deal with the High Justice again. Still, if Dmitrov thought she might know, he supposed it was worth a try. He couldn't be any worse off than he was now. "I guess I'll head for the Sirius quadrant then."

"Good hunting. *North Star* out."

"*Golden Stallion* out," Blaise replied automatically, his thoughts already turning to High Justice Perry and how to approach her. With Hendershott, he'd had the information from Harry. He hadn't needed anything to persuade Dmitrov; he'd known for some time that Sasha liked and approved of him. He had no idea what the High Justice would demand in exchange for whatever she knew. Actually, he did have an idea, and it turned his stomach to think of submitting to her. It had been bad enough when Peter was there, too, keeping her from trespassing too far. He'd just have to wait and see what her price was and hope it was something he could meet.

It took another week to reach the Sirius quadrant. High Justice Perry's face was just as beautiful and just as cold when he contacted her to request an audience.

"Mr. Risner. I must admit I'm surprised to see you," she said slowly, a gleam in her eyes that could charitably be called predatory. "Have you managed to get yourself into trouble again already?"

"Not any trouble that would see me before your court, Your Honor," Blaise replied politely, reminding himself that he couldn't afford to antagonize the High Justice the way he had the High Admiral. He didn't have any negotiating power here. "I had a request of a slightly more personal nature and hoped we might meet to discuss it in person."

"I'd be pleased to reacquaint myself with your person," Lapis smiled. "Dock your ship and have a court bailiff show you to my offices."

Blaise shivered at the expression on her face, suddenly not sure meeting her face to face was such a good idea, but he had to convince her to tell him what she knew. He just hoped Dmitrov was right and she knew enough to help him. Signing off, he piloted the ship toward the court docking port and steeled himself to keep his wits about him while he dealt with the High Justice.

A bailiff met his ship and showed him immediately to the High Justice's offices, a suite of rooms as luxurious as any royal boudoir.

"So, Mr. Risner," Justice Perry asked, rising from her desk and circling him as if she were inspecting a prospective purchase, "what 'personal request' is important enough to bring you back within my purview? I would have expected you to disappear as soon as Admiral Keller arranged your release."

"I did," he admitted, trying not to squirm at her leer, "but I discovered something after I disappeared, and I'd like the chance to share it with the Admiral myself. He's resigned his commission, though, so he isn't where I can find him, and Captain Dmitrov suggested you might know where he is."

"Peter resigned his commission?" Lapis exclaimed, momentarily shocked out of her prurient interest in the handsome example of manflesh. "He always swore he'd 'die in harness', as he put it." Her gaze hardening, she sank into her chair and pointed a slender finger at her visitor. "What in the name of the mother suns did you do to him?"

"Me?" Blaise squawked in protest. "I didn't do anything. He didn't give me a chance. He sent me back to the *North Star* as soon as he regained consciousness on Eudorae Prime and kicked me off his ship as soon as he got back! At the time, I was too angry to do anything but go, but...." He eyed the elegant green-skinned woman carefully. If she really was Peter's friend like Dmitrov thought, maybe the truth would sway her. "I should have fought for him, and I didn't. I shouldn't have let him push me away when he was down and hurting. I'd tell him all this except that I can't find the stubborn bastard."

The stare Lapis focused on the smuggler regularly reduced the accused before her bench to guilty squirming, but Risner met her gaze squarely. "I thought you were good for him, but if I'd known you'd abandon him when he needed you most, I'd have thrown you back on a penal planet instead of granting your release as he requested. Why would I tell you anything, even assuming I knew where he was?"

"*He* kicked *me* out!" Blaise all but shouted. "What part of that don't people understand? I didn't want to go anywhere except to his quarters to take care of him, but he threw my papers in my face and ordered me off his ship! I've been trying to find him for the past two weeks, since I realized I should have ignored him and insisted he let me take care of him, but he wasn't the only one hurting, and when he told me to go...." He paused and took a steadying breath. "You have absolutely no reason to tell me anything," he continued more calmly, "but ask yourself this. Why would I go to so much trouble to find him if I didn't care about him? I don't know what it will take to persuade you, High Justice, but name your price and I'll find a way to meet it."

"My price?" The Sirian walked gracefully back to Blaise and stood in front of him thoughtfully. "I never did get to put you through your paces properly on board the *North Star*," she considered, reaching up to coast her palms over his chest in evaluation. Her eyes widened when they encountered his nipples, returning to trace them through the layer of fabric. "What's this?" she demanded, sliding peremptory hands under the fastenings of his vest.

"A belated birthday present," Blaise replied slowly, forcing himself not to pull away from the touch of her hands. He'd said he would meet her price. If this was it, he would submit to whatever she demanded. He wouldn't enjoy it, and he'd pray Peter would understand, but he would submit. The Gavenelians had taught him that his body was separate from his heart and soul. Those belonged to Peter alone. "The Admiral gave it to me, Mistress."

Her eyes flashed at the address, and for a moment Blaise thought he'd gone too far, but the angry glare softened as she leaned closer to examine the new piercing, holding the ring away from his skin with a long fingernail. "A pretty piece of work," she asserted. "Fortunately for you, I recognize a claim when I see one. Peter and I may share the same tastes, but we've never poached in each other's preserves." She returned to her desk, sitting back at ease. "So, since you can't offer me your admittedly tempting person, what else do you have that might convince me to help you?"

They were the wrong fingers on the piercing, but his body reacted nonetheless, the longing for Peter's touch so strong it nearly drove him to his knees. Her words barely penetrated his thoughts. "I don't have anything of value to offer except my ship," he admitted before he could censor his words.

"I remember you seemed rather fond of your ship," Lapis agreed. "Give me the papers, and I'll see what I can do."

Heart breaking, Blaise didn't hesitate, reaching into the interior pocket of the loosened vest. He withdrew the deed Peter had returned to him along with his remission papers and tossed it onto her desk. "Tell me what you know," he demanded hoarsely.

Lapis scanned the document, considered Blaise for another long moment, then tossed it back to him. "And just exactly how would you find him without a ship?" she asked, a smile trying to curve the corners of her lips.

"Hire a ship, call in a favor from an old friend, find a public shuttle," Blaise enumerated, his heart pounding as he took back the papers. "Steal one if I had to. Please tell me you know where I can find him."

"If you stole one you'd wind up right back with me, and I doubt that's what you want," Justice Perry admonished. She leaned forward and held Blaise's gaze. "I don't *know* where to find him, but Peter always said that if he did ever manage to retire from the Admiralty, he'd settle on Petarus."

"Where?" Blaise asked, not familiar with the planet she named. "I've never heard of it. I've already been on one wild goose chase, Your Honor. I'd rather not go on another, if it's all the same to you."

"I have no idea where it is," the High Justice admitted. "I don't even think it's a member of the Confederation. He mentioned an old friend living there, though if he ever told me the friend's name, I don't remember it. The only reason I remember the name of the planet is that I told him I couldn't imagine him living somewhere so isolated."

"If it's on a star chart anywhere in the Confederation, I'll find it," he swore, thinking perhaps he understood Peter's choice. If he managed to get out, he'd want to get all the way out and stay out. A backwater planet on the edge of the Galactic Rim would be just what he'd want, especially if he had a friend there. Hadn't Blaise run to one of his oldest friends to lick his wounds? It made perfect sense that Peter would do the same. "I just hope you're right and he's there, because I'm out of leads if you're wrong."

"I hope I'm right, too." Lapis's voice hardened. "I've told you what I can because I believe you truly care about Peter. Prove me wrong, and you'd better hope you're never caught in my quadrant again."

"I won't make the same mistake twice," Blaise swore. "If he wants to get rid of me again, he'll have to remove me bodily from wherever I find him, and I'll fight him every inch of the way." He didn't say that in the state Peter was in last time he'd seen him, the Admiral wouldn't be in any shape to manhandle anyone.

"If you find him, give him a kiss for me," Lapis requested. "Now get out of here. I don't expect to see you in these courts again."

"Yes, ma'am," Blaise rejoined, flashing his trademark grin before returning to his ship to see what he could dig up on Peter's mysterious hideout. He believed the High Justice had told him everything she knew. He just hoped she was right.

Back on the *Golden Stallion*, Blaise keyed in a course away from Sirius, not particularly caring where he went at this point. He had research to do before he could choose a destination other than away from the High Justice.

Turning to the console he used for research, he typed in the name of the planet Perry had given him. It took far longer than he expected, but eventually, a reference came up to an Amalgamated Exploration log from ten years ago. He clicked on the reference only to find it blocked as classified. "Oh, no," he growled. "You're not going to let me get that close only to keep me out."

Setting the computer to hack the block, he leaned back in his chair and considered his options. He could continue to fly aimlessly until he knew where he was going or he could find a place to wait out the computer's search. Once, he'd have headed straight to Orion. The emperor's harem had been disbanded when it joined the Confederation, but its pleasure palaces rivaled any in the entire galaxy. That thought no longer appealed, though. Justice Perry's comment about his second piercing had hit far too close to home. Peter had claimed him and Blaise found he wanted no other's touch. He would have suffered it from the High Justice in exchange for the information she had, but he had no desire to seek it out, not while there was even a small chance that Peter might still want him.

Deciding he'd gone far enough from Sirius for his peace of mind, he brought the *Stallion* to a stop and let it idle where it was in the middle of nowhere. He set all the proximity alarms, shields at maximum, and left the computer to work while he went to get some sleep, hoping the dreams that followed him would be good ones now that he had a lead on where to find Peter.

It seemed like his eyes had just closed before his lover appeared, all golden hair and pale skin. The smile on Peter's face was soft, his green eyes shining like the lights of the Horsehead Nebula as they traced down the lines of Blaise's naked body. "I've missed you," he husked.

"I've missed you, too," Blaise replied, reaching for Peter and pulling him down into a tender kiss. They didn't speak after that. They didn't need to. Their hands, tongues, bodies spoke for them.

Peter's face was unmarked, his hands dexterous as they mapped Blaise's body with unaccustomed gentleness. Sliding slowly across the stubble on Blaise's chin, Peter's lips traced the contours of his neck, lingered at the pulse throbbing in the hollow of Blaise's throat. His fingers played with the rings adorning Blaise's chest, twisting, teasing, the touch tantalizingly light.

Blaise sighed softly, shifting beneath the lover's touch, offering his body and his heart to his Admiral to do with as he pleased. He knew instinctively that this man would never abuse that trust, would cherish both gifts the way they deserved. He stroked one smooth cheek softly, silently expressing the depth of his love.

Peter smiled at him—a warm smile, free of its usual cynicism—and continued lower, taking each piercing between his lips in turn, laving the spots where they entered Blaise's flesh until they tightened. Soft kisses nipped a lazy path between his ribs; a warm tongue defined the crease on each side of his abdomen, sliding closer to the dark thatch surrounding his cock while Peter's hands ranged up and down his thighs.

Blaise tugged at the short blond hair, trying to direct Peter's mouth to his cock, but he was ignored. His lover was apparently determined to drive him crazy in the slowest, most erotic way possible, brushing his lips across the sensitive skin of Blaise's inner thighs and then lower to tickle the backs of his knees. Blaise yelped and then smiled at Peter's chuckle, a sound he heard far too rarely. He subsided on the bed, consciously relaxing the tension that had invested his muscles at the tickling touch. His lover was careful to keep his caresses firm, though still loving, after that so he didn't accidentally tickle again.

The moist kisses and trailing touches continued lower, even his feet paid homage in this sensual exploration. With a final nip at each big toe, Peter began to work his way upward again with equal thoroughness, until Blaise was sure not a single patch of skin on his legs had not been anointed by his lover's mouth. The muscles in his abdomen jumped when Peter returned to the juncture of legs and torso, anticipating the touch that would surely come next to the one place his lover had neglected.

The touch came, but not to the place he expected, Peter's hands lifting his hips as his shoulders forced his legs farther apart, his lips ghosting over the heavy sac and then lower to blow hot air across the tightly furled entrance. He gasped in surprise, wishing he could wriggle closer, but Peter's hands kept him immobile, thumbs spreading his cheeks wide as his tongue darted out to taste and retreat, tantalizing Blaise mercilessly.

Just when he thought he would have to beg for what he wanted, Peter granted it, as if he knew exactly when he'd reached Blaise's limit. The agile tongue circled the ring of muscle a final time and then pierced it, plunging deep and withdrawing almost immediately, a maddening cadence that left him silently pleading for each incursion to probe just a little farther, each swirl to extend just a fraction wider, to reach the spot he knew would set him off like an exploding star.

"Peter!" he begged just as the Admiral gave him what he wanted, his body convulsing in ecstasy. He cried out again, the sound of his own voice rousing him from his sleep as hot fluid sprayed his chest and stomach. He curled around himself, reaching automatically for his absent lover. The empty space next to him struck him to the core, leaving him trembling helplessly on the bed. "I don't know where you are," he said to the phantom in his dreams, his voice aching, "but wherever it is, I will find you, and when I do, I'm not ever letting you go."

In the cockpit, the computer beeped quietly, and the coordinates for Petarus appeared on the screen.

CHAPTER 17
SOME LIKE IT HOT

IT had been a month since Peter showed up on his doorstep, Ryan realized as he steered his skiff toward home. Despite his warnings that he wouldn't be able to heal Peter completely, Juo had done wonders with the burns, giving Peter back most of his mobility in his hand and arm and eliminating all the swelling from his face and chest. The skin was still dimpled but no longer the flaming red it had been at first, and Juo was still hopeful that he could even erase some of that in time. Peter should have been happy, but it didn't take an empath to realize that he wasn't. He always had a ready smile for Juo, a smart-ass remark for Ryan, but when he thought they weren't looking, his face fell, thoughts turning inward to memories that clearly haunted him.

Sometimes at night, Ryan thought he heard Peter cry out, but the one time he'd gone to check, his friend had lashed out so harshly that Ryan hadn't gone back. If Peter wanted to deal with his nightmares alone, Ryan would respect that.

Peter needed something else to focus on, though, and Ryan had just the trick. The building permits for his house had finally been granted. Work could start as soon as Peter approved the final plans with a contractor. Ryan had called in a few favors to get his friend bumped up in the queue for new projects, and the contractor had contacted Ryan just a few minutes after the permits came through. All they needed now was Peter's approval.

Parking the speeder next to Peter's larger ship, Ryan hopped out with easy grace, comfortable now with most of the Petari vessels. "Peter," he called, walking into the house, "I've got good news!"

"You finally figured out how to throw an inside curveball?" Peter joked, a running taunt since their childhood baseball games back on Earth. He could feel a muted pleasure in his friend's good mood, whatever its cause, but it was the reaction of an outsider, a vicarious response to emotions Peter didn't think he could feel for himself anymore. Didn't think he wanted to feel. Numbness was definitely preferable to the fiercely painful memories he managed, for the most part, to suppress during his waking hours. He wasn't quite as successful in his dreams, though he hoped over time those would fade as well.

"Fuck you," Ryan retorted with a grin, the familiar joke bringing a smile to his face as always. He and Peter had been fiercely competitive, at baseball as at everything else, and that curveball was the one thing Peter had always been able to beat Ryan at.

"Juo isn't enough for you?" Peter couldn't help but grin back. "I wouldn't let him hear you say that if I were you. Those wings are stronger than they look."

Ryan chuckled. "You think I don't know how strong his wings are?" he teased. "Seriously, though, look what I got today." He waved the permits in the air. "As soon as you finalize the blueprints, construction can begin on your house."

"That is good news," Peter answered, his voice flat. He knew he'd been imposing on Ryan's and Juo's hospitality; if he was honest with himself, he'd been dragging his feet about looking for a contractor to build a home on the land he'd purchased years ago. He'd bought it on impulse when it came available because it was close to Ryan, but he hadn't expected to have to think about actually living there himself for years, when he was ready to retire from space. That retirement had come far sooner than he'd planned, but it didn't mean he'd accepted it yet. Breaking ground on a house that would never really be a home to him would make it all real. He'd have to face that he'd never get into space again. Never see Blaise again. He tried to arrange his face into a suggestive leer. "I'm sure the two of you can't wait to get your privacy back."

"What's that got to do with anything?" Ryan replied immediately, not caring at all for the implication that he wanted Peter gone. "You know you're welcome here for as long as you want to stay. I just thought you'd be happy to finally start getting settled. Was I wrong?"

And now he'd gone and pissed off the one friend he had left in the galaxy. "No, you're not wrong, and I appreciate everything you and Juo have done to help." Hoping to make Peter feel more at home, Ryan had introduced him to the small but growing enclave of off-worlders, most of whom had come for treatment or to study Petari healing methods, and to the planetary officials he'd had to work with to receive approval to settle permanently on Petarus.

"It's harder to get used to than I thought it would be," Peter shrugged, knowing Ryan would interpret that to mean only his leaving the Fleet.

"Just give it time," Ryan advised. "I just heard from the contractors today after the permits went through. Even if they break ground tomorrow, it'll be at least six months before you can move in."

Privately, he hoped he'd get the chance some day to take Peter's distress out on the damn pirate's hide. As if having to resign his commission weren't bad enough, Peter had to deal with a lover's betrayal. Yes, if Blaise Risner knew what was good for him, he'd give Ryan Nelson and Petarus a wide, wide berth.

"I'll call the contractors and let them know I'm ready to get started," Peter conceded. Finalizing the building design and overseeing construction would at least give him something to fill his days for the next six months or so. "The sooner they start, the sooner they'll finish." He'd worry about what he'd do after that when the time came.

"I just want you to be happy here," Ryan told him, feeling the hated helplessness in the face of a pain neither he nor Juo could heal.

Before he could say more, his comm link beeped. Glancing down, he saw a message from Nea-ta, his administrative assistant. "I'm sorry," he apologized. "Nea-ta-ri's calling. I've got to get back to work."

Peter clapped him on the shoulder, feeling only a twinge of residual stiffness in his damaged arm. "I'm a big boy; I'm sure I'll be able to manage without you somehow." He squeezed before letting his arm fall to his side. "Thanks, Ryan," he added. "It really is good news."

"Another month and your hand will be as good as new," Ryan commented as he walked out the door. "Oh, and Juo said to tell you he'd be home early today to try something different on your shoulder."

Without waiting for a reply—Nea-ta's message said it was urgent—Ryan ran back to his skiff and vaulted into the driver's seat, not for the first time wishing he had wings like his lover's. It made life so much simpler.

Ten minutes later, he set his skiff down outside the building that housed the Integration Authority, the agency charged with facilitating the transition of any off-worlder who arrived on Petarus, whether they stayed only a few weeks to receive medical treatment or intended to settle there permanently. The exterior of the building was covered with metal steps, reminding Ryan of the old fire escapes that had been added to so many buildings on Earth after a series of deadly fires. The Petari had no use for steps, each story of their buildings boasting an open landing where the natives could alight. One of Ryan's first requests as head of the Integration Authority had been the addition of these stairs on any buildings that regularly welcomed off-worlders. He didn't mind Juo carrying him from story to story when they were in a building without the accommodation, but he knew it was unsettling for those not used to the intimacy.

"What's going on?" he asked his admin as he stepped back into his office.

"We have a guest upstairs," the Petari explained, pointing toward outer space, "looking for an Admiral Keller. I thought you might want to handle this one personally."

"Did our guest give a name?" Ryan asked, his face hardening even as he smiled internally at Nea-ta's use of the slang he'd picked up from his boss. If it was the Admiralty looking for Peter, Ryan would simply pretend ignorance and send them on their way. If it was the pirate.... It had been a while since he'd been in a good fight.

Nea-ta consulted his notes, still not completely comfortable with all the unfamiliar names even after five years as Ryan's admin. "Captain Risner of the *Golden Stallion*," he replied after a moment.

It looked like Ryan was going to get his wish. "I'll be happy to deal with Captain Risner," he tossed over his shoulder as he headed to the exterior staircase that had been added to accommodate his inability to fly to his upper-level office. Taking the steps two at a time in his haste, he dropped into his desk chair and hit the comm button to open the channel Nea-ta had put through. "Ryan Nelson, planetary liaison office," he introduced himself gruffly. "Go ahead, *Golden Stallion*."

Blaise's sigh of relief was audible through the comm link as a human face appeared on his vidscreen. "Mr. Nelson," he said with a smile, "I'm looking for a friend of mine and a mutual acquaintance suggested he might have come to Petarus to recover from his injuries. Do you know Admiral Peter Keller? Is he there?"

Ryan tried to keep his anger from showing on his face as he examined the image on his screen. Disregarding the easy smile, he saw a well-built and powerful-looking dark-haired man, dressed in a sleeveless vest and cargo pants, a tattoo of some kind circling one muscled bicep. He could see what had attracted his friend's interest, though the thought of what this man had done to Peter's heart hardened his own. "What's your business with Admiral Keller?" he asked curtly, volunteering nothing. The man on the screen didn't deserve it.

"Personal business," Blaise replied, not sure how much Peter would want him to reveal of their past. If this was the friend the High Justice had spoken of, the man probably knew everything already, but he had no way of knowing if this Nelson was indeed the right man. "He disappeared before we could settle some accounts," he added vaguely, hoping that would be enough to sway the planetary official. "I just want to make sure he's okay."

Nothing in the other man's impersonal response was convincing Ryan to tell him anything about how Peter was doing, especially when he suspected he was looking at the cause of his friend's continued unhappiness. "Maybe he had a reason for disappearing. Maybe he doesn't want to be found."

"But it was all a misunderstanding!" Blaise replied, the passionate exclamation out before he could censor the words. "Please, if he's there, just let me talk to him, and if he's not, tell me so I can keep looking for him."

"You tell me why the hell I should tell you anything about Peter," Ryan growled, knowing his reaction wasn't going to let him continue to claim ignorance of the Admiral's whereabouts. But he still didn't have to give this pirate any information without a damn good explanation first. He owed his friend that much. If all Risner was going to do was make things worse, Ryan would shoot him back into space so fast his ears would bleed.

"Let me land and I'll tell you whatever you want to know," Blaise promised, sure now that he'd found both the right planet and the right man. Now he just had to convince Nelson to let him see Peter. "If I'm going to have to give an accounting of my sins, I'd rather do it face to face."

Ryan pondered whether it was wise to let the stranger land, deciding that it would make it easier to punch him out if he wasn't able to convince Ryan otherwise. "Set down on the landing pad outside my office," he agreed, transmitting the coordinates. If Risner didn't make a damn good case, that was as close as he'd ever get to Peter.

Blaise set the coordinates into the ship's nav computer, letting it guide him down through the planet's atmosphere. From the little bit of information he'd been able to find, he knew Petarus was tropical, a fact played out in the lush greenery that met his eyes as he broke through the layer of light clouds. As buildings came into view, the first thing he noticed was the multiple openings on the soaring, light beige structures. As he neared his destination, he saw that one had stairs on the outside in addition to the many openings. He set the *Stallion* down carefully at the indicated coordinates, seeing a man waiting outside. Opening the hatch, he stepped out, the heat of the day assaulting him immediately. "Some weather you have here," he commented to the waiting man, hoping to break some of the tension.

"You won't be here long enough to get used to it," Ryan retorted, irritated at the implied slur to his adoptive world. "Come upstairs. I'll give you ten minutes to convince me you have business that's worth disrupting Peter's recovery."

"Is he recovering?" Blaise asked immediately, following Peter's friend into his office and taking the seat indicated. "He was in such pain the last time I saw him." He took a deep breath and reminded himself that Nelson had no reason to trust him. "Look, I don't know what Peter told you, but I was with him on the *North Star* for awhile. We became... close. After he was hurt, he ordered me to leave. I didn't think. I just went, too hurt by the thought that he'd sent me away to think about why he might have done it. I know you don't have any reason to believe me, but I was a fool to let him make me leave when all I wanted to do was stay. There's more, but the rest is for his ears alone. Will you let me see him?"

Ryan held Blaise's gaze, searching for the sincerity behind the easy words. Before meeting Juo, he might have dismissed the other man's explanation, but he'd learned that while miscommunications could occur with alarming ease, the rewards of working for a relationship were well worth the effort. The pain and regret in the stranger's hazel eyes seemed genuine, and Ryan sensed he was feeling the separation as keenly as Peter was. If there was a chance for Peter to find the same completeness he'd found with Juo with the man across the desk, wasn't it worth taking a risk? Besides, he knew Peter well enough to believe that he could have pushed Risner away, too proud to let anyone else see his pain.

"I'll take you to him," Ryan decided. He supposed he could call first to ask if Peter wanted to see Risner, but if what his visitor told him was true, Peter might well refuse. "He's a stubborn bastard, but maybe you can talk some sense into him." He stopped the pirate with a grip of his arm, strong enough to get the other man's attention. "But if you hurt him again, you'll be answering to me. Got that?"

"If he won't take me back, you can do anything you want to me. It won't matter if he really is done with me," Blaise replied honestly, letting some of his own pain show in his voice and on his face.

Ryan didn't have an answer for that. If Risner was sincere, and he was beginning to believe the pirate was, it would be up to Peter to decide if he was willing to risk letting him inside the wall he'd built around himself after the accident. Ryan would put his money on Peter. His friend was stubborn, but he wasn't a coward. "We'll take my skimmer," he indicated the smaller vessel dwarfed beside Blaise's craft. And if Risner did anything to add to Peter's pain, Ryan would be escorting him right back here before his ship's engines had a chance to cool.

Blaise slumped back into the chair, relief making him weak. He'd been so afraid this gatekeeper would keep him from seeing Peter. "You won't regret it," he promised, following the taller man back out into the sweltering heat and down the stairs to the open-air land skimmer. They darted through the streets, passing only a few other vehicles but many buildings similar to the one where he'd landed, only without the exterior stairs.

"Are all those buildings still under construction?" he asked curiously, trying to think about anything other than the upcoming conversation with Peter. Dwelling on that would destroy what little composure he had left for sure.

It took Ryan a minute to figure out what his passenger meant. Apparently Risner hadn't done much research on Petarus before his arrival, and the sky over the residential area they were crossing was empty at the moment. "No, the Petari have a unique style of architecture," he answered as he set his skimmer on the pad beside Peter's ship. Once outside, he crossed the verdant patch that bordered their home and opened the door, gesturing for the other man to precede him in.

Wondering exactly what that meant since Nelson's comment was no explanation at all, Blaise crossed the threshold into the dimly lit interior, the sight that greeted his eyes almost enough to drive him to his knees in emotional agony. Peter stood in the middle of the room, bare-chested, one arm lifted over his head as the man behind him stroked him with huge, dark wings. Peter's eyes were closed, but the look of bliss on his face was apparent to even a casual observer.

"You could have just told me he'd moved on," Blaise gasped hoarsely. "You didn't have to be cruel enough to make me see it."

The expression on the younger man's face convinced Ryan as no words could have done how much he felt for Peter. "This isn't what you think," he said. "I'd forgotten my husband said he was coming home early for Peter's treatment." He reached out to touch Juo's shoulder gently, drawing his attention from the bond that linked healer and patient to the exclusion of any casual distractions.

Eyes opening, Juo looked from Ryan to the stranger darkening their doorway. It didn't take much to guess who he was. Letting his wings part and settle against his spine again, he nodded to the newcomer. "Juo-ta-dar-ri, assistant director of the Petari medical college," he said by way of introduction before turning to Ryan. "Should we perhaps make ourselves scarce?"

Peter opened his eyes slowly, prepared to be annoyed with anyone who interrupted a healing session with Juo, the only time he was fully free from pain. As his senses refocused on the here and now, he stared numbly at the man standing beside Ryan, sure for a moment he was still dreaming. Achingly aware of the scars marring his torso, Peter reached for his shirt, turning away from Blaise's gaze. "What are you doing here?" he asked harshly, ruthlessly crushing the spark of hope that flared at Blaise's presence.

"Looking for you," Blaise replied immediately, drinking in the sight of his lover after nearly a month apart. Very aware of the other two men in the room, men he didn't know and so didn't completely trust, he took a step forward, hoping to catch Peter's gaze. "Can we do this without an audience, please?"

Wanting to give the two men their privacy, Juo moved to Ryan's side, catching his hand and urging him gently toward the door, surprised when Ryan didn't immediately follow him. They were so obviously superfluous. "Ryan, shall we go?" he prompted again.

"Peter?" Ryan hung back, torn between allowing his friend privacy and making sure he wasn't going to be hurt again. "Do you—"

"I don't need a fucking babysitter!" Peter barked, knowing he was taking his anger out on the wrong person, but also knowing he could apologize to Ryan later. He was a good enough friend to realize that Peter lashed out in self-defense when he was feeling the most vulnerable.

"You know how to reach us if you need us, Peter," Juo said simply, drawing Ryan out the door and to the waiting skiff.

It was a long, tense moment before Blaise found his voice. "You look like you're feeling better," he began, taking a step deeper into the room. "Obviously whatever... Juo—is that his name?—was doing has helped."

"Juo-ta-dar-ri," Peter corrected, pulling a shirt sleeve over his damaged shoulder. "Only close friends have the right to shorten a Petari's full name."

Blaise filed that piece of information away for future reference. If all went well, he might well need to know the proper forms of address for the residents of Peter's chosen retreat. "I'll remember that, but are you doing better? I was worried about you."

"I'll live," Peter shrugged, refusing to let himself build on Blaise's words. "What do you want, Blaise? This is a long way to come to make sure I'm changing my bandages regularly."

There were so many different ways Blaise could answer that question, but he was done hiding behind his pride, and so his reply was simple. "You," he declared firmly. "I want you."

Peter wanted so much to believe that, but he still saw Blaise flinching away from his scarred face every night when he tried to sleep. "You couldn't get away from me fast enough once you had your ship back," he retorted. "Why should that have changed?"

"You ordered me to go!" Blaise retorted immediately, consciously clamping down on his anger as he felt it getting the better of his control. "I was stupid enough to listen once. I won't make the same mistake again."

"Oh, and you've always been so quick to follow my orders!" Peter sneered. The throbbing pain in his temples that had eased since his arrival on Petarus was back in full force.

"Well, forgive me for not quite thinking straight when the man I'd fallen in love with told me he didn't want me anymore," Blaise snapped back. "You ripped my heart out when you sent me away, and I was too angry and too hurt to realize that maybe, just maybe, you were as scared as I was." He took another step forward so he could reach out and touch Peter's uninjured shoulder. "Say what you like, Peter. I'm not leaving this time. Not now, not ever."

"Love?" The word started as a snort of disbelief, but transmuted as he spoke into nearly a plea. "You could barely stand to look at me on the *North Star*. Lucky I've healed enough for you to stay in the same room with me, eh?"

"Couldn't stand to look at you?" Blaise repeated incredulously. "Is that what you thought? God, you're as bad as I am. I was trying not to jump you in the middle of Engineering! I'd spent the past week worrying

I'd never see you again and then the first time I saw you, we were surrounded by your crew. I didn't figure you wanted a scene so I slipped out to wait for you in your quarters." He stroked Peter's scarred cheek, the closest thing to tenderness that had ever passed between them. "I don't care about the scars. I don't want you to be in pain, but the rest doesn't matter. Not to me, at any rate."

A shudder of need shook Peter's frame at the touch he'd thought never to feel again. His hand closed over Blaise's, holding it in place against his ruined cheek. "I was going to ask you to stay with me," he said hoarsely. "Before the Gavenelians attacked. After—" He shook his head, Blaise's fingers gentle against him. "After, I was sure you'd never accept."

"Ask me now," Blaise pleaded. "Forget about everything else that happened and ask me now."

Lowering Blaise's hand from his face and imprisoning it between both of his, Peter searched the hazel eyes for any sign of pity. "Stay with me?" he asked, almost too softly to be heard.

"For as long as you want me," Blaise promised fervently, squeezing the hand that held his tightly.

"Want you," Peter affirmed, leaning in until he was only a breath away from Blaise's lips. "Never stopped wanting you." He closed the distance between them, his mouth moving over his lover's in a kiss that began softly but quickly flared with all the heat and hunger of weeks apart.

"Thank God," Blaise groaned, biting at the lips that ravished his. His body reacted instantly to having Peter touching him again, the conflagration as hot as any galactic core. "Fuck me," he pleaded, his cock already swelling, his ass aching to be filled again. He rocked desperately against Peter. "Hot and hard and deep, the way only you can."

Peter's fingers worked awkwardly at the fastenings of Blaise's vest, desperate for the feel of flesh beneath his palms. "Take this off before I tear it off you," he growled in frustration, shrugging off his own shirt, fortunately still unfastened, in the meantime. He didn't need to hide his scars beneath it anymore.

Blaise didn't hesitate, jerking open the fastenings and dropping the vest to the floor, his pants following quickly as he reached blindly for Peter in his need to be close to his lover again. His eyes saw the scars, but his mind didn't even register them as he thrust urgently against Peter's hip.

Drawn like the irresistible pull of a black hole, Peter's hands flew to Blaise's chest, remapping the warm skin. His thumbs dragged over the pierced aureoles, fingers catching at the circlets marking the smooth planes. "You kept it," Peter husked, tugging at the ring of Zanian metal.

"It was all I had left of you," Blaise explained simply, hands flying over Peter's body, tugging at his pants, pushing them down until he once again had bare flesh beneath his hands.

The admission vaporized Peter's control like air through a hull breach. Thrusting a hand in Blaise's hair, he pulled his head forward and crushed their mouths together, groaning as skin dragged against skin. The friction not enough to slake his need, he pushed Blaise backward until they crashed blindly against a table. Peter ground himself between Blaise's legs, his tongue plundering his lover's mouth, his breath rasping through his lungs as he tried to absorb Blaise's essence through the kiss.

Now, now, now, Blaise chanted silently, unwilling to break the kiss long enough to press his demands. He reached between their bodies, fisting their cocks together, smearing the fluid leaking from their tips over Peter's shaft. Desperate to feel them joined again, he angled his hips so the head of Peter's cock bumped his entrance. "Now," he gasped, pulling away finally when Peter didn't move fast enough for him.

Once, Peter might have pushed inside without compunction, but however hard his need was riding him, he couldn't stake his claim through pain. Not anymore, and especially not this time. But neither did he have the strength to pull away. Spitting into his palm, he wet his shaft as best he could, urged on by Blaise's bruising grasp of his hips. Smothering another greedy "Now!" with his kiss, Peter sheathed himself in the hot clutch of Blaise's body, wringing a cry from deep in his lover's chest. His head fell to Blaise's shoulder and he froze, the tremors squeezing his cock nearly enough to set him off.

It hurt. Fucking hell, it hurt. Nothing had ever felt so damn good. He'd almost given up hope of finding Peter, of having his lover's touch again. Blaise's fingers dug into Peter's ass, holding him still momentarily as his body struggled to adjust to the swift penetration after over a month of no sex, but he didn't have the patience to wait long. It would just have to hurt. Easing his grip, he bucked his hips demandingly. "Fuck me like you mean it."

Peter didn't need to be asked twice. Hitching Blaise against the table, he pulled back, the friction so harsh it danced on the knife edge of pain, then thrust in fiercely, each stroke an effort to bury himself deeper, to touch Blaise's core as his own had already been claimed by the man in his arms. "Still... giving orders," he gasped before taking Blaise's mouth again.

It got me what I wanted, Blaise gloated silently as he returned the kiss eagerly. The fierce pounding did its job, driving him relentlessly toward his peak. He fought it as long as he could, but before long, he had no choice but to give in, rapture spreading through his body as he convulsed around Peter's cock. His fingers tightened again on Peter's hips as he felt the answering warmth of his lover's release filling him.

Sagging against Blaise's torso, Peter rode out the shuddering aftershocks of their climax, each twitch of the now-slippery channel around him sending another spark flaring along his nerves. When his softened shaft finally slipped from Blaise's embrace, he braced an arm against the table and levered himself up to ask, "That convincing enough for you?"

Blaise blinked once, then again as his brain struggled to catch up with the conversation. When it did, he smiled. "Oh, yeah," he replied appreciatively. He shifted a little, the wood tabletop digging into his back. "It's a good thing your friends have a sturdy table," he quipped, "or we'd be eating on the floor tonight."

That surprised Peter into a laugh, another emotion he hadn't indulged since Blaise had gone. "This is a replacement table. They broke the last one when I was visiting after they retired from AE."

"If you're not decent, you have thirty seconds to get that way," Ryan's voice called from outside. "I have a hungry husband who wants feeding."

"I guess that's our cue to disappear," Blaise said with a grin, not quite ready to have Ryan and Juo walk in on them still intertwined. "Bedroom?"

"Bedroom," Peter agreed, leaving their clothes on the floor as he led the way to his room. Ryan and Juo would understand. "I have everything I want to eat right here."

CHAPTER 18
SLOW BURN

PETER awoke slowly, the warmth of the body curved against his urging him to keep his eyes closed and ignore the noises that had interrupted his sleep. Once he opened his eyes, he knew the body would vanish as it had so many other mornings. He shifted deeper into his pillow, trying to smother the unwelcome return to awareness, when a muffled wheeze made his eyes snap open. His dreams had never snored, and even in the filtered light of a Petari morning, Blaise's presence was undeniably substantial. Peter's body tightened in reaction, a satisfied smile curving his lips as his muscles reminded him how often and how fiercely they'd joined the night before.

He ran a hand over the stubble shadowing Blaise's cheek, but the smuggler didn't stir, another snorted breath reminding Peter a bit of the horses his lover had tattooed around his bicep. Deciding Blaise needed his rest, he rose quietly and pulled on a loose pair of trousers, running a hand absently through his short hair as he closed the bedroom door behind him and headed toward the kitchen.

"So the dead awaken," Ryan teased from his seat when Peter shuffled into the room, even more bleary-eyed and mussed than usual in the morning. Tilting his head toward a pile of clothes in the corner, he added, "I think those are yours. If you want them washed, put them in the laundry room with the rest. I'm not your maid."

"I'll remember that the next time I find a pair of your shorts dangling from the skylight," Peter answered with only the hint of a smirk. Locating a mug from the cupboard, he poured himself a cup of the coffee Ryan imported from Earth and sank into a chair across from his friend. "I knew there was a reason I liked you," he added as he drank deeply of the life-giving elixir.

"Ah, but the difference is that I live here," Ryan reminded him with a grin. "I take it you worked things out with your pirate?"

"He'll be quick to tell you he's a privateer, not a pirate," Peter replied with a grin at just the thought of how they'd "worked things out."

"You did talk to him, didn't you?" Ryan pressed. "Fucking him instead of talking to him is what landed you in this mess to begin with."

"We talked," Peter insisted. He was pretty sure that *"more"* and *"harder"* and *"fuck me like you mean it, damn it"* wasn't the kind of conversation Ryan had in mind, but they were lucky to have managed that much.

"So is he going to stay here on Petarus with you?" Ryan asked. "He doesn't seem the kind to want to be grounded, but you've got at least another couple of months of treatment if you want to get the full use of your hand back. And what are you going to do about his smuggling? Even if you're not in the Admiralty anymore, I don't see you really being able to turn a blind eye to that. And have you talked about—?"

"We've got a few things still to work out." Peter rubbed the back of his neck, wishing he knew the answers to some of those questions himself. Blaise had said he'd come to find Peter, but did that mean he was willing to stay with him? It was hard enough for Peter to begin to adjust to being grounded. He couldn't imagine Blaise would be any more receptive, especially when he'd just gotten his ship back. And he couldn't see himself waiting patiently on Petarus like a good little wife while Blaise took off to wherever in the galaxy his trade demanded he go. Even assuming it was legitimate trade.... "Fuck," Peter muttered.

"Peter Mark Keller!" Ryan scolded with a scowl. "Did you at least tell him you love him?"

"I...." Peter hesitated, trying to remember if he'd actually said the words. Surely Blaise understood, from the way he'd reacted? "I think... I'm pretty sure I did."

Ryan's scowl deepened. "Turn around right now, march your lazy ass back in there, and tell that man you love him. And then apologize for not saying it sooner." He refused to see Peter make the same mistake he had almost made with Juo. Fortunately, his husband was a lot more intuitive than Blaise seemed to have been.

"You're as fucking demanding as he is!" Peter grumbled, standing to top off his coffee. He had a feeling he wouldn't be making it back to the kitchen any time soon. "You never used to be this bossy as a kid. Must be Juo rubbing off on you." Pouring a second mug for Blaise, he glanced over his shoulder at his friend before heading toward the bedroom. "Best thing that ever happened to you."

"Damn straight," Ryan agreed fondly, watching Peter disappear into the bedroom again. He was tempted to stay and keep an ear open just so he could pound on the door if they started making love again instead of talking like they were supposed to, but he thought that was probably taking meddling one step too far. He'd just needle Peter about it again when he got home and make sure they'd worked things out. With a last glance down the hall, he headed to work.

The body was still there when Peter returned to the bedroom, sprawled over the space he'd been lying in, sheet tangled around his delectable ass. Peter paused a minute just to appreciate the view. Blaise in his bed was a picture he could get addicted to opening his eyes to every morning. Setting the coffee mugs on the bedside table, he eased onto the mattress, his fingers returning to trace his lover's jawline. "Blaise...."

Blaise's eyes opened immediately, awareness following a moment later as the ache in his ass reminded him in the most glorious way how he and Peter had spent the previous night. He tilted his head into the caress, eyes fluttering shut again as he relished the feel of his lover's hand after fearing never to feel it again.

"Blaise," Peter repeated more insistently. He hadn't missed the flicker of dark lashes, and leaned closer to nip at the lobe of an ear. "Didn't figure a smuggler would be this hard to wake up." A hand skated below the sheet to find and cup a healthy arousal. "Though I see you woke up hard."

Blaise cracked his lids again, rolling onto his back. "If you hadn't kept me up all night, I might not be so sleepy now," he groused, a slow smile taking the edge off his words. One hand snuck out from under the sheet to find the apex of Peter's thighs. "Looks like you've still got your morning wood, too."

"Wasn't a problem until I walked back in here." Peter pulled the sheet free, baring Blaise completely to his hungry gaze. Any words he had meant to add froze on his lips as he reached out to trace the ring of twisted metal glinting through the dusting of hair on his pirate's chest. "I still can't believe you're here."

"Is it that difficult to believe that I might care about you?" Blaise asked seriously, fingers twining with Peter's other hand even as his body reacted predictably to the caress.

"We didn't exactly have the easiest of beginnings." Peter's fingers followed the wedge of hair lower, to where Blaise's cock was already stiff against his flat stomach. "Or of endings."

Blaise had to admit the truth of both those statements. "But the middle part meant something," he reminded Peter. "We managed to make things work once we stopped playing the roles we thought we had to maintain. We did it once. We can do it again." He gasped as his hips arched up toward Peter's fingers. "Can't we?"

Peter knew his answer without question. Once he'd finally admitted his feelings for Blaise, they'd only grown stronger, even during the time they'd been apart. He only wished he could be as sure Blaise felt the same. He wanted to believe that his ring still marking Blaise's chest meant what he hoped, but saying the words was proving even harder than resigning his fleet commission. "I'm not the man I was then," he said slowly. "The scars may never get any better than this."

"Do you really think they matter to me?" Blaise asked, sitting up and taking Peter's hands in his. "I'm not here because of the way you look, you know. And the scars aren't enough to make me leave."

"You can't expect me to believe you'd be happy staying planetside when you just got your ship back," Peter challenged.

Blaise shrugged. "The way I see it, I have two choices, at least until Juo-ta-dar-ri releases you from medical treatment. I can stay here with you, or I can fly around in an empty ship without you. Staying here with you is no hardship, and after spending a month alone on the *Stallion*, I've discovered it doesn't hold the same appeal it once did." He squeezed the hands he still held. "What's it going to take to convince you I want to be with you, whatever that means?"

"I want to believe it." Peter stared out the window at the lush Petari landscape, the words coming easier when he wasn't lost in Blaise's hazel eyes. "Fuck, you have no idea how much I want to believe it. Your being gone hurt worse than the damned burns. I just...." He shook his head, swallowing hard. "I just need you to be sure."

"Sure of what?" Blaise pressed, lifting Peter's hands to his lips. "Sure that I want to be here? I argued with High Admiral Hendershott and High Justice Perry to find you again. I certainly didn't do that for kicks." He pressed a tender kiss to the burned knuckles. "Sure that I'll never leave again? I didn't fly halfway across the galaxy and back to find you just to turn around and disappear again." Tugging gently, he leaned forward and kissed Peter quickly. "Sure that I love you? I told you I do, but only time can prove that to you." Releasing one of Peter's hands, he let his hand rest on his lover's scarred shoulder. "Sure that the scars don't matter? I know how to prove that to you. Will you let me?"

"You faced down both Hendershott and Lapis?" Peter shook his head. "You're even braver than I thought." His smirk softened as Blaise's subsequent words registered, a warm tingle sparking in his chest. "You... love me? Last night... did I...? I told you, too, didn't I?"

"No," Blaise replied with a grin, "but I kinda figured you might, given the fact that you didn't let me out of reach for the entire night."

"I didn't dare. I left the restraints back on the *North Star.*"

Blaise chuckled. "I hope you at least brought your toy collection with you," he retorted. Sobering, he went on. "I know we have things to work out, and I know some of them won't be easy decisions to make, but I also know that there's no one I'd rather be with and nowhere I want to be if you're not there. If you feel the same way, then we can make this work."

"I couldn't stop thinking about you," Peter admitted. "Even when I was mad as hell at you, I wanted you there, fighting me, if that's all I could have." He pulled Blaise into his arms, one leg draping over his pirate's to wrap their bodies together. His cock throbbed beneath the thin fabric separating them, but he ignored its insistent ache for the moment. It would be so easy to give in to their lust, but as difficult as he found it, the words needed to be said. "We might be headed for the biggest explosion since the big bang, but I want to try. I... do too. Love you, I mean." He rubbed a hand through his hair and then reached for Blaise, pulling him forward roughly. "Ah, fuck," he grumbled, letting the ardor of his kiss communicate his feelings instead.

Blaise returned the kiss eagerly, knowing how much the awkward declaration must have cost the Admiral. "I don't need flowery declarations of undying love," he assured Peter earnestly, breaking the kiss to scatter butterfly kisses over his lover's face. "You've said it once. You don't ever have to say it again. You do, however, have to make love to me. Immediately."

"We're better with action than words," Peter agreed, his palms splaying over Blaise's warm, honey-bronzed chest. Lowering his head, he nipped at the cords of his lover's throat, encouraged by Blaise tossing his head back to give him better access. Biting and suckling, he latched onto the ring that marked his claim. Maybe someday he'd let Blaise mark him the same way, but that would have to wait for another morning. Right now he was too intent on proving their commitment in a far more primal manner. A hand slid around Blaise's back and lower, cupping a buttock, fingers teasing at the shadowed crease.

Blaise's back arched and he cried out, pulling away when Peter's fingers probed his aching opening. "I don't think I can take you again," he apologized. "We were a little too energetic last night."

Eyes glittering, Peter regarded his lover. "You think that will stop us?" he retorted. Once, that might have meant forcing himself on a resistant prisoner, but though Peter knew Blaise wasn't unwilling, even welcome pain wasn't how he wanted to prove his admission. And he still had other scars, far older than the plasma burns, that he suspected only Blaise would be able to heal. With a slow smile, he offered his pirate what he had allowed no one else since escaping his abusive past so long ago. "You'll just have to make love to me instead."

Blaise's mouth opened, shut, then opened again, but no sound came out as he struggled to assimilate the novel suggestion. In all their months together, he'd never had the slightest hint that Peter might consider reversing their roles. "You... you mean...."

"Speechless?" Peter grinned. "You've always wanted to give the orders. This is your chance to take the controls."

"You'd really let me top you?" Blaise asked, too thrilled by the possibility to summon a glare at his lover's teasing. "I didn't think you'd ever want that. We can just suck each other off. It's still making love."

Shaking his head, Peter rolled onto his back, taking Blaise with him so his lover landed on top. Peter spread his legs, letting Blaise settle between them. "I won't *let* you. I *want* you. Want this." His hips rose beneath Blaise's, grinding their cocks together, the damp spot leaking through the thin fabric of his sleep pants testament to the truth of his words. "No games, no toys, no roles. Just you."

Blaise's mouth crashed down on Peter's, sealing them together possessively. He lifted his hips enough to reach between them and push down Peter's pants. He wanted bare skin to bare skin, and he wanted it now. The cloth out of the way, he settled his weight back on Peter, fingers drifting over the scars. Impulsively, he kissed the edge of the pale skin, his tongue tracing the line where the burn started. When Peter did not stop him, he kissed his way lower, his lips never leaving the marks left by the plasma.

Unaccustomed as he was to ceding control, Peter couldn't deny how good Blaise's hands and mouth felt on his body. A shiver wracked him when the kiss ghosted over the scars from the explosion, which had faded after weeks of Juo's treatments but would never completely disappear. They had a sensitivity he'd never noticed before, or maybe it was just Blaise's touch making him tremble. "Blaise," he said softly, not asking for anything, just needing to acknowledge what his lover was making him feel.

"Are they too sensitive?" Blaise asked, concern lacing his voice. "I don't want to hurt you. Don't ever want to hurt you."

"The only way you could hurt me would be to leave again," Peter assured him, threading a hand into Blaise's hair to guide his head back to his chest. "There's no part of me that doesn't crave your touch."

Taking Peter at his word, Blaise returned to his meandering path along the cicatrices, covering every inch of them in tender kisses and caresses, following them across his chest, over one scarred nipple until he came again to smooth skin and another peaked nub. His hand continued to wander, stroking skin, scarred and smooth alike, as he licked and nipped at the tight pink bud. Lifting his head for a moment to meet Peter's eyes, he confided, "When I escaped from the Gavenelians, I felt like my body belonged to a stranger. My first piercing was a way to reclaim myself. Something like that might help you, too."

"They left their mark on us both," Peter admitted. "I'd like to bear your mark too, the way you wear mine." Peter's fingers tugged at the slender Zanian ring, urging Blaise closer. "But right now, I'd rather feel you inside me."

Blaise nodded, feeling himself falling in love all over again at this unexpectedly vulnerable side of the usually bristly spacer. He grabbed the lube from under the pillow where it had ended up the night before, coating his fingers liberally with the cool gel and beginning to work one into the tight passage while his lips returned to their wandering ways, coasting over Peter's stomach and lower to capture the head of his leaking cock.

A sibilant breath hissed from Peter's lips when Blaise's mouth closed around the tip of his arousal. It took all his considerable control not to buck up immediately into that moist suction. He clutched at Blaise's shoulders, focusing instead on the tantalizing fingers slickening him. The invasive burn was offset by Blaise's mouth sliding downward, taking in more of his cock, sending tendrils of pleasure curling around his limbs. "More," he groaned, not sure which of the two sensations he needed most.

Blaise smiled around his mouthful, working his fingers deeper inside Peter, seeking the bundle of nerves that would drive his lover wild. The sudden jerk of the blond's hips and the deep groan told Blaise he'd found it. He exploited it mercilessly, fingertips rubbing back and forth across the sensitive spot until Peter was thrashing beneath him.

"Fuck," Peter panted, trying to get enough of a grip on Blaise's spiked hair to pull him upward. Shooting stars were coloring his vision, and he was going to explode like one of them if Blaise kept doing what he was doing. That normally wouldn't be a problem, but if Blaise's fingers alone could send him rocketing this high, he couldn't wait to feel what having Blaise's cock moving inside him would do. "Up here," he grunted, the effort to string entire sentences together beyond him. "In me. Now."

Blaise moved immediately, sliding over Peter's body sinuously, rubbing their bodies together as much as possible until he could rub his cock against Peter's balls. He kissed his lover, a slick hand running the length of his shaft as he pulled back, only to rut against the Admiral again. He wanted Peter as frantic as the blond always made him before finally joining their bodies.

Opening to Blaise's kiss, Peter tried to accede to his lover's control, but when the cock he wanted to feel impaling him slid forward against his balls for the third time, he groaned into Blaise's mouth and grasped the teasing ass as tightly as his damaged hand would allow. Thrusting his hips upward, he ground them together, the friction still not enough to ease the empty ache no one else had ever made him feel. Only this man—this infuriating, inimitable, inflaming man. "You," he insisted again, tearing his mouth away and pushing Blaise's groin down until the head of his shaft bumped against its target. "Only you. Now, damn it!"

"Some people have no patience," Blaise scolded as he pushed inside, hissing as the constricting heat opened to welcome him in. He paused with just the head inside, fighting for control as he let Peter's body grow used to the stretch. When he felt the tension ease, he began rocking his hips, working deeper inch by inch until finally, they were as close as two men could be.

Fuck, it hurt, and for a moment Peter remembered why he hadn't let anyone do this to him since leaving Earth. He'd rationalized that submitting to another man would have undermined the authority of his position, but it had been fear, he admitted to himself, and determination never to allow anyone that power over him again. As the burn eased, the knot of anger and betrayal he'd carried inside since the first time he'd been hurt unraveled beneath Blaise's tender care, his lover's caress as healing to his soul as Juo's wings had been for his body.

Blaise didn't push his advantage, giving Peter time to remember how to relax enough to accept the invasion. He hitched his hips a fraction, letting the thick shaft shift enough to slide a fraction deeper. Slowly, inevitably, Blaise filled him, and when his balls brushed Peter's ass, he wrapped his legs around his lover's, pulling him down into a kiss that joined their mouths as deeply as they were joined below.

Blaise let Peter control the kiss, his attention on other aspects of their lovemaking: the slow, steady rocking of his hips against his lover's, the feel of Peter's hands, one strong, the other less so, against his back, the tug on his nipple rings as they caught against Peter's body. Never breaking the kiss, he balanced on one arm so the other was free to trace up and down Peter's scarred arm, trying to invest every touch with the reassurance that the burns did not matter. All that mattered was their being together.

Intent on savoring every molecule of his own saltiness mixed with the taste of Blaise's mouth, Peter couldn't say at what point the pain turned to pleasure. He only knew he needed Blaise to keep moving, each withdrawal its own torture until he thrust deep again. The cool metal of Blaise's rings scraped over his chest, catching where tufts of hair had started to regrow around the scar tissue, sensitizing the puckered skin. Clenching around the steady, insistent pressure, he found the cadence that let him push back against each thrust, taking a little more of Blaise into himself with each roll of his lover's hips. It surprised him to realize he felt no drive to push for a climax. Through the slow, deliberate joining, they were forging a link that was more than merely physical. Blaise's fingers caressed his scarred shoulder, making him shiver with the emotions elicited by the touch.

"You all right?" Blaise asked, lifting his head when he felt the shiver run through Peter. He could tell it had been a long time since Peter had bottomed from the way his passage clenched even now. Nothing in his lover's actions made him think his attentions were unwelcome, but he wanted to make sure. While he hoped someday to turn some of Peter's toys around on him, this time he wanted only pleasure between them beyond the inevitable burn of that first penetration. They weren't playing games now. They were making love, and that made all the difference in the world.

"Good. Better than good." Peter shook his head, the words to describe what Blaise was making him feel eluding him, if they even existed. He rocked his pelvis, gasping when the change in angle drove the head of Blaise's cock over his prostate. "Just... don't stop," he gasped, reaching to draw Blaise's head back down to his. Actions definitely trumped words at this moment.

If Blaise could have spoken, he would have assured Peter he had no intention of stopping. Not now. Not ever. His lover's tongue twining with his made speech impossible, however, so he simply picked up the speed of his thrusts, making his intent clear in his movements. Feeling the hitch in Peter's breathing every time he moved a certain way, he tailored his motion to his lover's needs, the tip of his cock brushing repeatedly against Peter's prostate. His own release suddenly imminent, he fought to hold back until Peter could climax, wanting the satisfaction of knowing he'd brought his lover pleasure first.

Each snap of Blaise's hips stole a little more of Peter's control, and he fought not to roll them both over and take what he was beginning to need so desperately. But he'd taken Blaise more times than he could count. This time, at least, he was going to give instead. His cock leaked between their bellies, the slippery fluid letting him slide a little more easily. An electric charge was building inside him, needing just a touch to set him off. Breaking the kiss, he arched beneath Blaise, trying to reach for the contact he needed. "Blaise, please," he rasped, pride forgotten in the imminence of his climax.

Slipping a hand between them, Blaise fisted Peter's cock in time with his pounding thrusts, the rod of flesh heavy in his hand. His thumb swiped over the tip, capturing the leaking fluid and spreading it over the head and down the shaft. "Anything you want," he murmured. "Anything and everything you want."

"Only you," Peter ground out, and then the world imploded around him and even breathing became impossible. His body stiffened in a rictus of ecstasy, his cock pulsing a thick white stream over Blaise's hand. The clenching fist managed one or two more unsteady strokes over his twitching shaft and then froze in turn, the hot surge of Blaise's release filling him.

Blaise's shout echoed through the room, and probably through the house, as he collapsed on top of Peter, chest heaving with the force of his orgasm. His head slumped forward into the curve of his lover's shoulder, his breath ruffling the ends of Peter's regulation haircut and blowing across his damaged skin. Blindly, his hand searched for Peter's, twining their fingers together, only the odd texture making him realize he had found the injured hand. With a smile, he squeezed softly, thinking it appropriate that he should have found that hand and not the other.

When he had strength enough to inhale again, Peter drew a deep breath, smiling at the resistant weight of Blaise's body pressing his into the mattress. Returning the squeeze of Blaise's fingers as best as he could with his damaged hand, he used the other to turn Blaise's chin until he could once again reach his lips. "We'll have to do that more often," he murmured with a wry smile. Someday, he'd explain to Blaise why it hadn't happened until now, but he wouldn't mar the contentment of the moment with memories of a past he'd finally put behind him.

"Any time you want," Blaise replied immediately. "Any time we want," he corrected, feeling Peter tense beneath him. He pushed up on his elbow so he could peer down into the green eyes still hazy with pleasure. "Don't just tense up on me every time I say something you aren't sure you like. Talk to me, Peter. Tell me what you're thinking. I'm not your prisoner anymore. If I'm going to be your partner—and I *want* to be—you have to stop feeling like you have to deal with everything alone."

"I want it to be what *we* want," Peter insisted. "I'm used to being in command, and that's not going to change overnight. But part of why I love you is that you never back down," he continued, the admission coming much more easily this time. "We'll have fights that will rattle the airlocks, I have no doubt, but we'll work things out together." His hand skated over Blaise's back to tweak an ass cheek, making Blaise jump inside him. "And just think how much fun we can have making up after."

Blaise chuckled. "I can't wait. I know we'll fight sometimes, but my grandmother always said she didn't worry about couples she heard fighting occasionally. She worried about the ones who never fought because they didn't ever clear the air between them." He rolled to one side a little, curling into Peter's side and squirming to get comfortable. "The Gavenelians tried their damnedest to break me and couldn't. Everything we've done together, from the very first time, has been with my consent. You didn't force me into anything I didn't want when you were my jailer. You're certainly not going to do it now that we're on equal ground. What I meant earlier, when I said any time you want, was just that I'd be happy for a repeat of today as long as you are. That's all."

"Let me give my ass a chance to recover first," Peter grumbled, though in truth the thought that he'd feel Blaise's claim throughout the day appealed to him.

"Your ass?" Blaise interrupted. "*Your* ass? You've got some nerve complaining about your ass after you fucked me how many times last night?"

"I didn't hear you protesting at the time," Peter retorted. "And you're not as out of practice as I am. Something I'm sure you'll take great delight in remedying," he added with a grin before turning on the pillow to face Blaise directly.

"Oh, I'll whip you right into shape," Blaise agreed with a leer.

Peter smiled. "Speaking of asses, if I don't want Ryan to kick mine from here to the galactic core, there are some things we need to talk about."

Blaise's jaw-cracking yawn stopped whatever Peter would have said next. "I know we still have decisions to make, but do you think Ryan would mind if we slept a little more first? We can solve the universe's problems when we wake up."

Shifting nearer, Peter settled Blaise's head back on his shoulder, his arm holding his lover close. "Sleep," he agreed, letting his own eyes drift shut. He had no doubt they'd find a way to work through the challenges facing them, together.

And if Ryan didn't like it, he'd just have a word with Juo.

✺ EPILOGUE

BLAISE walked through the corridors of the *Golden Stallion*, still shaking his head at the sight of all his hidden compartments now clearly labeled as shipping holds. "I still can't believe we pulled this off," he said over his shoulder to his partner, lover, mate. "Stallion Transport, exclusive shipping company to and from Petarus. I never really thought it was possible."

"Without Ryan's help, it likely wouldn't have been." Peter followed the *Stallion*'s captain into the bridge, taking the co-pilot's seat. "Two strangers approaching the Petarus planetary council might never even have been granted a hearing. The Petari are cautious about opening their world up to outsiders. But they trust Ryan. Between his being Juo's mate and his position as offworld liaison officer, he's practically an adopted Petari himself."

"I know we don't have Ryan's stature on Petarus, but it couldn't have hurt that we're willing to base our company on planet and employ Petari at the landing pad and loading docks, too," Blaise pointed out, checking the control panel to make sure everything was in order. "We're not just making a living for ourselves. We're helping out the local economy as well, not to mention streamlining the bureaucratic process on imports by eliminating the need to check every ship as it comes in for contraband."

"As idyllic as it is here, I can understand why the Petari want to control who and what they let on their planet." Peter set the pre-flight sequence, double-checking the coordinates for their first cargo run to the Sirius sector. "And since they aren't part of the Confederation, they aren't bound by free-trade regulations."

"Damn good thing for us!" Blaise agreed. "We'd never be able to make a living if they were. The steep tariffs they charge for any unapproved shipping means we can charge our customers enough to make a living, and they still come out ahead by avoiding the Confederation surtaxes." Seeing everything was ready for takeoff, he gave the command to the ship's nav computer and leaned back in his chair to watch their new home recede into the distance. "You sure you're ready for this?" he asked, turning to face Peter.

"Juo's done as much as he can," Peter shrugged. The scars on his face and body would never fade completely, but he'd regained nearly full use of his damaged hand and shoulder. He could live with the rest, especially since they didn't matter to Blaise any more than they did to him. "And say what you will about the Confederation, they did take out the Gavenelians quickly enough once Harry's tinkering let them track the homing devices back to their homeworld."

"So how long before Captain Dmitrov makes Admiral?" Blaise asked curiously, setting the autopilot as soon as they cleared the planet's gravity well.

"We're completely alone on our maiden voyage, and you want to talk about Sasha Dmitrov?" Peter stood to lean over the captain's chair, his arms caging Blaise as he loomed over him.

"Well, when you put it that way...," Blaise drawled, leaning back in his chair and spreading his legs. "Maybe I can think of other, more interesting things to talk about." With a flip of a switch, he activated the autopilot feature and shut down the rest of the control panels. "At least here, we don't have to worry about scandalizing Ryan and Juo. There isn't anyone to hear us."

"You might be surprised at how much it takes to scandalize those two," Peter grinned. Straddling Blaise's legs, he lowered himself onto his lover's lap, rubbing suggestively. "But by the time we get back from this run, the house should be finished. Our house," he added, leaning back until his cock nudged the matching hardness beneath his mate's cargo pants.

Blaise's grin was as bright as a supernova. "I can't wait. As much time as we spent on the plans, I just know it'll be perfect." He circled Peter's waist, his hands coming to rest on the rocking ass. "Nobody to hear us, nobody to worry about if we want to walk around naked, nobody to care if we leave our clothes scattered all over the place. Just us."

"Naked sounds good." Peter's hands unfastened the toggles of Blaise's vest, coasting a palm over the hard planes, fingers lingering over the ring of Zanian metal that marked his lover. His other hand dipped into his trouser pocket, tapping the control device hidden there. "Naked and screaming sounds even better."

A deep groan escaped Blaise's lips as the Eridani plug in his ass shivered to life, sending a jolt of lust through him. He'd been waiting, on edge, since Peter inserted the plug early that morning in the 'fresher after nearly fucking him through the wall, never knowing when Peter was going to hit the control and set him ablaze like the twin Talixin suns. He'd counted himself lucky that his lover hadn't fastened the matching cock ring on him at the same time. He reached for Peter's shipsuit, fumbling with the fasteners until he could find bare flesh, pulling Peter toward him so he could latch onto the ring bisecting his mate's unscarred nipple. It didn't quite match his, but it didn't need to for them to understand what it meant.

"You can do better than that," Peter chided, though just the touch of his lover's fingers on the piercing that claimed him as much as he'd claimed Blaise set flares of heat licking along his nerves. He leaned forward until their bare chests met, his mouth tracing Blaise's jawline while he nudged the plug's control to max.

"Ah, fuck!" Blaise wailed, body arching off the chair, rubbing his aching cock against his lover's. "Peter!"

"Much better." He could feel the vibrations himself, shuddering through Blaise's body to his. They must be driving his lover wild, which was just how Peter wanted him. He crushed his mouth to Blaise's, plundering with the familiarity of experience, though each time they kissed he discovered some new sensitive spot, Blaise's or his own. When his own need started to approach the frenzy of Blaise writhing beneath him, he broke off the kiss reluctantly, pushing off the arms of the captain's chair to his feet. "Get naked. Now." When Blaise didn't move fast enough, Peter pinched an erect nipple. "Unless you want to wear that plug all the way to the Sirius quadrant."

Blaise rose unsteadily to his feet, pushing his trousers down with shaking hands. "You wouldn't do that," he taunted, "because you can't fuck me when I'm wearing it." Turning around and bracing his hands on the arms of the captain's seat, he wiggled his ass. "Please tell me you brought the dildo from the Orion pleasure harems." The thought of the twisted alien stone spearing him had him leaking.

Peter was already stripping out of his own flight suit as quickly as he could wrestle away the fabric. "I packed a few toys, but damned if I'm going to hunt them up now. You'll just have to settle for me." He palmed a perfect globe, admiring the natural tan of Blaise's skin beneath his paler hand. His lover wriggled impatiently, demanding a swat that Peter didn't hesitate to give. "Or I could leave the plug."

Blaise shook his head immediately. "Fuck me," he pleaded immediately. "Fuck me hard. This thing's been driving me crazy all day."

As impatient as his lover, Peter didn't tease, grasping the handle and pulling the thick implement free in a single tug. Letting it fall to the floor, he molded himself to Blaise's back, his cock sliding under the captain's heavy balls while he nuzzled Blaise's cheek until he turned his head into the kiss.

The emptiness when the plug popped out was almost painful, but Blaise reminded himself that Peter wasn't cruel. He leaned into the kiss, waiting for the hard cock to fill him again. When the kiss continued and Peter still didn't take him, Blaise pulled away, turning in his lover's embrace and pushing the blond back against the control panel. Straddling his lover's thighs, he positioned Peter's erection at his entrance and sank all the way down in one long stroke. His breath hissed out of him as he captured his mate's lips again for a quick kiss. "You were taking too long."

"Still giving orders." The observation had become a private joke between them, since Peter certainly had no complaint with the result of his lover's actions. His hips arched up in response, palms gripping Blaise's cheeks without pulling him forward, letting Blaise set the pace... at least for now. "Just be... careful... we don't bump something that sends us halfway across the galaxy," he panted between Blaise's increasingly energetic thrusts.

"Everything's on autopilot from my seat," Blaise gasped as he fucked himself on Peter's cock. "The only sparks flying in here today will be the ones we set off between us." He tugged lightly on Peter's piercing. "I'm doing all the work here."

"Thought that's what you wanted." Not reluctant to take a more active role, Peter rocked upward in synch with Blaise's downstroke, driving deeper into Blaise's slick heat with each slap of their bodies. When that quickly led to a tightness in his balls that meant his own climax was near, he worked a blunt finger into the flexible passage alongside his shaft, angling for the spot that would send Blaise into freefall.

Blaise cried out at the additional stretch. He loved it when Peter fingered him at the same time he fucked him, the slight burn adding to the overwhelming pleasure. He'd toyed with the idea of suggesting they find a dildo flexible enough to fit inside him alongside Peter's cock, but he was never coherent enough to suggest it when Peter was fucking him. Then Peter's finger found his prostate and he wasn't coherent at all, all thought leaving him as he came in a rush, spewing creamy fluid over their bellies and collapsing hard against Peter's chest.

As soon as he felt the first splash of hot come against his stomach, Peter tightened his grip on Blaise's ass, holding him still. As close as he was to his own climax, he wanted to savor Blaise's first. When the shuddering around him lessened, he flipped them about, his arm protecting Blaise's back from the console while he pounded into him fiercely, lasting only a few thrusts before his orgasm consumed him with the ferocity of a solar flare. Spent and panting, he sagged against Blaise with a sated grin. "That's rechristened her well and proper."

Blaise grinned. If this was an omen for the success of their business venture and their new life, he thought it was a pretty damn good one. "So, the captain's cabin next?"

Peter's answering smile was equally wolfish. "Just let me unpack the toys first."

Read Ryan and Juo's story in "Healing in His Wings" by Ariel Tachna, available in *Size Matters: Short Stories Long Enough to Satisfy* from Dreamspinner Press.

Growing up in Chicago, NICKI BENNETT spent every Saturday at the central library, losing herself in the world of books. A voracious reader, she eventually found it hard to find enough of the kind of stories she liked to read… and decided she needed to start writing them herself.

ARIEL TACHNA lives in southwestern Ohio with her husband, her daughter and son, and their cat. A native of the region, she has nonetheless lived all over the world, having fallen in love with both France, where she found her career and her husband, and India, where she dreams of retiring some day. She started writing when she was 12 and hasn't looked back since. A connoisseur of wine and horses, she's as comfortable on a farm as she is in the big cities of the world.

Visit Ariel's website at http://www.arieltachna.com/